This
lates
peric

- Ph
- Vis

D

THE CAPTAIN'S GIRL

Cornwall 1793. As the French Revolution threatens the stability of England, so too is discontent brewing in the heart of Celia Cavendish. Promised to the brutal Viscount Vallenforth, she must find a way to break free. Inspired by her cousin Arbella, who followed her heart and eloped with the man she loved, she vows to escape her impending marriage. She enlists the help of her neighbours, Sir James and Lady Polcarrow, to make a new life for herself. But can the Polcarrows' mysterious friend Arnaud, captain of the cutter *L'Aigrette,* protect Celia from a man who will let nothing stand in his way? And will Arnaud himself be friend ... or foe?

THE CAPTAIN'S GIRL

THE CAPTAIN'S GIRL

by

Nicola Pryce

Magna Large Print Books
Long Preston, North Yorkshire,
BD23 4ND, England.

British Library Cataloguing in Publication Data.

A catalogue record of this book is
available from the British Library

ISBN   978-0-7505-4677-5

First published in Great Britain in 2017 by Corvus
an imprint of Atlantic Books Ltd.

Copyright © Nicola Pryce, 2017

Cover illustration © Lee Avison/Arcangel by arrangement with
Arcangel Images

The moral right of Nicola Pryce to be identified as the author of this
work has been asserted by her in accordance with the Copyright,
Designs and Patents Act 1988

Published in Large Print 2018 by arrangement with
Atlantic Books

Magna Large Print is an imprint of Library Magna Books Ltd.

Printed and bound in Great Britain by
T.J. (International) Ltd., Cornwall, PL28 8RW

For my children:
Moreno, Angharad and Hugh.

Family Tree

PORTHRUAN

PENDENNING HALL (Acquired 1787)

Sir Charles Cavendish MP	m.	Lady April Montville
b.1743		b.1750

Celia	Charity	Georgina	Sarah	Charles
b.1773	b.1774	b.1780	b.1789	b.1791

Sir Richard Goldsworthy	*Guest: Bow Street Stipendiary magistrate*
Major Henry Trelawney	*Guest: Major in the 32nd Foot Regiment*
Mr Phillip Randal	*Steward*
Mrs Jennings	*Governess*
Walter Trellisk	*Coachman*
Ella	*Housemaid*

FOSSE

POLCARROW (Baronetcy created 1590)

Sir Francis m. 1) Elizabeth   2) Alice
Polcarrow   Polcarrow   Polcarrow
b.1730 d.1782   (née Gorran) (née Roskelly)
           b.1749 d.1770 b.1763 m.1780

James Gorran m. Rosehannon   Francis
Polcarrow   Pengelly   Polcarrow
b.1765   b.1772   b.1781

Jenna Marlow *Companion*
Joseph Dunn *Master of Horses*

Bespoke Dressmaker (Est. 1792)

Madame Merrick *Dressmaker*
Eva Pengelly *Seamstress*
Elowyn *Seamstress*

HMS *CIRCE*   *L'AIGRETTE*
Captain Edward Penrose   Captain Arnaud Lefèvre
Lieutenant Frederick Carew   Jacques Martin
Nathaniel Ellis
Jago

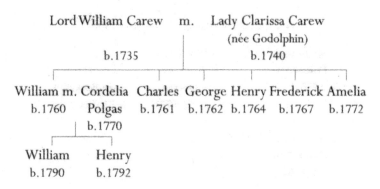

Lord William Carew   m.   Lady Clarissa Carew
(née Godolphin)
b.1735   b.1740

William m. Cordelia Charles George Henry Frederick Amelia
b.1760   Polgas   b.1761 b.1762 b.1764 b.1767   b.1772
b.1770

William   Henry
b.1790   b.1792

BODMIN

Mr Matthew Reith	*Attorney of law*
Mrs Sarah Hambley	*Guesthouse proprietor*
Hannah Hambley	*Daughter*
Mary	*Maid*
Adam Tremayne	*Friend of the family*
Robert Roskelly	*Convicted murderer in Bodmin Gaol*

We only part to meet again.
Change as ye list, ye winds; my heart shall be
The faithful compass that still points to thee.
John Gay

South-East by South

Chapter One

Pendenning Hall
Thursday 7th November 1793, 3:00 p.m.

'Come, Charity, I'll race you to the folly.'

'No, Cici, it's too far. It's getting late and it feels like it's going to rain.'

Always the same sense of duty. Always reigning in when I wanted to gallop. 'I don't give a fig if it rains. Let it pour.'

'I think Miss Charity's right, Miss Cavendish. The weather's turning ... and–'

'And?' I turned to face him. He may be a groom but, for all of that, he was our gaoler. He looked nervous, pulling at the reins, edging in front of us so we would turn back. *Do not let them out of sight of the house,* was that what he had been told? They were both right, of course, the sky was darkening. We should return to our dressing rooms and prepare for the evening. I should dress in my blue organza, the better to show off the huge ring now glittering on my finger. We should sit stiffly with Mama, eat Madeira cake, drink sherry and bask in my wonderful fortune. I knew what I *should* do.

I looked up at the folly. 'Itty, Viscount Vallenforth's horse is tethered outside the folly – he hasn't left the park. He must be waiting for us, hoping we'd ride that far.' My heart began

17

pounding. Father had negotiated a brilliant settlement, well exceeding Mama's expectations, but perhaps Viscount Vallenforth felt the same as I did? The same empty longing? The dream there was more to marriage than legal negotiations and formal settlements? I felt suddenly so happy. He, too, must regret we had never been left alone together. He must be waiting, hoping I would see his horse and ride over.

'I know you have your orders,' I said, using as much of Mama's tone as I could bear, 'but think how *displeased* Viscount Vallenforth will be if you stop me. Take Miss Charity home – she's getting cold and she's tired. I'm only going to the folly and Viscount Vallenforth will accompany me back.'

The groom bowed, reluctantly turning away. I knew it was unkind to speak so sharply. He looked kind and was certainly good with the horses. 'Very well, my lady,' he replied, giving me every indication he recognised a prearranged tryst when he saw one. Charity looked anxious, turning to me in distress.

'I won't gallop, Itty, I promise. I know about the rabbit holes and I'll take the greatest care.' I could not go back, not now, not with him waiting for me like that. This was a tryst – a real tryst, like proper lovers, and he had chosen the folly – how wonderfully romantic. Perhaps he would kiss me. I felt breathless, gripping the reins tightly, tapping my mare forward. She was a lovely chestnut, my favourite in the stable, and I knew she was itching to canter. Sensing my excitement, she needed little encouragement and I spurred her on, ignoring Charity's frown of concern.

I loved the folly; I could watch it all day. In fact, I frequently did. I loved the light, the changing colour. Early sun turned the marble a brilliant white, evening sun bathed it in glowing red. Moonlight turned the columns ghostly silver. Should I kiss him back? We had met twice, both formally, and on both occasions he had seemed so reserved, so very distant, but perhaps that had been for appearances. Perhaps, beneath that impeccably embroidered waistcoat was a heart beating with passion. I was blushing now, the banned books from the library distressingly vivid.

The ground was growing steeper, the final rise before the top. This was my favourite place. In a moment, I would turn round and gaze across the river mouth to the harbours below; Fosse and Porthruan – two opposing towns, fighting for dominion of the river mouth. I would see the jumble of stone houses rising steeply from the quaysides; some days, so clear, I could see the shuttered windows, the grey slate roofs, other days, smothered by a fog so thick, they would disappear completely. Today was perfect. In the evening light I could see the masts of the ships, the church tower, the solid outline of Sir James Polcarrow's house with its sturdy walls and pointed windows. Best of all, I could see the sea – miles and miles of open sea; the clouds now gathering, the waves turning an ominous grey.

Go to Cornwall? Mama had been aghast. She never intended Father to come. Buy the house and estate and become the Member of Parliament, certainly, but to expect her to *go* there? The

19

thought had left her reeling – that was until she realised how very opportune it would be. My marriage was her prime concern, and to be within visiting distance of Viscount Vallenforth and his powerful father was enough to rouse her. It had taken seven years for her to venture down here, but only three months to secure the engagement. Once the wedding was over, Mama could leave this godforsaken wind-blown wilderness and return to her beloved Richmond.

Full-bellied clouds blew across the land, the folly nearly indistinguishable against the overcast sky. I could see Charity dismounting at the house below and knew she would be anxious. Only ten months separated us, we could not be more different and I loved her all the more for that. Neither of us called Pendenning Hall home. It was certainly a beautiful house with perfect symmetry – all four aspects equal, three rows of seven windows, the top windows slightly smaller than the ones below. It had the obligatory large front door, framed by a particularly ornate portico and a circular drive, large enough to please Mama. Even the huge fountain, brimming with nymphs and watery goddesses, had met with her approval. Terraces stretched down either side, statues eyeing each other from across the formal gardens but I felt no love for it. Father had owned it for seven years. For five months it had been our home, for the last eleven weeks, it had become our prison.

How had Arbella left the house in broad daylight – our beautiful cousin, exactly five months younger than me and five months older than Charity? I missed her so much. For a few weeks she had filled our hearts with talk of sun-drenched, turquoise seas, of blistering heat, of butterflies and humming birds; of vibrant flowers and exotic fruits growing in the gardens of Government House. She hated Dominica but I thought it sounded so exciting. How could she just walk out of our house in broad daylight, plead a headache, go to her room and escape unseen? Even more puzzling, how could she know she loved a man quite so much to be prepared to give up everything?

The mare hesitated and stopped. Rabbit holes were everywhere but the ground was still firm so I urged her on, choosing our route with care. She seemed strangely jumpy, throwing back her ears, her nostrils beginning to flare. The folly was less than fifty yards away, Viscount Vallenforth's horse tethered on the other side, but still she hesitated, ignoring my repeated commands.

Slipping from the saddle, I grabbed her halter, examining her carefully for signs of injury. There was nothing – no limp, no reason to stop, and I began edging her forward with more force than necessary. It was strange; I always chose to ride this mare because she was so fearless. Suddenly I stopped. I could hear whinnying from the other side of the folly – the unmistakable sound of a stallion in distress. The sound unnerved us both and my hands began shaking. The mare's fear was rising and I knew she would bolt if we got any closer. I began calming her, turning her round, desperate to get her safely tethered.

A small wood ran down the side of the hill and I ran to it, tying the mare safely to a trunk, returning quickly across the uneven grassland, grateful for my sturdy boots. The stallion was straining against the post, rearing on his hind legs, the whites of his eyes stark with fear. He was clearly petrified, his mouth frothing, his nostrils flaring in panic. My alarm increased but I knew to show no fear. To reach Viscount Vallenforth I would have to walk calmly in front of the terrified stallion, edge round the columns and enter the arch at the other side.

I stopped. I could hear a slow, rhythmical sound coming from the folly – the sound of a whip whistling through the air, meeting its target each time, the same speed, the same relentless ferocity. Worse still, I could hear grunting, the terrible grunting of a man using all his effort. I put my hands over my mouth to stifle my scream. I was right. Dear God, I was right. I had seen the cruelty in his mouth. I had sensed his coldness. In my heart, I had known.

The boy he was thrashing had long since stopped crying, his white face seemingly lifeless; his tiny, thin frame lying half-naked across Viscount Vallenforth's knee. Angry red wheals covered his back and buttocks – all of them oozing, all glistening with bright red blood. There was blood on Viscount Vallenforth's arms where his sleeves had been rolled and a smear of blood across his forehead where he must have wiped the sweat from his eyes. I drew back, my stomach retching.

It was the most vicious thing I had ever seen, but it was the look on Viscount Vallenforth's face that sickened me most – that glazed, lustful look, that smile, the gluttonous, satisfied curl to his lip. The pleasurable grunting. I could see his enjoyment in such a cruel act and I bent over, trying to stop myself from vomiting. Hateful, vile man – just one more lash and he could kill the boy. Pulling myself together, I rushed in and grabbed his arm as it rose towards me. 'Stop this at once!'

His arm went rigid, his eyes unable to focus on my face. He was looking through me, not at me, his chest rising and falling, his thin lips creased in their tight smile. I gripped his arm, wrenching it towards me, his white knuckles clenching the riding crop so tightly. As if coming to his senses, he stood up, letting the boy fall to the ground. 'That'll teach him. He won't poach again.'

'It's not your land. Father should punish the poachers.'

'I'll punish who I like.' His voice was hard, unrecognisable from the voice that had only an hour ago been sweet-talking Mama. 'I'll whip anyone who sets a snare and threatens my mount – whoever's land he's on.' His eyes were focussing again; cold, cruel, staring straight at me as he began rolling down his shirt sleeves, carefully fastening the pearl buttons above the lace, flicking some dirt off his satin waistcoat. He turned to retrieve his carefully folded jacket. 'You shouldn't be here.'

I knelt on the ground, gathering the whipped boy in my arms, 'He might die.'

'I doubt it. They're stronger than they look. Goodbye, my dear, I'll see you in church.'

The boy was deathly white for all the dirt covering his face. He lay limp in my arms, his wounds bleeding, his chest barely rising. I took

23

off my cloak, wrapping it round him, cradling him softly. How old was he, nine, ten? His thin body seemed just skin and bones as I held him to me, trying to get some warmth into his fragile frame. Poor, poor boy, I could imagine him watching Viscount Vallenforth fold his jacket, the fear in his eyes as he saw him roll up his sleeves. Had Viscount Vallenforth petrified him even further by testing the crop in the air? Somehow I knew he had.

I had hoped. I had really hoped. I had tried so hard to supress my instincts, believe in my good fortune. I thought he must be cruel. I could tell by his thin lips, his humourless face, by his arrogance, his hauteur, his distain. I had seen the cruelty, but never believed him such a brute. At thirty-nine, there must be a good reason why he remained unmarried. Others must be privy to his true character. Others must know.

The boy stirred, opening his eyes, staring at me with little comprehension. I rocked him gently, his two dead rabbits on the floor beside us. He was clearly starving, desperately in need of food and shelter but, first, his wounds must be dressed. He was almost weightless when I picked him up, almost lifeless when I carried him to the mare. She was nervous; the smell of blood clearly causing her distress. Calming her as best I could, I led her to a broken tree stump and eased myself carefully into the studded saddle. The boy barely moved.

I looked round, scanning the contour of the trees. The wood sloped gently to the river below. I had not ridden there before, the folly marking our furthest boundary, but halfway down the hill, a narrow track led straight into the woods. I urged the mare forward, slowly picking our way towards the tiny opening. Just as I thought – fresh hoof prints, digging deeply into the soft mud at the entrance. I stared at the hoof prints. Viscount Vallenforth must have been cantering. To canter, he must know the path to be sound. It must be a shortcut out of the park.

West of the river, all the land belonged to Sir James Polcarrow, east of the river, everything belonged to Father. I stared at the path as if mesmerised – the fallen leaves, the twigs snapped in half. For the first time in my life, I was un-accompanied. I could follow that path. I could walk away. In the wood, the birds were singing. The boy stirred in my arms and I flicked the reins, digging in my heel to urge the mare forward. She hesitated, as if questioning my command.

'Walk on,' I said, turning her westwards.

Chapter Two

The boy's head rested against my shoulder, his tiny frame shivering. My tears were drying, my resolution hardening. I would never marry Viscount Vallenforth. Never. I would go to Polcarrow and beg Lady Polcarrow to take me in. I would write to my parents, telling them I would not come home until I was released from my engagement. It was the only thing I could think to do. The boy needed help, I needed sanctuary and, without the threat of scandal, my parents would take no notice.

'It's not much further. You'll be safe soon,' I whispered. I could visualise the way: I had stared down at the house often enough and my memory never failed me. Polcarrow was three miles from Pendenning Hall, only two miles from the folly. The path was already getting flatter, the ground growing softer by the minute. We must be half-way there.

Through the trees I glimpsed the river. The tide was out, only the thinnest stretch of water showing black against the muddy banks. It seemed strangely eerie – the trees' roots gnarled and twisted, seaweed hanging from the white branches like long black fingers. Broken trunks lay stranded along the shore, an abandoned rowing boat with planks missing, but it was so beautiful, so peaceful. Fast grey birds darted across the glistening mud, tall white birds looked down from the trees. I forced my eyes away, turning with the path, following the fresh hoof prints pointing my way.

The path widened and stopped, the growing dusk making it hard to know where I was. Gradually I recognised a rough stone wall, a crooked post. Turning left would take us back to the gate-house, turning right would take us along the river to the bridge. Ahead lay the ford, used only when the tide was out. Our coach had driven through it, but only once. The water had been deeper then, almost to the steps of the carriage.

'Walk on...' I urged, kicking the mare forward, forcing her down the muddy slipway, keeping her head steady as the inky black water rose above her fetlocks. I knew not to stay on the road – if they came searching, they would come this way. For the past few weeks I had seen wood-smoke rising from these woods. Trees were being cleared; I knew to look for a small path that would take us straight to Polcarrow.

The path was smaller than I expected, hardly wider than the horse. The light was fading, the trees merging together in the gathering darkness. I could see lamps burning through the trees and knew exactly where I was. We had never been invited to Polcarrow, the animosity between Sir James and Father saw to that, but Arbella and I had gazed down from the hill, studying the stables and the coach-house, thinking she would soon be mistress of the old house. How very secretive she was then; I wished she had told me the truth, but how could she? Everyone had to believe she was to marry Sir James – how else could she run away with the man she truly loved? Her plans must have been so intricate, borne out of desperation, yet now I understood her. Dearest Arbella, to keep so silent, not telling a soul.

How very different Polcarrow was to Pendenning Hall – here was ancient woodland, a long-established house, a family name stretching back for generations. Our house was so new, Father's baronetcy straight from the boardroom of the East India Company. *Trade,* as Mama would say, had she not depended so entirely upon it.

The mare saw the lights and increased her pace, picking her way more readily through the dense overgrowth. We were heading straight for the stables – unseen, uninvited, a terrible affront, but it was my only chance.

'We're here – you'll be safe, now. Sir James's a good man.' The boy's small arms clasped my neck and I felt him shake. 'You're safe, I promise. You'll be well looked after.' I sounded reassuring, but I was surprised the place seemed deserted, no-one there at all. 'We just need to find someone.'

Not far away was a hitching rail and I decided to dismount. Wrapping the boy carefully in my cloak, I slipped from the saddle and carried him in my arms. Lamps were burning either side of the stable entrance; other lanterns lit the path to the house and more lamps burnt against the coach-house, but there was no-one to be seen.

I crossed the courtyard and entered the stable, at once met by the familiar smell of fresh straw. A well-run stable, that was obvious – no corners cut, no laziness tolerated. Deep straw lined every stall, the horses contentedly nudging their hay-bags. Buckets of water stood inside each gate and newly oiled saddles hung against the dark wooden stalls. My eyes were immediately drawn to two saddles lying on the flagstones. They looked to be flung to the ground and abandoned in haste, clearly at odds with the immaculate surroundings. Stranger still, two black stallions stood bridled and steaming with sweat.

A tiny glow of light lit the end stall – the flicker of a single lantern. I could hear a woman sobbing and whispered voices. The last two stalls were empty, the voices coming from within the furthest one. I knew I ought to walk away, or make my presence known, but curiosity drew me forward.

It was always like this. It would be easy to slip into the second stall, hide in the shadows where no-one would see me. Knowledge was power – I had learnt that as a child. How else could I know the truth from the lies they peddled me? Cocooned in silk, the newspapers hidden? Told only what they wanted me to hear. Without listening at doors I would never know what was really going on.

I crept silently forward, stepping over the freshly laid straw without a sound. A chink of light showed through the wooden stall and I knelt down to peer through the tiny crack. There were two men, three women and a boy of about twelve. James Polcarrow had his back to me, with Lady Rose Polcarrow by his side. I did not know the blonde woman or the huge red-haired man, but I recognised Alice Polcarrow, Sir James' step-mother. She was kneeling in the straw, sobbing, clutching her son to her.

'When was this, Alice?' James Polcarrow sounded furious.

She looked up, tears streaming down her cheeks, 'This morning ... at ten o'clock.'

'Ben came to you in the garden and gave you this?' He held up a small brown paper package.

'Yes.'

'And the message was, *"You know what to do".'*

'Yes.'

'Alice, Ben's not the best of messengers, he can barely get his words straight. How do you know what it means?'

A fresh burst of sobbing met this question. 'I know exactly what it means,' she stammered. 'I've been dreading it for months. It's from Robert – it's poison. When he was arrested, Robert told me he'd get poison to me, to put in your drink.'

'Dear God, Alice, your brother's an evil man – you should've told me this long ago.' James Polcarrow's jaw clamped tight, his face thunderous.

'I thought it would never happen. I just prayed and prayed, hoping we'd hear of his hanging, but when it was postponed I began to feel such dread. I was going to tell you when I heard he'd escaped from Bodmin, but you left in such a hurry.'

She wiped her tears with the back of her hand and leant forward, scooping something up from the straw. My heart froze. A spaniel dog lay with his head hanging limply to one side, his big brown eyes glazed and lifeless. She buried her face in its immaculate coat.

'He's poisoned Hercules as a warning I must do exactly as he says ... he told me to use the poison on you, and if I didn't, he'd take my son. He takes everything – everything. First he killed your father, now my dear, sweet Hercules and he'll take Francis, I know he will. He just takes and takes and takes. I hate him.' Pain caught her throat, her words barely audible. 'He said I'd never see my son again ... he'd kidnap Francis, sell him to some ship's captain.'

'The man's insane.'

'He's always controlled me ... always. You weren't here. You were miles away. Your dear father was dead and as Francis' guardian he took everything into his own hands. He ran the estate with such cruelty and I was powerless to stop him. I thought only to get by until Francis came

30

of age. His greed knows no end – he wants to control Francis just like he controlled me. You're in his way.'

I leant back against the wooden stall, clutching the boy closer. They were speaking so quietly, their voices hardly above a whisper. Robert Roskelly – I knew the name. Father had done business with him when he lived at Polcarrow and I had watched him from the window when he had come to dine. Father had liked him but Mama thought him *frightful*. Neither had spoken of him since he was arrested for the murder of Sir James' father.

'How did he escape?' It was Lady Polcarrow's Cornish accent, the beautiful Rose Pengelly, not three weeks married. 'Will he come to Fosse, James?'

'No. He'll not come anywhere near here – he won't risk being recognised.'

I peered through the chink again. James Polcarrow was pacing backwards and forwards, one fist tapping his mouth, the other held tightly against his side. Lady Polcarrow was kneeling on the ground, her arms round Alice and Francis. The boy looked petrified. He was tall and dark like his stepbrother. Sir James' scowl deepened. 'Alice, have you any idea where your brother would hide? Who would your brother trust with his life?'

She looked up, pain deep in her eyes, 'I've been trying to think – perhaps Rowen Denville. I think he'd trust her. They were ... well ... you know, rumour had it...'

'Where does she live?' James Polcarrow knelt in

the straw, encouraging Alice in her distress.

'Falmouth.'

'Then that's where he'll be. My guess is he won't sail until he knows I'm dead and Francis will inherit Polcarrow. Whoever gave Ben that poison will have instructions to wait and see if you use it. If I don't sicken, he'll have instructions to take Francis–'

'Dear God, James. No.'

'Our only option is to make them believe you've used it. Rose and I will pretend to be ill and while Robert Roskelly waits to hear of our deaths, I'll go to Falmouth and find Rowen Denville. I'll base my search round her. I will find him, Alice. Your brother *will* hang for the murder of my father and Francis will come to no harm. That, I promise.'

I held the boy carefully against me, afraid he might whimper. Sir James turned to the other man. 'Joseph, send to Truro for Dr Trefusis – we can't trust any of the local doctors ... and stay with Francis at all times. Sleep in his room and never let him out of your sight. Never.'

'Yes, Sir James.'

He turned to the blonde lady. 'Jenna, tell everyone Rose and I are fighting for our lives. Insist on being our only nurse and stop anyone coming into our rooms. Cry a lot and say we're getting worse.'

'Yes, Sir James.'

'Rose,' his voice once again softened as he looked at his wife. 'You must stay in our bedroom and make sure you aren't seen by anyone.'

Rose Polcarrow looked back at him through the

darkness. Her chin lifted, her beautiful eyes flashed. 'I'm coming with you, James.'

'No, Rose, it's too dangerous. I insist you stay here.'

She smiled, seeming to take no notice. 'I won't let you go alone.'

I could not believe it. Rose Pengelly, the seamstress's daughter, contradicting her husband, yet he was smiling back at her; a deep, loving smile, the two of them exchanging a look of such love. The rumours he had hastened their marriage were true – he did love her, he adored her. I closed my eyes, trying to shut out the sight of Viscount Vallenforth's terrible thin lips, curling in their cruel smile.

Lady Polcarrow's voice grew urgent. '*L'Aigrette's* still in harbour, James. I've been watching her from the terrace. The wind's northerly, the tide's about to turn – it's perfect for Falmouth. If we hurry we'll catch Captain Lefèvre.'

I leant against the stall, holding the boy in the darkness, the sound of their footsteps receding along the cobbles. My mind was racing. Could I? Would I dare? I remembered Arbella's hastily scribbled note. I had burnt it, as requested, but I remembered every word – *we'll be married straight-away, but so we can't be traced we're going to call ourselves Mr and Mrs Smith. We've got respectable lodgings in Falmouth, in Upper Street, with Mrs Trewhella, but don't tell anyone, will you, Cici? Not a soul.*

I took a deep breath. Arbella's elopement was all the courage I needed. If she could escape, so could I.

Chapter Three

Polcarrow
Thursday 7th November 1793, 5:30 p.m.

The footman looked incredulous but he took the boy in his arms, gaping in disbelief.

'See to him straightaway, if you don't mind. He needs urgent attention.' Behind him, the blonde woman was running down the stairs clutching a pile of clothes. Bobbing a petrified curtsy, she hurried away.

'Could you take me to Sir James?' I called after her.

She stopped abruptly. 'Sir James's not at home, m'lady,' she replied with wide-open eyes.

I crossed the polished black and white marble floor, and lowered my voice. 'We both know he's at home and we need to be quick if we're going to catch the tide.' She went as white as a sheet but made no protest, turning instead down the panelled corridor. I followed close behind, stopping outside an ornately carved door. 'Tell him Miss Cavendish would like a word.'

The remaining colour drained from her face. 'Miss Celia Cavendish?'

'Yes,' I replied.

The house was certainly ancient, Sir James' study particularly dark. Dense wooden panels lined the walls, an assortment of ruffed ancestors peering down from their frames. A large fireplace dominated the furthest wall and heavy beams crossed the low ceiling. The furniture was solid, intricately carved, the flagstones highly polished. Only the drapes looked new. Sir James looked up.

'Miss Cavendish! What brings you bursting in like this?' For such a young man, James Polcarrow could look stern at the best of times; when he was angry, he looked petrifying.

'Forgive me, Sir James. I've just witnessed Viscount Vallenforth whip a boy half to death and I've brought him here – for his safety.'

'For his safety?' His eyes sharpened beneath his frown.

'Well, mine as well, I suppose.'

Lady Polcarrow was by his side, watching me. She was breathtakingly beautiful – perfect oval face, high cheekbones, her piercingly intelligent eyes somehow magnetic in their power. Her chestnut hair was coiled beneath her lace cap, her gown definitely Marseilles silk. She had risen so far, but with looks like that, it was hardly surprising. We knew one another only slightly from when she worked at the dressmaker's, but I liked her very much and felt sure I could trust her.

'I imagine Viscount Vallenforth does that rather a lot,' she said with evident distaste.

'I can't go back, Lady Polcarrow.'

'How can we help?' Her voice was cautious, wariness darkening those beautiful eyes.

'Take me with you to Falmouth,' I said, watching their astonished faces. 'Forgive me... I know it was wrong to listen – I was searching for a groom and heard you talking. I didn't mean to eavesdrop but I heard everything. As it happens, it quite suits my plans. When we get to Falmouth, I'll leave you in peace and your secret will remain safe.'

Sir James looked furious. 'Miss Cavendish, if you think for one moment–'

'No, wait, James...' Rose Polcarrow put her hand on her husband's arm. 'Miss Cavendish must need our help very badly, or she'd never suggest such an idea. How's the boy?'

'Thrashed to within an inch of his life. I can't go back, Lady Polcarrow – if I do, my parents will take no notice of my pleas. They won't let me break my engagement – I need leverage, some kind of bargaining power.'

Lady Polcarrow nodded but James Polcarrow remained thunderous, his handsome face scowling at me with dislike. 'Miss Cavendish, I'll take no part in your running away.'

'But she's welcome to stay here, isn't she, James?' Rose Polcarrow clearly understood. She understood and she cared. 'We can't do anything now, but when we come back, we'll try to help ... only stay here, don't go to Falmouth.'

She meant well, but if they were in Falmouth they could not keep me from my parents. It would only be a matter of time before Father barged his way in and dragged me back. Arbella had known her only hope had been to run. 'It's very kind of you, Lady Polcarrow, but my parents will only listen to me if they fear scandal. I have to go to Falmouth and if you don't take me, I'll make my own way.'

'Where in Falmouth?' barked Sir James.

'I'm afraid I'm sworn to secrecy.'

'You're going to Arbella! How could you be so foolish?'

'Please Sir James, I don't do this lightly. I know the consequences but I believe I'll be safe with Arbella and her husband – I have their address.'

Sir James shrugged his shoulders. 'It's your choice, Miss Cavendish. Ruin your reputation along with your cousin's – it's no concern of mine.' He turned to Joseph. 'Move the bookcase, if you don't mind and when we're through, put it back exactly as it was. Jenna, if you could order our supper on trays and tell everyone we've gone to our room ... tell them we woke unwell and you've sent for the doctor. We may be gone several days – four, maybe five.'

Jenna nodded. She was sifting through the pile of clothes, holding up one garment, then another. They were working men's clothes, coarse jackets and breeches. A pair of boots stood on the floor, two large hats ready on the table and I stared in disbelief, hardly believing my eyes. Jenna was unfastening Lady Polcarrow's laces, Sir James already pulling off his coat and I turned quickly away, staring at the huge wooden globe in front of me.

'Are you ready, Miss Cavendish?' The beautifully elegant Rose Polcarrow had disappeared and in her place stood a tall, gangling youth wearing brown corduroy breeches and a worsted-wool jacket. Her hair was scraped back beneath the large hat, her boots scuffed and covered in mud. Gone, too, were Sir James' finely tailored clothes. A sailor stood in his place, wearing a dark blue jacket and baggy breeches, a red scarf tied around his neck. I stared at them, my heart racing.

'Take those diamonds off your ears, Miss Cavendish, and if you value your life, get that ring off your finger. Put them in your purse. Where's your cloak?' James Polcarrow opened the top drawer of his desk and began filling a leather pouch with coins.

'I don't have a purse and the boy's wrapped in my cloak.'

'Then take this,' he said, sliding the purse across the desk towards me.

'Thank you. That's very generous. I'll pay you straight back.'

'It's not generous, it's worth nothing – just pennies and half-pennies but it's what you'll need. Hide your jewellery down your bodice and wear this.' He reached for a cloak folded across the back of a chair. 'Keep hooded at all times. No-one must know you're on my boat.'

I wrapped the cloak around me. It was black and coarse but covered me completely. I lifted the hood to hide my face and turned at the sound of scraping. Joseph had his back against a book-case and was heaving it slowly away from the dark wooden panelling.

'Thank you Joseph.' Sir James strode across the hall, buckling up the strap of his leather belt. A large bag lay slung over his shoulder, a pouch hung from his waist. 'The catch is here – this bit that looks like a knot. Press that and the spring releases.'

Joseph pressed the knot and a panel sprung

open, a dark entrance gaping in front of us. It was about three feet across and as black as a grave. Rose was watching me. 'It leads down to the sea – to the rocks beneath the rope-walk, but James won't let you see where it comes out. He'll blindfold you at the entrance.'

'I don't mind,' I said, my heart hammering.

'It's cramped and dirty. Water drips from the rocks and there are deep pools of water – your boots'll get ruined.'

'I don't mind,' I repeated.

'The lantern's likely to go out and bats might fly down at you.'

If she thought she was putting me off, she was not succeeding. 'I'll manage.'

'Of course you will,' she replied, smiling. She handed me a lantern. 'Just stay very close.'

I crouched at the tunnel's entrance, catching Joseph's eye. 'My horse's tethered by the coach-house. Could you stable her tonight and return her to Pendenning? Perhaps you could say you found her wandering?'

A voice echoed through the tunnel, 'Keep close, Miss Cavendish.'

The tunnel smelt damp, airless. It was icily cold, the walls solid stone, the floor roughly hewn flagstones. We were going down, the tunnel widening to the width of two men. I leant forward, bending almost double to avoid the rocks jutting down from above. A drop splashed my cheek and I stopped just in time. A vast pool of water glistened ahead of me; black, stagnant, smelling of damp earth and putrid mud.

I put down my lantern and pulled up my skirts,

hitching them high above my knees. It felt strangely wonderful. No-one was watching me.

For the first time in my life, I was free.

Chapter Four

Rose undid the red scarf from around my eyes and smiled, handing it quickly back to her husband. The wind was blowing against our cheeks, the waves surging against the rocks we were standing on. Everywhere was wet and slimy, covered in cockles, and it was hard not to slip. Rose seemed so sure-footed, Sir James dragging a rowing boat behind him. At the water's edge, he pushed the boat into the foaming waves. 'Get in, Miss Cavendish – sit in the bow.' I held my breath, summoning my courage. As the boat tipped, I gripped the sides, edging forward as Rose and Sir James got in behind me.

'We're away,' shouted Rose as Sir James pulled on the oars, skimming through the white foam, the tip of rocks just visible beneath us. Seaweed swirled round the boat, swaying in a black mass. I could see barnacles, limpets, an encrusted chain. The salty air smelt so good. It was so fresh, so raw, a million worlds away from the stuffy rooms I hated so much.

We were at the widest stretch of the river, pointing east towards Porthruan. Both harbours were busy. Ships lay three abreast along the harbour walls, their masts rocking in the swell of the waves. Vast pulleys stretched high into the air, hoisting sacks onto the decks and into the holds. Men were rolling barrels along the quayside; mules were waiting, their carts piled high with produce. The spray was wetting my cloak, soaking my hood. My boots were wet and muddy, my hem just saved from ruin, yet I felt like pinching myself. I was living, not watching. For once, doing, not dreaming. Across the water, the church bells chimed half past six.

Sir James pulled hard on the oars, his face streaked with spray. 'The tide's on the turn. Where's *L'Aigrette* anchored, Rose?'

'This side ... behind that brig. I hope she hasn't left.' Her words were lost to the wind.

Sir James heaved on the oars, his pace quickening. The waves were mounting, our boat low in the water. Huge black hulls towered above us, lanterns hanging from their sterns, lights dancing across their decks. It was clearly time to leave. Men were climbing the rigging, heaving on ropes. Shouts were ringing across the darkness, sails unfurling, anchors rising from the water.

Sir James' words were clipped with exertion. 'When we're aboard ... don't use our names. Captain Lefèvre will recognise us but the crew mustn't know who we are. Can you see her, Rose?'

'She's there – she hasn't left.'

I looked up, my heart sinking. The boat we were rowing to seemed so small – only a tiny one-masted cutter, not a ship at all. I could hardly believe it. 'Not that one, surely?'

Rose smiled. 'Wait till you sail on her.' We were alongside her now, her black hull glistening in the water beside us. Sir James lifted the oars and grabbed the hull.

'What the hell?' came a voice from the deck.

'I've urgent business with Captain Lefèvre,' shouted Sir James.

A second man leant over the rail. 'And that business is?' He, too, sounded French and distinctly annoyed.

'Captain Lefèvre, I need to speak to you.' The figure disappeared and a ladder slammed against the hull. It was made of rope, the wooden rungs secured by huge knots. Sir James caught the ladder and pulled it tight, the two boats knocking together in the considerable swell.

'Go first,' urged Rose. 'Hold very tight as the rope can get slippery. Sir James will keep it steady.' I pulled my hood over my head, grabbing the ladder tightly.

The sea looked ominously dark, the boats rising and falling at different times. The swell was lifting first one, then the other and it was hard to judge the timing. I put my foot on the bottom rung and held my breath. On the second rung, I felt my boot tug against my skirt and realised I had caught my hem. I tried kicking my foot free, but the corduroy was wet and clinging to my leg. I tried again. I had never done anything like this before. I had rowed the Thames at Richmond, but never dangled from a boat in open sea.

My only option was to tug my skirt free but the waves were swirling beneath me, and letting go with one hand much harder than I thought. The captain was watching from above, James Polcarrow standing in the boat below; both men must think me so foolish. Only Rose would understand how difficult it was, hauling yourself up a swaying ladder in a heavy riding dress. I pulled at my skirt but a large wave rolled beneath me, swinging me violently round, knocking me against the hull.

The captain swung himself over the side; one hand holding the ladder, the other reaching towards me. 'Give me your hand,' he said, leaning as far down as he could.

I would have reached up, but another, stronger, wave crashed the two boats together and I clung even tighter to the rope, scared to be thrown off balance. I was normally so fearless, but the waves were unpredictable, and the foaming black sea suddenly so terrifying. I looked up, preparing to reach out my hand, but Captain Lefèvre was already halfway down the ladder, his arm encircling my waist. His strong arm held me, his body safe behind me and I began kicking my foot free. At once, I heard his command. 'Put your arms round my neck.'

His arm loosened from my waist and reached round my thighs, gripping me tightly and I could do nothing but comply. I slid my hands round his neck and felt myself lifted effortlessly up the ladder, pinned closely against his chest. At the top he swung me over the rail, holding me carefully until my feet touched the deck. I looked up. His eyes were searching the shadows beneath my hood and I turned swiftly away, pulling my cloak closely round me.

Though he could not see me, I saw him clearly. He was tall, fine-boned, his clean-shaven face browned by the sun. Wisps of brown hair blew across his face, the rest tied neatly in a bow behind his neck. His jacket was blue silk, well cut, made only for him. His breeches were leather, his boots highly polished. His movements were quick, decisive, his body at one with the swaying boat. Already he was helping Rose over the side. I saw him nod to Sir James but when he looked back at me, his eyes looked watchful.

'This way, mademoiselle,' he said. 'Down this hatchway – but I'll leave you to yourself, this time.'

The steps opened to a small kitchen, an iron stove standing at its centre, a black pipe leading to the deck above. Cooking utensils hung from large brass hooks and plates and pans lay neatly stowed behind carved wooden grilles. Bottles of wine lay cradled in a curved rack and lemons swung freely in a knotted rope. Rose and Sir James gave it barely a glance but I was struck by the beauty of the glass-fronted cabinets.

'Go through, mademoiselle,' he said, pointing the way.

A brass lantern drenched the cabin with light. It was bigger than I expected and just as intricate. There were no windows, but a raised hatch and a table beneath it. Everywhere was wood – all highly polished and gleaming in the lamplight. Down both sides of the table carved benches were upholstered in rich blue velvet. It was so neat, so compact. Another lantern hung above a desk in the corner, the swaying light making the clock and barometer glint. Shelves of books filled the alcoves, the desk covered with overlapping charts. A pair of compasses lay open, a book creased along its spine.

Rose Polcarrow was already seated, Sir James on the bench opposite. 'We need to go to Falmouth, and we need to go now,' he said as we entered.

Captain Lefèvre did not reply but I thought I saw a flicker of annoyance cross his eyes. He was young for a ship's captain. I expected him coarser, a lot more whiskered – certainly a lot less refined. He turned quickly and mounted the steps, calling loudly from the top step. 'Set sail for Falmouth.'

'Falmouth?' came the astonished reply.

'You heard me.'

Lady Polcarrow patted the bench next to her. 'Come and sit here.'

I slipped next to her on the plush cushion. 'Your boat's certainly very beautiful, Lady Polcarrow.'

She smiled proudly. 'My father built her. She'll do eleven knots when pushed.'

I presumed that was good. 'Your father must be very clever. Did he build her for you?'

She smiled across at her new husband. 'She was meant for the Revenue but was stolen. Sir James tracked her down and bought her for me. We've not been long off her. We spent the first nights of our marriage on her – Captain Lefèvre sailed us to Jersey.' I saw another look of love pass between them and a knot of jealousy tightened in my stomach. I could not help it. I felt hollow, as if betrayed. If Lady Polcarrow knew of Viscount Vallenforth's cruelty, then Mama must also have heard the rumours.

Captain Lefèvre was halfway across the cabin, a bottle of wine tucked under his arm, two glasses held in each hand. They were exquisite glasses, very finely engraved, and as he put them down I recognised the opaque, twisted stems at once – David Wolffe, Mama's favourite engraver. I watched him pour the wine, the dark red liquid making the cupids blush. 'Good wine requires good glasses, don't you think?' he said, smiling at me.

He was clearly at ease with his new companions, showing no surprise that Rose was dressed as a man, but sat leaning back against the velvet cushion, his outstretched arm resting on the polished table, his thumb and forefinger slowly turning the glass in front of him.

'I'm afraid Captain Lefèvre has rather expensive tastes,' laughed Sir James, holding his wine to the light. 'Though I'm not complaining. I met Captain Lefèvre when we were bidding for the cutter. He was determined to outbid me – gave me quite a run.' He took a sip of his wine and smiled appreciatively. 'In the end, we had to compromise. I would buy her, but Captain Lefèvre would be her master. As it happened, it's quite the best solution. But I think you win, don't you, Arnaud? Your money stays safely in the bank *and* you get to sail her!'

'I win indeed, Sir James,' Arnaud Lefèvre replied, raising his glass and sipping his wine slowly.

'And with all that money in the bank, you can afford the finest wines and the very best brandy. Not that I'd have it any other way – I'm quite happy to be the recipient of your trading, but that last crate of cognac cost me a fortune!'

Captain Lefèvre's smile broadened. 'We could

halve the price, Sir James.'

'Halve the price and be had for smuggling? You know my rules – everything above board. If I'm to stand for Parliament, my boat must pay His Majesty's taxes. Where were you bound?'

'Jersey – I've several consignments to collect and deliver.' His blue eyes remained creased in their laughter lines, looking out from beneath their dark lashes. 'Fortunately, the war's not stopping people buying – trade's good and there's profit to be had. But I'm forgetting my manners ... would you like something to eat? I've cold roast beef, or I could boil you some fresh crab?' His English was fluent, his French accent making his words sound strangely intimate.

'I'll have anything you can lay your hands on. I've ridden straight from Bodmin and not eaten since breakfast – I'm starving.' Sir James took another sip of wine, turning back to me. 'You must taste Captain Lefèvre's food – it's quite outstanding. He dives for his own lobsters and cooks them to perfection.'

I smiled, shaking my head, my mind wrestling away the thought of Arnaud Lefèvre, stripped naked to the waist, diving from a rock into clear blue water. It was hot in the cabin, too hot, the oil lamps burning, the stove giving off far too much heat. I felt on fire beneath my cloak. I wanted to rip it off but Captain Lefèvre was looking at me. There was something too watchful about him – something too impeccable, too correct. Sir James may believe he did not smuggle, but I was sure he must.

'Are you too warm? May I take your cloak,

Miss...?' It was as if he could read my thoughts.

'No, thank you ... and nothing to eat... It's ... *Miss Smith.*' I felt suddenly so foolish, regretting my lack of imagination.

We were well underway, the cabin rising and falling, my stomach matching the movement of the boat – dipping, swaying, going up, lurching down, the circular movement taking my stomach with it. It had been a mistake to drink my wine. My lips felt dry, my mouth full of salt and I gripped the stem of my glass, breathing deeply. What was the point of a strong will, if it was accompanied by a weak stomach?

'Nothing to eat at all?' Captain Lefèvre sounded disappointed.

I shook my head. It was definitely getting rougher – the table sloping dangerously towards me, the wine in my glass at a terrible angle. The others seemed oblivious, Sir James and Rose sitting back, enjoying their wine. Captain Lefèvre was busy in the kitchen, opening drawers, reaching for utensils, standing quite upright among all the pitching. At last he finished and came swaying back, placing a huge platter on the table in front of us.

'That looks good,' said Sir James, reaching forward with a smile.

I could barely look. A huge pile of roast beef lay bleeding in front of me. It could have been raw. 'How long's this journey going to take?' I managed to ask.

Captain Lefèvre seemed amused, 'Our passage? No more than three hours – we've got wind and tide–'

'*Three hours!*' The beef was swimming in front of me. I put my hand across my mouth.

'Quick!' whispered Rose, sliding her arm beneath my elbow, 'Come with me. You need some air.'

Chapter Five

On board L'Aigrette
Thursday 7th November 1793, 7:30 p.m.

The fresh air helped, but not completely. Two sailors sat in the open cockpit, one holding the tiller, the other coiling a rope round a wooden peg. There was no moon, no stars, just the vast darkness and the wind whipping the waves into curving white crests. Spray crashed against the bow, the bowsprit plunging beneath the water. 'This can't be safe,' I said, clutching Rose's arm. 'We're sliding into the sea.'

She smiled, genuinely amused. 'This's gentle, I promise – the wind's perfect. The boat's designed to sail like this.' The larger of the two sailors finished coiling the rope and stood to let us sit, but Rose shook her head, leading me instead to the high side of the boat. She beckoned me down. 'Squeeze yourself here – wedge your feet against the coach roof. There you are – you'll be quite safe. My father always designs boats with high bulwarks – it gives this sense of security.' I did as I was told but was not convinced. Foam frothed across the lower deck, spilling out through the gaps in the side.

'That can't be right.'

She laughed again. 'We're not going to sink – she's fast, that's all. You can see why the Revenue wants her back – her name's *Egret* and she's flying.' The boat did seem to be flying, her sails arching above us like wings. Rose Polcarrow seemed so at ease, her legs in their borrowed breeches crossed in front of her, her eyes shining. 'Have you been to Falmouth before?'

I shook my head. The truth was I had not even been to Truro. We had sailed from London to Fosse, five months before and, apart from church, and a few rare visits to the dressmaker, we had been nowhere. Mother had accepted no invitations to socialise with anyone from the town and Father's dislike of the Polcarrows denied us our nearest neighbours. Even during my uncle and aunt's visit, we had not ventured out of the park. 'Mother only came to Cornwall because Viscount Vallenforth's father suggested our marriage.' The nausea in my stomach increased.

Rose stiffened. 'I've only seen Viscount Vallenforth once, but I didn't like what I saw.' Her well-known hatred for the aristocracy rang in her voice. 'If you really don't like him, then you should refuse to marry him – we're not chattel to be bartered with. You should just say no.' Her father was a dissident boat builder, known for his radical views, her mother, a dressmaker; she was proud, quick-tempered and questioning. Just the sort of woman Mama sought to keep me from.

'It's not that easy – I wish it was. We've always

50

known Mama will choose who we marry.' Was it pity, contempt or a flash of irritation crossing those eyes? I felt strangely belittled. She had no idea what my life was like. She had risen from her father's bankruptcy; her skilled book-keeping paying her bills, but I could do nothing. I was a pawn in my parents' hand, my marriage serving solely to align our family with those in power. Could she not see I had no say? Why else would I be running away? I gripped the polished wood, breathing the salt-laden air. It was the air I so longed to breathe. 'Why does Sir James dislike me so much?'

The wind blew her hat, her collar flapped against her face. She seemed genuinely surprised. 'D'you really not know?' She frowned, looking away.

'No, I don't.'

'It's not you he dislikes, it's your father.' She turned to face me, 'Your father, Robert Roskelly and their two land agents have formed a company called St Austell Trading. Your father owns the greatest share, but between them, they've taken the leases of large parcels of Polcarrow land – land they should never have been offered. It's rich in china clay and the leases are illegal. James wants the leases declared void. He's contesting them and intends to drag your father through the courts.'

I felt struck by the anger in her voice. No wonder they hated Father. I knew nothing of Father's affairs, never questioned how he provided for us. He was a hard man, twenty years had taught me he was barely likable, but was he corrupt? Taking land through illegal practice? I gripped the rail, my sea sickness making it hard to talk. 'I'd no idea...'

Rose Polcarrow could sense my distress. She put her hand on my arm and squeezed it gently. 'No, of course you didn't, or else you'd never have come to us.' Her smile was shy, yet defiant. 'But I'm glad you did. That means a lot to me – not many of the gentry will accept me the way you have.'

I took another deep breath and tried to return her smile. 'They will ... just give them time. Forgive me, but surely Robert Roskelly could not expect his sister to poison Sir James, just so her own son could inherit Polcarrow?'

Her mouth hardened. 'Robert Roskelly knows no bounds. He murdered James' father – made it look like a riding accident. He had James transported for grievous bodily harm and attempted murder. James was only seventeen at the time and Alice had only just had her baby. But the baby was a boy and that was all that mattered. Robert Roskelly was named as guardian.'

'And so he took over the estate?'

She nodded. 'For eleven years he's done exactly what he wants – his hold over his sister absolute. I believe he thought she'd use that poison. Alice lives only for her son and we all know Robert Roskelly's threats are real.' She paused, a slight falter in her voice, 'He wants Sir James dead – he always has. That's why we *have* to find him and get him back to Bodmin. If we don't, he'll go abroad and change his name. We all know what he's capable of doing.'

Nausea gripped me. Father was in business

with Robert Roskelly. His land deals were corrupt and illegal. No wonder there was such animosity between him and Sir James. She said no more but left me clutching the rail. Perhaps Father was corrupt. His business dealings had always been kept from us but I remembered the hushed whispers and quickly shut newspapers.

Sir James had come up on deck and was on the helm, watching Rose make her way effortlessly down the swaying deck. He handed her the tiller and they sat looking up at the set of the sails. The beautiful Rose Pengelly, what an extraordinary woman. She seemed so free, so capable, controlling the boat as easily as any man. Her confidence seemed to accentuate my weakness, their obvious love making me feel so empty.

I was meant to be the strong one, the one to champion Charity but, in reality, I was weak and foolish. Rose would have gone straight to her parents. She would never allow herself to be traded like chattel. I should have stayed, not run, certainly never left Charity. My nausea was now unbearable, the thought of Charity bringing tears to my eyes.

'Hot peppermint might help – it's good for calming the stomach. We're just rounding the Dodman, so we're halfway there.' Captain Lefèvre was behind me, holding out a steaming china cup. 'And with the wind behind us, it should get more comfortable.' I had not seen him come. He seemed oblivious to the deck plunging beneath him, holding the cup as steadily as if he had been handing me tea in a drawing-room.

The scent of strong mint rose from the delicate

53

cup. It was Chinese, the rim gold, the exquisitely painted birds far too delicate for a heaving boat. Even through my nausea, I could appreciate its fine glaze. 'Big ships are just about bearable but this's terrible. I don't feel safe.'

'You *are* safe,' he replied, 'and with luck, you'll be ashore before you feel worse.'

He was staring at me and I realised, too late, that my hood had slipped. I pulled it closer. 'Thank you.' I took a sip of the peppermint. It was hot and strong.

'Can I get you anything else?' He stood with one foot on the deck, the other on the bulwark, smiling down on me.

I shook my head. 'Just get us there as quickly as you can.'

Egrets: I had been trying to remember the name of the tall white birds by the river. Perhaps the peppermint was helping. If I stayed completely still, my sickness could be held at bay. I put my chin on my hands, watching our movement through the waves. The white crests rose and fell, and I followed the flashes of green light swirling through the water beside me – whole streams of brilliant green light, tumbling beneath the surface. It was mesmerising, almost soothing – like being rocked to sleep in a cradle.

Only twice did I look away; once, when Captain Lefèvre hauled against a heavy rope, once, when he took control of the tiller. Somehow, I felt safer with him on the helm. He hardly seemed to hold it at all, his long fingers seeming only to rest against the highly polished wood. I shut my eyes, trying not to remember how effortlessly he had carried me up the ladder. How strong those arms were.

'Lights ahoy,' shouted the man called Jacques. He was leaning on the bowsprit, straining his eyes across the black sea, 'Falmouth in sight – Pendennis Castle right on the nose.'

Chapter Six

Falmouth
Thursday 7th November 1793, 11:00 p.m.

Shouts echoed across the water. 'There's fighting on the quayside – stay close to me, Miss Cavendish. Don't let them see you.' Sir James manoeuvred the rowing boat along the harbour wall. Above us, the new moon showed briefly through the racing clouds. We were in the inner harbour sheltered from the wind. Rose reached for a large iron hook hanging next to some steps and secured the rope with a deft knot, tugging to see if it held. 'Take care, Celia, the steps will be slippery.' I stared up at the quay above us; the fight was in full swing and once up those steps, we would be in the midst of it.

'Falmouth!' muttered Sir James behind me. 'Don't say we didn't warn you. I'll go first.' I clasped the wet rung with one hand, my skirt with the other, following him up the worn steps with Rose close behind me. The quayside was heaving, encircling bystanders goading the fighters on, their shouts rising with every fresh blow. Men watched from behind the brazier, their faces lit by the burning coals. Others spilled from the tavern, the crowd thickening as we watched; everyone looked roughly dressed and unkempt. No lamps lit the harbour wall, only the two braziers and a soft glow coming through the leaded windows of the tavern behind. I drew my cloak around me. 'Keep to the back,' urged Sir James.

The circle parted as the two fighters lurched forward; shoulders interlocked, their fists pounding the life out of the other. The stronger of the two seemed unstoppable. Sensing his advantage he redoubled his efforts, his increasingly furious blows meeting their target with ease. The weaker man's eyes were too swollen to see. He staggered aimlessly about, his legs collapsing beneath him, his body falling in a crumpled heap. Blood from his broken nose dripped onto the cobbles by my feet.

'This way.' Sir James seemed so calm, ushering us forward with hardly a look. I followed him, running quickly along the quayside, skirting the backs of the yelling crowd. Behind us, I heard a large splash, followed by a howl of laughter and my stomach sickened – the man had no chance. He could not move, let alone swim.

The alley we were in was no wider than two men, the walls close together. We were going steeply uphill, the cobbles rough and uneven. It was very dark, the oil lamps too few and far between, their light barely penetrating the darkness. I could make out archways with steps leading from them and wooden crates stacked against the wall. Men were leaning against the crates, their shoulders hunched, legs sprawling across our path. Drunk or asleep, they looked like lifeless mounds of filthy clothing. It was reeking, foul and I put my hand over my mouth, trying not to breathe.

The alley gave way to a street just as badly lit and uneven, but wider, with taller buildings over-hanging both sides. The buildings were crammed with sailors toppling drunkenly out of the doors. I could hear laughter, shouting, the sound of brawling. Men were weaving their way down the cobbles and I watched in horror as two men used the wall as a latrine, not ten feet away. I was too shocked to hear what Sir James was saying. He was staring at me, his brows drawn tightly. 'Where are we to take you, Miss Cavendish?' he repeated.

'Upper Street.'

'This *is* Upper Street. I hope to God it's the other end. What number?'

It was the question I had been dreading ... *we've got respectable lodgings in Falmouth, in Upper Street, with Mrs Trewhella* ... that was all Arbella had written – she had not said the number. Somehow I envisioned we would find it easily. 'I'm sorry... I don't know exactly. They're staying with Mrs Trewhella.'

Sir James looked furious and with good reason. I was delaying him. They were here to find Robert Roskelly, not play nursemaid to me. He turned in exasperation to Rose. 'Wait here, both of you – I'll have to ask.' He crossed the street, walking quickly through the door of the nearest tavern.

Rose put her hand on my arm, 'Someone will know where Mrs Trewhella lives. Don't mind James, he's in a hurry, that's all. We've got to catch Robert Roskelly off guard and we mustn't make ourselves obvious.'

I smiled back, but my fear was rising. I had always been shielded from the streets, conveyed everywhere in a sedan chair or carriage. I had never seen anywhere like this, nor felt so unsafe. Falmouth was a horrible place and Arbella must hate it. A crowd had already started to gather. Rose was attracting no attention, her slim body easily disguised by the jacket and breeches, but I was clearly an object of interest. Men began leering, coming towards me. They were laughing, spitting on the street, wiping their hands across their mouths. 'He's coming back,' whispered Rose.

Sir James pushed his way through the watching men, and grabbed my arm. His eyes were blazing, 'It's number fifty-five. She runs a boarding house, but I warn you – it's the wrong end of town.' He ran quickly up some steps to an even narrower street, and I followed as fast as I could. Rose kept close behind me and when he stopped, we stared in equal horror. 'As I said – wrong end of town.'

Dismay filled me. I could not imagine how Arbella must have felt being brought to such a place. It was a tall house, the eight windows and front door in desperate need of repair. Every sill was rotting, the paint peeling, dark patches of mould growing thickly down either side of the portico. It was eleven o'clock but lights were burning in two of the rooms upstairs and a light

58

showed behind the shutters on the ground floor. For that, at least, I should be grateful. I saw the look that passed between Sir James and Rose and tried to hide my fear. 'When did you receive your information? Who gave it to you?' His voice was polite, but terse.

'Arbella ... when she left.'

'But that's nearly three months ago! They'll be long gone. Miss Cavendish, this farce must end. I'm not leaving you here. I suggest I take you to a friend of mine. He's a packet captain and lives in a good neighbourhood – his wife will take you in.' His hand tightened on my arm. 'I'm not prepared to leave you unaccompanied in an inn and you can't stay with us – we're dressed to merge with the crowds, but you'll be a target for thieves.'

Everything was going so horribly wrong. I forced back my tears, desperate to find Arbella. 'Sir James, please ... I know what you say is right but let me at least just *see* if they're still there. If they are, then I won't be alone and if they're not, then I'd be more than grateful for your friend's hospitality. Perhaps they need money – perhaps my coming is just what they need.'

Sir James seemed to soften. 'If they're still here, then you're right, they must be desperate. Perhaps your diamonds can help them!' His concern seemed genuine, his sudden smile full of compassion. I had heard talk of his generosity, his desire to see his workers well housed and I smiled back, but my heart was hammering. If he was to knock on that door, Arbella would never come forward – she would hide and refuse to see us.

'I promised Arbella I wouldn't tell anyone ... if

you ask for them, they'll hide and pretend they're not in. Could I knock on the door by myself? Would you watch me from over there?' I turned, pointing to the shadows of the opposite doorway.

Sir James clearly did not like my suggestion but turned, drawing Rose with him as he crossed the road. They remained swallowed by the darkness and I grabbed the brass knocker. It was green and rough. Within minutes, a woman stood scowling at me from under a filthy mob cap.

'Yer business? Don't know what time ye'd call this, but I'd call it late.' She was a large woman, untidy, about forty, with greying blonde hair, and two teeth missing. The light from her candle showed thick stains down her apron. She glowered at me, staring at my hood. 'Show yerself – ye've no business hiding yer face once ye've knocked on my door.' I let my hood slip to my shoulders. I was wearing my riding hat and must have looked a sight; my dress wet and filthy, my hat pinned so securely in place.

'I would like to speak to Mr and Mrs Smith.'

'Mr and Mrs Smith?' She was looking over my shoulder, searching the street, 'Ye by yourself? A friend or somethin'?' She was obviously protecting them, keeping them safe and I felt immediately grateful, heartened by her concern. I nodded quickly, angry with myself for judging her so fiercely.

'Yes, I've no-one with me. I'm her cousin – she told me where to find her.'

'Quite alone?' I nodded again and she turned. 'Well, ye'd better come in.' Her thick Cornish accent was hard to understand, her words whistling through the gaps in her missing teeth. Excitement made me almost lose my fear. I would soon be with my dearest cousin and meet her new husband. I hoped I liked him, but even so, what sort of man would bring his new wife to such a place?

I turned quickly, smiling back into the dark recess of the opposite doorway. It seemed so ill-mannered to leave Sir James and Rose without thanking them properly but at least my smile would show them I had found Arbella. Mrs Trewhella was well ahead of me and I hastened to follow her down the dingy corridor. Her candle sent shadows across the ceiling and I could see large patches of brown mould encircling huge cracks in the plaster. It smelt damp and musty 'Wait in here,' she said, 'while I see if they be awake.'

The candles must have been tallow as the room stank of burning fat and I caught my breath, hardly wanting to enter. Two men sat staring at me through thick tobacco smoke, both hunched over clay pipes, the smoke rising in thick coils around them. Mrs Trewhella watched me from the door. 'Which Mr an' Mrs Smith? We've got two. Yesterday we had three.'

My heart jolted, the rancid air beginning to choke me. I tried to keep calm, think her words through, but my head was spinning. This must be a place known to eloping lovers. They would book themselves in as Mr and Mrs Smith with no questions asked. They would pay for their anonymity with foul, stinking rooms, but they would never be traced. 'Mr *Morcum* and Mrs *Arbella* Smith,' I replied, trying to hide my rising panic. Mrs Trewhella remained staring at me, her eyes flicking from my face to my hat. My hair must look a mess, but surely she need not stare so openly? I cleared my throat, my voice thin and strained. 'Mrs *Arbella* Smith is very beautiful ... she has hair the colour of gold.'

Mrs Trewhella sniffed. 'Ye may know what gold looks like, m'lady, but the likes of us never see gold. Wouldn't know gold if 'twas handed us on a plate.' She was staring at my hat and I suddenly remembered my hatpin. The shaft was gold, the head encrusted with diamonds. It had been my birthday present.

'But you must know who I mean. She's very beautiful, with blonde hair ... about my height ... blue eyes—'

'Oh, we know who ye mean, don't we, Mrs Trewhella?' The man rose from his chair. He began knocking his pipe against the fireplace, glowering at me. 'The rich bitch who refused to stay – said we weren't good enough. Left without paying even though we'd kept them our best room.' He began filling the bowl of his pipe, re-lighting it with a taper from the candle, sucking at it until the tobacco sparked. Thick smoke curled from his mouth. 'Falmouth be rowdy on a Friday – especially late like this. She's best to stay, don't ye think, Mrs Trewhella?'

The woman was blocking my exit, her husband edging slowly nearer. I had to get out. Both had their lips pursed and evil in their eyes. 'As it happens, I'm not alone,' I said, fighting the rise in my voice. 'I've perfectly good lodgings and there are three men waiting for me outside. I've been sent here as a trap. I was to lure my cousin out, but I see we've wasted our time. Let me pass.' I caught their glance, my heart pounding. There was less certainty in the way they looked at me. I must keep my nerve; they would have to let me out.

The man's clothes stank of sweat, his breath of rum and decay. He was stocky, powerful, the kind of man to win any quayside fight. 'Then, I'll 'ave to see ye back to yer friends, won't I? Wouldn't want *a lady* going unaccompanied – not round here.' He began leading me down the dismal hall, one hand on my elbow, the other pushing against my back. As the door opened, I peered desperately into the shadows of the opposite doorway. Sir James and Rose must have gone. There was no-one there, just shouts echoing down the alley and shuffled footsteps of a man too drunk to know where he was going.

Mr Trewhella's grip tightened. Forcing my arm behind my back, he began pushing me across the street, his hips pressing roughly against my skirt. 'Perhaps yer friends are waitin' over here?' He jerked me so violently I almost fell, his foetid breath making my stomach turn. A blade was pressed against my throat. 'That fancy tart owes us money.'

I could barely breathe. 'How much?'

'Everythin' ye've got, ye stupid bitch – the whole bleedin' lot.'

My legs were shaking. I was trying to think. He could have my hatpin, my earrings, but if he got hold of Viscount Vallenforth's ring, my life would be over. 'I've nothing else ... only my hat pin ... you can have my hat, too.' My jewellery was down my bodice, not two inches from his knife.

'The likes of ye always have more.'

At once I remembered the purse. 'Alright ... alright ... you can have everything. I *have* got money ... a whole purse full of gold sovereigns ... you can have them all ... *and* the hatpin. Just let go.' I began undoing the top of my riding jacket, my fingers shaking so fiercely, I could hardly grip the buttons. 'You can have the lot.' The purse was heavy in my hand and I gripped it tightly. 'There,' I shouted, throwing it deep into the shadows behind him.

He heard the thump of a heavy purse and fell to his knees. If I was quick, I would stand a chance. I grabbed my skirts, hurling myself back the way we had come. I could remember the details – left at the inn with the blue door ... right at the house with the crooked lamp ... straight ahead at the drinking trough with the broken spout. Right, down the alley ... past the three lamps ... round the back of the inn. I weaved through the sailors lurching towards me, ignoring shouts from the doorways, the drunkards trying to delay me. In the last alley I jumped over the legs sprawling across my path and stopped, gasping for breath. I was nearly there. Just the second brazier, the pile of lobster pots and then I would know.

I hardly dared look down. The rowing boat was still there, the oars safely stashed. I almost flew down the steps and pulled at the knot. The rope slipped free and I grabbed the oars, pushing myself away from the harbour wall. Men shouted down from the dockside but I was free, gliding through the black water, working my way past the moored boats. My rowing was erratic, the oars splashing noisily in the water but I did not care. I was moving and that was the only thing that mattered.

Not quite the only thing. Captain Lefèvre had better be there.

Chapter Seven

Falmouth
Friday 8th November 1793, 00:00 a.m.

The anchored ships looked different, *L'Aigrette* nowhere to be seen. The wind seemed fiercer than before, clouds racing across the thin outline of the moon. Even the current seemed stronger, pulling me out to sea. We had rowed straight from the boat. I remembered looking round and seeing the light on her stern. My fear began rising.

A log trailing seaweed from its branches knocked against the boat and I realised my mistake. The ships had turned with the tide and were facing the other way; the large naval frigate was blocking my view. I began pulling on the oars. *Please, please, be there.* I rounded the hull and fought back tears of relief – three lamps were burning on a sleek black cutter. What had I been thinking? No money, no luggage, no protection? Women in my position might gallop but we could not run. We could stand at the door of our gilded cage but we could not fly. I had been so foolish, so utterly stupid.

The rope-ladder hung from the deck. Securing the boat as I had seen Sir James do, I hitched up my skirt, holding it firmly away from my boots. I had learnt my lesson well. The sea was more sheltered than in Fosse, the climb easier than I imagined. I swung myself over the top rail and glanced along the decks. The boat was pulling against her anchor rope; everything was tidy – the ropes neatly coiled, the sails rolled away. There was no one on deck but a light was shining in the cabin below. I walked quickly to the hatch, turning to face the steps like I had seen everyone do. The kitchen looked clean and tidy, the plates stowed neatly away. In the cabin, the light shone on the uncluttered table. Surely someone must be on board.

He was sitting at his desk watching me, one hand holding a quill, the other resting on a book. His jacket hung over the back of his chair. He was wearing a white shirt, open at the collar, loose at the arms and even in the half-light I could tell it was silk. There was surprise in his eyes. Or was it annoyance? Whatever it was, he covered it well. 'Is Falmouth not to your liking, Miss Smith?' He looked watchful, no longer smiling.

'My friends have changed their lodgings and I became separated from the Polcarrows. You must take me straight back to Fosse.'

'I'm not going to Fosse.'

'I'm afraid you must.'

'I run a business, *Miss Smith,* not a ferry. I'm already six hours behind my planned departure and I cannot, and will not, leave it any longer.' He stood up, putting on his jacket, flicking his hair free of his collar. 'I'm sorry but you'll have to–'

'No, *I'm* sorry, Captain Lefèvre, I insist you take me straight back. Falmouth is a foul, stinking place, full of thieves and brawling drunks.' I was wet and scared and did not like the look in his eyes. It showed a distinct lack of respect. 'And I'm not *without* influence ... you don't know who I really am.' I pulled the hood from over my face.

'But I do know who you are,' he said, walking slowly towards me, carefully adjusting the lace at his cuffs. 'You're Miss Celia Cavendish, eldest daughter of Sir Charles and Lady April Cavendish, granddaughter to Earl and Countess Montville ... elder sister to Charity, Georgina, Sarah and baby Charles.'

I stared at him. 'Sir James was meant to keep my identity a secret.'

He fastened his collar. 'You go to Porthruan church every Sunday. You wear three different dresses – one green, one apricot and one blue. I prefer your blue one. You fidget when you're bored. You curl your ringlets round your right forefinger and nudge Charity with your elbow. The two of you have difficulty suppressing your giggles. You don't like Reverend Bettison – you think he goes on too long and you long to be out in the fresh air...'

I could not believe what he was saying. He had been watching me, studying me. I took a deep breath, wishing I had my fan. 'You seem to know a lot about me,' I snapped.

'You find your middle sister Georgina rather annoying but you love Charity and you're extremely fond of your governess, Mrs Jennings.

67

You never look at your mother but every now and then you glance at your father with dislike. You fear him.'

'That's quite enough!'

'When you stand outside the church, you look up at the trees. You're watching the birds. That's why I chose the china cup with the birds on it. I knew you'd like it.'

His tone was soft and intimate, his French accent making his words sound strangely thrilling. He had been watching me, studying me. I felt confused, almost pleased. I had watched him too. I knew the set of his shoulders, the way his jacket stretched. I had imagined him diving through the sea, his hair streaming behind him, his arms reaching in front of him. I had even tasted the lobster. 'Well, what you don't know ... and I think it important you *should* know ... is that I'm engaged to be married to Viscount Vallenforth.'

There, I had said it. The words seemed to stick in my teeth, but I had said it. Captain Lefèvre would have no choice but to take me home. A flicker crossed his eyes. He bowed respectfully. 'Now, that I didn't know,' he said softly. 'Please accept my sincerest condolences.'

His words sent a wave of shock straight through me. I felt wounded, stabbed. Viscount Vallenforth must be known for his cruelty – Mama *must* have heard the rumours. I took a deep breath, strengthening my resolve. I would go straight back and tell her there could be no engagement. A boat scraped along the deck and Captain Lefèvre looked up, walking quickly to the bottom step. 'Any luck?' he called.

''Fraid not,' Jacques called down the hatchway. 'Seth's still bad – must've eaten a bad oyster.'

'Then Nathaniel will have to sail with us.'

'Are we to stow this other boat, sir?'

'Tie it to the coach roof and secure it well – the wind's picking up. When you've done that, we'll leave.' He may have been talking to Jacques, but he was staring at me. 'Stay below, Miss Cavendish. We're sheltered here, but once at sea, your other voyage will seem like a walk in the park.'

He was taking me home and I should have been grateful, but the thought of rough weather filled me with fear. It seemed too harsh a penance for a lesson already learnt. *Between the devil and the deep blue sea* – my uncle always said that, but I had never appreciated it quite so keenly. Captain Lefèvre must have seen the fear in my eyes.

'Come,' he said more kindly, 'let me make you comfortable. Give me your cloak.' His eyes seemed genuine in their concern, his long eyelashes as dark as his hair. 'I'll show you around – it's really very civilised. In here we have washing facilities...' He opened a door to a small cabin. A washbasin rested in a beautifully crafted cabinet, a jug hanging from a brass hook beside it. Above the basin was a mirror, beside it, a towel neatly folded over a brass rail. 'The jug's full of fresh water, but I'll boil you some hot. This seat lifts up, look, there's a bucket underneath.' I looked away, my embarrassment making him smile. 'We empty the bucket over the side, but I don't expect you to do that. We sailors don't mind slops – we're trained to keep things ship-shape.'

I followed him out. 'There's no kitchen on a ship, it's called a galley and the privy's called the heads. There's no left and right ... just port and starboard ... and on my boat the master has the right to call the crew by their first names. Shall I show you my galley, Cécile?'

I looked up. It was the way he said my name – it sounded so much nicer. I had always hated Celia, yet *Cécile* sounded strangely exciting, as if I was a different person. It could do no harm to humour him so I smiled, indicating the galley would be a nice place to visit. 'The water's kept in this barrel. The kettle's here ... and the stove's always lit – we'll soon have hot water for you.' There were rails round the stove, thick ridges round the wooden surfaces.

'You must like lemons,' I said looking at the huge basket hanging from the deckhead.

'Lemons keep scurvy at bay. Lemons or limes, but you probably already know that. While the water's boiling, I'll show you the cabins.' He was smiling, his head already dipping beneath the beam separating the galley from the walkway. For such a tall man, he must find boats difficult.

'Were you keen to buy this boat because she's so fast, or because you can stand up in the galley?'

'Both, Cécile – how very perceptive of you.'

How strange to be thought perceptive – most people just thought me nosey. We crossed the main cabin, stopping outside the first of two narrow doors. He smiled again, his eyes mischievous. 'This is my cabin – you're very welcome to use it.' Down one side lay a long wooden berth, a pillow at the end, a red damask cover stretching

70

along its length. Somehow it seemed too intimate and I looked away, my face uncomfortably hot.

'I won't need a bed,' I snapped.

'I think you might – it's going to get rough.'

'I'll be quite comfortable on the bench by the table, Captain Lefèvre.'

'Call me Arnaud,' he replied, his voice strangely compelling.

'Another ship's rule?'

'It is now.' His face turned serious. 'You shouldn't be here, Cécile.'

'I know that, thank you, Captain Lefèvre. Just make no record of it in your log.'

His eyes held mine; watchful eyes making me uneasy. 'No record whatsoever. I'll leave you in peace – you'll be quite private. Jacques won't come down, he'll remain aft.' He picked up the kettle and began filling the washbasin, the steam rising, misting the mirror. 'There's a spare bucket under the basin and a blanket in the locker under the port bench. Once we're underway, I'll check you've everything you need.'

I smiled my thanks. He had been very attentive, almost as if he anticipated a longer voyage. I took off my riding jacket, plunging my hands into the warm water. It felt so good. There was soap resting on a porcelain dish and I rolled it between my hands, the soft foam smelling of almonds. I was already feeling better – we would be back while it was still dark and I would tell everyone I had been thrown from my horse. I would say I had been too dazed to know where I was.

We were clearly underway now, the boat rising and falling, throwing me off balance. I jammed my feet against the sides of the cabin and gripped the basin. The water was tipping over the edge, slopping onto the floor. I had filled it too full and must empty some out. Picking up the jug, I tried scooping it up, pouring the hot soapy water into the empty privy bucket but I could feel my nausea rising – great waves of sickness swelling within me. The same salty taste, the same dull headache; I needed to lie down. Opening the locker, I grabbed the spare bucket.

It was so much rougher; the cabin floor was slanting in front of me, the boat rising and falling, crashing sideways. I lurched forward, throwing myself onto the bench as it rose to greet me and lay rolling with the motion of the boat – if I moved, I would be sick. I clutched the bucket against my chest, closing my eyes. Dear God, three hours. *Let it be quicker.*

'Let me take off your boots.' I could do nothing but lay there, my eyes tightly shut. 'Wrap yourself in this.' I felt the blanket warm around me. 'Use this as a pillow. Do you need–' I clutched the bucket and leant forward, the contents of my stomach turning inside out. 'Oh, here, take my handkerchief ... now let me empty this–'

'Don't take it,' I cried, retching again, the smell of vomit making everything worse. 'Leave me... I'll be–' I began straining again, my stomach heaving. I wanted to cry, curl up and die. He took the bucket. 'Don't be long–'

He must have rinsed the bucket and come straight back, sitting on the bench next to me. I know I was moaning. 'Try some of this – it's preserved ginger. It's good for sea sickness.' I opened my eyes to see him handing me a fine Chinese jar covered in delicate blue blossoms. I could do no more than glance at it.

'That's beautiful ... quite old.'

He untwisted the carved mahogany lid. 'It's very old but the ginger's fresh.' He was smiling, pushing a stray ringlet away from my face. 'Have as much as you need. I'm sorry you don't like sailing.'

'Just get me back to Fosse ... make it quick.'

A shadow flicked across his face. 'As quick as I can. Are you feeling better?'

'No.'

'Then lie very flat – I'll come back and check on you.'

'Captain Lefèvre, are we safe?'

He put his hand on mine, his touch warm and comforting. 'Yes, Cécile, we are – this boat's been through far worst. She's as stable as they come and we're not going to sink.' I watched him climb the stairs, his voice soaring across the wind, 'Starboard, south-east by south. Take down the foresails – we'll fly by night.'

I took a deep breath. We had been sailing for about an hour, only two left to go.

I gripped the bucket, every fresh fall making my stomach dive, every rise making me want to heave. I lay anticipating each movement, not knowing which was worse – the drop, the twist, the rise. My head was throbbing; my stomach was empty, but I could not stop retching. The lantern had blown out long ago and I lay in the dark, listening to the wind howl around me. The timbers were creaking. At any moment the boat could flip backward and tip us into the sea.

'Are you any better?' Through the darkness I saw the outlines of a dripping cape. I could not speak. If he had come telling me to abandon ship, I could not have moved. He bent towards me, holding another cup. I could not even look at it but lay back, groaning. 'Drink this, Cécile, I think you need it.' He helped me raise my head and put the cup to my lips, holding it gently so I could sip its fiery contents. It was thick, syrupy, tasting of ginger and exotic spices, burning my throat as I swallowed. I was too weak to refuse. I thought I might throw it straight back up, but I finished the cup, the contents warm in my stomach.

He took the bucket, turning me to my side, tucking the blanket round me as if I was a child. I felt so sleepy, the sounds of the storm receding around me. There was nothing but a gentle burr, the faintest whirr. I was weightless, floating, a sense of calm spreading right through me. I was no longer sick but felt so content ... so wonderfully at peace. I could hear my breath rising and falling. It was so warm, so comfortable. I was weightless, drifting, perhaps I was flying. Part of me wanted to giggle – Reverend Bettison ... he had got that wrong. I was watching the buttons on his waistcoat, waiting for them to pop. One day they would pop. Pop. I was smiling, laughing. What a funny boat.

A voice came and went. It was here again. 'Here's someone to keep you company – I'm afraid you've got her blanket.'

I was not sure I could talk. I think I was giggling. I would like to have said *the more the merrier.* Perhaps I did. Something soft rubbed against my cheek and I opened my eyes. There was nothing there, just two green eyes staring at me through the darkness. No face, nothing, just two huge green eyes.

Now I knew I was giggling. Green eyes. Nothing but huge green eyes. What a funny boat.

Chapter Eight

On board L'Aigrette
Friday 8th November 1793, 11:00 a.m.

There was a loud buzzing in my ear and the smell of coffee. Men were talking and I could feel a gentle swaying. My legs and arms felt heavy, my head unable to move. I tried opening my eyes but they seemed glued together. If I was awake, my body was still asleep.

'We've made good time. Slack water will be in an hour.'

'Where are we?'

'Here ... that last bearing had the church north-west by west. In fifteen minutes we'll turn up tide. Landfall in half an hour gives us two hours of slack. We'll heave-to. I don't want to anchor unless we have to. We've lost enough anchors, don't you think, Jacques?'

The voices were familiar, the smell of strong coffee clearing my head. A jumble of images were flashing through my mind – green eyes, a man's head resting on his arms on the table next to me.

'Normal signal?'

'Should be straightforward, now the storm's over.'

'What about Miss Smith?'

'Let's hope she goes on sleeping. With luck, the cargo will be landed and we'll be heading home.' I remembered everything now – the howling wind, the storm, the terrible nausea. 'Is Nathaniel still asleep?' The voice was familiar but wrong. It sounded more furtive than it should be, less trustworthy.

'Yes. He's got another three hours off watch. He's a good sailor. I'll give him that – knows his stuff.'

'I'd rather it was Seth. You better get back, Jacques. Keep the tiller tied to this course – I'll be up in fifteen minutes with some coffee.'

The loud, persistent buzzing was coming from somewhere very close and I forced my eyes open. A black cat was resting against me, her eyes tightly shut, her paws tucked beneath her. It was no longer dark; daylight streamed through the hatch, filling the cabin with light. Arnaud Lefèvre was at his desk, his right hand twisting a pair of dividers across a chart. He seemed pensive, pre-occupied, his frown too furtive for legitimate trading. Sir James was more gullible than I thought.

Captain Lefèvre must have seen the cat jump. He looked up, catching my eye. 'Are you thirsty, Cécile?' He crossed the cabin, holding out a tall, finely etched crystal glass. My mouth was parched, my stomach rumbling, but I shook my

76

head and he laughed, sitting down on the bench opposite me as I struggled to sit upright. My hair was everywhere, my ringlets in a tangled mess. 'It's freshly squeezed lemon with a touch of honey – it's perfectly safe,' he said, smiling. 'I'll drink half and you can finish the rest – that way you can be sure. You heard us talking?'

'Where are we?'

'Twelve hours from Fosse.'

'Twelve hours!'

'I told you I didn't run a ferry.' He glanced briefly at the brass clock above his desk. His eyes looked bluer in daylight, fine stubble shadowed his chin. 'I'll get you back first thing in the morning.'

'Which morning?' I reached for the remaining lemon juice, draining it in one go. It was sharp, refreshing, absolutely delicious.

'Saturday morning, we'll make landfall at about four.'

'Saturday! But I left on Thursday ... that's ... that's ... thirty-six hours. How could you do this to me?' I was furious. Thirty-six hours would be impossible to explain. At least from Falmouth, I could have sent an express, but now they would be so worried. Charity would be beside herself. 'I was a fool to trust you. You're a smuggler and you've put my life in danger. I thought you better than that.'

'You put your own life in danger, the moment you decided to run away. I think we should make that clear.' He was no longer smiling, his voice no longer mocking. 'You saw at once how things were – I saw it in your face. *Not quite as they*

77

should be yet you chose to come back.'

'Believe me, only the direst necessity brought me back.'

'Was it? Or was it the belief there's more to life than four walls?' He was staring at me, his blue eyes edged with brown. I saw the challenge in them, the danger – the invitation to drop all pretence and answer truthfully.

'That's a very impertinent question.' My heart was pounding. I was used to false politeness, the veneer of social niceties, not saying what you really meant.

'Sir James would never just abandon you – he would have offered you a safe option. You ride, don't you, Cécile?' he leant back against the cushion, one hand resting on the table. It was strange, his movements on deck so quick and decisive, yet below, so studied and watchful.

'Of course I ride. You probably already know that.'

'Do you gallop?'

I could see exactly where his question was leading. It was as if he knew my mind. Yes, I galloped. Yes, I wanted to go faster than was safe. Yes, I looked with envy at the birds flying above me, the white sails on the sea. Of course I felt my house a prison, everyone my gaoler. Who would not long to break free from rigid protocol, endless hours of embroidery? 'I was a fool. I acted on impulse and I regret it – thirty-six hours alone on a boat with three men rather hints at complete ruin, don't you think?'

His smile returned. 'You're no fool, Cécile. You notice details – that ginger jar is Ming, by the way.'

'Of course, I just didn't see it properly.'

'You'll see everything properly now you've got your sea-legs. We both have a secret. You can trust me – not one word will pass my lips. I'll get you back to Fosse as soon as I can, but, believe me, you'd have been in far more danger if I'd left you alone in Falmouth.'

Half of me was petrified, half of me thrilled. As a child, I had always longed for the forbidden, always wanting to see what lay beyond the gates. *With luck, the cargo will be landed and we'll be heading home.* The thrill of conspiracy seemed strangely compelling – the same heady mix of anticipation and trepidation which spurred my gallops. I was not looking out of the window, I was breathing the air. It smelt exciting, the cries of the seagulls loud with warning. Perhaps he was right. Perhaps I *had* been courting danger. 'Sir James will hear nothing from me – you can be sure of that.'

'Then we have an agreement,' he said, the approval in his eyes making my cheeks flush. He glanced back at the clock, his face at once serious. 'There's coffee in the pot, roast beef and fresh bread in the galley ... and the kettle's nearly boiled. By the time you've eaten and washed, we'll be heading home. Help yourself – there's mustard above the stove and horseradish, if you must.' He turned to go.

'Captain Lefèvre, we're not in any in danger, are we?'

He paused. 'No more than usual ... but I suggest you remain below.'

He left the galley, an earthenware mug in each hand, the smell of coffee following him up the stairs. I had slept so well. I felt refreshed, bursting with energy, my senses buzzing. Most of all, my stomach was rumbling, the thought of rare beef suddenly irresistible. I jumped from the bench, not noticing the slight sway, the floor rising and falling. I had never been anywhere near a kitchen, but a galley looked perfectly simple. A large wooden platter lay on the surface, a big clay pot strapped to the cabinet beside it. I opened the lid. Inside was the beef, wrapped in brown paper. It felt surprisingly cold and smelt so good. I unrolled the paper, the gnawing in my stomach almost unbearable. Pulling open a drawer, I grabbed a large knife and began slicing the rare beef as quickly as I could.

I tore at the bread, stuffing both the beef and bread into my mouth, amazed at how good they both tasted. The cat was rubbing my skirt. Did cats eat roast beef? I suppose they did. I had never been anywhere near a cat before. Dogs, yes; Father's gun dogs and Mama's beloved pug Saffron, but cats? There might be cats in the kitchen but I suppose Saffron chased them away. I looked up. Was Saffron too overfed to run? Perhaps she just barked at them.

Cats did like beef, plenty of it. I poured some coffee. There was steam coming from the kettle. For the first time in my life I was doing something for myself. I picked up the kettle, carrying it carefully across the cabin to the heads. A bright swathe of colour caught my attention and I looked up through the hatch.

A huge red, white and blue flag fluttered in the wind above us. It was partly surrounded by blue and red and I stared at it, trying to recognise its message. My uncle had taught us all the code flags, yet this flag eluded me. I filled the basin, stripping off my jacket, plunging my face into the hot water.

Immediately, a painting at home flashed through my mind. A ferocious sea battle. Huge seas. Cannon fire. Blazing galleons bearing French flags.

Chapter Nine

On board L'Aigrette
Friday 8th November 1793, 12:00 a.m.

I stared through the hatch at the flag and grabbed my cloak. It was dry, the mud carefully brushed from the hem. I searched for my boots. They, too, were dry and newly polished. I pulled my hood over my head and climbed the steps into beautiful sunshine. The sea was intensely blue, the sun glinting like thousands of tiny mirrors. 'Miss Smith, I suggest you remain below.'

'I can't, Captain Lefèvre. I'm desperate for fresh air.'

I could sense the tension in him. His mouth was drawn tight, his brow creased. He put the telescope back to his eye, clasping his pocket watch in the other hand. We were not moving, the boat still in the water. Just one small sail caught the sunshine, the rest were rolled away.

Jacques was tying down the tiller, his short, stocky frame hunching away from me. He was in his mid-thirties, maybe younger; it was hard to tell with the weathering of his face. He had thick, curly hair, cut short, barely contained under his black scarf. His red shirt was rolled to the elbow, his powerful arms covered in tattoos. He nodded, his manner respectful, but he spoke to Arnaud. 'Not like him to be late.'

'Our position's perfect. Where is he?'

'Perhaps our delay's unsettled him.'

'No. We're on time and in the right place.'

The other sailor was no longer asleep. He was in the bow, tidying the ropes, coiling them next to the sails. He looked to be in his forties; a thick-set man, powerfully built, about my height, his hair shaved, his bald head browned by the sun. His movements were swift, sure. He was twisting and turning the rope, tucking it neatly in place but he seemed watchful, full of hostility. He must be Nathaniel, the replacement crew, not privy to the plans.

We were in a bay, the land sweeping round us in a gentle curve. Vast swathes of marshland fringed the shore and I stood gazing at it, my eyes blinking in the sun. Arnaud came to my side and took my arm, leading me to the coach roof where he beckoned me to sit. 'We don't usually have to wait. They row straight out to the boat. I'm sorry for the delay.'

'That's France, isn't it?'

'Yes.'

'You must be insane. Smuggling from Jersey's one thing, but from France? It's ludicrous. No amount of brandy can be worth this risk.'

'I'll get you home, Cécile. I've promised you.'

I looked across at the fringe of marshland and the huge wall running the length of the shore. There was an abbey at its centre, grey and austere; its tall, steeply sloping roof merging into the land around it. Cloisters huddled against one side, a walled garden against the other. Vast orchards stretched both in front and behind, reaching down to the huge wall which encircled everything. 'It's beautiful, though. I'll give you that.'

'Use this.' Arnaud handed me his telescope and I held it to my eye. I could see the slates on the roof, ornately decorated cornices and window panes glinting in the sun. There were pointed arches in the cloisters, some roses in the rose garden. Dark purple grapes still clung to the vines; beehives dotted the orchard. Sheep grazed the grass. Small grey birds with yellow legs were running on the dunes by the wall. It was all so beautiful. I took a deep breath, breathing in the scent of herbs drifting across the sea.

'I saw birds like that by the river in Fosse.'

He took the telescope, pointing back to where I had been looking. 'They're sandpipers, they nest in the marshes. And that's a marsh hawk,' he said, following a bird across the dune. Suddenly he swung the telescope round and, even without the aid of a lens, I saw a red flag waving. He stood up, making his way quickly back to Jacques. 'Three waves, two rests, three waves.'

Jacques nodded. 'That must be him.'

'He should be directly south – it's wrong.'

'But if it's his signal–'

'No. Something's wrong.' Arnaud spoke sharply, the anxiety in his voice making my stomach knot. He hurried down the hatch, returning almost immediately with a large chart. Spreading it out, he began comparing it to the land. 'It puts him here – that's too near the village. If we go any further along the coast, we're in danger of being seen.' He glanced across at Nathaniel. He was wringing out a cloth, hanging it from the ropes to dry. Nathaniel returned his look, all nods and smiles, but as Arnaud turned away, I saw his face change.

Arnaud pointed to the chart and dropped his voice. Perhaps he did not trust Nathaniel either. 'I'll not risk going any further towards the village, nor must we be seen to row ashore. If we're being watched, we must look as if we're waiting for the tide to turn – nothing more.' His voice was barely above a whisper, I missed most of what he said but I heard ... *have to swim ... will signal back...* I rushed quickly to his side, my heart thumping.

'Captain Lefèvre, I hope you're not thinking of going ashore–'

He reached for my arm, pulling me to the hatchway, descending the steps so quickly, I almost tripped. 'Cécile, I have to.'

'No, you don't *have* to. You absolutely don't. You can just hoist up those sails and take me straight back to England. I'll not be put in danger ... not for greed and profit.'

'I can't just sail away. I need to search the area.' His mouth was stern, his words urgent.

'You're not thinking of swimming ... it's November. The water will be freezing.'

'It's no more than two hundred yards.' He was silencing me, the authority in his voice telling me not to question. 'If no-one's there, I'll swim straight back and if I need the rowing boat, I'll wave this flag.' He pulled open the top drawer taking out a folded red cloth. 'I'll wave twice, followed by a rest, followed by four more waves. Only that – no other signal.' He held the red flag and grabbed my hand. His grip was warm, firm, more like a grasp. 'I *have* to do this, Cécile, I have no choice.'

I drew my hand angrily away. 'You do have a choice and you're choosing to leave me on a boat with two men. I don't trust that man, Nathaniel. He's been staring at me and I don't feel safe.'

His eyes narrowed. 'You won't be alone, you'll have Jacques. Nathaniel's probably just superstitious – sailors don't like women on boats, they think it brings bad luck...'

'He doesn't like you, either ... or Jacques...'

I thought he would brush aside my words, but his eyes turned strangely sharp. 'Jacques will look after you ... but you'd better have this. I see no reason why you'll need it, but if it makes you feel safer...' He bent down, opening the bottom drawer, reaching under a velvet cloth, drawing out an elaborately decorated pistol with an ivory handle. 'Use this, if you have to. Here, I'll get it ready. All you have to do is aim and pull this trigger. Have you learnt to shoot?'

'No,' I replied, staring in horror at the pistol. 'I refuse to shoot game birds.'

'Just hold it firmly. Keep it steady, don't wave it about. I'll leave it here, under the cloth. Are you alright?' I said nothing, but stood scowling at the velvet cloth. Adventure was one thing, pistols and smuggling in France quite another. He could see I was scared. 'Cécile – I have to search the cove. I'll be back within the hour; if we don't sail by half one, we'll risk running aground.' As he spoke, he began taking off his jacket, stripping away his neck tie, undoing the top buttons of his shirt. He crossed quickly to his cabin, returning with a canvas bag. Taking off his boots, he put them in the bag, tying the ropes tightly before slinging it across his chest. 'If I need the boat, Jacques will send Nathaniel. You'll be quite safe. What's the signal?'

'Two, rest, four.' He smiled at my prompt reply, turning to climb the stairs, taking them two at a time. I glanced at the clock. Nearly half past twelve. A whole hour to wait.

He lowered himself from the stern, dropping silently into the blue water and I held my breath, waiting for him to surface. Across the long sweep of the bay the red flag was signalling – three, two, three. The person waving that flag was watching us, waiting for one of us to row ashore.

Chapter Ten

He surfaced forty yards from the boat, immediately diving beneath the water again.

'He's a good swimmer and he won't be seen behind the reeds.' Jacques had come to my side. His voice was gruff, his French accent more pronounced than Arnaud's. 'He knows what he's doing. My orders are to sail in one hour. If he's not back, he's instructed me to return you to Fosse.'

'What?' I stared at him in horror. 'Not back? He must be coming back.'

His eyebrows formed a thick black band across his forehead. 'Those are my orders.'

My heart seemed to stop. 'You'd leave without him?'

'Yes.'

I could barely breathe. I felt sick with anxiety. Leaving without Arnaud Lefèvre would be unthinkable. 'Well, he'd better come back.'

Jacques watched the waving flag through the telescope, the tension in his body almost palpable. Nathaniel scowled from the bow, his eyes full of hostility. I pulled my hood further over my face. I did not like that man. I did not trust him. The midday sun was shining on the deck – warm, autumnal sunshine with still enough strength to penetrate my cloak. Glad it was keeping me hidden, I sat watching the shoreline, searching the water, watching intently for a figure to surface and swim towards us.

The sea was the colour of sapphires, the air fresh, blowing across the land with the smell of manure. Gulls swooped across the water, birds darted through the reeds, but my eyes remained fixed on the small outcrop of rocks – exactly south on the compass. Jacques tied the tiller to the gunwale and came back to the coach roof, a pipe clamped between his teeth. He began splicing a rope. He seemed restless, like a dog waiting for his master. The heat of the sun was increasing, the hideous black cloak far too heavy. I needed to go below, splash my face and hands.

I glanced at the clock – a quarter to one. On the desk lay the velvet cloth, the shape of the pistol visible beneath it. Below was the chart. I pushed the pistol carefully to one side, trying to make sense of the swirling outlines but the land and sea seemed indistinguishable from each other; it was impossible to differentiate one from the other. There was nothing marked – no towns, no ports, no villages. I looked up, annoyed. Where were we?

In the alcove above the desk a row of books crowded together. One caught my eye. It was smaller than the others, pushed further back, and I reached forward, taking it from the shelf. The spine was creased, the book immediately falling open where a folded page had been inserted. It was the book Arnaud had had open when I arrived and I unfolded the page. It was a song – the words carefully written beneath the notes of a musical score. *Oh, come with me and be my love. Let not thy heart be timid.*

The thought of Arnaud Lefèvre composing love songs was somehow intriguing and I looked at the carefully drawn notes, trying to follow them. I looked again. The key kept changing, there were too many beats in some bars, it was discordant, impossible to sing and clearly impossible to play. I re-folded the page, tucking it quickly back into the book. It was wrong to pry into something so personal.

The cat was sprawling across the bench, her long black limbs stretching across the blue cushion. She was pretending to sleep but was watching me, too indolent and hot to move. I entered the washroom and poured water into the washbasin. The water was tepid and far from refreshing, the temperature in the cabin warmer than on deck. I would be better going back above. Suddenly the cat leapt from the bench. A shadow crossed the skylight and the cabin plunged into darkness. I edged forward, looking up at the hatch. Jacques' red shirt was writhing against the glass above.

I grabbed my cloak, pulling it round me and ran to the desk. The pistol was much heavier than I expected, the ivory handle smooth and strangely cool. I was surprised by how calm I felt, how steady my hands were, as if waiting for danger was more frightening than having to face it. Nathanial had been biding his time. I should have known that my coming below would give him his chance. I put my foot softly on the bottom step, slowly inching my way up the stairs. The two men were equally matched in size: both stocky and powerfully built, both holding knives. Jacques was on his feet again, Nathaniel wiping blood from his nose. They were facing each other, their chests rising and falling. Nathaniel's hatred was no longer hidden but blazed across his face. Sweat streaked down their foreheads. Their shoulders were hunched, their arms outstretched, their knives held high in front of them. I took a deep breath, keeping my hands steady, watching the fight from the shadows. Jacques had his back to me, his hunched figure stepping from foot to foot, dodging, ready to spring. Neither had seen me.

Nathaniel's knife flashed in a silver arc. 'Take that, you French bastard.'

Jacques dodged sideways, backing towards me. Nathaniel seemed the heavier man, Jacques the quicker. As his heel struck the mast, he leapt sideways, running quickly down the narrowing deck, turning, ready to spring once again.

'Damn the whole bloody lot of you,' shouted Nathaniel, swinging to face him. His back was turned to me. Nothing lay between him and my pistol and I knew it was my chance.

'That's enough. Throw down your knife or I'll use this.' My voice was firm, authoritative, strangely like Mama's. I stepped onto the deck, pointing the pistol at Nathaniel's chest.

He swung round, glaring at me. 'I should've bloody known.'

'Yes, you should've *bloody* known,' I snapped. 'Drop your knife – now!' I had never sworn before but somehow it seemed right, more threatening, as if I was used to doing this all the time. 'Jacques, get a rope and tie this man up.' He, too, was staring at me, too surprised to move. 'Jacques, get a *bloody* rope.' It felt good to be swearing. Somehow it relieved my tension, gave me the courage I so desperately needed. 'Now step away from that knife. This pistol has a habit of going off when I'm angry.'

I sounded like my mother, but was using Father's words. Between the two of them, I had enough to go on. It seemed to be working. I saw the fear, even respect, in both men's eyes and it spurred me on. 'Put him in the hold, Captain Lefèvre will deal with him when he gets back.'

Jacques grabbed a coil of rope. Nathaniel was muttering, swearing under his breath, blood dripping from his broken nose. For a moment, I thought he would call my bluff, start fighting again. He stood, glowering, waiting to spring, spitting blood onto the deck at Jacques' feet. Jacques was cursing as he uncoiled the rope, but Nathaniel was too quick. He leapt to the deck, throwing himself headlong towards the gunwale, vaulting over the side before Jacques could reach him. I heard the splash and ran to look. He was thrashing in the water, making headway. If he was not exactly swimming, he was not drowning.

Jacques came to my side, his chest heaving. 'I'm sorry, that thieving bastard took me by surprise – must've thought he could steal the boat ... he jumped me from behind, damn him.' His frown softened. 'It's good you had that pistol. Shall I take it from you?' He could see my hands were shaking.

My knuckles were white. Somehow I could not let go. I watched the splashing figure heading towards the shore. 'I'm glad he's gone, I knew he was trouble.'

'I'm not glad he's gone – he should be punished.' He touched the swelling on his lower lip. 'Bastard's got clean away. Pardon my language.'

My body was tingling. Fear, excitement, I could hardly tell. I felt exhilarated, proud, flushed with triumph. I had prevented a thief from seizing the boat. It was thrilling, scary, my heart was racing. I should be drinking tea with a packet captain's wife, waiting for my parents to collect me. I should be arranging my trousseau, trying on my wedding dress. I should be staring out of the window, watching the sun light up the folly, but I was holding a pistol. I was in France and I was on

91

board a smuggling vessel. Even if I pinched myself, I could hardly believe it.

'Can one man sail this boat, Jacques?'

He shook his head. 'Two at the very least.'

'Then that settles it. We're not going anywhere until Captain Lefèvre comes back.' I was flushed, my breathing rapid. I was far too hot. I threw back my head, shaking out my hair, flinging the hideous black cloak right off me. I was free at last and wanted to feel the sun on my cheeks. I did not care if Jacques saw me, or the whole world for that matter. 'How much longer have we got?'

He seemed shocked, his eyes wide with surprise. 'I'm sorry ... how much longer? No more than half an hour.' He seemed to recover. 'In three hours, all this water will be gone – there'll be just a tiny channel winding through the sand to the river mouth.' He pointed to a path leading down from a gate. I could just make out a small jetty jutting through the reeds. 'The rest will be sand, scattered with rocks. When the tide comes in, it's faster than any man can swim. Even Arnaud never risks it.'

The splashing figure had almost reached the land. 'He thought you were French.'

'He's an ignorant pig. I'm from Jersey ... he should know the difference.'

We sat in silence, our eyes scanning the reed beds. He was looking further up the bay to where the red flag had been waving; I was staring more to the left. There was no-one there, only the sheep grazing above the abbey and a solitary monk walking among the beehives in the orchard.

Suddenly Jacques stood up. 'We're drifting too

much – those rocks have sharp teeth beneath the water. We're getting too close.'

I looked at the rocks, a wave of fear twisting my stomach. 'Can we move back?'

'No, we'll have to anchor. I'll get it ready. I may need your help.'

A movement caught my eye and I swung round. A red flag was waving – two waves, followed by a rest, followed by another four. 'It's Arnaud,' I shouted. 'Get the boat. He needs your help.'

Jacques frowned, looking towards the rocks, turning back to the waving flag. 'We're leaving it too late. I have to anchor. The tide's going out ... we're being sucked towards those rocks. Can you row?'

'No ... a little – not very well.'

'You'll have to.' He was untying the rowing boat, pulling it across the deck. 'Get the oars. They're stashed under the thwart – the seat at the back.' He bent over the side, heaving the rowing boat into the water. 'I'll tie this – then I'll lower the ladder.' He was working fast, collecting what he needed, dashing from one side of the boat to the other.

I was still holding the pistol. 'I'll take this. I might need it – Nathaniel's still out there.'

'Don't mind him, he'll be long gone. Just keep the boat pointing to the end of that wall ... see there? With this current it's better to go upstream. Those reeds are very thick so drift in front of them, don't get stuck in them. Arnaud will wade out to you. It won't take long. I'm going to hand you down the oars – then I'll anchor. Are you alright?'

'Yes.' I climbed down the rope ladder as if I had done it all my life, keeping the rowing boat steady beneath me. I reached up for the oars, locking them in place. Lining the boat up with the end of the walled garden, I pulled with all my strength. My heart was pounding. I was one of them now – a smuggler. No longer watching, but rowing. I would have to face Sir James, knowing I had helped his captain smuggle contraband back to England.

The oars were heavy, the handles smooth. Along the shore, newly exposed sand glistened in the sunshine, beneath me, rocks darkened the blue water. I pulled with all my might. The current was weaker than I expected and I looked up, anxious of my direction. The end of the wall seemed too far to the left. Time was against me and I had to hurry. I changed direction, pointing to the outcrop of rocks.

The reed bed was taller than it seemed from *L'Aigrette*, the dense, impenetrable stems standing rigid in the water. I skirted its edge, pulling with all my might, the exertion making me sweat. I had studied the land from *L'Aigrette*, but from the surface of the water I could see nothing but reeds. I looked back. From the position of the sun and the boat, I must be nearly there. I heard a shout. Not twenty yards from me Arnaud was chest-deep in water, pushing his way through the reeds.

'What happened?' He stared at the pistol on my lap, grabbing the boat with both hands.

'Nathaniel tried to steal the boat. I threatened him and he jumped overboard. I've got the pistol in case he's here.' There were flies everywhere, landing on my face, my mouth, and I shook my head, spitting them out. Arnaud pulled the boat backwards through the towering reeds. The sleeves had been ripped from his shirt. There was blood on his collar and across his shoulders. 'Arnaud, you're getting scratched – you're injured.'

'It's not my blood. Where's Jacques? Why hasn't he come?'

'He's anchoring – the boat's drifting too near the rocks.' He scowled at my words, turning to face the shore, dragging the boat behind him. The boat scraped the sand and I prepared to jump out. 'Why are your sleeves torn?'

'Because I needed bandages. Quick, we've got to hurry.' He pulled the boat further onto a small beach, hidden from sight. On one side was the reed bed, on the other, a swathe of long grass, as tall as any man. A group of rocks stood to our right, at their base a small cave. I saw a set of footprints leading across the sand, the imprints too deep for one man alone.

In the shade of the overhanging rock a monk was lying on his side, his cassock badly stained with blood. He was deathly pale. Congealed blood matted his bushy eyebrows, discolouring his long grey beard. Stooping to pick him up, Arnaud eased him onto his shoulder. For such an old man, he was well built and heavy. 'I'll carry him – you bring the bag.' I looked around, grabbing the bulky bag, pulling the strap over my head, slinging it quickly across my shoulder. There was nothing else there.

'Has everything been stolen?'

Arnaud looked quickly up, his eyes narrowing, 'You mean the brandy? All gone – they must have left him for dead.' He walked quickly across the beach, easing the man gently into the bow. The monk made no sound, his face seemingly lifeless and I stared in horror, helping Arnaud push the boat back into the sea. 'Get in, Cécile. Don't get any wetter.'

I climbed next to the monk, squeezing by his side, putting his head in my lap, my hand against his nose. 'He's hardly breathing.'

'He's got a nasty head wound and I think a bullet's passed right through his shoulder. He's lost a lot of blood. I found him in the orchard.' He began heaving against the stern, pushing the boat through the water, the dense reeds reluctantly parting to let us through.

'Will he live?'

'I hope so.'

Stalks were decaying beneath the water. It smelt dank, earthy, dragonflies darting across the boat. I waved off the flies that landed on the monk's beard and watched his blue lips closely, desperate for him to take the next shallow breath. 'He's bleeding through your bandages – they're not staunching the blood.'

'I know. We need to hurry.' He steadied the boat, the muscles in his arms clenching as he heaved himself over the stern. We began skimming the surface of the clear blue water, racing across the bay. He was breathing hard, pushing himself to the limit, the distance to the boat getting shorter and shorter.

Jacques was watching the land through the telescope. He pointed to the left and I looked round in fright. Along the shore a group of men were running to the rock we had just left. 'Arnaud, look!'

'I know. I've seen them.' He quickened his pace, 'And I've seen *them,* too.' He was looking over my shoulder to the entrance of the bay. I turned round – two boats were rounding the headland, their sails bright in the midday sun.

'Are they after us?' I gasped.

'I rather think they might be.'

We were nearly at the boat. Jacques was leaning over her side, pointing across the bay. 'Two luggers – north-west.'

Arnaud flung the oars to the sides and grabbed the rope ladder, holding it firmly with both hands. He looked up. 'I've seen them – we'll have to cut and run ... prepare the sails.' He looked back at me. 'You go first.'

'No, it's alright. You go – I'll follow you up.'

He seemed surprised, pleased. Bending down, he lifted the monk carefully onto his shoulder, gently shifting his position so he could take hold of the ladder. 'Let this boat go, Cécile – let it drift.'

I reached back for the pistol. 'Will they catch us?'

He was halfway up the ladder but turned at my words. 'Catch the fastest cutter in the Channel?' He smiled. 'Not a chance.'

Chapter Eleven

He laid the monk on the bed. 'We'll have to leave him – we need all hands on deck.'

I followed him out of the cabin, watching him grab a knife from the galley. At the top of the stairs he held it towards me, pointing to the bow. 'Use this to slice the anchor rope ... then come back and hold the tiller. Point it towards that church spire and hold your course ... it's into wind. I'll set the sails.'

I nodded and grabbed the knife, running as quickly as I could along the deck to the bow. My hands were shaking. The anchor rope was on the other side of the bowsprit and I had to lean over and stretch. The rope was taut in the water, the weight of the boat pulling against it. It was a large rope, the tension considerable. I began slicing through it, sawing backwards and forwards, my mouth clenching with the effort. Though the rope was thick, the knife was razor sharp and it began splitting, fraying. I kept slicing, the last strands now stretching thinly in front of me. One last cut and it fell away. I heard the splash as it landed in the water and ran back to the stern, dodging under the ropes that hung from the sails. I grabbed the tiller and held it firmly, my eyes scanning the bay, searching for the church. From the corner of my eye I saw the luggers. Their sails were wide and full. They seemed to be gaining on us.

With my eye firmly on the church spire, I clutched the tiller in both my hands. Arnaud and Jacques were hoisting up the main sail. Ropes were creaking, the sail flapping. They pulled it taut and it started to swell, curving above us in a graceful arc. The sail glowed in the sunlight and I felt the boat shift. 'Keep us to the church,' shouted Arnaud, his voice breathless with exertion. 'Keep us to wind.'

Four of the five sails were up and I could feel the boat moving through the water. I grasped the tiller tightly, pulling it towards me, swinging the boat back on course. We were facing the steeple again, the sails of the two luggers swelling before us.

'Keep her like that. We're almost done.' Arnaud was tying down a rope, Jacques hoisting the final sail – five glowing sails and the huge French flag; the same flag as the ones flying across the bay. Arnaud was watching them, his voice urgent. 'Point away ... point north-east by east. Be ready to hold her – she'll heel to the right. As soon as we've set these sails, I'll take over.'

I looked at the compass. North-east by east would take us straight between the rocks and out to open sea. I held tight, feeling the soft caress of air against my face. *L'Aigrette* was moving, the waves rippling across her bow. We were sailing, skimming through the sea, leaving a wake in the clear blue water. Arnaud came to my side. There was admiration in his eyes and I could feel myself blushing. He put his hands over mine, his shoulders strong behind me. His hands were warm, firm, holding mine against the tiller. 'That's right,

Cécile. Hold her just like this. Are you sure you haven't done this before?'

'I've watched others,' I said.

His hand tightened over mine. '*L'Aigrette* can sail on breath alone ... just watch us leave those creaking tubs behind.' He smiled down at me, his eyes laughing. 'We can sail closer to wind than any other boat – no ship can point as close.'

'Will they fire at us?'

'They'll try – but by the time they turn broadside, we'll be out of range. They don't stand a chance.' His bare arms stretched against mine, his chest so close behind me. For a moment, I wanted to lean back, feel his strength, let his arms slide round me but I stared ahead, holding my course. He reached down, his face almost touching mine. I could feel his breath on my cheek. 'Thank you, Cécile. You've just saved my life.'

I drew my hand quickly away. 'And you've just put my life in danger.'

I stared at the grey beard coming away in my hands. I dabbed at it again, whole handfuls of hair clumping together. I rubbed harder with the soft cloth, dipping it again into the warm, soapy water. The skin was I red where the beard had been glued. His chin and head were freshly shaven. He was young, not old, the grey eyebrows every bit as false as the beard. I pulled them away, the wisps of hair floating on top of the bucket. Under his cassock he wore strong working men's clothes, stout shoes and a belt with a knife in it.

He must be only middle thirties. He was strong, well nourished, his bone structure fine, his hands elegant. His chest was rising, his breaths shallow. I wiped the blood from over his eye and felt his eyelids flutter. Blood was already seeping through the bandages so I grabbed his knife, pulling it from its sheaf, ripping his jacket to expose his wound. Arnaud came to my side, holding the jacket rigid so I could cut through the coarse cloth.

'You must've realised he was too heavy to be quite so old. Do monks shave their heads?'

'I think they might.' He was watching me.

I was surprised by how calm I felt. I had once had a mare with a rip to her fetlock, but had never seen wounds like this. 'I'll need fresh bandages and some brandy...'

'Brandy?' He seemed surprised.

'Yes and quickly. Ship's surgeons have noted wounds washed in fresh seawater heal better than those washed in barrel water ... and bandages soaked in brandy can prevent suppuration.'

'How do you know that?'

'Never mind how I know. Just help me off with this jacket ... have you some cotton bandages? And I'll need a clean bucket of seawater.' I pushed up my sleeves, looking at the wounds again, trying to decide where to start. The shoulder wound was deep and badly burnt, bleeding through to his back. I would start with that.

Arnaud put the brandy on the side and started tearing up some cloth. I took a deep breath and began dabbing at the burnt skin, picking out the fragments of charred clothing, rinsing away the black shot. The wound was deep, the path of the bullet straight beneath the shoulder bone. It was still bleeding so I grabbed a thick wad of bandages, pressing them firmly to staunch the blood.

I thought the smell of burnt flesh, the sight of so much blood, would turn my stomach but my mind was racing, trying to remember what I had read. I knew to force the brandy-soaked strips of cotton as deep into the wound as possible. Both sides would need to be done. My hands were trembling, my heart beating. He must not die. He must not.

I reached over, holding the man against me, forcing the bandages deep into the wound, packing it solidly. The brandy was strong, the pungent fumes filling the cabin, making my eyes water. I stood back, examining my work, surprised by how practicality had stemmed my usual queasiness. The bleeding seemed controlled – perhaps I had stemmed it. Either way, I would use all the bandages. I would force them in so tightly until there was no more room.

Arnaud was behind me. 'Where did you learn to do that?'

'I haven't I just read about it. Father's library's full of very useful books. He didn't collect them, George Pelligrew did, but I've learnt a lot... I think it was *The Recommendations of the Sick and Hurt Board.*'

'Thank you, Mr Pelligrew,' he replied, smiling.

I smiled back, suddenly proud of what I had done. 'Are the luggers still chasing us?'

'They're long gone. We're making good progress.'

I turned the man gently away from me. The second wound was deep, curving in an arc across the back of his head. It was full of sand and large bits of grit; the edges jagged, the surrounding skin bruised and swollen. 'I'm going to clean and dress this now.'

Arnaud nodded and left. The boat was swaying beneath me – gentle, yet deliberate. It felt safe, comforting, a lovely rhythm. I carefully cleaned away the sand and grit and pressed a thick pad against the wound, securing it tightly. Wrapping a large bandage round his head, I hoped it would hold. I had no notion of time; all I knew was that this man must live. He made no sound, no movement, but his body was strong, his skin healthy. I hoped he stood a chance. I dabbed some brandy to his lips. They were cracked and dry but his breathing seemed stronger. Covering him with a blanket, I pulled down my sleeves. I would leave him to sleep.

The cat had been sitting on the cabinet beside the bunk watching my every movement. She must have sensed I had finished as she sprang to the floor, rubbing against my skirt. I picked her up, holding her to me. 'Help him live,' I whispered. 'We've had enough bad luck for a while.'

I felt incredibly hungry. A delicious smell was drifting into the cabin, drawing us both out to the galley. It was four o'clock, a cast-iron pot simmering on the stove, a pile of freshly baked rolls lying in a stack. There was beer in a jug and a cheese in danger of oozing off its board. Arnaud had washed and changed. He was freshly shaven. Over his blue silk jacket he wore a huge white apron. 'How is he?' he asked.

'I think ... well, I hope, I've stemmed the bleeding.' He smiled and my heart seemed to stop. I felt breathless, almost dizzy. I looked down at the cat. 'That smells delicious. What is it?'

'Crab – but we've just caught a large sea bass. I'll cook that for supper. Perdue will love it.'

'Perdue?'

He nodded at the cat, a small plate of crab meat held in one hand. 'She turned up one day. I found her on the deck. There's a saying that if a black cat finds a ship, that ship will never sink.'

The hairs on my arms stood up. Shivers ran down my back. 'Honestly,' I laughed, 'you sailors are far too superstitious!' Perdue seemed to understand my words. Springing from my arms, she jumped on the desk. Her tail flicked, her green eyes stared at angrily me.

Arnaud Lefèvre sucked in his cheeks and shook his head. He handed me the dish of crab meat. 'Oh dear, I think you better give her this,' he said.

I held the dish out for her, feeling immediately sorry. She had stayed by my side all through the storm, she had sat watching me dress the man's wounds and, only minutes ago, I had been asking for her intervention. I needed all the luck I could get. If we had been alone, I would have gone down on my knees and begged her forgiveness.

Chapter Twelve

On board L' Aigrette
Saturday 9th November 1793, 00:30 a.m.

L'Aigrette's movement was smooth and rhythmical, plunging us gently through the water. I held the tiller, watching the foam swill across the deck, hearing the waves break against the bow. The wind was on the port side, smelling of salt, of vast oceans and distant lands. It was as if I had been sailing all my life. I glanced at the compass; north-north-west. It was just past midnight – only four hours until landfall.

'Jacques, take your break, I'll keep watch – I won't sleep tonight. I'll wake you when the coast's in sight. How's your wrist?'

Jacques shrugged. 'Better all the time. That fish was delicious – I'll wash the pan.'

'No, I'll do it. You get some rest.'

Jacques nodded to us both. 'Goodnight, Miss Smith.'

The night was so dark, the tiny crescent moon giving no light. Arnaud pushed the pan to one side and edged closer to my side, his jacket pressing against my cloak. I could feel the warmth of his body through his clothes. He was too close, his position too intimate. A lifetime ago, this was how Rose and Sir James had sat. I must draw away, hand him back the tiller. Now we were alone, I must go below, but somehow I felt so reckless, as if the coast of England would come too soon.

'The fish really was delicious. I've never tasted anything so good. Jacques doesn't know who I am, does he?'

'No, your secret's safe. Why?'

'It's just I thought he might have recognised me – he looked surprised when I took down my hood.' Arnaud smiled, his eyes almost black in the darkness. 'Why do you smile? I'm being serious.'

'I told him you were a middle-aged governess with a pock-marked face and a disfiguring scar which you liked to keep hidden. I told him it was better for us all if you kept your hood up!' He grinned broadly, his eyes alight with mischief.

'That's a terrible thing to say.'

'I know, I'm sorry, but I wanted you to be safe. You're a born helmsman, Cécile. Are you sure you haven't done this before?'

I handed him the tiller, leaning back, feeling the wind on my face. The wind of my dreams; the wind I had always imagined. I felt so free. 'I've only ever sailed on my bed in Richmond. I used to sail Charity to China – we often went there.'

'China?' he turned round, smiling the same tender smile.

'Yes – we've a lot of things from there. Father works for the East India Company and one of the captains brought us back some fans. When Charity broke hers, I told her I would sail her straight to China to get another one. That was the first time.'

'Did Charity like sailing to China?'

'No, she hated it! She was scared we wouldn't

find our way back. She thought we'd be eaten by tigers. I told her I had a compass and I'd take a gun.'

'So you *do* know how to shoot.' He was laughing now.

'Only tigers!' I replied, laughing back. 'The compass was a brass badge I found on the terrace. I think it was a naval button – it could have been military – but it had four points on it so I knew it was really a compass. I told Charity all we had to do was point east and then we'd come back pointing west. Poor girl, I used to draw the curtains round the bed and she would cry all the way.'

'So you did *get* to China?'

'Oh yes, we always got to China, but Charity was too scared to open the curtains, so I'd have to sail her all the way home again. She never let me stay long enough to get her another fan. I had to give her mine in the end.'

'Did you sail by the stars as well?' His tone was soft, strangely hoarse.

'Just the North Star,' I said, looking up. The cloudless day had given way to a cloudless night. Above us, the black sky was ablaze with countless stars. 'It's that one, isn't it?'

'Yes,' he replied softly, 'and that one? Do you know who that is?' He pointed to the brightest star, outshining all others with a brilliance of its own. 'She's the goddess of love and beauty.'

'She must be Venus,' I said gazing up at her.

The wind was ruffling his hair. He was pointing up to the stars with one hand, the other hand lightly holding the tiller. 'And that's Orion – those three stars form his belt ... can you see that's his right hand ... and that bright star marks his sword. He's hunting – that's his left hand, holding up his shield. He's chasing the nymphs, the Pleiades, but they remain safely out of his reach.' He leant closer so I could follow the direction of his gaze. His cheek was next to mine, his breath soft against my skin. I caught the scent of almond soap and forced myself to look away.

'Then Orion's a fool,' I said. 'He should know better than chase nymphs who're beyond his reach.' This was too dangerous. I was being seduced. I must go below.

Suddenly a flash of light caught my eye and I looked up. A brilliant light was flashing across the night sky; a bright red light, blazing so intensely, arching across the sky, leaving a trail of light in its wake. It was so quick, so dazzling, vanishing almost as quickly as it had come and I stared at its path, willing it to reappear. 'Did you see that?'

'Yes. A shooting star ... a red one – they're very rare... I've never seen one before.' He was no longer smiling but had turned away, staring at the waves breaking against the bow.

My stomach knotted. 'Why are you scowling? Is it a bad thing? What does it signify?'

'Good fortune, long life and happiness.' The bitterness in his voice seemed at odds with his words.

'But ... I don't understand – that's a good omen. I thought you were going to tell me something awful's going to happen.'

He turned round. There was pain in his eyes. 'Can't you see something awful *is* going to happen?' His chest was rising and falling, the intensity of his gaze making my heart race. 'Cécile, don't marry Viscount Vallenforth – the man's a vicious brute, for all his wealth and position. You were right to run from him.' He turned away, his mouth hardening. 'I just wish I wasn't taking you back to him.'

I turned to face the wind. I needed to cool the heat in my cheeks, hide the tears filling my eyes. He had voiced my very thoughts. For thirty-six hours, I had been the woman I wanted to be – brave, adventurous, able to do things for myself. I loved everything about this boat – the smell of the sea, the wind in my hair, the sun against my cheek. I loved the sense of adventure, the way my body tingled with excitement, the hint of danger. I did not want to go back.

I wanted to learn how to haul up the sails, navigate by the stars. I wanted to swim in clear blue water, dive for lobsters. I wanted to make bread from beer froth, catch sea bass and cook it on a bed of herbs. I wanted to watch the gannets, shooting like arrows through the air. I wanted to smile back at the dolphins as they rode the bow waves. For a woman with everything, I wanted so much. I fought the lump in my throat, forcing out my words as if they would choke me. 'If I don't marry Viscount Vallenforth, Mama will soon find me another suitor.'

'Then I hope the next one doesn't whip his stable boys.' His voice sounded bitter.

'I hope so, too.' I held back my tears, forcing myself to sound indifferent, watching the white crests disperse into fine spray. 'Arnaud, what does a red shooting star really mean?'

His voice was no more than a whisper. 'When Venus sees two people who should be together, she tells Cupid to send an arrow. It's his lover's dart – then nothing can keep them apart.' His eyes held mine and I clutched my cloak round me. I felt so empty.

'Then it's a shame it was wasted on us.' My voice sounded so much like Mama it frightened me. 'I need to check our patient and get some sleep. I'll be glad to get back to dry land – thirty-six hours on a boat is quite long enough. Goodnight, Captain Lefèvre.'

It was the wine, that was all – the bottle of Chablis that had gone so well with the sea bass. Between us, we had drunk the whole bottle. It was the wine, the stars, the beauty of the night. I was not like those silly girls in novels. I had read those books – long before Mama had them removed from the library. *Sicilian Romance... The Old Manor House...* I had read them all. I could not be fooled by talk of Cupid's arrows.

The lanterns were lit in the cabin, the wood gleaming in the soft light. A fresh chart lay on the desk, the brass dividers stretching open across it. I would be home soon. Perdue was lying on the cushion, well fed and purring. I opened the door to Arnaud's cabin and checked my patient. He was breathing deeply, some colour returning to his pale cheeks. The bandage on his head was clean and dry. I pulled back the blanket. The shoulder bandage looked fresh, no signs of seepage.

'Are you comfortable?' I whispered in his ear. There was no response. *'Est-ce que vous êtes confortable?'* I repeated. For a moment I thought I saw his eyelids flicker. I tucked the blanket carefully round him and trimmed the lantern, the brass gleaming like everything else.

I turned to go but two books in the wooden alcove above the bed caught my attention. I reached over, bringing them nearer to the lantern. They were small books, beautifully bound, their red leather bindings worn soft with frequent use. I opened the first. It was a book of poetry. I opened the second and a searing pain shot through me, so sudden, so violent, it felt as if my heart was on fire. The book was a compendium of birds – almost identical to the one I kept by my bed.

I could hardly see the pages. Through my tears I glimpsed the beautiful etchings – egrets, sand-pipers, curlews, cormorants, marsh harriers ... the collared doves...

I closed the book. The next three hours could not pass quickly enough.

Chapter Thirteen

Porthruan
Saturday 9th November, 4:00 a.m.

'Wake up, Cécile. The coast's in sight.'

I had not been asleep. I had been watching him through closed lids – the way he held the papers to the light, the way he held the quill. He had been too absorbed to realise I had been aware of

111

his every move. 'How's our patient?' I said as I took the china cup of coffee.

'Not awake, but he's been talking in his sleep. It won't be long before he comes round. You saved his life, Cécile.'

Perdue stretched and I stroked her little round belly. 'I'm going to miss this little cat.'

'She's never taken to anyone else before.'

'I think the roast beef and crab might have helped!'

There was no joy in his smile. He seemed distracted, passing his hands through his dishevelled hair. Rough stubble covered his chin, dark circles shadowed his eyes. 'Everything's ready, wash when you like – you've about thirty minutes. We'll soon be passing Polperro.' A terrible emptiness filled me. It was still dark and I glanced at the clock. Half past four.

'Thank you.' There was tension in the way he spoke, formality in the way I replied. It would need to stay like that.

He had prepared everything – hot water, fresh soap, a silk cloth, a tortoiseshell comb. I stared at my reflection, lifting my chin for courage. In my hand, I held my jewels. I would secure my hat with the pin and wait until I reached Pendenning to wear my diamond earrings, but the huge sapphire ring with its circle of diamonds? I knew Arnaud Lefèvre needed to see it on my finger.

I checked my patient. Arnaud had changed him into working-men's clothes, his heavy jacket now hiding his shoulder wound, his hat drawn low over his bandage. He was not awake but seemed restless, tossing his head, his brows contracting in

112

pain. His breathing was easier and his colour improved. I unbuttoned his jacket and checked his wound, enjoying a sudden rush of pride. It was clean, no fresh blood, the bandages still tightly in place. I redid the buttons, noticing the top button on the right was missing.

'Are you ready, Miss Smith?'

I pulled my cloak tightly round me. Freshly squeezed lemons lay on the galley top, coffee warming on the stove. Perdue rubbed against my skirt and I bent to pick her up. 'Goodbye, Perdue,' I whispered. 'Thank you for keeping me safe.'

'Two at the bow, three on the mast – take these for the stern.' Through the hatchway I could see Arnaud handing lanterns to Jacques. He reached for a rope. 'All sails down except the fore sail – it's a lee shore so we can't get too close.'

I hurried up the stairs. Arnaud was leaning against the bulwark, staring at the mass of black land just visible through the greyness. I pulled my hood firmly over my hat. 'But we're still sailing! I thought we'd be anchoring – or at least tying up along the quay.'

'Not this time!' He sensed my alarm and his face softened. 'It's better you leave *before* the excise men welcome us home – they'll search this ship from top to bottom.'

'Will you row me ashore?'

'Someone will be along shortly.'

'But I mustn't be seen. Arnaud, you promised me.'

'You'll not be seen. Not if you keep your hood up. I'll tell him you're a maid who needs to get back to Pendenning. Our passenger must go,

113

too.' His voice dropped. 'Take that ring off – at least until you get home.'

I slipped the hateful ring from my finger. 'They'll be cross there's nothing here.' My voice was firm, no quavering, no sign of how empty I felt. 'What were you meant to bring back? Brandy ... lace ... Marseilles silk?'

He shrugged his shoulders, but his eyes looked wary. 'There'll be more, soon enough.' He turned to search the shore. 'Our lanterns will soon be seen – watch out for a signal.'

The wind was full of moisture, the black clouds heavy with rain. In the east, the first streaks of dawn were lifting the night sky. It was so wet, so cold – a far cry from the beauty of the reed-fringed bay. I pulled my cloak around me, staring across the darkness. We were hardly moving, just rising and falling, the smallest sail fluttering in the wind above us. 'There!' I shouted.

A lamp flashed and went out – another flash, then two, then four. Arnaud slipped from my side, holding up a wash board in front of the lowest lamp. He counted three, flashing the light six times. The light on the shore dipped three times. Arnaud responded with another three flashes. The lamp on the shore was raised to the right.

'Put the ladder down, Jacques – I'll get our passenger.'

Across the darkness, I could see a lamp come slowly towards us, low on the waterline, one moment there, the next hidden by the waves. Arnaud held the man carefully in his arms, balancing with one foot on the gunwale, the other on deck. The splashing of the oars got closer, a boat bumped against the side.

'There's nothing for you,' Arnaud shouted over the side. 'Everything was taken – there's just this anker of brandy for your trouble. But we've a lass to get home and this gentleman needs our help. Defending his brandy has left him in need of attention.'

'Better get him aboard then, sir.' The man sounded displeased. He had broad shoulders, a thick-set neck and white hair beneath his cap. Tying the rowing boat to the ladder, he stopped when he saw me. 'Who is she?'

'A maid from Pendenning – it's alright, she won't talk.' Arnaud smiled and I felt myself blush. 'They knew we were coming – took the lot before we got there.'

'Best get them ashore. The Revenue's sniffin' about like no-one's business – all hell's let loose. Ye can't breathe now without some idiot askin' questions ... no ... stay as ye are, I'll bring him down.' He climbed over the gunwale with the agility of a man half his age and relieved Arnaud of his burden.

Arnaud's voice sounded strained. 'Are you ready, Miss Smith?'

I felt strangely like crying. No, I was not ready to go back to those stuffy rooms with windows through which I could only look. To doors that locked. To have my every thought dictated, my every move controlled. Only Charity was draw-ing me back – my love for Charity, nothing else. The rowing boat tossed against the hull, the two men safely on board. This was how it began, how I tasted how life could be lived.

'Yes, of course I'm ready. Goodbye, Captain Lefèvre.'

I could not thank him. He was a smuggler, a profiteer, disobeying Sir James' express instructions, his gain more important than my safety. How could I tell him I appreciated his gentle manners, his intelligence, his humour? The way he cooked. His beautiful wine glasses, his delicate china. How could I thank him for making me feel so alive? For allowing me to be the person I had always yearned to be. I held the rail with both hands, preparing to descend the ladder.

'That's no way to say goodbye,' he said, lifting me high in his arms, his lips brushing against my ear. 'A maid would snatch a final kiss and we must make it look real.' He swung me over the side, carrying me down the ladder, placing me gently in the rowing boat next to the injured man. His eyes were burning, staring at me with the same intensity they had done the night before. He reached for my hand, holding it against his lips. 'Goodbye, Miss Smith.'

I snatched my hand away, turning my face to the cooling breeze, staring across the sea to the hidden cove, stiff, upright, refusing to look back. I was heading back to my life of privilege and plenty, to my beloved sister, yet I wanted to cry. I was not some lovelorn maid, seduced by a smile, by burning eyes. I was not going to make a fool of myself over a smuggler who knew maids would come back for one last, lingering kiss. I would forget the birds we might have watched, the seas we might have crossed. I would forget the way my heart jumped, the way he seemed to read my thoughts. My tears were selfish, indulgent, that was all – I was crying for my freedom.

This was the second time the man's head lay in my lap. Fine cheekbones, strong chin, long fingers with manicured nails, but my eyes were so blurred, I could hardly see. The boat scraped shingle, Jago secured the oars and leapt from the side. Behind him stood a yawning black cave, a wagon at its entrance. 'I'll take him. Wait in the wagon with him while I hide the boat.'

It was a small wagon, just a farm cart, full of straw and chicken feathers. Jago whipped the reins and we jolted forward, the mule struggling up the steep incline. A thick canopy of branches arched above us; the wheels splashed through water. It smelt dank, of mouldy leaves and rotting vegetation, each jolt bringing a curse from Jago and a frown on the face of the man lying beside me. He was covered with a rough sack, his face only just visible, but the jolting was clearly waking him.

'I'll take ye as far as the east gate...' Jago was scowling round at me. 'It's not like the captain to get distracted by a woman – not one word, ye understand? One squeak and ye're as good as dead. Understand?' I nodded, drawing the cloak round me. He could be sure of that. Not one word. I would never tell anyone, not even Charity. I was far too sensible to risk the scandal.

The canopy was thinning, the trees parting as the ground levelled. We were on the cliff-top, the clouds black in the grey sky. The air smelt of grass and I took a deep breath, desperate to control the fear rising within me. The thought of my reception churned my stomach. The wagon became steadier, the path growing wider as we left the cliff-top, dropping down to a vale. Horned cattle grazed the pastures, large white goats stood tethered to the wayside. Cold penetrated my cloak. Ahead of us lay a gate-house. A bucket clattered, a cockerel called hesitantly into the early dawn. In a pen two pigs lay sleeping in a muddy sty. Across the yard, a dog barked and a woman stopped drawing water from a well to turn and watch. The injured man opened his eyes. He looked terrified. *'Où suis-je? Qui êtes-vous?'*

'Vous êtes en Angleterre … vous êtes en sécurité,' I replied. He seemed to hear me, falling back against the rough sacking, clearly having exhausted all strength. Jago was watching me, his eyes hostile.

'Ye speak French?' I did not answer, but climbed quickly out of the wagon, balancing on the small ledge before I jumped. In front of me, the long road stretched through the park.

Yes, I spoke French. I read Latin. I was educated. I played the pianoforte to perfection. I had a trained soprano voice. I could embroider exquisitely, sketch moderately and knew exactly how to behave at dinners. I had a fine figure, impeccable breeding, and, give or take the odd outburst, never put a foot wrong. I was an accomplished horsewoman, had good teeth, a straight back and excellent child-bearing hips.

My parent's most valuable asset had returned.

North-West by North

Chapter Fourteen

Pendenning
Saturday 9th November 1793, 4:45 a.m.

The heavy clouds were passing, daylight slowly breaking. It had been raining, puddles pooled on the drive and droplets still lingered on the grass. With every step my fear rose. No-one could disappear for thirty-six hours without dire consequences. Across the parkland I could see the outline of the house ahead of me, the clock tower silhouetted against the dawn. I looked round, hesitating. A well-used track lay to my right but if I crossed the park, I could be seen from the house.

Fear clouded my thinking but, wrapping my cloak around me, I stepped over the stile and braved the muddy path. It began to get firmer, drier, more structured as it neared the house. Privet bushes began lining the sides and I thought the bench in the alcove looked familiar. I turned a bend, relief flooding through me – of course, the Little Cottage. Fate had taken me to the exact spot where I should have thought to go.

George Pelligrew had built the cottage for his wife. Charity and I often visited it to take tea with Georgina and Mrs Jennings, but we left it for Georgina to play in. It was perfect for a twelve year old, a grown-up dolls' house really; the thatched roof, the pointed windows, the stone porch – fashioned more like a witch's house than a cottage. In the half-light gargoyles grinned down at me, grotesque and evil but I stared at the ornate door, my heart soaring. It was ajar, candle-light filtering through from the room behind. I crept carefully forward, peeping through the leaded windows – a maid was tidying the room.

She screamed as I entered, clamping her hands against her mouth. 'Oh, ye made me jump. Scary enough without ye frightenin' me like that.' I must have looked a sight. I pulled my hood from my head, checking my hat was still in place. Her eyes widened, her shoulders hunched and her hands flew to her mouth. She dropped a curtsey, as pale as if she had seen a ghost. 'Oh ... m'lady...'

'Don't be scared, I've been for a walk. Are there rumours I'm missing?'

'Ye was missin' – ye was thrown from yer horse ... ye've been recoverin'...' She could hardly bring herself to look at me but stood staring at her feet, her thin hands clutching the starched white apron that seemed to swamp her. What was she, twelve, thirteen? Her jet black hair was scraped beneath her mob cap, dark shadows circled her eyes. She was pale, painfully thin, her hands red and sore.

'It's alright, you can stop curtseying. What's your name?' I had never asked a servant's name before.

'Ella, if ye please...'

I looked round the room – a recent fire, dis-turbed cushions on the chaise longue. The re-mains of a tea tray – four cups and saucers, three

122

plates with cake crumbs, one with an un-tasted slice of Madeira.

'Shall ... shall ... I carry on, m'lady ... only we're that pushed. That's why I've come so early... I should of cleared all this yesterday but with all the fuss...'

'The fuss of my accident?'

'No, the extra cleanin' ... gettin' the rooms ready fer guests ... it's been that hard...' She looked as if she would cry, her thin lips puckering in fear.

'Carry on, by all means – don't let me stop you.'

Georgina's dolls' house stood open – a beautiful Palladian dream, three storeys high, nine windows wide with a portico, a colonnade, and seven Greek statues guarding the roof. She had insisted on bringing it with her. The interior was decorated to match our Richmond house, wallpapered in Chinese silk, replica tapestries, matching drapes. The figures were made of porcelain, dressed in silk and lace. I picked them off the floor, putting them carefully back on their delicate mahogany chairs.

There was only one candle, so I lit another and left Ella sweeping the grate, entering instead the tiny back room. There was nothing there, just a simple pine table with a pewter jug and a clay candle stick. There was no window, just a small cupboard with a round brass knob. I turned to go, but the brass knob glinted in the candlelight, catching my eye. My curiosity rose – the brass was worn smooth with the patina of regular use. I could not resist a second look so, squeezing round the table, I pulled the knob. Not a cupboard, but a narrow staircase with small wooden steps twisting out of sight. Jars, a block of soap and a few cloths lay tucked against the sides, but they were definitely steps.

I gathered up my skirts, ducking my head to squeeze through the narrow door. The steps were steep, turning sharply, opening to a tiny attic tucked beneath the eaves. I held the candle up. A huge unmade bed took up most of the space, the bedclothes tumbling to the floor in a jumbled mess. Who could possibly have the audacity to come up here? One of the servants, no doubt, perhaps someone from the stables; either way, my cheeks began burning, my imagination taking flight. None of us knew this room existed but whoever had found it knew it made the perfect lovers' nest. I began smiling, amazed by my good luck. I would have to tidy it up, of course, unrumple the sheets, tuck in the eiderdown.

Downstairs, the room was back in shape, the grate gleaming. 'Have you finished?'

'Yes, m'lady–'

'Don't keep curtseying – you'll upset your tray. Here, let me take it, you've got far too much to carry.' The maid seemed reluctant to hand me the tray but I gripped it firmly, surprised by how heavy it was. 'Can you get me back to the house without anyone seeing me? My morning walk's ruined my gown and I don't want to be seen in such a state. I like early morning walks, don't you?'

She looked at me as if I was insane. 'I've too many jobs to go walkin'.' Her dark eyes looked exhausted, her face pinched and thin. 'Do ye want to use the servant's stairs? Only no-one will see ye then – it's just the maids what's up – Mrs Pumfrey don't come down till six.'

'That will do very well. I'd rather people didn't see me like this.'

'Don't mind me, m'lady. I'll not tattle.' She searched in her apron pocket, bringing out a large key.

'Thank you.' I put the tray down, pulling the hood back over my face. Behind me, the clock started to chime. Half past five.

The household was slowly waking, lanterns beginning to glow in the courtyard. I knew the stables well but had never ventured into the myriad of outbuildings with their painted doors and grilles across the windows. Ella put down her mop and bucket, turning to take the tray. 'I'll put this in the scullery then we'll go through the laundry.'

I stayed back in the shadows watching two maids fill buckets from the pump. They looked so young, barely awake as they lifted the arm and pumped the water. There must be twenty buckets to fill. Two wheelbarrows stood piled with logs and I could hear a man whistling across the courtyard. Ella returned. 'This way ... if ye please... I needs take up the laundry so I might as well do it now.' She smiled, her sweet face eager to please, her eyes plummeting to the cobbles when she saw me smile back.

The laundry room was vast, longer than Mama's drawing-room and twice as wide. Ropes and pulleys as complicated as any ship stretched high above us. Pipes ran down the length of the side wall and huge water tanks crowded the furthest end. Vast copper cauldrons sat gleaming in a row and mangles stood at each end of the long tables. I hurried behind Ella, the smell of lye catching my throat, stinging my eyes. The next room was equally wide, though half as long. We hurried past the fireplace and a battalion of black irons, dodging beneath the sheets hanging from above.

Three large wicker baskets stood crammed with freshly ironed linen. Ella grabbed one of them and began to pull. She saw my face and stopped. 'We drag 'em – it's not far.' She pushed open a small door, dragging the basket behind her. The corridor was long and narrow with red floor-tiles and white-washed walls. Candles in brass lanterns gave sporadic light and at the fourth lantern the corridor widened, opening out to a vestibule. Two more baskets stood squeezed against the wall, a narrow staircase leading to the right. Ella positioned her basket next to the others and picked up a heavy armful. 'Yer room's two sets up – on the second floor.'

I looked at the huge pile of laundry. 'Are you going to take *all* that upstairs?'

I thought she might cry. 'Yes, m'lady ... I needs do it yesterday but with all the fuss...'

I scooped up an armful, following her up the narrow staircase. The steps were steep, the linen heavy; my muddy hem in danger of tripping me up. The stairs opened to a lobby where a series of trolleys stood empty. Through the dim candle-light, I could just make out two corridors leading into darkness. 'Where do they go?'

126

She looked appalled that I was holding the linens. 'That corridor's to her ladyship's drawin' room – that's to her parlour.'

'Does the whole house have these corridors?'

Once again she looked at me as if I was insane. 'Yes, m'lady.'

At the top of the next set of stairs, Ella opened the vast cupboard and placed her linen neatly on the empty shelf. I followed suit, surprised by how heavy the linen had been. She adjusted her mob cap, her eyes huge in the darkness. 'It's not yer bedroom, so much as yer washroom...'

'That'll do perfectly.' I sounded calmer than I felt. I could hear footsteps running down the stairs. 'It's very dark. Do you have a candle?'

'Only parlour maids gets candles. It's this way. Best touch the wall as ye walk.' I followed closely through the darkness, trailing my fingers along the wall. I could feel bumps, indentations, a sudden left turn. It was stuffy, the heat intense, only just wide enough for two people to pass. When she stopped, I almost bumped into her. 'This is yer room – the third door after the second bend.' I heard her fumble for the latch.

The door opened into my washroom. The candles were lit. Folded on the chair was my crisp white nightdress. It was as if I had not been away and I could not stop smiling. This was how Arbella had done it. This was how she had slipped from the house as if by magic. She had discovered these corridors and planned her escape, knowing no-one would see her leave. Clever, clever girl – all that time plotting and we never suspected.

'Could you help me out of my clothes?' A look

of panic crossed Ella's face. 'No ... it's alright, I suppose I can manage. Carry on with your work – you've a lot to do.' If I could fend off a thief and dress a man's wounds, I could certainly learn to undress.

I looked back at the carefully concealed door. It was so clever, tucked away in the shadows, the lines of the wallpaper exactly matching the contours of the door. Unless studied carefully, it would never be seen. I took off my hat and shook out my hair. There must be a catch – but where? I took hold of my hatpin and ran it along the thin gap in the wallpaper, first one side, then the other. It struck an obstacle and I forced it upwards. The latch lifted and the tiny door swung open.

Behind me I heard the bedroom door open. 'Is that you, Cici?' whispered Charity.

I pulled the bedclothes round us. Charity listened in silence but was clearly shocked. 'It's alright, Itty, the boy was saved.'

'But it's so horrible.' A tear dropped to her cheek. I put my arms around her and held her tightly.

'That's why I ran away. I was so horrified, I acted on impulse. I thought if I went to Lady Polcarrow I could leave the boy with them and prepare to face Mama. I will never marry Viscount Vallenforth, not after that.'

'No, of course not ... but Mama will be furious. She's already furious and Father's in such a rage. They searched everywhere. Mr Randall set up a hunt and when the mare came back everyone thought you were dead.' She held me tightly, her flood of tears returning. 'Honestly, Cici, it's been so awful. I've been beside myself. Where were you?'

As a child, I vowed never to lie to Charity. If I took something of hers, ribbons to match my dress, her special hairclip, I always told her. If I heard something, saw something, she would be the first to know. I had lied before to Mama, but never to Charity. The words stuck in my throat. 'Lady Polcarrow couldn't see me. I think she was ill...'

'She *is* ill ... they're both dying. It's awful. They ate some poisonous mushrooms and aren't expected to live.'

'That's terrible.'

'I know, it's too awful to contemplate. Did you know Father hates Sir James? He says Sir James is a Jacobin. I heard him telling Mother that Lady Polcarrow and her father sympathise with the French.'

I had to watch my words. 'Father hates Sir James because they have a land dispute, that's all. It's probably just in his interest to spread rumours.'

She nodded. 'I hope you're right. Where did you go for all that time?' She dabbed her eyes. She looked so tired, her face as white as her cap.

'I was going to write to Mama and tell her I would only return if I could be released from my engagement ... but things went terribly wrong.' I took a deep breath. 'When Lady Polcarrow couldn't see me, I decided to come straight back but it was dark and the mare was getting jumpy. I decided to lead her across the ford – the one that cuts across the river?' Charity nodded. 'Halfway across I tripped and let go of the reins. The mare ran in fright and I couldn't call her back.'

'But you must've seen everyone looking for you?'

'I saw them, Itty – but I didn't want to be found. I was in a terrible state. I thought the threat of scandal was my only option.'

'They're so cross with you. Mama's convinced Arbella's behind it. Where did you sleep?'

'In the cottage – the door was unlocked. There's a room up in the eaves and I slept in the bed. I was upstairs when you came to tea with Georgina. I wanted to catch your attention but Mama and Mrs Jennings were there. I was going to come back but the maids were too busy cleaning and they locked the cottage. I couldn't get out and the windows don't open. I was locked in and no-one passed so I had to wait until the maid came this morning. She's just brought me in through the servant's stairs. They've a whole network of corridors and stairs running behind our rooms.'

'There's a bed in the witch's cottage? You must've been petrified. Oh, Cici, if I'd only known. I could have got them to open the door. I've been so scared.'

'I knew you were worried – too worried to eat. I ate your slice of Madeira cake, so you did help!' She smiled and I began to relax. It sounded so plausible. Her head lay on my shoulder – my dearest, timid sister who I had just put through the worst of nightmares.

'Promise you won't go anywhere without telling me first.'

'I promise. I absolutely promise.' I settled

further down the bed. 'Are you alright?'

She nodded. 'Father's told everyone you had a fall and needed to rest. Mama's furious. She's written to Aunt Martha asking if they've found Arbella. She thinks you went to find her. She went straight to bed with one of her headaches and wouldn't get up but Father insisted she should act as if nothing's happened – that's why we had tea in the cottage. He's worried Sir Richard will suspect something.'

'Sir Richard?'

'Sir Richard Goldsworthy. Cici, you're back just in time. Sir Richard and Major Trelawney are to come as house guests. They were meant to stay at Polcarrow but of course they can't. Father's insisted they come here.'

'Who are they?'

'I don't know, but Father's very keen to have them ... and they must be of some importance or Mama would never have agreed. I've been sick with worry. I thought I'd have to face them on my own.' She smiled a watery smile, looking up at me like when we were children. 'You won't run away again, will you?'

I thought my heart would break. 'I promise.' They would search the cottage and find the room. If I stood firm, my story could hold. It was nearly seven o'clock; we would not be woken for another two hours. 'Itty, shall we try and catch some sleep?'

The bedclothes were warm, the bed soft beneath me, but it was too still, too silent. The room was too hot, the dusty bed curtains closing me in. There was no gentle rocking, no waves breaking against the bow. No breeze, no salt-laden air. I had to stop myself from crying. I wanted the smell of freshly brewed coffee, bread baking in the oven, fish sizzling in the pan. I wanted seagulls to screech, shackles to jangle, the mast to creak as the wind filled the sails. I wanted piercing green eyes to stare at me through the darkness.

Chapter Fifteen

Pendenning
Saturday 9th November 1793, 11:00 a.m.

'You slept in the play cottage?' I was always more scared of Mama when she used this tone. It was so much better when she shouted. Icy-calm politeness was her greatest weapon. 'And did you find the cottage *comfortable?*' She had dismissed her maid, only Saffron remained.

'Mama, I'm not going to marry Viscount Vallenforth ... and if you'd seen the look on his face as he was thrashing that boy, you'd not want to speak to him again either.'

'I doubt that. But then I'm not a foolish, ungrateful child. I'm a woman who knows that a great man like Viscount Vallenforth can do what he likes. It's his business, no-one else's. Servants need discipline. Daughters need discipline.' She fed Saffron another piece of chicken and rested back against her pillows. A silk shawl lay loosely round her shoulders, the plate of chicken on the bedclothes beside her.

'He wasn't a servant. He was just a boy – a child. He beat him nearly to death.'

'I doubt that.' She looked up, her furious, cold eyes slicing right through me. 'But then you've always had a bad habit of exaggerating. Does it mean nothing to you that we were worried out of our wits?'

'I was going to come back after you had taken tea. Mama, please listen to me. I was wrong to put you through so much anguish. I'm really sorry ... I didn't mean to stay away so long.'

'Yes, I know. You were locked in the cottage.'

The shutters had been drawn back. Thin sunshine filtered into the room, lighting the red wallpaper, the cherubs, the ornate plaster round the door. Gold leaf glinted on the chairs, the mirrors, the posts of the bed. Hanging against the wardrobe was the gown she would wear; on the dressing table stood the wig she had chosen. It would be another two hours before she would get out of bed, a further two hours before she would finish dressing.

'I won't marry him. I can't.' My voice was breaking. After half an hour of her displeasure, I was finding it hard to stay calm. 'Mama, please release me from this engagement. There must be other men of equal rank.'

'Equal rank, but not equal influence. I had thought you sensible, prided myself you were not like your empty-headed cousin. But I was obviously wrong.' She looked older without her make-up, years of discontent etched across her face. Even now, her mouth was tight with dis-

133

approval. 'You're too foolish to recognise your own good fortune. Viscount Vallenforth belongs to a powerful family. Through him, your father will receive the peerage he deserves and Charity can, at the *very least*, hope for marriage. Your selfishness will have far-reaching consequences ... but I believe you don't care one jolt for your family's name or reputation.' She handed Saffron another piece of chicken.

'I care deeply for our family and, of course, I want my marriage to advance our prestige, but find me someone I can at least *respect*. I'd never be able to free myself from what I saw. Every time he came out of the stables or returned from a ride, I'd be looking for signs of his cruelty. It would destroy me.'

She looked up. 'Do you think me so heartless I don't understand your revulsion? Things are best left unseen, that's all – that way there's a chance of happiness.'

I fought my fury, biting back my anger. She had heard the rumours yet she was prepared to turn a blind eye, throw her daughter like a lamb to a wolf. I had to match her icy-calm. No emotion, just straight refusal. 'There'd be no chance of happiness and I'll not marry him.' I had to maintain my composure; if I did not, she would accuse me of *outrageous temper*.

She sat stroking her beloved pug, the veins prominent in her slender hands. There was a glass vial by her bed, a crystal decanter, an ivory comb. Her beaded slippers lay ready on the floor. She only ever allowed Georgina into her bedchamber and I felt strangely uncomfortable in the intimate surroundings. Suddenly her voice softened. 'You'd better hand me that ring. I'll speak to your father.'

I could hardly believe it. I looked up, smiling, reaching across the bedclothes to place the ring in her outstretched palm. I thought I might even kiss her. 'Thank you, Mama. Thank you so much. Will you explain everything to Father?'

'I *will* talk to your father, but you cannot expect me to discuss it tonight. He's angry enough at your wilful disobedience and he's engaged with Sir Richard until dinner. I cannot risk furthering his anger, not while we have guests – Sir Richard's an important man and his stay with us must *not* be compromised. At the very least you'll agree to that.'

'Of course.' My heart was beating. I had done it. I had held firm, drawn on every ounce of courage. Lady Polcarrow had been right. I was my own person and I had a right to refuse to marry a man I hated. I looked at Mama as if seeing her for the first time. Without her wig and rouge she looked pale, the hair beneath her cap thinning and grey at her temples. Perhaps I had misjudged her. 'I'm sorry ... I thought you wouldn't understand. I've been very foolish and should have come straight to you, not put you through such anxiety.'

'You'll not be so foolish again.' She was holding up the ring, watching the stones sparkle in her hand. Almost at once, her face hardened and she thrust it back towards me. 'You must wear this tonight, Celia. If your father notices you aren't wearing it, he'll ask you why. Everything must be as it should be. Your appearance at dinner will scotch any rumours but if you aren't wearing your ring, people will notice. Viscount Vallenforth must not hear rumours. After church tomorrow you can give me back the ring and your father will write to Viscount Vallenforth. *That* is the *correct* way of doing things.'

I put out my hand, knowing I must make amends. She watched me place the ring back on my finger and nodded to dismiss me. I curtseyed, turning to go. At the door, she stopped me. 'We'll be dining later than usual tonight. Sir Richard Goldsworthy prefers it. He's a personal friend of Mr Pitt but I believe we can show him how equal we are to his society.'

'And Major Trelawney?'

'Major Trelawney's merely a local man, but your father assures me he is sufficiently well mannered. I expect both of you in the drawing-room at five minutes to seven. You must look your best – your blue organza – and tell Charity I do *not* expect to see her wearing her glasses.'

'But, Mama, she can see almost nothing without them.'

'After dinner you will play Mozart – I don't mind what you choose. Charity will sing "Ridente la calma".'

'But, Mama, Charity's never sung that before ... she doesn't know it.'

'Then I suggest you tell her to find Mrs Jennings,' she replied, trying to coax Saffron to eat another delicate morsel.

Mama seemed oblivious to the anxiety she would be causing. Charity would be absolutely terrified. I had to brave her anger. 'Couldn't Mrs

Jennings play and Charity and I sing together?'

'Charity will sing "Ridente la calma".' The irritation in her voice left me in no doubt our conversation was at an end. I closed the door, leaning against it in near exhaustion. Charity was waiting, her face pale with fright.

I squeezed her hand. 'Mama will tell Father after church tomorrow, until then I have to wear the ring.' I slipped my arm through hers. 'But we need to find Mrs Jennings – Mama wants you to sing tonight.'

I was wrong. Mama knew exactly how much anxiety she was causing. My penance was to watch Charity suffer.

The bedroom lay cluttered with discarded gowns. Mrs Jennings took a step back. 'Hold still, Charity, let me pin this brooch a little higher. There, you look perfect.' Her face relaxed. 'Just remember, you've the voice of an angel and no-one can sing more beautifully. You've learnt it perfectly.'

'But I might forget the words.'

'No you won't, but if you do, I'll be right beside you and sing them for you.' I was wearing my blue organza, my satin shoes. Charity was wearing her lemon gown. She seemed so fragile, so ethereal, her blonde hair framing her face in a mass of tiny ringlets. I knew how nervous she was. Without her glasses she could see only colours. With her glasses she could see outlines and shapes. This was her first formal dinner and the first time she had been asked to sing in front of Mama's guests.

Mrs Jennings smiled. 'Just remember Lady April's rules, my dears. Smile if you're addressed,

137

reply quickly and courteously to any direct questions, but otherwise keep silent. Leave all talk of politics to the men and *never* give your own opinion. And, Celia...' Her eyes sought mine for yet another reproving glance. 'Not a foot wrong, you understand?'

Georgina looked up from her sulky silence. 'Yes, Celia. Not a foot wrong. You're in terrible trouble. Papa's furious. They won't forgive you. You'll be shut in your room for running away.'

'I *didn't* run away. I was locked in the cottage... And you can sneak straight back and tell Mama.'

She tossed her head, her hair curling down her back, her lips pouting in their customary fashion. 'I can't, can I? I'm not allowed downstairs. I've got to go to the nursery to have my meal with the *babies* and Mrs Mackerel.'

Mrs Jennings almost jumped, her eyes flashing with disapproval. 'Mrs *McCreal*, really, Georgina! Calling people names is beneath you.'

'It's what Celia calls her. I heard her laughing with Charity – it's her name, not mine.'

'Then all three of you are at fault and no-one's to repeat it.' Mrs Jennings wiped her brow with her handkerchief. I could see she was exhausted. It had been a very intense day; the room was as hot as a furnace. The fire had been lit to dry our hair and what with the tongs and the four of us, and at least as many maids, the air was stuffy and unbreathable. I crossed to the window, lifting the sash, breathing in the welcome freshness, the hint of salt.

The ring-necked doves were sitting on their narrow ledge. Charity came to my side. 'I fed them

138

for you. I saved my bread and left it – just like you do.'

'They pair for life, Itty. If one dies, the other will pine.'

She put her arm through mine. 'You seem so sad, Cici. Are you alright?'

She was so perceptive; I could never hide my feelings from her. 'Mama never asked how the boy was, or if I'd taken him anywhere. She must've presumed I just left him for someone else to find.'

She squeezed my arm. 'In a way, that was good.'

'It let me off the hook... I ought to be grateful, but it makes me sad.'

'Time to go downstairs ... don't forget your fans. Come, Georgina, time to see your baby brother and I wonder what Sarah's been doing today. Perhaps she's drawn us a picture.' Mrs Jennings stood by the door, her black gown and purple brooch as impeccable as ever, her cap just a little to one side. Georgina remained slumped across the chair, her podgy fingers smoothing out several of my ribbons. She had clearly picked out the best.

'It's not fair. I'm twelve, I'm not a baby. I'm *always* left out. Celia and Charity have all the fun. I don't have any beautiful dresses or ribbons as lovely as these. They have everything. It's so unfair. And Celia's never nice to me.'

I took a deep breath. Of course I understood, but even so, everything I said or did went straight back to Mama; her eyes, her ears, always watching. 'Take whatever you want,' I snapped. 'Put it with my tortoiseshell comb and ivory hair clasp –

139

and everything else you have of mine.'

I had been back for less than twelve hours and already the walls seemed to be closing in on me.

Chapter Sixteen

Major Trelawney swung his leg stiffly behind him as he handed Charity to her seat. Charity smiled, no doubt wishing she could see the details of his scarlet coat, his white sash, blue collar and cuffs, the gold lace on his shoulders. Sir Richard was on Mama's right, Major Trelawney on her left. I would be on Father's right. At some stage he would have to speak to me but, for the moment, I was enjoying his frosty silence.

'Lady April, this is splendid. Your hospitality's most welcome. To dine with you and your charming daughters is an honour indeed.' Sir Richard's shrewd eyes looked at each of us in turn.

Mama's intention was always to remind her guests she was an earl's daughter. We were using the Sèvres china, the finest silver, the crystal candelabra. Huge tureens and silver platters crammed every available space and a large silver urn brimmed with exotic fruits and nuts. She caught his appreciative glance and shrugged her shoulders. 'You join us as family, Sir Richard, nothing more. In London we're used to greater society – I'm surprised our paths haven't crossed, but you know my brother, I believe.'

'I've had the pleasure of Lord Edwin's company – at the races.'

Father clicked his fingers. Wine could never be poured quickly enough for him. 'My brother-in-law has a nose for the horses – or maybe just the devil's own luck. Well, here's to your good health,' he said, raising his glass and making short work of the contents.

Major Trelawney held his glass to the candle to admire the beautiful engraving and my heart jolted. I was in the cabin, Arnaud Lefèvre handing me a glass of wine. Sir James was holding his to the light. *Good wine requires good glasses, don't you think?* I looked up to see everyone staring at me. 'I'm sorry ... I didn't hear your question.'

'Do you enjoy riding, Miss Cavendish?' repeated Sir Richard.

'Very much, especially here in Cornwall. The park's so beautiful and the air so fresh.' I knew I was blushing. To be caught like that. To look such a fool.

'Very fresh, but you know about that, don't you, Major Trelawney?' Sir Richard had turned his attention from me. He had ruthless eyes, terse, impatient actions. He seemed self-important, cruel, playing with me like a cat would play with a mouse.

'There's no finer air, Sir Richard,' replied Major Trelawney. 'Lady April, I hope you've enjoyed your stay in Cornwall. Sir Charles tells me you intend to return to London after the wedding.'

I felt the blood rush to my cheeks and looked down. There had already been too much talk of my engagement, Mama going out of her way to stress her delight. 'We must return to London

141

before the roads become impassable. We came by ship, from Portsmouth, but we return by coach.' She was answering Major Trelawney, but addressing Sir Richard. 'It's such an interminable journey. Cornwall's so far from anywhere. You're from London, Sir Richard? You're in Parliament?'

'My seat was East Grinstead but I left when I was called to the bar. I received silk in '89 – the Western Circuit.'

'And is there a *Lady* Goldsworthy?' Mama's coquettish tone made Charity stiffen.

'My wife likes to know every detail,' said Father, waving his fork at the footman. His mouth was full, his words hard to distinguish. 'Mutton for Sir Richard and pass him the powdered rump – eat, gentlemen, I can't be the only one trying this ... what is it? Pigeon?'

'I have no wife, as yet, Lady April. My job takes me away for long periods.' Sir Richard shook his head at the dish the footman offered him. He was in his early forties, Mama's age, yet seemed older, his hooked nose and persistent frown showing evident displeasure. Perhaps it was the sight of father's plate piled high with food, or the knowledge there were poisonous mushrooms in the vicinity. 'What about you, Major Trelawney? Are you a married man?'

Major Trelawney smiled. 'I am, Sir Richard... I've three fine sons – the youngest not quite seven.'

'And your regiment?'

'The thirty-second though I'm no longer in active service. Cannon fire saw to that ... but I'm grateful I can still serve my country. I believe the work I'm doing will prove vital.' His soft Cornish accent was thick with pride.

Father drained his glass, indicating for it to be refilled. 'You're here to visit every household and make a list. Is that right? A poll of eligible men, fit for military service – should the need arise?'

Major Trelawney's smile vanished, his handsome face turning serious. 'The need's already arisen, Sir Charles. The French have instigated a *levée en masse* and England needs to act quickly or we'll be found wanting. France has mobilised the entire nation.' The gravity in his voice sent a chill down my spine. Charity looked petrified.

Even Mama looked shocked. 'They've mobilised the *entire nation?*'

'I'm sorry to scare you, Lady Cavendish, but every French person's been requisitioned – even the sick aren't exempt.'

'Good God, man. Are they to fight from their sick beds?'

'They're to aid the cause, Sir Charles – the young unmarried men will be sent to battle, the married men will forge arms and transport supplies ... the women will make tents and uniforms and serve in hospitals and the sick will roll bandages. The children will pick rags and the old have been instructed to preach the hatred of kings and the unity of the republic. There, I have it by heart!'

'Dammed murdering barbarians,' Father drained another glass of claret, his face getting redder by the minute. 'So you're preparing a force? How many?'

'As many as we can muster. First we must repair

143

the batteries and build the redoubts, then we must train men to take charge of our coastal defences. Major Bassett's establishing a corps of Fencibles and I'm setting up the Volunteer Forces. Helston and Hillidon are already established.'

'We're an island nation. We *have* defences.'

'We may have them, but most are woefully neglected – some batteries are even derelict. Our coast's exposed and vulnerable to attack.'

'Then use the local militia, for God's sake. We don't pay them to stand idle. Get them to man the defences.'

A flash of irritation crossed Major Trelawney's face. He took a deep breath. 'The regular militia are over-stretched and needed where they can do the most good – in Ireland or France. They can't be everywhere and we believe local volunteers should fill the gaps. My job's to muster a strong well-armed, well-drilled body of men capable of defending this coast.'

'Do you really expect us to sleep better at night, knowing half the estate's armed with rifles?' Mama's icy-politeness cut through the air. 'Handing out arms seems rather foolish, Major Trelawney. The Radicals will be first in the queue, rubbing their hands in glee, unable to believe their good fortune.'

'I believe it's time to allow the people of our country some responsibility. If a man has the safety of his wife and family at stake, I believe he'll defend his country to the last.'

'Defend his country?' Mama sniffed. 'Arm the *people* and there'll be anarchy and revolution, just like France.' She fanned herself furiously, 'Thank goodness we shall be in London.'

'Your talk of arms is frightening my wife.' Father's words were slurred and sweat covered his brows. There was gravy on his waistcoat. At any moment he would belch and Mama would stare at him with loathing. 'Your work'll be wasted, I can tell you now.' His wig moved as he scratched his head. 'An armed citizenry is downright dangerous – they're damned Jacobins, the lot of them.' He slumped back in his chair, scowling at Major Trelawney.

'Cornishmen aren't Jacobins, they're just poor. There's no employment and prices are rising. All they want is a fair wage, food on their table, clothes for their children. They've no appetite for revolution – they're as appalled as anyone at the butchery in France.'

Mama turned her back on him, smiling quickly at Sir Richard. 'Mr Windham's assured me poor Louis Charles will soon be released. He's told me the Comte de Provence has a very large army and we're going to his aid. That's where we should be sending our arms – to the Vendée. Don't you agree, Sir Richard?'

Sir Richard leant back, his meal discarded. 'The monarchy must be restored, but the *old* regime?' He shook his head, his lips pursed. 'France's grown too powerful. There's little support for the old regime – especially in the circles I frequent.'

'But Mr Windham's adamant... The Comte de Provence is the king's brother! He's already being called regent. We *must* come to his aid.'

'The savagery must stop, but I do not believe

restoring the old regime would serve England ... and England's interests *must* take priority.' Sir Richard's tone had sharpened, his look of displeasure deepening. 'The old regime's long been our enemy.'

Major Trelawney leant forward. 'I take it you mean support the Duc d'Orléans?'

'If the Duc d'Orléans is spared then I believe we should support him. He's a personal friend of the Prince of Wales and our spies tell us he's open to certain reforms.'

Major Trelawney nodded. 'A constitutional government? Is that feasible?'

'Why not?' Sir Richard wiped his mouth with his napkin. 'A constitutional government under a Bourbon king must be the way forward – anything else and our interests will remain threatened.'

The room was hot and stuffy, the talk of war taking away my appetite. Charity had hardly touched her food. The war had previously felt so remote, everyone promising it would be soon over, but Major Trelawney and Sir Richard seemed so well informed and their words quite terrifying.

The dining room was one of the largest downstairs rooms, certainly the most ornate. Painted cherubs looked down at us from the plastered ceiling, turquoise and gold stripes covered the walls. The sideboard was Chinese, the table and chairs Chippendale, the fireplace Adam. The Pelligrew family were watching us from their huge gold frames. They did not look amused. Neither did Mama. Major Trelawney was addressing her and her dislike of him was becoming obvious.

'I'd like to prove your husband right, Lady

April – about the waste of my time – but I fear not. My instructions are to make a list of every man willing or able to serve...'

'Every man?' she said, not looking at him.

'Between the ages of fifteen and sixty–'

'Good God!' Father spluttered into his glass. 'You're going to call every man to do his duty?'

'No, Sir Charles ... it's merely a list of vital information which the government can call upon. In the future there may be ballots – or, indeed, compulsion ... but, for the moment, I'm to record everyone and their occupations.'

'You're not expecting the gentry to go on your list?'

'Everyone's to go on my list – even unbaptised infants. I need to record every horse and wagon, all livestock – dead or alive, every boat and barge. I'm to check the barns and record the produce. I need a list of all bakers and millers. I need to know where the mills and the wells are...'

'Good God, man. You'll be here for ever!'

'If I may trespass on your hospitality for just a few days longer. My men are hard at work – the fort will soon be habitable.'

Mama waved her hand for the plates to be removed. Father and Major Trelawney had eaten well, Sir Richard less so. She kept her back turned on Major Trelawney. 'I hope you've saved a little room for the trifle, or the almond pudding – perhaps these sweetmeats? What can we offer you, Sir Richard?' Her lips squeezed into a teasing pout. 'My husband tells me you're a magistrate.'

'A *stipendiary* magistrate,' said Father, pulling the bowl of trifle towards him, 'from the Home

Office. He's got sweeping powers, my dear, so we'd best be careful.'

Sir Richard took one mouthful and pushed his almond pudding aside, reaching instead for his gold toothpick. 'I'm from Bow Street. Yet more government business, I'm afraid. My office is to regulate all foreigners entering our country. Every foreigner – including the Irish – needs to register with the appropriate officials and sign a declaration of arrival at their port of entry.'

'But surely, Sir Richard, you don't intend to treat émigrés like criminals? Some of them are very distinguished – the Marquis de Chavannes, for instance, Chevalier de Anselme. They've been brutally treated and have lost everything. They need our help.'

'We need tighter control. Émigrés are still free to enter but they must register and obtain their declaration form. No-one's exempt. All house-holders housing émigrés must supply details and anyone making enquiries about foreigners seeking nationalisation must register the enquiry with the Alien Office.'

Major Trelawney nodded. 'It's well overdue. Our borders need protection and travel must be curtailed.'

Sir Richard nodded. 'I'm here to instruct local mayors and magistrates. They need to know it's their duty to fine or imprison anyone without an official declaration. These French need watching and it's my job to watch them.'

Sir Richard had been wrong to push his plate aside after just one mouthful. Mama was no fool. Refusing her food was his way of snubbing her.

She nodded to the footman, taking Saffron back in her arms. 'Gentlemen, forgive me. This talk of politics has quite exhausted me. We'll leave you men to your port. Come, girls, let the men finish their talk of business.' The footmen pulled back our chairs. Major Trelawney rose stiffly to his feet. He looked deeply troubled.

'Lady April, it's you who must forgive me. I'm sorry about my talk of war. I thought you were interested. There's so much more we could have discussed.'

I held my breath, expecting Mama to say her favourite words – *I doubt that.* Instead she managed a smile. 'Will you be coming to church tomorrow, gentlemen?'

'Indeed, Lady April ... that would be delightful,' they replied, almost in unison.

'Excellent. Well, gentlemen, I'll see you tomorrow.'

She left with a flutter of smiles. I took Charity's arm, both of us curtseying as we left the room. We were free, spared from having to perform the music we had been practising all day. Charity squeezed my arm and I tried not to smile.

We both knew Mama would be heading for one of her headaches.

Chapter Seventeen

Pendenning
Sunday 10th November 1793, 1:30 p.m.

The two coaches waited on the drive – the first, very splendid, hired from Truro for the duration of our stay, the second, far less grand, much older, with suspension that had probably seen better days. It had been Mr Pelligrew's coach, which we had acquired along with everything else.

Father looked furious, stabbing the floor with his cane, his face as red as the coachman's livery. 'Lady April's headache shows no sign of improving. She regrets she's too unwell to accompany us and sends her apologies. I'm sorry to keep you waiting. Shall we go?' Sir Richard was pacing the drive, Major Trelawney entertaining us with stories of his children. I could tell Mrs Jennings liked him.

'Papa, can I travel with you in the big coach? Mama did say I could. She promised me I could go with her and I'm wearing my best ribbons.' Georgina's well-practised tears filled her eyes, her mouth trembling in its heartbroken pout.

Father's face softened. 'Major Trelawney, could I ask you to accompany the ladies? Now I think about it, vagrants have set up camp in the woods and it's not such a bad idea. My steward's dealing with them but we can't be too careful.' Major

Trelawney smiled, walking with us to the second coach. How very clever of Mama. A military escort. No chance of escape.

The Cornish weather never ceased to amaze me. It was always so variable, changing day to day, even hour to hour. Yesterday had been so wet, yet driving the three miles to church, the sun was shining, the sky a beautiful azure blue. We climbed the hill, surprised at the strength of the wind. It was so sheltered in the vale, yet on the top of the hill the branches of the trees were swirling ferociously.

'It's really windy, Charity. The field's been ploughed and men are sowing corn but it's blowing all over the place and the seagulls are swooping down, getting buffeted by the wind.'

'I'm surprised they don't wait until the wind drops.'

Major Trelawney smiled. 'I agree, Miss Charity, but they probably think yesterday's rain will help set the seed. It's winter wheat and I'm surprised by that. Does wheat do well here, do you know?'

Charity and I had no idea but Mrs Jennings had obviously heard talk. She leant forward, smiling politely. 'I believe not. The harvest's been very bad and bread is scarce. You seem to know a lot about farming, Major Trelawney. Is it your interest?'

'My brother and I have land near St Kew – along the River Amble to the Camel Estuary.'

'And do you grow wheat?'

'Wheat, barley, corn – we're fortunate the land's good for both crops and grazing. We've sheep and more cattle then we're used to. Demand's rising. The navy's devouring everything we can send and

151

where we used to send our calves to Somerset for fattening, we're keeping more and driving them to Plymouth.' He smiled, his handsome face alight with passion.

'Do you ever feel torn between your land and your regiment, Major Trelawney?' I asked.

'I'm a military man and proud of my achievements but, yes, as I grow older, I feel the draw of the land. I find myself wishing for peace and prosperity.'

Father's coach was pulling well ahead, the scarlet coats of the footmen still visible on the back. His horses were strong and lively, our horses, by comparison, seemed tired and overworked. The road was widening, the verges full of ripening blackberries; the square tower of Porthruan church just visible ahead. A grassy track joined us from the right and we pulled slowly to a stop. Father and Sir Richard were waiting impatiently, Georgina all smiles and happiness. Father and Sir Richard turned to go but Major Trelawney offered us both an arm. Mrs Jennings grabbed Georgina's hand. We had kept Parson Bettison waiting for fifteen minutes. Last week it had been thirty.

Father insisted on writing Parson Bettison's address and today it seemed to go on forever. *'Timely preparation,* both on this earth and for where we are to follow,' the parson shouted. *'Duty,* the path of *obedience.* Your God sees your every move. You must give allegiance to your betters so that the enemy, when they come bearing down on you, will not kill your children and burn your houses. Be ready, so that the enemy, when they come rushing through your doors, can be repelled with force...'

Vaulted timbers arched above us like the ribs of a ship. I held Charity's hand. I could tell she was scared. The church was crowded, bursting at the seams. The men looked stirred, ready for action, the women weeping, the children growing more petrified by the minute. If father wished to frighten everyone, he had certainly succeeded.

'Think how you would feel if the enemy landed *before* you learn to *defend* yourselves. Attend, therefore, with alacrity, to the calls of your betters. They are the ones who will point you to what services you may, in your various situations, most effectively perform...'

To my shame, I barely listened. I was wearing my blue organza, my straw bonnet framed with silk flowers and matching ribbons. I felt excited, restless, wanting to turn round and search the benches. It was as if I knew Captain Lefèvre was watching me, laughing at me from beneath his hooded eyes. I could almost feel his eyes burning my back.

'We serve a monarch whom we love and a God whom we adore. We are not *barbarians,* bloodthirsty *revolutionaries* like the enemy we face. No. The laws we revere are our Father's laws. The faith we follow teaches us to live in the bonds of charity and die with the knowledge of bliss beyond the grave. In the name of the Father and of...'

He had finished. Father looked pleased, nodding to Sir Richard, leaning back to talk to the man sitting behind him. Parson Bettison stood patiently for Father to finish, waiting to lead the procession with his customary pomp. I took

Major Trelawney's proffered arm, following them down the aisle, glancing quickly down each row as we passed. I could not help myself. What had happened to me? Celia Cavendish, looking for a smuggler.

He was standing on the end of the last pew, his hair tied neatly behind his back, a dark green jacket stretching across his shoulders. He looked impeccable, his cravat the finest silk, his cuffs Belgium lace. His cream waistcoat was silk, embroidered with silver thread, his boots highly polished. To be dressed so well could only draw attention and I looked stiffly ahead, prickles of fear running down my back. My heart was racing. He must not give me away. Please, please, do not look at me.

Father slowed his pace, believing he ought to know the well-dressed stranger, giving him the slightest nod in case he did. Captain Lefèvre bowed in response and we passed within a foot of each other, my eyes fixed firmly on Father's back.

'Are you alright, Miss Cavendish? Only, you don't look well...'

'It's just the heat, Major Trelawney – it's very crowded. I just need some air.' We reached the church porch. 'I'm fine, honestly I am. Mrs Jennings's just behind so do feel free to leave me – I know you've a lot of people you want to meet.'

The wind was strong, blowing the trees, the sky so piercingly blue. Bright autumn sunlight flooded the churchyard, casting shadows across the grass. It was too windy for the birds and nothing to watch, just the dazed look on the people's faces as they poured out of the church. I needed to compose myself so slipped my arm through Charity's, pulling her aside. 'Come, Itty – it's horribly crowded. Let's go for a walk. Are you coming, Mrs Jennings?'

'Yes ... but keep to the path, the ground's still soggy.' Mrs Jennings reached for Georgina, tucking her arm firmly through her own. 'Wait, Celia, don't rush – there's no fire. Dignity, girls ... goodness me, with everyone watching and you run off like racehorses!'

It was so fresh, so wonderful to be in the open air. I loved this squat little church with its square tower and elaborate sundial. It was so peaceful, so rooted in time. Tombs went back for generations, the same names repeated, the quarrels long-forgotten. Goats bleated behind the hedge-row, oxen stared at us from across the farmyard. Cows were in the milking-shed, the smell of dung drifting from the fields. So rooted in time – all the hard-working people now resting in peace, their wars long over, their fear eased.

We reached a fork. The inner path would lead us back to the church, the outer path would skirt the churchyard. In the distance, I heard a black-bird. 'Did you hear that, Itty?' I said, guiding her up the path towards the stile. 'A blackbird's sitting on the gate though he can barely balance in the wind. His feathers are being ruffled but he's determined to sing.'

I turned round in surprise. Two ladies were placing a bunch of wildflowers in a vase by a tomb. My surprise turned to pleasure. 'My goodness, Itty, there's Mrs Pengelly and Madame Merrick. That's so lovely. Come, let me introduce you.'

Charity pulled me back. 'Mrs Pengelly, Lady Polcarrow's mother? She must be so distraught... Have we heard any news?'

I had spoken light-heartedly and realised my mistake. 'Maybe there's hope of their recovery.'

Charity's face lifted, 'Let's hope so. If they were dying, she'd be at their bedside, wouldn't she?'

'Either way, it would be unpardonable not to ask after their welfare.' Mrs Jennings had caught us up and was also watching them. 'Charity will like Mrs Pengelly, won't she, Mrs Jennings?'

Mrs Jennings' face was full of compassion. 'Perhaps we shouldn't trespass on her grief.'

We stood watching them arrange the flowers. I had only been twice to their dressmaking shop, both times with cousin Arbella and Mrs Jennings. Madame Merrick was the proprietor and Mrs Pengelly one of her best seamstresses. Madame Merrick always dressed exquisitely. Today she was wearing a shimmering green silk gown with a large matching hat. She had extraordinary hauteur and composure and I was desperate for Itty to meet her. 'You've got to meet Madame Merrick, Itty,' I whispered. 'Honestly, she's quite remarkable ... you like her, don't you, Mrs Jennings? Or is it just her punch you like?'

'Really, Celia! Yes, I admire Madame Merrick considerably, but *not* for her punch. She's the best dressmaker I've come across and the shrewdest woman I've ever met.' Mrs Jennings smoothed her black silk skirt, drawing her shawl firmly around her. She always wore the same – black silk on Sundays, black taffeta for visits and afternoon tea, black worsted wool on every other occasion. Her

156

only brooch was a dark amethyst, set in silver, the ribbons on her bonnet always a matching purple – silk on Sundays, satin for visits and tea parties. Somewhere in her late thirties, her hair was still brown, her figure quite beautiful, her face often filled with compassion. In repose, it became etched with sadness. I knew she liked both Mrs Pengelly and Madame Merrick and would be delighted to renew their acquaintance.

They saw us approaching and curtseyed, Madame Merrick with the grace of a duchess, Mrs Pengelly with a flash of pain.

'This is my sister, Miss Charity Cavendish... Mrs Jennings you know, of course, and this is my younger sister, Georgina.'

'Miss Cavendish, this is such an honour,' replied Mrs Pengelly, her tiny frame dwarfed by her taller companion.

'We've come to enquire after Lady Polcarrow. We've heard the terrible news.'

Mrs Pengelly looked down, wringing her hands. She was as timid as she looked fragile, her face still beautiful beneath her plain grey bonnet. 'We must pray for their recovery ... but there are signs of improvement – so I believe.'

Mrs Jennings and Charity smiled, voicing their delight. Did Mrs Pengelly know Sir James and Rose were only pretending to be ill? Or had they kept the truth even from her – for the safety of young Francis? The thought that Robert Roskelly could be so evil to tell his sister to poison Sir James or never see her son again was still too terrible to contemplate. The wind was blowing our skirts, tugging our shawls; wisps of grey hair were escaping from under Mrs Pengelly's bonnet. She smiled up at me and I smiled back. Madame Merrick was as immaculate as ever. 'I'm wearing your gown, you notice, Madame Merrick – it's become my favourite – I never seem to wear any other.'

She dropped another curtsey, her proud head bowing with modesty, her movements smooth and unassuming. 'Material *that fine* is always a *pleasure* to sew and seeing you wearing it makes it all the more pleasurable.'

'We must come and visit your shop again, Madame Merrick. I did so enjoy our visits. And Charity needs a new gown, don't you, Charity? You missed out last time so it's only fair. Don't you think so, Mrs Jennings?'

Charity's face lit up. 'Do you think we could ask Mama, Mrs Jennings?'

Mrs Jennings was clearly not going to be hard to persuade, 'Well ... perhaps we should – why not? You could do with another gown.'

Georgina was staring at us in sulky silence. As usual, she would need to be appeased but Madame Merrick was already looking at her as if she knew Mama's eyes were watching. 'Perhaps Miss Georgina should have some *new* ribbons?' she said softly. 'I believe I have some *very fine* silk to match that *beautiful* dress – perhaps a little pocket for you to carry ... with a *pearl* button?'

Georgina had the grace to nod and Madame Merrick turned to Charity. 'As it happens, I have recently acquired some very *fine* fabric, *quite as lovely* as your sister's organza.' She dropped her voice to a conspiratorial whisper, a slight flicker of a smile, 'or maybe even finer. I have peach and apricot ... *both*, I believe, are colours you should wear.'

Charity blushed. I loved to see her as the centre of attention but I knew she hated it as she always shied away from fuss. I put my arm through hers, smiling my delight. From the corner of my eye a flash of green caught my attention and I turned in surprise, my heart leaping. Arnaud Lefèvre was walking round the bend, not thirty yards from us, and our eyes locked. He stopped, standing rooted to the spot, the wind blowing the lace at his cuffs, the leaves swirling past him from the tree behind us. He looked so handsome, every inch the gentleman and a thrill of excitement passed through me.

But what was he doing here? This part of the churchyard was furthest from the lych gate; it was hardly ever used, the path overgrown with weeds. We had come upon Mrs Pengelly and Madame Merrick by chance but no-one else had come this way. Surely he had not thought to follow me? No. If he had followed us, he would have taken the same path we had chosen. Was this chance – an unintended meeting or was he expecting only Madame Merrick and Mrs Pengelly? He seemed to recover and nodded politely, turning quickly away. He had clearly come to meet Madame Merrick.

Madame Merrick, for her part, seemed hardly to notice, inclining her long neck to hear Georgina's exact requirements. I felt suddenly breathless, shock making me want to gasp. I had been blind; surely I had been so blind? Madame Merrick was no ordinary dressmaker – her straight back, her effortless curtsy, her flawless deportment had all been drilled into her from birth. All Sir Richard's talk of France and still I had not guessed – Madame Merrick was an aristocrat, an émigré. She must be. I felt thrilled, excited, as if somehow it mattered. I tried to keep the excitement from my voice. 'We'll try very hard to persuade Mama to let us visit you.'

'Or I could come to *you*, Miss Cavendish. I can bring as much material as I can up to the Hall...'

I was barely listening. My heart was leaping. Nothing was as it seemed. Surely Arnaud Lefèvre had the same arch to his neck, the same elegant, long fingers? He was refined and educated, those clothes more suitable to a grand house than a ship. How blind could I be? I felt breathless again; Arnaud Lefèvre was not after brandy – he was no common smuggler. He risked his life to save others. He took me to France only because another man's life had depended on him. I suddenly felt so happy. He was in league with Madame Merrick, he must be. He was brave, courageous, honourable – as good as his word.

He had almost reached the bend and I stood watching his retreating back, a terrible sense of loss ripping my heart. I had dismissed his advances, been so aloof. He knew me to be engaged and now he was leaving and I may never see him again. I slipped my fingers quickly through the ribbons of my bonnet. The silk slid easily through my hands, the wind catching it in an instance, 'Oh, no! Help ... my bonnet!' I shouted.

He turned and saw my straw hat flying towards

him, the blue ribbons streaming in the wind behind. Jumping quickly, he caught it in his outstretched hand and started walking back, holding the bonnet in the air like a trophy. I stared back at him. He was smiling, his glance conspiratorial, his eyes full of laughter. 'Your bonnet, I believe, madame.'

I smiled back. In the sunlight his eyes were intensely blue, fringed by long black lashes. His chin was closely shaven, his hair held neatly back. I could almost smell the almond soap. 'Thank you, Mr...?'

He bowed a low bow. 'Captain Arnaud Lefèvre and very glad to be of service.'

I wanted to smile, laugh. No, worse than that, I wanted him to sweep me up in his arms and carry me away. 'Are you French, sir?' I managed to say.

He seemed to hesitate. 'No, I'm from Jersey.'

Madame Merrick was watching us through those hooded lids, Mrs Pengelly was smiling broadly. 'We've Captain Lefèvre to thank for all Madame Merrick's fine silks. We don't know how he manages to find them with all the blockages but they really are quite the loveliest. He's master of Sir James' cutter – a boat my husband built.'

I felt so alive, every pulse in my body pounding. 'Is that so?' I replied. 'Then we'll definitely have to avail ourselves of your spoils, Captain Lefèvre. We can't have you going to so much trouble for nothing, can we?' I held out my hand but Arnaud seemed reluctant to give me back my hat. I put out both my hands and took the bonnet, my heart jolting in pleasure as our hands touched.

161

'Tie the ribbons tightly this time, Miss Cavendish,' he said, slowly relinquishing the bonnet.

I wanted him to tie them for me. For a brief, glorious second, I imagined him stepping forward, standing closer, his fingers brushing my neck. I felt so giddy, so wonderfully light-hearted. My stomach was fluttering. 'I'm sorry to cut short our conversation but I'm afraid Father will be waiting,' I said, tying my own ribbons, 'and we'd better not keep him any longer. Goodbye, Mrs Pengelly, Madame Merrick. I hope we see you again soon.' I glanced at Arnaud Lefèvre. 'Good day, captain.'

I slipped my arm through Charity's – not to help her, but to have her support. I could barely breathe. My head was spinning, my heart turning cartwheels. I had to stop myself from smiling. Everything had changed. Three things were certain: Arnaud Lefèvre was no smuggler, he was certainly no common sailor and he was not from Jersey.

The carriage jolted us from side to side. I was deep in thought, my fingers playing with the beading on my bag. Of course he was an émigré – it was obvious he was born to quality. His taste was perfect. I sat hugging my secret, almost too excited to breathe. I had helped save the life of a man fleeing the guillotine. How incredible, how completely thrilling. I had to look out of the window to hide my excitement.

Charity and Major Trelawney were deep in discussion. 'We grow barley because barley bread's cheaper than wheaten bread, but we use it as fodder as well – for weaning the cattle and, of course, it's used for malting.'

'Do you make cream?'

'Only enough for our farm – the boys love it but we're quite some distance from the market and it doesn't travel. It spoils too soon.'

'Do you grow turnips and rotate your fields?'

'You know a lot about farming, Miss Charity,' he replied, smiling. 'Two years for the corn, a year for manured turnips, four years for dressed grass. My father learnt it from his father and my grandfather before him. What on earth–?' The carriage slammed to a halt. Someone was shouting, yelling orders. Major Trelawney pulled down the window and frowned. He opened the door and lowered himself without the aid of steps.

'There's quite a crowd,' I told Charity. 'They're in rags. They look filthy.'

The colour drained from her face. 'Are they vagabonds?'

'I think they must be. They look starved to death.' I stared in horror. Philip Randall had his whip held high in the air. Two baskets, piled high with blackberries, stood in front of him, the crowd slowly backing away from them. Children were clinging to their mothers' skirts. They were caked with mud; poor sparrow-framed children, their hollow eyes full of terror. A man was on his knees, begging Philip Randall to stop. Two other men stepped forward, trying to plead.

Mr Randall's whip slashed the air. 'Get off this land before I whip the lot of you.' He was taunting them, walking slowly forward, one hand on his hip, the other ready to lash.

Major Trelawney stormed to his side. 'I beg you, sir, have some pity. These people are starving.'

'They're stealin' and should be hanged – the lot of them.'

Father leant from his carriage, his face purple with rage. 'Do whatever you need, Mr Randall. Just get them off my land.' He pointed to the baskets. 'We'll take those. You can get back in now, Major Trelawney, our way's been cleared.'

Father's carriage pulled ahead of us. The footman let down the steps and Major Trelawney swung himself into the carriage. He tried to smile but the fury in his face was hard to hide. Behind us, we heard the baskets being strapped to the back and I let go of Charity's hand. I would describe everything to her later but, for now, none of us could speak.

Chapter Eighteen

Pendenning
Monday 11th November 1793, 1:30 p.m.

The footman bowed politely. 'Lady April will see you now.'

I had been waiting for over an hour, sitting on the tapestry chair outside Mama's drawing-room. No one had gone in or out, so I knew she had kept me waiting. She was standing by the window, sunlight streaming onto a letter in her hand.

'You've reconsidered, I presume?'

My mouth went dry. 'No, I've not reconsidered.'
I held out the ring, walking slowly towards her.
'I'm not going to marry Viscount Vallenforth.'

She ignored my outstretched hand, looking instead at the letter she waved in front of me. 'I've been sent two letters – one from Lady Clarissa, the other from her son, Lieutenant Frederick Carew. They arrived together, though they were posted several days apart. Lady Clarissa's a cousin of my brother's wife – she's practically family. I knew her as a child though, after her marriage, our paths no longer crossed.'

I took a deep breath, trying to fight my panic.

'With your marriage imminent, I wrote to Lady Clarissa reminding her of our family connection. She has five sons and a daughter – Lieutenant Carew is the *fifth* son and therefore has no great marriage expectations.' Her eyes pierced me like daggers. 'There are not many mothers who would seek to marry their daughter to a fifth son, even though his father does own vast estates. Are you following me, Celia?'

My mouth tasted of salt. Yes, I was following her, following her exactly.

'Connections arc what I'm talking about. As sister-in-law to Viscount Vallenforth, Charity has some value.'

'Mama, how can you say that? Charity's priceless ... she's so beautiful ... so clever.'

'She's all but blind – she has little, if any, marriage hopes. You know that, Celia.' She walked angrily across the room, almost throwing Saffron to his cushion. Reaching her desk, she snatched the second letter. 'I've written to Lady

165

Clarissa, explaining Charity's blindness is due to a childhood illness and would have no effect on any child she may bear. No ... hear me out. Your father's offered a substantial dowry. Lord Carew knows your father's well connected in Mr Pitt's government and could be of great use. They also know your uncle's Vice-Admiral and Governor of Dominica. Through our patronage, Lieutenant Carew could expect a glittering career... And, quite rightly, Lady Clarissa has instructed her son to pay his respects.'

I clamped the ring in my fallen hand. I knew to stand straight, shoulders back, chin held grace-fully in the air. Mother held up the second letter. 'And here's Lieutenant Carew's very prompt re-sponse – he clearly has manners and has done what his mother has asked. His ship, HMS *Circe*, is arriving in Fosse to await orders and he sees this as a perfect opportunity to call. I've asked him to dine with us on Friday.'

The salt in my mouth turned to nausea. This game of chess. My move. Her move. She was the knight, I was the pawn. She had no intention of freeing me from my engagement – she had not even spoken to Father. I felt furious, the strength of my anger hard to control. She was staring at me, expecting my defiance. I bit my lip – I must breathe, take a leaf from her book; icy-calm politeness was a potent tool. I would not give her the satisfaction of seeing me plead. The rush of fury was abating, the giddiness passing.

I would never marry Viscount Vallenforth and I would certainly never abandon Charity to an am-bitious family who saw attaching themselves to

Viscount Vallenforth as worthwhile. I would wait. I slipped the hateful ring back on my finger, furious at the gloat in her eyes. I was biding my time – that was all. 'Did Georgina tell you we met Mrs Pengelly and Madame Merrick after church yesterday?'

'You shouldn't have spoken to them.'

Of course Georgina had told her. She told her everything. 'We passed within feet – I thought it rude not to acknowledge them.'

'Well, you were wrong.'

'There's unrest and great poverty in the town. Major Trelawney thinks the town needs our patronage–'

'I don't care what that odious man thinks.'

'Madame Merrick, for example, the dressmaker, her gowns are as good as any we can find in London.'

'We don't require her services. You can go now.'

I stood my ground. 'Mama, I think Charity should have a new dress. If Lieutenant Carew's to be snared, she needs to look beautiful.'

Mama flinched at my words but I could see her deliberating. 'Perhaps Charity could do with a new gown.' She picked Saffron up, rubbing her nose against her little squashed face, laughing with delight as her pink tongue licked her face. 'I'll think about it. Before you go ... those are Mrs Pumfrey's menu plans. They're virtually unreadable. Cross out almond pudding and add venison and rib of beef. Tell her there'll be one extra on Friday and I want sorbet. I don't care if the ice-house's empty. I want sorbet.'

I wrote as asked. Well, almost. *We have another*

guest on Friday. I suggest venison, a rib of beef and sorbet not almond pudding. On another note, employ two more under-maids and make sure all the maids have at least three good meals a day. And issue them all with lanterns. I held out the paper, knowing she would not read it.

'Give it to the footman.'

'Can we go to Madame Merrick tomorrow, Mama? She won't have much time if she's to make Charity a new gown.'

'Only if your father doesn't need the carriage.' She kissed Saffron and caught a glimpse of her reflection. A curl on her wig needed tweaking. Her lips needed attention. Perhaps a little more rouge.

The thought of going to Madame Merrick was enough to give me wings. I rushed down the staircase, past the alabaster urns, the marble plinths, the vast Chinese vases, racing past poor Atlas with the world on his back. My footsteps echoed across the polished floor. We were going to Madame Merrick. My heart was soaring. I had never expected Mama to agree. Hurrying across the hall, I had to wait for the footmen to open the door.

It was a beautiful day, the sun brilliant in the sky above. I would go riding but, first, I would arrange for the carriage. I loved Madame Merrick's fabrics, the huge warehouse, the bustle of the town. My silence had bought this treat. On Friday I would tell Father the engagement was over, Lieutenant Carew could scuttle back to his ambitious mother and Charity would be safe.

I skipped down the steps of the terrace, weaving

between the box hedges, passing under the arch to the stables. The tower of the coach-house rose high above me, the clock-face gleaming in the sun. Father's carriage was newly washed, the wheels free of mud. I looked about for the coachman, expecting him to be not far away. He was nowhere to be seen. I would go instead to the stables and tell the groom to saddle my mare.

I crossed the courtyard. It was strangely quiet, no sign of grooms, certainly no stable boys. 'Good day, m'lady. Can I be of service?'

A man in his late thirties was standing behind me. He took off his hat, holding it in both hands. His freshly washed hair was tied neatly behind his neck. He looked wholesome, honest, his face browned by the sun. He was wearing a small leather apron, a leather belt; a bucket of water was on the cobbles in front of him. I was sure I had never seen him before. 'I want my groom,' I said. 'The one I ride with. I think his name's John.'

He twisted the hat in his hands. 'John's been dismissed, m'lady.'

'Dismissed?' A cold grip clutched my heart. 'Then find his replacement,' I managed to say.

He could barely look at me, his eyes darting nervously around him. 'I wish I could, m'lady, but he's not been replaced.' A flash of sympathy crossed his eyes, 'There's no grooms ... not no more ... because there's no horses. All the ridin' mares are returned to the farms ... there's just the carriage horses, an' Mr Randall's stallion ... an' the old nag that pulls the cart – just the six. All the others are back on the farms.'

I spun round, walking quickly to the stable. The

first six stalls were empty, newly scrubbed, the bridles and saddles missing from their hooks. 'No riding at all?' I felt breathless, suffocated, the walls of my prison closing in on me. 'Where's the coachman?'

'I've taken his place, m' lady.' He was a small man, undernourished, with callused hands and bowed legs. Without his hat, he squinted into the sun. 'I'm that sorry about yer mare – she was a real beauty, quite the nicest chestnut I've seen.'

'Yes, well. It can't be helped.' I wish he had not been so kind. Tears stung my eyes, I wanted to cry. The doors were shutting, the locks turning. I stared through blurred eyes at Father's coach. 'We need the carriage for tomorrow. Is it free at one o'clock?'

'I believe so, m' lady.'

'Then I'd be grateful if you could take us to the dressmaker in Fosse. You'll need to wait an hour or more.'

'Pleasure, m'lady.' He was smiling, his face full of pride. He had nice eyes, deferential, kind. He seemed calm, pleasant, no signs of cruelty. He was sure to be good with horses.

'I'd like you to take a message to Madame Merrick. Tell her we're coming at half past one and I don't want other people there.'

'I'll send a boy, straightaway. An' I'm sorry about the ridin', m'lady. Wish it was otherwise.'

I was still reeling. This was no chess game and Mama was no fool – she knew I had run away. I felt increasingly petrified, knowing her next move would be to search my room. Perhaps she had already searched my room while we had been at church. The coachman picked up his bucket. 'One moment...' I said. 'I've an alteration that Madame Merrick might as well do for tomorrow. Tell the boy I've a parcel for him to take – I'll get a maid to bring it down.'

I knew to walk slowly across the terrace. Mama would be watching from her window. Georgina would be watching from the school room. I would walk calmly up to my room, wrap the cloak in my torn shawl and address the bundle to Mrs Pengelly. It was the best I could think to do.

Charity slipped into my bed, pulling the bed-clothes round us, her beautiful face full of anxiety. 'Do you think he'll be kind? Is there any chance he might be nice?'

'If he's not kind, you're not to marry him.'

'Is Mama making him come? Cici, be honest. Is it for money? Is he poor? Are they buying me a husband?' She looked so vulnerable, her hair curled in silk strips, her lace night-cap flopping over her face.

I blew out my candle, my heart in turmoil. It would be so cruel to tell her the Carews were only interested in her because they believed she would be Viscount Vallenforth's sister-in law. Viscount Vallenforth still thought us engaged and no doubt word had spread. 'Mama says he's family – and families help each other. He's a young naval officer and we've got the connections he needs. He needs patronage – you need a husband. It could work very well.' I hoped I sounded encouraging. 'If he's worth his salt, he'll snap you up.'

For a moment she was silent. 'I've always

dreaded growing up. I don't want us to part.'

I pulled her closer. 'We must stay firm ... we must insist they find us husbands we like.'

She nodded. 'Anyway, I don't suppose Madame Merrick can make a dress in four days. I'll have to wear my green dress – would that look alright?'

'I think Madame Merrick can do anything.'

'Mrs Jennings likes her and Mrs Pengelly. Do you think Sir James and Lady Polcarrow will get better? Only yesterday, at dinner, Father said they were dying.'

Charity was set to chatter. I loved it when Charity slept in my bed, but tonight I wanted to be alone. I had not told her the mares had been returned, nor had I the heart to tell her my marriage to Viscount Vallenforth had obviously sparked Lady Clarissa's interest. I felt so angry. We were chattel, nothing but chattel. I must not let Charity hear me cry. The room was stuffy, the bed curtains oppressive. I wanted to throw open the window and listen to the owls.

I closed my eyes. The wind was blowing our clothes, ruffling our hair. I was running, glancing over my shoulder, knowing he would spin me in his arms when he caught me. My hair was loose around my shoulders, my hat long blown away. Soon he would catch me. He would spin me round and hold me in his arms. Soon he would kiss me.

Chapter Nineteen

Pendenning
Tuesday 12th November, 1793

The carriage was newly polished, the four greys immaculately groomed. They stood shaking their manes, their hooves shining with fresh oil. We were ready to go, our skirts spread out around us. I glanced out of the window and my heart sank. Philip Randall was striding towards us, his cane tucked angrily beneath his arm. Dressed in a greatcoat and gloves, he swung himself alongside the coachman, shouting a string of orders.

Charity heard his voice. 'I'm afraid we've company,' I said with distaste.

It was overcast, dull, the sky a dark grey. I thought it might rain but the ground was hard. Horned cattle looked up as we passed, sheep ignored us. At the gate-house a small boy took off his hat and tugged his forelock. We reached the river and the tide was out. The coachman urged the horses across the ford, the wheels splashing noisily through the water and I leant against the window, searching the muddy banks. I could see the birds – egrets, curlews, sandpipers. Last night I had felt like crying, but this morning my heart was singing. Arnaud Lefèvre must think he had a chance of winning my hand. Why else would he be so bold?

We turned the bend, descending the first of the narrow streets dropping steeply to the harbour's edge. I was hoping to see Lieutenant Carew's ship lying at anchor but, for the moment, we had no view. On either side, rows of houses huddled together, clinging precariously to the cliff. Shoulder to shoulder, they bore the ravages of wind and sea, the thick stone walls, the small leaded windows somehow defying the strength of the westerly gales. A sewer ran in the front of the houses. It was black with filth, the smell so appalling I had to hold my vinaigrette up to my nose.

In London we never drew unwanted attention, but in Fosse we were like a magnet for hostile stares. People spat as we passed or turned their backs in sullen silence. The coach slowed to a walking pace, crawling to a stop, and I pressed my cheek against the window, trying to see what was causing the delay. 'It's so crowded,' I said. 'There's a cart in front – the man's trying to back up but the oxen won't move.'

Mrs Jennings had seen the expressions on the faces of the people passing. 'Draw the curtain, Celia. Don't let them see you.'

We eased slowly forward, gradually pushing our way down the narrow lane. Through a small gap in the curtain, I watched this unfamiliar world where men and women could go as they please. The women had baskets on their heads, the men great bundles of firewood balanced on their backs. A pack of heavily laden mules were trying to squeeze past us, the mule leader cursing and shouting. There were children in rags, dogs sniffing at rubbish. One man looked like a peddler, another a pie seller, but most seemed to be labourers or fishermen. The younger men had rope keeping their breeches from falling, patches of canvas on the elbows of their jackets. The older men had stooped backs, weathered faces. They looked gaunt, joyless, all of them scowling as they stood in the sewer to let us pass.

At the turn in the road, we could hear shouting, cheering, the beat of a drum. Charity looked up. 'That's a regimental fife,' she said. 'It must be Major Trelawney.'

I pulled back the curtain. 'It is ... I can see him. He's recruiting – there are posters everywhere.'

The town square was heaving. Major Trelawney was standing on a cart, fully dressed with bearskin and sword. Six soldiers stood in front of him, facing the crowd, their brick-red coats and white sashes dazzling the onlookers despite the grey day. One soldier was playing the fife, one banging a drum, the others standing stiffly to attention. Our coach had reached a standstill, hemmed in on all sides, but no-one jostled us. All eyes were staring at Major Trelawney. The music had stopped and he raised his hands. To no avail, it seemed. He reached for a long, thin pipe and blew it. Immediately, the crowd stopped and listened.

'You ask how much you should give? Well, let me tell you.' His voice was strong, full of authority and I opened the window so Charity could hear. 'I urge you to give as much as you can. Times are hard, I know. You may not have a lot to give, but I urge you to give what you can. To muster a force we need money to pay the company.' He held up a large leather-bound book. 'I've opened a book of subscriptions. Place your name here and pledge as much as you can, so everyone will know you've helped defend your country.'

Charity leant back from the window. 'He's a good way of talking, don't you think, Mrs Jennings?'

'He's a clever man. He's got just the right mix of authority and compassion. I like him, he makes me feel safe.'

Major Trelawney put the book down. 'The money you raise will pay for clothing and training. It'll pay for arms and ammunition. Helson's mustered a company of sixty privates – they're to have one drummer and one piper. Hillidon are raising a company of *one hundred* men – they're to have two drummers, two pipers. What will Fosse raise? Here, let me show you this...' He held up a letter, waving it high above his head. 'These are my orders. They state quite clearly, that where batteries are to be erected, an allowance of *one shilling a week* will be given to every man who enrols into such a corps. I have it in writing. One shilling a week.'

A huge cheer drowned his last words: those jeering moments before looked plainly astonished. They began pushing forward, elbowing themselves to the front of the queue. Major Trelawney was finding it hard to be heard. He had both hands in the air, 'Hear me out. Your enthusiasm does you credit ... but hear me out. We must be vigilant, keep watch at all times. Our coast is threatened and we want strong, able-bodied men to man the batteries. The guns are heavy. It's demanding work. You'll train for three hours a week. You'll be drilled, marched. Discipline will be tight.'

Again, the men started cheering, pushing forward towards Major Trelawney who tried to shout louder. 'But first we need funds ... we need your subscription ... we need...' He seemed to sense the time for talking was over and nodded to the piper. A shrill fife soared through the air. The drum followed and the soldiers started marching on the spot. With whoops of delight the crowd started marching in time to the drum, two small boys jumping quickly into the cart next to Major Trelawney. They looked so proud, their chins held high, their dirty faces aglow with excitement.

Our carriage pulled forward. It would not do to get stuck behind this marching rabble. As it was, we were already late for Madame Merrick.

It was hard to know which jumble of buildings was which. The different businesses merged together in the vast warehouse, overlapping one another, towering above us. We stood in the courtyard looking through an arch, *Pengelly Boat Yard* written above us in bold paint. Hammering filled the air. I could hear men shouting, the rattle of heavy chains, the creak of the pulley as newly planked wood was hoisted in the air. Smoke from the forge filled my nostrils. It was noisy, smelly and I stood breathing in the acrid air, envying their sense of purpose.

The boat yard's office was on the ground floor and could only be reached through the arch. They had no windows looking out to this side. On the first floor, Madame Merrick had vast windows stretching the whole length of the building and I could see her looking down, watching us through her lorgnettes. The door opened and a thin girl stood nervously on the top step.

'Take care, Charity, keep hold of the rail. It's the first floor and the steps are quite steep.' Mrs Jennings took Charity's arm and started walking towards the steps. I would have followed but a beggar caught my eye. He was lying on a filthy coat under the overhang of the building opposite – an old man, rough and unkempt, his left leg amputated below the knee, the left arm of his jacket hanging empty by his side. He was looking down, mumbling, no doubt asking for alms. I was holding a purse of money to buy Georgina some ribbons and felt suddenly compelled to give him something – a farthing, at least.

Mr Randall joined me as I crossed the yard. 'Miss Cavendish, I advise ye not to.'

I opened my purse, retrieving two farthings. 'A farthing or two, Mr Randall, surely you don't begrudge him so little?'

The man's head was bowed, his hand lying across his heart. He looked up and sudden shock stopped me in my tracts. I stared back at him, holding the coins tightly in my hand, reluctant to let them drop. He was a beggar, yes, filthy, definitely. He was crippled and unkempt, but he was not desperate. There was no vacant stare, no hollow lack of hope. I threw the coins down and walked away. As I climbed the steps, my heart was hammering.

Madame Merrick was deep in curtsy. 'Miss Cavendish, this is such an *honour*. Elowyn, take

Miss Cavendish's cloak.' She looked unusually distraught, glancing down to the courtyard below. 'I am *so* sorry, Miss Cavendish, that beggar will be the *ruin* of my business. I have asked him *repeatedly* to leave and I cannot apologise enough. My establishment is for genteel ladies and his presence is *very* distressing.' She had clearly prepared for our visit. She was wearing a very fine blue gown with lace foaming round her neck and cuffs. Her hair was immaculately curled, a cluster of feathers dancing above a silver hair pin. On the table a glass punch-bowl stood in pride of place, five delicately etched glasses hanging from the rim.

'The beggar's no consequence,' I said, smiling at the warmth of her greeting. I nodded at the girl taking my cloak, 'We've slipped from Mama's clutches and that's all that matters.' Charity and Mrs Jennings looked shocked, but I did not care. I loved this place, part shop, part warehouse, with its polished tables, tall looking-glasses and cabinets filled with every type of ribbon. I loved the neat rows of lace, the spools of thread, the chatter, the excitement, the feeling of freedom it gave me.

'Good day, Miss Cavendish, Miss Charity, Mrs Jennings.' Mrs Pengelly curtsied.

'Ah, Mrs Pengelly, how lovely to see you – I hope that punch is for us.' Mrs Pengelly smiled and began to spoon the amber liquid into the glasses. The punch smelt strong, full of freshly squeezed lemons and plenty of cognac. 'We thought you might not be here,' I said as I took the glass from her.

'I'm glad to tell you 'tis very good news. My daughter and Sir James show signs of recovery and we've every reason to believe they're on the mend.' She smiled shyly. 'But you're quite right – I have stopped working here. I've only come to help Madame Merrick with Miss Charity's gown.'

We took a sip of our drinks, Charity clearly shocked by the strength of the cognac. It was delicious. Madame Merrick was no fool – the more her customers drank, the more they would spend.

'Perhaps we should make a start?' Madame Merrick turned to the young woman who had taken my cloak. 'Elowyn, bring through the satin, then the Chine and the Pompadour – only be *careful,* they are very *delicate* … so carry only one at a time. Then go back for the taffeta and the tulle.' Madame Merrick's voice softened, 'This way, if you please, Miss Charity – to the window where the light is better. *Tell me,* do you see colours?'

I stiffened, watching the blush spread across Charity's cheeks. No-one had ever spoken so intimately to her before but she smiled and lifted her chin. 'Yes, I can see colours – if they're very distinct. With my glasses, it's a bit better – I see blurred outlines, but I'll have to take your advice, Madame Merrick, as I've no idea what colour I should wear.'

'You have brought your glasses?'

'I never wear them out. They're very ugly and Mama says they make me look a dim-wit. She says my eyes will weaken if I wear them too much.' Charity did not see Madame Merrick's eyebrows shoot upwards or the flash of fury cross her eyes, but she heard her sharp intake of breath. 'Oh, I don't mind...' she added hastily. 'Really I don't.'

Elowyn came hurrying from the back room, her arms laden with the last of the silks. There were so many – dusky pinks, apricot, cream, soft blue and green, all as beautiful as each other. She straightened each roll, leaving the exact same gap between each of them and stood back, smiling. My eyes were immediately drawn to the end roll of silk, a beautiful soft peach with a shine of its own. Mother's gown of Persian silk was very similar. 'That top one ... let's look at that first.'

Madame Merrick smiled. 'Ah, the shot silk taffeta. Indeed, Miss Cavendish, I *thought* you would like that one. It's from *Persia,* but no doubt you knew that. It's quite my *finest* and just the one I had in mind ... but the apricot satin beneath is also of the finest quality and the dusky rose comes from Italy...'

Charity's blush deepened. 'Perhaps it's too fine for me?' she said.

'Oh, Itty! Nothing's too fine for you. It's perfect. It's the softest, creamiest peach, quite the most beautiful colour you've ever worn. It'll make you look so pretty.' Charity looked eager, vulnerable, searching our faces, desperate to hear our approval.

Mrs Pengelly began unrolling the delicate material. 'Miss Cavendish's right. It's definitely your colour.'

Mrs Jennings came, smiling, to her side. 'Feel the quality, Charity. It's as light as air and almost iridescent when it catches the light.'

'Shall I choose it?'

181

Outside, Mr Randall was pacing up and down, banging his cane impatiently against his thigh. He could see me staring down at him. 'I think so,' I replied. 'But just because we *think* we've chosen the right fabric doesn't mean there might not be a better one. We mustn't rush. We must look at every roll just to make sure we've seen everything. Then we'll look through all the ribbons and lace.' I turned away, holding up my glass. 'And we've hardly begun the punch, have we?'

Madame Merrick smiled. There was something in her look – not fierce, not disapproving, but watchful, almost conspiratorial, as if we shared a secret. I smiled, holding my glass carefully as Mrs Pengelly refilled it. I loved this place, I really did. My heart was singing, my mind full of mischief.

'And when we've been through all the fabrics, we'll go through all the patterns. We'll need to go through them at least twice – maybe even three times.'

Chapter Twenty

Despite Elowyn's attempts to keep the rolls in order, the table piled higher and higher, the fabrics cascading to the ground like a pastel waterfall. Madame Merrick held each in turn, praising its quality, explaining the intricate interweaving of warp and weft. I loved seeing them fuss round Charity. 'Of course we can finish it in three days. You will have this gown by Friday, even if we have to sew all day and all night. Am I right, Mrs Pengelly? A *naval* lieutenant, did you say? How wonderful, we must make sure you look your *very* best.'

I stood by the window, watching the crowd dispersing from the town square. I could see the river mouth and the sea beyond. A patch of sun glistened on the sea, lifting it from grey to blue. Several large ships lay docked against the town quay, one flying naval flags, but I was not looking for HMS *Circe*, I was searching for the fastest cutter in the Channel – home to the man who filled my every thought.

Madame Merrick saw me staring out of the window. She stood behind me, looking across the sea as if searching for the same boat. 'Miss Cavendish, do you remember the last time you came you asked if there was a *circulating library* in the town?'

'And is there?' I replied.

'Not *as such,* but it left me thinking. I thought it might be a good idea to start my *own* library – just a small selection of novels for those attending my establishment. And, as it *happens,* I have managed to obtain some *very suitable* books.' She held her tape measure in one hand, her measuring pole in the other. 'Elowyn and I will be *quite a while* with these measurements. If you like, why don't you go through to the back? The books are on the shelf in the corner.'

It was not so much her tone that caught my interest but her sense of conspiracy. As if she was telling me, not asking me. I felt increasingly curious, knowing she had waited until I would be

183

unaccompanied. 'Thank you, perhaps I will.'

The store room was crammed with a criss-cross of wooden shelves, every bit as confusing as a maze. Each shelf was piled high, stacked with rolls of fabric, the tall, dark shelves crushing together, jutting out in all directions. Ahead of me lay the shelf of books and just one glance at them made me smile – they were the highly *unsuitable* books Mama had banned from our library. A basket lay next to the books and I saw my mended shawl. No sign of the cloak. That must have been what Madame Merrick was trying to tell me.

The rooms were divided by a wooden partition, polished smooth on the shop side but rough on the store side. A tiny hole caught my attention, small enough not to be seen but big enough to look through and I put my eye to it, watching everyone on the other side. Charity looked so happy.

The floorboard creaked behind me and I jumped in fright. A hand slid quickly over my mouth, another round my waist, Arnaud's cheek brushing gently against my hair. 'Come,' he whispered, drawing me deeper into the dark maze of shelves. There was hardly any light. It was cramped, confined, the lack of space pressing us together.

'You've been watching us,' I whispered.

'Only you,' he replied, 'and it's been torture, watching you, not being able to hold you.' His arms slid round my waist, drawing me closer and I looked down, thrilled by his terrible boldness. My wish had been to see him again but never in my wildest dreams did I think it would be like this.

184

'Madame Merrick must think me so bold.'

'She was young once – or so she tells me!' He leant nearer, his arms tightening around me. 'Your hat came to no harm, I hope.' He was so close, our lips almost touching. 'When I saw your smile ... that look in your eye, I knew you'd done it on purpose.'

'No harm. And it was only luck you were there,' I whispered.

He laughed softly. 'Well, you're not to worry. I'll chase any number of hats for you.' I could feel his breath against my lips. 'You know that, don't you?'

I felt so alive, every part of me tingling. 'Arnaud, I think you should know I'm not going to marry Viscount Vallenforth.'

His lips brushed my forehead. 'Well, I'd rather guessed that might be the case.'

'And you don't have to pretend any more. I know who you are and what you were doing.' I felt him stiffen, pull slightly away. 'No, it's alright, I haven't told a soul. I know you and Madame Merrick are émigrés. I think what you're doing is wonderful. Rescuing men from the guillotine. It's very brave and...' I could no longer speak, he was kissing the side of my mouth.

'And very foolhardy,' he murmured, his lips travelling softly down my throat, kissing my neck, behind my ear.

I was alone with a man I was deeply in love with. It was wrong, so wrong. He had chosen our position well – a blind end, blocked from sight, no light penetrating through the rolls of fabric. No room to step away. His arms tightened round me, his lips closing over mine. I could feel the power of his body, the strength of his arms. So this was what it felt like to be kissed. I began yielding, unable to resist, giving way to the pressure of his lips. I could not stop myself, nor did I want to. His kiss deepened and I returned his passion, so powerfully, so completely, overruling all sense of decorum.

We drew apart. In the darkness, his eyes held mine. 'I've something for you,' he whispered, reaching inside his jacket. 'Open it later.' He handed me a small parcel wrapped in gauze and I slipped it carefully down my front. 'That's where it belongs,' he whispered, 'right there.' His fingers touched it through the silk of my bodice.

The touch of his fingers, that soft brush against my breast; I was galloping, going dangerously fast. I should control my recklessness, rein it quickly in. 'Arnaud, I must warn you. Sir Richard Goldsworthy's watching all foreigners. From now on, émigrés need to register and sign a declaration of arrival at their port of entry. That beggar outside isn't a beggar – he's a spy and he's been sent to watch you.'

Arnaud's arms stiffened. 'How d'you know?'

'There's no desperation in his eyes, no lack of hope. And his arm's only tucked beneath his shirt.'

'Is that so?' he replied, drawing me to him. I shut my eyes, feeling his lips brush against my forehead, my eyes, my ears. He lifted my chin, bringing me closer, and I realised then that he had been holding himself in check. He kissed me hungrily, deeply, his passion igniting in me such desire, such unrestrained longing, I could not hold back. Suddenly his arms stiffened and he pulled away.

Footsteps sounded behind us, the scrape of fabric being placed on a shelf. Through a small gap we saw Elowyn walking back to the door. 'Come, Cécile,' he whispered, lifting my hands to his lips, 'our precious time is over.' He kept hold of my hand, leading me back through the maze of shelves and I followed him, my body still tingling from his touch. As I reached the shelves, my heart raced – Mrs Jennings was coming through the door. Somehow, I managed to grab a book.

'Have you found one? There seem to be quite a few – perhaps I'll get one for myself.' She looked suddenly appalled, 'No, Celia! Not that one.' In my haste, I had grabbed the first book I could reach. I glanced at it now, *Les Liaisons Dangereuses*. Mrs Jennings was shaking her head, 'No wonder you look so flustered. I hope you've not been reading it – it's highly unsuitable.'

She put it back on the shelf as if it might burn her. My body was still on fire from Arnaud's touch. Poor Mrs Jennings, she need never know I had read it long before Mama had it removed from the library.

Mr Randall looked at his fobwatch and scowled, climbing angrily next to the coachman. The footmen helped us in and stood stiffly on the back rail while Madame Merrick glared furiously at the beggar. Mrs Pengelly and Elowyn were smiling happily, waving as we left. Charity looked radiant. 'I'm so excited. It felt so delicate and the lace's so light.'

'The material's lovely, but it's you, Itty, who makes it look beautiful. Lieutenant Carew will be a complete idiot if he's not to be completely captivated.'

The coach pulled forward and I leant against the window, curious to have a closer look at the warehouse. Arnaud had vanished so completely – appearing and disappearing in the blink of an eye. He obviously had not used the front steps but there was no door round the other side, just overlapping wooden planks and a series of steps leading to the third floor. A pulley jutted out from an open arch and a covered chute ended about four foot off the ground. But no obvious way in. There must be a back entrance some-where. Perhaps the secret doors in Pendenning had gone to my head but, either way, it was a good thing the spy only watched the front.

We pulled away from the town, Charity and Mrs Jennings chatting happily. My life had changed. I loved Arnaud Lefèvre so completely. I loved everything about him – his mischief, his energy, his total disregard for propriety. I loved the way he held me, the way he kissed me. I loved his sense of danger, the thrill of the forbidden. Already I ached to see him again.

'Do you think Madame Merrick's right about my glasses? You've got the name of that man she recommended?'

'I have it safe. Her lorgnettes are very lovely. He's in Truro, so that's very near. A pretty pair of glasses would make all the difference.'

'And wearing my hair that way?'

'Absolutely,' Mrs Jennings looked as excited as Charity, 'It's definitely worth a try.'

'And colouring my lips to draw attention from

my eyes?'

'No. Definitely not. That would look wrong.'

As we drove through the gate-house, Charity touched my hand. 'Cici, you weren't listening, were you? Did you hear what Mrs Jennings just said?'

'No, sorry, I was miles away.'

'Mrs Pengelly has a boy in her charge. He's been badly beaten and has no family but she's going to take him in. He's going to stay with her. Isn't that wonderful? Mrs Pengelly's making him a new set of clothes and she's set to spoil him.'

I stared at the sheep grazing the lakeside. I had never believed in destiny before – people like us did not leave things to chance. We forged our own futures, slicing away the weak, aligning ourselves with the powerful. Chance meetings never happened – everything prearranged. I could not stop smiling. My misgivings about the poor boy could end. He would be fed and loved, good would come from evil.

I was meant to run away. That boy needed a home and my fate was to meet Arnaud Lefèvre. I realised that now.

Shutting my bedroom door, I tiptoed back to my bed and took Arnaud's gift from my bodice. The gauze was tied with a beautiful blue ribbon, inside a slip of paper and a small silk purse. My hands began shaking as I unfolded the paper.

We only part to meet again.
Change as ye list, ye winds: my heart shall be
The faithful compass that still points to thee.

I read and reread the words, holding them first to my lips, then to my heart. Picking up the purse, I carefully undid the pearl button, tipping the contents into my hand. It was a silver locket on a silver chain and I held it to the candle, smiling. The front was engraved with a cutter in full sail – *L'Aigrette,* no doubt about it. It was so beautiful, the etching so delicate, the silver glinting in the candle light. I pressed the clasp to release the spring and caught my breath.

It was not a locket at all, but a beautiful compass, set in diamonds and sapphires that sparkled like the sea. I wiped my eyes, staring through my tears at the four words engraved inside. *To China and back.*

Chapter Twenty-one

Pendenning Hall
Friday 15th November 1793, 5:00 p.m.

Madame Merrick was as good as her word, bringing the newly finished dress by twelve, finishing the minor adjustments by one. Charity looked radiant, her delicate beauty enhanced by the simplicity of the dress, the soft peach giving warmth to her skin. She seemed to glow, her new curls framing her face, her diamond hair pins sparkling on either side of her brow.

'You look gorgeous, Itty, just be yourself and

everything will be fine.' The footman opened the door to the drawing-room. 'He'll be here any minute. Sir Richard's on the terrace with Father and Major Trelawney's talking to Mama.'

At our entrance, Mama's eyes widened in surprise. Even Major Trelawney stopped mid-sentence and bowed in greeting. I could see his delight in Charity's transformation. He smiled broadly, stepping quickly forward to offer us each an arm. Outside, horse's hooves came to a halt and we heard a man dismount and give his reins to the groom.

Charity looked petrified, the colour at once draining from her face. Major Trelawney smiled, guiding us gently to the fireplace, his voice dropping to barely a whisper. 'If he's not good enough, we'll see him off, won't we, Miss Cavendish?'

'We certainly will,' I whispered back.

The footman bowed. 'Lieutenant Frederick Carew.'

He was tall, fair-haired, his broad frame filling the room with sudden vigour. He was in full uniform – blue jacket, white waistcoat and breeches, highly polished boots, his hat held beneath his arm. I searched his face, my heart soaring. He had kind eyes, a gentle smile, perhaps a touch of shyness. No hint of vanity, no sense of cruelty. Bowing deeply to Mama, he turned to the three of us.

'This is Major Henry Trelawney and Celia, my eldest daughter, soon to be married to Viscount Vallenforth.' I curtseyed. 'And this is my second daughter, Charity.' I held my breath, watching as he bowed to Charity. She smiled, looking so beautiful, her eyes serenely gazing from him to Major Trelawney. 'How lovely you're both wearing uniform. I can see the colours.'

Frederick Carew's eyes softened. 'Mother tells me you lost your sight in childhood. I can't image how awful that must have been.' There was something in Frederick Carew's tone which seemed to cut through all pretence, something so honest, so friendly, like a weight lifting from the room.

'Not so awful,' Charity replied, smiling up at him. 'I could have died. I can walk and ride and my hearing's more acute. I can sing and my sense of smell is very good. I've got used to having no sight.' Charity had never spoken so openly. Mama always forbade us to speak of her blindness.

'Charity has a rose garden at Richmond,' I added quickly. 'She's a large selection and recognises them all by their scent.'

Frederick Carew's eyes had not left Charity's face. 'My sister loves to paint roses. She, also, has a rose garden. Perhaps you grow some of the same variety?'

'I have one very special rose – a Bengal rose, all the way from China. They're very rare.'

His reply was interrupted by Father and Sir Richard coming in from the terrace. He bowed to them in turn. Major Trelawney smiled broadly but, even so, did not relinquish Charity's arm. I put my hand on Lieutenant Carew's arm, following Mama and Sir Richard into the dining room.

The table was lavishly decorated, overflowing with flowers and fruit. The glass was gleaming, the silverware shining. Taking our seats, the line of footmen began filling the table with roast venison, ribs of beef, fricassee of chicken, carps in court-bullion. The tureen dishes held white soup, celery and spinach in oyster sauce. There was enough for an army. Mama smiled. 'I hope you're hungry, Lieutenant Carew. Sir Richard, I trust there's something to your taste.' She handed Saffron to the footman. 'Eat please, gentlemen. We're just family.' She smiled at Lieutenant Carew. 'How's Lady Clarissa? Is she well?'

'Very well, thank you. My eldest brother has two sons – they keep her and my sister busy. Amelia enjoys their company.'

Father put down his empty glass, leaning forward to fork some venison. 'Been in the navy long? Five years? Six?'

'Five years, Sir Charles. I entered straight from Oxford.'

'What was your degree?' Chewing hard, he indicated for his glass to be refilled.

'Botany.'

'A naval botanist! That's a waste of time.' He took another mouthful.

'I'm not a naval botanist, Sir Charles, but I always enjoy the voyages when we take one.'

'Have you ambition, young man? Want to rise to the top ranks?'

'Certainly, sir, I intend to serve my country to my utmost. It's an honour to work alongside such brave men.' He looked at his plate, wondering whether to take his first mouthful.

'I've got contacts. You've heard of my brother, I take it?'

'Indeed, sir. Most people have.'

Father sniffed. 'Who's your captain?' He leant

forward, stabbing a rib of beef, dripping gravy across the table.

'Captain Edward Penrose, sir.'

'Never heard of him.'

Lieutenant Carew took a deep breath. I was beginning to admire him – most men would be faltering under father's grilling. 'Captain Penrose has suggested I invite you to dine with him on board HMS *Circe*. He'd consider it an honour.' He smiled at Major Trelawney, 'I believe you already know Captain Penrose but, Lady Cavendish, can I persuade you and both the Miss Cavendishes to venture on board?' His eyes went straight to Charity. Mama was watching.

'Please eat, Lieutenant Carew – you've not touched a mouthful.' She turned to Sir Richard. 'Is your work proceeding?' Mama was much more guarded tonight, less flirtatious, though the sight of Sir Richard slowly eating his plate of carp obviously pleased her.

'There's much to be done. Not just the French, but the Irish. There are pockets of them hiding in this area. We need better surveillance.'

'Bloody United Irishmen,' growled Father, 'Papist, the whole damn lot of them. Dammed Jacobins – inciting riot and open rebellion. They didn't get my vote and never will.' Father slammed his hands on the table, his clenched fists gripping his knife and fork. 'The Irish *must* be crushed before they join forces with the French. We need harsher control.'

Sir Richard sat back against his chair, swirling the claret in his glass. He took a sip. 'Harsher control is why I'm here. Immigration may be my avowed purpose, but my government duty is to smother even the merest whiff of revolution. My powers are absolute. Until Habeas Corpus is officially revoked, I've the power to hold any violator without bail.'

'Then you must use your powers.' Father's face was flushed, his eyes blazing, his fist once more striking the table.

'I intend to.' By contrast, Sir Richard remained pale, icy-calm. Slowly sipping his wine, his coldness seemed somehow worse than Father's outrage, certainly more frightening. He seemed to enjoy inflicting fear.

'You have your own court and jury?' asked Major Trelawney.

'Revolutionary intentions are too heinous a crime to require the ordinary process of justice through the courts.'

'So your power is absolute? You can imprison on suspicion?'

'I have informers and act on their testimony. I can imprison on suspicion and have discretionary powers to apprehend people, examine them, and commit them to prison without further trial. I do not need a jury.'

Lieutenant Carew looked up, a frown creasing his forehead. 'But they go to the assizes? They have proper representation?'

'No, Lieutenant Carew, they do not go to the assizes. My powers are absolute. If the case against a perpetrator is treason and witnesses can testify that the state's security is under threat, then the perpetrators can expect the harshest of sentences. They will hang.'

'That's exactly what's needed. Mr Pitt's got it right – harsher penalties and make them swing.' Father's clenched fist reached forward, stabbing another rib of beef.

I suppose it was inevitable the conversation would be dominated by politics. I tried not to let Frederick Carew see me watching him. He was certainly glancing at Charity, but what did he make of Father's uncouth manners, Mama's cold politeness? There was too much food, the large centrepiece blocking any direct vision. My heart sank. Mama nodded to the footman and took Saffron back on her lap, feeding him pieces of chicken from her plate.

Sir Richard stared at Frederick Carew in cold dislike. 'Your father's an assize judge?'

Lieutenant Carew did not seem surprised by the question, 'And his father before him.'

'He keeps up to date with government policy?'

Major Trelawney coughed politely. 'Lord Carew has an exceptional reputation, Sir Richard. His judgements are considered very sound.'

'Sound?' Sir Richard raised his eyes.

A slight flush gave a hint of Lieutenant Carew's displeasure. A pulse beat in his neck, but his voice remained calm. 'My father's reputation for leniency is for those who are starving, not those who seek to undermine the security of our nation. You know my father, Major Trelawney?'

'I've met him on a number of occasions. My brother's estate adjoins yours.'

'I've not had the honour of meeting your brother but I know of his reputation. He breeds very fine cattle – I believe my father's bought several bulls from him...'

The conversation had at last turned pleasant. Major Trelawney and Lieutenant Carew could talk to each other while at the same time glance at Charity. She was following their conversation, turning first to one and then to the other, smiling when Major Trelawney complimented her on her knowledge of farming.

'How are the repairs to the fortifications, Major Trelawney?' Father interrupted.

'The place is in a state of ruin, Sir Charles – funds are missing and our job's the harder for the lack of those funds.' His accusation hung in the air.

Father pushed his unfinished meal to one side and reached for his glass. 'The Corporation work tirelessly for the benefit of this town!'

Major Trelawney's eyes grew stern. 'So everyone tells me.'

'And your Company of Volunteers?' asked Sir Richard.

'Our list of subscriptions lengthens each day and we've no shortage of men enthusiastic for the muster.'

Mama bristled. 'That's hardly surprising! Tell your parents to be careful, Lieutenant Carew – Major Trelawney's arming the labourers.'

Frederick Carew smiled. 'My father's Lord Lieutenant of Cornwall and my brother's to be the Lieutenant of Division. The volunteer companies will be under their direct supervision. You're responsible for the returns, Major Trelawney? What have you found?'

The savoury dishes were removed. Lemon syllabub, trifle, apple turnover and a rather pale blancmange now vied for our attention. 'There's sorbet as well ... perhaps you should try a little of everything.' Mama handed Saffron back to the footman. 'What will you have, Sir Richard? Lieutenant Carew, some syllabub?'

The more I saw of Frederick Carew, the more I liked him. His manners were impeccable. He would not be rude, but neither would he be bullied or intimidated. He had counteracted Sir Richard's criticism of his father and had not buckled under Father's questioning. He was not as gentle as his boyish looks would have us believe. He had strength, inner resolve. Best of all, he could hardly take his eyes off Charity.

The head footman brought in the sorbet. Father looked up. 'Ah, blackberry sorbet, I've been looking forward to this.'

I felt ill, my stomach contracting in distaste. The footman reached forward with the spoon and I held out my hand to stop him. Charity and Major Trelawney did likewise. Father and Sir Richard nodded for more and I could see Frederick Carew sense something was wrong.

The footman refilled Father's dish. 'Splendid – yes more, you don't know what you're missing. This is good, my dear, very good.'

Major Trelawney put down his spoon and turned to Frederick Carew. 'You ask me what I've found? I've found a level of poverty far greater than expected. Every house is in need of repair. Buildings are crumbling, rents have been raised. Non-payers are whipped and there have been forced evictions. There's no provision for common grazing, no land for labourers. No barley is grown to make bread. There are no alms-houses. The sick are left begging, the homeless to wander. Children collect whelks and eat limpets.' He turned to Father. 'The Corporation's failing in its duty and only Sir James Polcarrow's trying to put things right. He's instigated the repair of all his cottages and is building others. He has plans for a school, for alms-houses. It would be an un-imagined loss if those mushrooms were to kill him.'

Father's face matched the purple sorbet. 'James Polcarrow may masquerade as a liberal reformer but it's him that needs watching – him and that new wife of his. Her father is a known trouble-maker, a seditious snake. I shouldn't speak ill of the dying but they're Jacobins, the lot of them.' He finally pushed his plate away, draining his glass.

Sir Richard tapped a small leather case on the table, his eyes hardening. 'We're infiltrating Pascoe Pengelly's meetings and he'll soon be arrested, but as for Sir James – you must have evidence to make such a claim. I'm here to root out sedition and revolution but the lily-livered abolitionists and reformers I must leave to Mr Pitt.' He opened the case, taking hold of his gold toothpick.

One glance at the toothpick and Mama stood up. 'Gentlemen, it's time for us to leave you to your port. When your talk of politics is over, please join us in the music room. Celia and Charity have prepared a concert for your entertainment.'

Chapter Twenty-two

Mama swept furiously into the music room, flapping her fan indignantly. 'That man must go. I've had enough of his bumpkin manners. How dare he?'

'Lieutenant Carew, Mama?'

'No, of course not, Celia, Major Trelawney. Criticising your father like that. The man's an upstart. Pretending to know Lord Carew – I'm sorry Lieutenant Carew had to be exposed to his company.' She flapped her fan. 'Celia, open the terrace door, prepare the pianoforte. Charity, are you ready?' She paced the room, Saffron looking quite petrified.

I had barely time to arrange the music. A maid brought in a tray of tea, another with two decanters and four crystal glasses. 'Sir Charles says the gentlemen's to have their port in here.'

Mama flapped her fan more vigorously. 'Oh, for goodness sake! Get me a brandy.'

I took Charity to the piano. 'He's very handsome. He has kind eyes and blond hair – a bit like yours. He's very distinguished, very tall, holds himself well. He's got a lovely smile and he's kind. I know he is.'

Charity squeezed my arm. 'Does he like me?'

Lieutenant Carew entered the room, his eyes immediately seeking Charity. Yes, he liked her. I only wished she could see his gaze. I could say nothing but watched Mama put down her empty glass and turn with her most radiant smile. 'Frederick ... may I call you Frederick?' He smiled, nodding his consent. 'Does your sister, Amelia, play the pianoforte?'

'Yes, we love music. It's an important part of our family life. Mother holds concerts on the pavilion overlooking the river – people row into the creek and listen from their boats.'

'How very charming. Trenwyn House overlooks the river, does it?'

'It's on the bank of the River Truro – just round the bend from Falmouth. As children we spent most of our time splashing about in boats, rowing over to Falmouth to see the Navy ships. Sometimes we were allowed on board.'

I could hardly stop smiling; a musical family, just wait till he heard Charity sing. Major Trelawney and Sir Richard took their seats. Mama positioned Frederick next to her. The music was in place, Mrs Jennings no doubt listening on the terrace outside. I took a deep breath. Charity knew exactly when to turn the pages. A programme lay on each of the chairs so there would be no need to interrupt. I hated interruptions. When I played, I became absorbed by the music and needed complete concentration.

My fingers began racing over the keyboard, the notes rising and falling, evoking emotion in me I could never voice. With certain pieces, I found myself aching. Sometimes I would want to cry. Tonight I was playing for Charity and thought my heart would burst. He was watching her, realising how clever she was. She was following the music in her head. I did not even need to nod. She knew exactly when to grip the corner and turn the page. The Haydn Sonata finished, I went on to Mozart. I did not need the music – I had the piece by heart. How else could I do it justice? I just had to remember to breathe. My heart was racing, my mind absorbed by the beauty of the composition.

I smiled at their applause and Charity took up position, holding her hands in front of her, the hem of her dress shaking against the swirling pattern of the carpet. I played the opening bars and her voice rose with such sweetness, filling the room with a purity that made me ache. The yearning in her voice was so intense it almost hurt to listen. Frederick Carew looked captivated. She smiled shyly at their prolonged applause, blushing as she curtseyed, finally giving way to their collective plea to sing another song.

At the end of our concert Mama could barely conceal her triumph but Charity's singing had torn at my heart and I found it hard to hold back my tears. I wanted Arnaud Lefèvre to be there, gazing at me as tenderly as Frederick Carew now gazed at Charity.

'How about some fresh air?' Frederick Carew was smiling at me. 'It's a beautiful night – shall we take a turn round the terrace? He held out both arms, leading us away from Mama's watchful eye. A light mist drifted across the lawn, gathering at the foot of the steps. Above us, stars stretched as far as the eye could see. I thought I would cry. 'I wish my sister could have heard your concert. I know she'd love to meet you.'

Charity smiled. 'And we'd love to meet her.'

Frederick Carew looked thrilled. 'Would it be too much to ask ... could Mother invite you both to stay? My sister's desperate for company – five brothers and two nephews leave her longing for feminine society.'

Charity smiled. She looked so beautiful. 'I'm sure Father will consent.' She sounded so happy. 'Are there stars out tonight? Is it still a crescent moon?'

'It's waxing now. The sky's full of stars, there are no clouds at all,' replied Frederick.

A lump formed in the back of my throat. 'Lieutenant Carew, have you ever seen a red shooting star?'

He laughed softly. 'I think they're very rare.'

'Do sailors have a saying about them? Do they bring luck?'

'Now there you have me, Miss Cavendish.'

I fought back my tears. 'Do you believe they're Cupid's arrows, sent from Venus?'

He looked puzzled at the tears in my eyes. 'I'd like to think so.' His gaze turned to Charity. 'I think Venus has a way of striking when we least expect it. It's not up to us to question her powers.' He smiled and my heart soared. If she loved him, I could part with her to such a man.

I felt torn with anxiety. His talk of his sister, his invitation to visit – things were moving so fast and Charity must not get hurt. Major Trelawney was at the door, at any moment he would walk towards us. I had to tell Frederick the truth.

'Lieutenant Carew,' I whispered, 'I'm not going to marry Viscount Vallenforth. I despise the man.'

Frederick Carew's smile turned mischievous. 'Really, Miss Cavendish? Well, that *is* good news.' His eyes returned to Charity. 'Extremely good news. Ah, Major Trelawney, are we being summoned back inside?'

When we returned to the drawing-room Mama was smiling. There was no doubt her matchmaking would bear fruit. Lieutenant Carew was eminently suitable and he was clearly smitten. She knew it would not be long before she heard from Lady Clarissa.

I lay waiting for Charity, desperate to go over every detail. The night had been her triumph and there was so much to say. Frederick Carew could not take his eyes off her. I would describe the white lapels on his blue jacket, the brass buttons on his waistcoat, how he parted his hair, the scar he had on his hand. I would tell her everything so she could see him through my eyes. The candle guttered and went out. It was later than I thought.

Slipping from the bed, I crossed to the washroom, trying the door to Charity's room. She never locked her door. 'Itty, it's me,' I said, pushing the handle harder. There was no answer.

I went slowly back to bed, staring into the darkness. Surely I had not heard sobbing?

Chapter Twenty-three

Pendenning Hall
Sunday 17th November 1793, 4:00 p.m.

Of course he would not always be at church. He was a sailor; he went with the tide and returned with the wind. What else could I expect? I felt listless, agitated, unable to eat, wanting him in a way I found hard to understand.

I stared out of the window. Charity and Mrs Jennings were talking to Mrs McCreal, staring into the pram, admiring little Charles. Sarah was holding up both her arms and I watched Charity bend to pick her up. I felt so empty. Did she not like Frederick Carew? I had tried to tell her how much I esteemed him, how I thought he would be a wonderful husband, but she seemed so sad, smiling and kissing my cheek but not seeking my company.

I always sought sanctuary in the library but today the stuffy curtains and rows of books seemed dusty and oppressive, the wing-neck chair hard and uncomfortable. I rose quickly from the chair – of course! Mr Pelligrew had an eclectic taste, how silly of me not to think of it; there must be plenty of poetry books. I knew Arnaud's verse by heart, but where did it come from? Book-shelves flanked both sides of the huge marble fireplace. There seemed no logic or order to the books, most of them dreary tomes, sermons, a few naval lists and plenty of maps. A good number were in Latin and I was surprised to see so many in French, but no poetry books.

The marble fireplace was quite magnificent. Two goddesses held the mantle with the touch of their fingers and my thoughts raced. What did it feel like to stand naked, only the flimsiest of veils caressing your skin? Did women do that behind closed doors? I could feel myself blush and turned away. Suddenly I noticed a line running down the marble fireplace – it was a narrow door, almost undiscernible, but once noticed, very obvious. My curiosity sharpened; yet another of the servants' entrances, how very clever. There must be a way to open it, a hidden catch somewhere in front of me.

I began pressing the surrounding marble, sweeping my hands along the top, down the sides, determined to find the catch. Taking out my hairpin, I ran it down the narrow crack. No, it was more sophisticated than that. I stood back, grateful the footman could not see me. He would be laughing at my attempt. Perhaps it only opened from the inside? I stood back again. No, there would be a way of opening it, I just had to think. If it was not a latch, it would be a handle, but not one I would recognise.

I looked again, my excitement growing. The bookcases reached to within a foot of the fireplace. Perhaps I should search for a book that looked different. I began running my hands across the spines, feeling the leather. A group of books caught my attention and I pulled, all four spines coming away as a single book. Just as I thought, behind them was a brass lever, well-polished and obviously well used. I pulled it and the tiny door clicked open.

I felt completely elated, opening and shutting the hidden door. I would love to have met Mr Pelligrew. Even better, the shelf in front of me held a row of poetry books, two of them with the creased spine of a favourite book. I reached for one, glancing round at the sound of laughter filtering through the open door. The nursery group had reached the fountain, Mrs Jennings chasing Sarah round and round. I looked again. Georgina was striding towards them looking very cross. Mrs Jennings shook her head at her arrival and pointed her towards me in the library.

She began hurrying back across the lawn, her scowl to be avoided at all cost. I pulled the secret lever and replaced the books. The tiny servants' door lay open. Poor Georgina, it seemed I had at last found the perfect hiding place.

Chapter Twenty-four

I was in the servants' corridor, behind the fire-place. It smelt of soot but there was plenty of space so I stood to my full height, my eyes adjusting to the semi-darkness. Piles of firewood lay stacked against the wall, baskets of faggots, two brushes and a wooden pail tucked against the side. Large bellows hung from a hook and a pair of leather gloves lay neatly folded on an iron scuttle. Pools of light lit the corridor leading to the left.

Above me a small grid was the main source of light, but further patches of light filtered through tiny eye-level holes drilled through the bookcase. I often hid from Georgina, diving behind curtains or hiding behind chairs, but this was disappearing at its very best. Picking up my skirts, I crept slowly towards the first hole and stared back into the library. Georgina was searching everywhere, scowling, stamping her foot, looking behind the curtains. She swiped her arm across the table, sending the books crashing to the floor and threw herself onto the chair, frowning back at the secretive smiles of the two Greek goddesses.

She was clearly in no hurry to leave. I looked further to my left. The row of peep-holes led like tiny beacons to another pool of light further along the corridor. I could hear angry voices and knew they must be coming from Father's study. I stood listening, catching almost nothing of the raised voices and decided to edge nearer. Somehow it seemed important to know who was so angry with Father.

The narrow corridor widened to an alcove with light shining through a circle of tiny holes. I leant forward, putting my eye against one of them. Again, I was behind a bookcase, Father's desk, just in front of me. I pressed closer against the panel. The wood felt smooth and I knew instantly I was not the first to stand there. I could smell polish, leather oil, the faint hint of tobacco – the scent of a man, leaning there, not once, but time and time again. Someone else was used to spying on Father.

Father had his back to me, his bandaged leg resting on a stool. Gout always brought out his temper but it was the man opposite who must have unleashed his anger. 'A misunderstanding – and that's the end of it!' Father shouted.

The man looked furious. He was dressed with more expense than taste, his blue jacket too bright, the lace at his cuffs unnecessarily fussy. His waistcoat was too tight, his gold watch too obvious. 'I must strongly protest, Sir Charles. Two weeks ago yer expressly told the Corporation we could buy that tenement and start clearin' the area.'

'And now I've changed my mind. You should've waited until you signed the deeds.'

The man was clearly horrified. 'But you gave us yer word. We've evicted everyone, removed half the rottin' timbers.' He wiped his handkerchief across his brow, his face livid. 'We've spent money ... and now yer tell me it's not for sale?'

Mr Randall glowered across the desk from his seat beside Father. 'Another bidder, a higher offer.'

'Then we'll match it. This's good land we're talkin' about – prime waterfront position.'

Father waved his hand in the air. 'Too late. The land's already sold.'

I watched the man rise angrily from his chair, his face purple with rage. Mr Randall saw him to the door, a self-congratulatory flicker crossing his eyes. He removed his jacket and placed it on the back of his chair. I had underestimated this man's influence. He wielded such power; for seven years he had taken charge of the estate and his word must be law.

The door closed and Father removed his wig, flinging it on the desk to scratch his bald head. Without his wig he seemed older, almost insignificant, except for the power in his voice. Philip Randall unrolled a series of carefully drawn plans, spreading them across the desk and the two of them studied them carefully.

'Who is Alexander Pendarvis?' Father winced, shifting his leg on the stool. 'Bloody foot – pass me some brandy.' He reached forward, retrieving his snuff box, taking a pinch before grabbing the proffered glass. 'The man must be a complete idiot, offering us all this!'

'A fool an' his money are easily parted,' replied Philip Randall. 'He's Sir Alexander Pendarvis, a retired admiral, to be precise. He wants to build a house where he can gaze out to sea – reckons the view will be like a ship. I've checked the naval list an' he's genuine. He's seen action, but he's wounded an' out to grass ... yet he yearns for the sea.'

'Wealthy?'

'More money than sense – he's got a charity named after him.'

'That's no use. He'll be an abolitionist, some bloody Quaker. I don't want a damned do-gooder – I want a vote I can count on.'

'He's promised you his vote. More to the point, he's promised this row of cottages.' He pointed to the desk. 'These are the plans, they're for the top road leadin' out of town ... an' he's plans drawn up for an alms-house. Here. Both the cottages and the alms-house will bear your name an' his donation will remain anonymous. He clearly wants that land.'

'Ten cottages and an alms-house for ten – I must appear generous.'

Philip Randall helped himself to a glass of brandy, raising the crystal glass in mock salute. He was a sallow man, dense eyebrows, thin lips. His shirt was silk, his embroidered waistcoat fastened with mother-of-pearl buttons but his hands were rough, stained with tobacco. His body looked taut, his movements firm, like when he lashed his whip at people too weak to run away.

'I was expectin' that. It's already done. Here, written clearly … ten cottages … an' the provision for ten in the alms-house. The timing's perfect. Those last evictions caused trouble and that major isn't helpin'. The Corporation won't like it but they know we'll rack up their rents if they complain.'

Father hardly glanced at the drawings. 'What's happening with the Polcarrow attorney?'

'He's goin' ahead. He's filed to attest the leases at the next assizes – Polcarrow against St Austell Trading. He's declared the leases illegal. Claims the land was never negotiable, his point of law; Robert Roskelly failed in his fiduciary duty. In other words, he didn't act in the best interests of his nephew.'

'I know very well what it means. Buy his silence – everyone has a price.'

'Not this one. Matthew Reith's a life-long friend of James Polcarrow. His father's Sir George Reith, the attorney who got Sir James pardoned.'

'Then disgrace him. Stir something up. Get

him ridiculed.'

The confined space, the darkness, the stale air seemed to press against me, making me breathless. I rested my head against my hands, breathing deeply, a horrible sense of betrayal turning my stomach. Rose Polcarrow was right. Father was corrupt, a bully, reneging on agreements, prepared to conjure up false accusations and slander.

Phillip Randall lit his pipe, sucking at the glowing bowl, breathing the smoke across the desk. I could smell the fumes through the peep-holes and my heart jolted. It was the same tobacco permeating the wood around me. Did he stand here, spying on Father? I looked back through the holes. He must know everything. He was so assured, so much at ease, even his look held contempt. 'Polcarrow will be out of the way soon,' he muttered, clamping his pipe between his tobacco-stained teeth, 'It can't be much longer.'

'It's taking too long. I thought you said the dog died straight away.'

The blood rushed from my head. I began shaking, gasping for breath. Falling to my knees, I gulped the confined air. Murderers. They were both murderers, prepared to poison an innocent man. I thought I would scream. My legs were shaking, my hands trembling.

A footman entered and I took a deep breath. It was not a visitor, but an express, carried in on a silver salver. Father grabbed the letter and broke the seal, his face darkening as he read the contents. He waited for the footman to close the door.

'Damn it – Roskelly's been found. They're bringing him back to Bodmin. Damn it. Get to Falmouth. Find his share certificates. For God's sake, don't come back without them – if the shares go to the boy, he'll own half the company.'

Philip Randall reached for his jacket, buttoning it quickly. 'Who found him?'

Father crumpled the letter in his fist. 'Doesn't say. Damn him, he should've sailed days ago.'

'He was waitin' to see if he was to take the boy.'

'Damned idiot – he should've sailed the moment he knew the Polcarrows were sick. We'd have sorted the boy out – go at once, leave now.'

Phillip Randall nodded. 'I'll be quick.' He pointed to the parchment with a seal on the bottom of it. 'That contract's ready to sign. You'd best get on with it.'

Father leant forward, his chin resting on his interlocked fingers. 'How much commission is Alexander Pendarvis paying you? You must be a rich man by now.'

Phillip Randall straightened his cravat. 'No commission, Sir Charles. I work only for you.' His crocodile smile revealed his brown teeth; lying, murderous thieves the two of them.

Father seemed satisfied. 'When you've got the shares, draw up a bill of sale. Forge Roskelly's signature and date it two months before he was imprisoned. We'll take half and half.'

The crocodile smile broadened. 'Thank you, Sir Charles, that's very generous.'

'I want that clay and so do you. Damn the man – he'd better not talk.'

Philip Randall picked up a leather bag and

213

walked across the room. At the door he paused. 'Might I suggest you write to Viscount Vallenforth and bring the weddin' forward? Tell him you've to return to London.'

Father grabbed his wig. 'That's exactly what I intend to do. And I'll chase up Lieutenant Carew – Lord Carew's more powerful than I realised. I need both weddings.'

The library looked empty. I shut the tiny door and ran to the chair, desperate Georgina might still be around. She must never know what I witnessed. Nobody must ever know. I was shaking, the tremor in my legs making my skirt quiver. Names jumbled in my mind. Not accusations, but names of business contacts, suddenly missing and never found. I tried to think but my mind was blank. Rumours of business contacts never seen again, vanishing without trace. My mouth was dry, my stomach sick with fear.

'Ah, there you are, my dear. Georgina said she'd already looked in here. Are you alright? Celia, you look very pale.' Mrs Jennings knelt by my side, her hand going straight to my forehead. 'You're sweating ... do you feel unwell?'

'What's happened?' Charity knelt by my other side, taking my hand.

'A bad dream,' I said, trying to laugh. 'I must've fallen asleep. I was being chased – I was running and running but my legs weren't moving. I was stuck in the ground.'

Charity put my hand to her lips. 'I'll stay with you tonight. That way, if the dream comes back, I'll be there for you.'

This dream would never go away. Behind us, angry footsteps came to an abrupt stop. 'So, here you all are. Well, that's not very nice – running away and hiding from me. Mama will be very cross. She wants you, Celia – you're in trouble. And she wants you, too, Charity. Not you, Mrs Jennings.'

'Where is she?' asked Charity.

'In her drawing-room. You better hurry – you've kept her waiting and she's furious.'

Chapter Twenty-five

I took Charity's arm, rushing down the corridor. Tonight, I would tell her everything – the poisoning, *L'Aigrette,* about Arnaud and how much I loved him. The footman opened the door. I was still trembling as we curtseyed. Mama was standing by the window, frowning down at the groundsmen raking the gravel. Saffron was on her cushion.

'I expected you half an hour ago,' she said, staring out of the window. 'Leave us.' The footman closed the door and Mama turned to us. 'I have written to Lady Clarissa, telling her how charmed we were by her son, and Lieutenant Carew has written very effusively to thank me, telling me how much he enjoyed his visit and inviting us to dine on board HMS *Circe,* on Saturday.' She looked up, her frown returning. 'The rest is up to you, Charity. I expect you to leave him in no doubt as to your pleasure in the prospect of your union. You will tell him how much you want to meet his mother and how much you look forward to enjoying his sister's company.'

Charity's hand trembled in mine. She turned pale. 'I'm ... I'm sorry, Mama, but I can't do that.'

'What?' Mama looked incredulous. Charity never refused anything.

'I can't marry him and I'm sorry but I won't go to his ship either.'

I stared at her in disbelief. She was standing so firm, her chin held high, resignation not defiance showing on her face. Taking both her elbows, I swung her round, not caring if we had our backs to Mama. 'Itty, don't be afraid,' I whispered. 'He likes you, I know he does. He'll be kind to you – he'll make you happy.'

She shook her head, tears filling her eyes. 'I can't, Cici. You know I can't.' She reached forward, kissing my cheek, pulling herself free from my grip. 'Mama, Celia must marry Lieutenant Carew. There's clear attraction on both sides – it's Celia he has regard for, not me. She must marry him.'

'Itty?' I suddenly understood. She heard me tell him I was not going to marry Viscount Vallenforth – our talk of Venus. She had not seen how his eyes softened when he looked at her. 'Itty, you silly goose ... don't you realise–'

'That's enough.' Mama held up her hand, her eyes brittle and cold. 'I don't care which one of you marries Lieutenant Carew, because the other will marry Viscount Vallenforth. Perhaps Charity's right. I think I may have underestimated her charms – judging by the way that major falls at her feet. Vulnerability can be very appealing. Perhaps, Celia, you should marry the Carew boy and Viscount Vallenforth should spend more time with Charity. I'm sure she would better fit his expectations of an obedient wife.'

I thought I would scream. I saw his thin mouth, the whip flashing. If I refused to marry Viscount Vallenforth Mother would make her take my place – my beautiful, vulnerable sister handed to him on a plate. She could never run away. Every night she would lie waiting for the sound of his footsteps.

'No, Mother! Absolutely not! You know what that brute will do to her.' I held Charity to me. 'You wouldn't hear her screams. No-one would. Everyone would be looking the other way. It's disgusting.'

'Celia, that's enough.'

'You'd sanction that? Just so Father can get his peerage?'

'Then it must be you, Celia. You still have the ring and you're still engaged.'

Panic clouded my thoughts; I had to think clearly, persuade Celia of Frederick Carew's regard for her. Then I could plan my escape. Once Charity received her invitation, an engagement must follow and I would run away. It would be easy. I would slip unseen from the house, take the path past the cottage, the shortcut across the park. I would go to Fosse, search the harbour. If Arnaud was not there I would go to Madame Merrick.

The door opened and Mama turned her icy-calm eyes on Father as he limped across the floor. Charity was so ashen, I thought she would faint. Until Mama gave us permission, we could not sit. 'This is a pleasant surprise,' said Mama coldly. 'To what do I owe this honour?'

Father slumped on a chair, staring back at her with reciprocal dislike. 'I've just received an express,' he said, scowling.

'I know. The horse's hooves made an appalling mess of the gravel.'

'Important business calls me back to London. I can't delay.'

'You'll be back for the wedding, I presume?'

Father sniffed, wiping his handkerchief across his forehead before blowing his nose. 'The weather warrants just one journey. We must bring the wedding forward and the whole household must return to London within the week.'

Mama looked down at Saffron, kissing him on the nose. 'That won't be possible. The wedding will take place as planned on Friday week, in St Mary's Church, Truro ... followed by a ball in the Vallenforths' town house. The invitations have been sent.' She looked up with barely concealed loathing. 'Every family of consequence has been invited. There will be upward of fifty guests so your business in London will have to wait.'

'I think Viscount Vallenforth would agree to bring the wedding forward.'

'Men do not organise weddings.'

They glared at each other and, for once, I was grateful for Mama's intransigence. Father had obviously not known the wedding plans were so well advanced. I would need a dark dress, perhaps a black one; maybe one of Mrs Jennings'. Soon I would be free from them all. I would wake to the sound of seagulls; feel the swell of the waves. I would be in his cabin, watching him through the door. He would be pouring coffee or squeezing lemons and would turn and smile. I tried not to blush. My dreams were too vivid, too full of yearning.

All at once I understood. I knew how a woman could know she loved a man, quite so much, to be prepared to give up everything.

For the first time in my life, I took notice of how the maids came and went. Parlour maids and ladies' maids slid quietly through the main doors if they were carrying trays, but under-maids entered only through the servant doors. Timing would be crucial. Between two and three in the morning seemed a good time. 'Shall I do yer hair now, m' lady?'

I nodded, my mind elsewhere. I would need a bag, big enough to take my treasured possessions – my silver brush and comb, my mirror, my jewellery, my mother-of-pearl fan and, definitely, my bird compendium. But first, Charity must be assured of Frederick's affection. She had stood up to Mother with such bravery, putting her own happiness before mine. I heard her stick tap against the washroom door and I leapt from the chair. She looked distraught, as if she had been crying. The maid left and she burst out, 'Cici, you mustn't marry Viscount Vallenforth.'

'You silly goose, of course I'm not going to.' I led her to the safety of my heavily draped bed. 'I

219

wish you could see the way Frederick looks at you – it's like there's no-one else in the room. He's clearly enamoured by you and shows only the friendliest regard for me – I can't bear you to think otherwise.'

'You really think so?'

'I know so. He's perfect for you – he has presence, Itty. Under those boyish looks, he has gravitas. He's an intelligent man and he's clearly honourable.'

'But that doesn't help you ... the thought of my own happiness is selfish ... it's you I worry about.'

I squeezed her hand. 'Once Lady Clarissa's accepted you and Frederick's proposed, I'm going to run away – and not to China.'

She looked terrified. 'You can't ... you've got nowhere to go! You'll be brought straight back.'

'No I won't, Itty. I've been giving it a lot of thought. Madame Merrick will hide me, I know she will. There's so much more to her – she's an émigré, you know.'

Charity's jaw fell. 'How do you know? Why is she a dressmaker if she's an aristocrat?'

'There's something she's hiding, but I trust her. She would never give me away. And it won't be for long ... when you're safely married, I'll come to you.'

I had to lie. I had to cross my fingers and blatantly lie to my dearest sister who deserved better. I almost told her the truth. I wanted to tell her everything about Arnaud Lefèvre and how much I loved him, but too much was at stake. Charity would just about sanction me running to the safety of Madame Merrick, but she would never approve of me running away with a man I barely knew. To ensure our safety, I must keep my secret to myself a little bit longer.

Chapter Twenty-six

Pendenning Hall
Tuesday 19 November 1793, 12:00 p.m.

Father's cruel eyes filled my dreams. I was being chased down twisting alleys, held up before a court accused of a crime I had not committed. I was pleading for my life. I had not poisoned the Polcarrows – Father was accusing me of something I had not done.

Mrs Jennings put her head round the door. Behind her, a maid carried a tray. 'How are you, my dear? Charity tells me you've a headache.'

'I'm practising for when I am a viscountess. I intend to have a lot of headaches and I'll take laudanum, just like Mother – no, don't shake your head – I've seen the vial by her bed. Did you know I'm to wear Arbella's wedding dress? We're not even going to have the pleasure of visiting Madame Merrick again.'

'Celia, dear – you look so pale. You haven't been eating. Here, I've brought you some broth.'

'Thank you – put it down there, please.'

Mrs Jennings lifted the lid off the silver tureen, the smell of rich broth turning my stomach. I screwed up my nose, picking up a slice of bread

221

and going straight to the window to open it wide. The birds were still on their ledge. 'Collared doves are more beautiful than white doves, don't you think?' I said, crumbling the bread to entice them down. 'I don't know why they stay. Why don't they fly while they have the chance?'

Mrs Jennings came to my side, slipping her arm through mine. She was watching me, not the birds. 'They're very beautiful. Thank goodness the rain's passed – that was quite a storm last night.'

The folly was shrouded in grey mist, the top arches lost to sight. 'Why do you stay, Mrs Jennings? Why don't you fly when you've the chance?'

'What a strange thing to say.'

'I mean it.'

'My home's with you. I don't want to be anywhere else. The regard I have for you and Charity goes far beyond my personal wishes.' She spoke softly and I turned, leaning my head against her shoulder, letting her hold me. She was the one in need of comfort, not me. I could see her heart was breaking. 'Ten years is a long time and I'm not ready to let you go.'

'You mean you don't want me to go to that brute of a man – you've heard the rumours and I can assure you they're all true.'

'If you'll have me, I'd like to come with you. I'll write my resignation letter to Lady April and I'll do everything in my power to keep you safe.' She was fumbling for her handkerchief, turning away so I could not see her tears. 'Come, Celia, drink this soup – don't let it get cold.'

The doves would not fly down if I was there, I would watch them from the table. The soup was lumps of white chicken, floating in a congealed pea-green sea. I pushed it away, rolling the bread between my fingers. I had no appetite and took Mrs Jennings' hand in mine, drawing her to the chaise longues so we could watch the doves. Everything had changed. She was no longer my governess; she was offering to be my companion and I knew how difficult it must be for her to choose between the two of us.

She must have read my mind. 'Charity will be very happy with Lieutenant Carew. I was watching them from the terrace. They look so well together, and he's certainly a very charming man.' Her smile filled her face. 'I've just had the very great honour of reading her his first letter. He writes very tenderly, assuring her of his great regard.'

'A letter? Just now? Oh, I'm so happy for her. We only hoped to respect our husbands – but to love them seemed an impossible dream. It's terrible to witness your parents' hatred – they can barely look at each other. Why did Mother marry so far beneath her?'

Mrs Jennings hesitated, avoiding my eye. 'I try not to listen to gossip.'

'But you read the newspapers. It's alright, I already know. Burlington Hall is in need of repairs, the estate's woefully neglected. Grandfather's an inveterate gambler – and so's my uncle. Father's growing fortune and limitless ambition was clearly enough to persuade Mother. She knew her family name would buy him honours – it's just taking longer than she thought.' I could only think of her as Mother now, Mama seemed too benign.

'She's only done what most women have to do.

Women need to secure their futures – and the future of their children. Passion may keep you warm at night, but when it's over, cold can kill. Try not to think badly of her, I believe she has your best interests at heart.'

'*I doubt that.*' It did not matter, I no longer cared. I would be free of Mother soon. The fire was crackling in the fire place, the room warm despite the grey day outside. It was not like my room in London; in Richmond I had my own belongings, here everything still seemed to belong to the previous owners. 'What happened to Mr Pelligrew, Mrs Jennings? You must have asked – it would've been your first thought when we arrived. I know it was mine.'

She stood up, straightening her skirt. I could see I had unsettled her. 'By all accounts he was a very pleasant and forward-thinking man, but he ran into terrible debt.'

She stopped. 'And?' I prompted.

'His schemes cost money. He was looking to dredge the river and build a new harbour. All I know is that to finance it, he decided to sell his shares in your father's company and take a mortgage on the house.'

'Why did he want a new harbour?'

'He realised the clay on the Polcarrow estate was the finest kaolin – he had it tested. He knew anyone mining the clay would need to transport it to the potteries in the north and the sea was the best option. He was a very clever man.'

'So why did he go bankrupt?'

'He didn't go bankrupt. He mortgaged everything, believing he would recoup the money once the harbour was built. He invested in a dredging company but had a terrible accident. He was found drowned in the river.'

My heart began thumping. 'A dredging company?'

'He must have been inspecting the creek and slipped. Your father held the mortgage on the house. He had also lent him a considerable sum of money for the dredging – he was the main creditor. When the extent of his debt was revealed, your father did the kindest thing and wiped the slate clean. He took the house and grounds and settled Mrs Pelligrew in a very comfortable house at his own expense.'

'Where?'

'Near here ... but she was inconsolable and went mad with the grief. Are you alright, Celia?'

No, I was not alright. My hands were trembling. Father knew about the clay and had lent Mr Pelligrew money to invest in a fabricated dredging company. Philip Randall must have lured Mr Pelligrew down to the creek and held him under the water with those sinewy hands. Phillip Randall would have been so plausible and Mr Pelligrew had fallen for it entirely, giving them all his money. Father could enter Parliament from a borough with two members and stay in London while Phillip Randall saw to the land deals. The clay would be theirs.

My mind was whirling. I could remember now – the names, the whispers, the hidden newspapers. 'Mrs Jennings, that man last year ... the one who came to Father for help? Mother hid the newspaper from me but I had already read the headline. He went missing, didn't he? Father bought his company off him and the man was never seen again.'

'Mr Arthur White. They say he left for America. His wife went mad with grief.'

'And before that? The ginger-haired man who waited outside the house? Who kept shouting that Father had ruined him? He was going to take Father to court. What happened to him?'

'It never went to court.'

'Convenient, wasn't it? What happened? Did he drown?'

The colour drained from her face. 'Celia, stop this.'

I felt faint with fear. 'Does Mother know Father's a murderer?'

She grabbed the chair for support, her knuckles white. 'Celia, this is madness.'

'Don't you see?' I heard a slight movement and looked around. Georgina was standing at the door.

'You've to hurry and get dressed. Lieutenant Carew's ship's been given orders to sail. He sends his apologies but asks if tea would be convenient. Mama says you've an hour to get ready.'

Mrs Jennings ran to pull the bell. 'Have you told Charity?'

'Yes, she's already dressed.'

'Go to her, Mrs Jennings,' I said quickly. 'Make sure she wears her lemon dress and cream bonnet. And stop staring at me, Georgina, the wind will change and you'll be left looking like one of those hideous gargoyles on your cottage.'

Chapter Twenty-seven

It was to be just the three of us. Father's stamping backwards and forwards across the hall, thumping his stick on the marble floor had been to no avail. Mother was not going to be summoned at such short notice and yet another headache kept her from joining us. We were halfway to Fosse, Father slumped in furious silence, his foot resting on the seat next to me. Charity sat opposite, her face glowing with nervous excitement. We did not dare speak in front of Father. I could hardly bring myself to look at him.

The face of a killer, not that he would ever do the deed himself; he would pay others to do it for him. So much made sense now; his friendship with Robert Roskelly, his sudden acquisition of the Pendenning Estate, his entry to Parliament. No, I could not look at him. If I looked at him, he would see the accusation in my eyes.

We watched the park give way to woodland, the dry riverbed widen behind the trees. The rain had obviously been very heavy. Pools of rainwater collected in the ruts forming deep puddles along the road. We splashed through some, avoided others, the horses slowing to a steady walk. As the carriage drew near Fosse, Father straightened himself and glared through the window at the passing townsmen. One by one, they turned their backs on us. No wonder they hated Father. I

227

hated him. Hated and feared him.

The crowd grew thicker and our pace slowed. The coachman urged the horses forward, the whip cracking in the air above. Our pace turned to the barest crawl. Around us people began jeering and I felt the stirrings of uneasy fear. Charity gripped her shawl.

'Bloody peasants, blocking our way.' Father banged his cane against the roof, his signal to go faster. 'Draw the curtain.'

We were in the centre of the town, past the town square. The houses were bigger here, shops on the ground floor with premises above them. Signs hung from overhanging buttresses, goods proudly displayed in the large bay windows. I could see a bank, a milliner, a shop selling household goods. The Ship Inn stood at the end of the lane, but we were going nowhere, the crowd gathering around us. Some were jeering, a man waving his fist. They looked so ragged, their clothes filthy, cloths binding their feet instead of shoes, sacking covering their shoulders instead of jackets. There was hunger in their eyes, that desperate lack of hope. I slid next to Charity and clasped her hand.

A thud slammed against the window and the crowd roared with laughter. Another clod hit the door, and another. Father banged his cane furiously against the coach roof but we remained at a standstill. The horses were whinnying, the crowd pressing forward, my fear turning to terror. Just like France. Aristocrats pulled from their carriages, dragged screaming through the streets. I clutched Charity's hand. There was no lock on the door, nowhere to run.

A movement of red caught my eye and I pulled back the curtain. 'Major Trelawney's there,' I said, my eyes filling with tears. 'Major Trelawney's coming.' A sullen silence met his arrival; the crowd stopped jeering, parting slowly to let him through. Father leant forward, reaching over to open the window.

Major Trelawney bowed in greeting. 'Sir Charles, I'm afraid it's bad news – the whole side of that tenement's collapsed. The heavy rain last night was too much for the roof and the whole lot's come crashing down. These people have nowhere to go. Their homes are destroyed and they're desperate. The Polcarrow steward is trying to find somewhere for them to sleep tonight and we're awaiting his return.'

'Open the door, dammit!' shouted Father, struggling to get upright.

'Are you sure, Father?' asked Charity.

'Of course I'm sure,' snapped Father. 'D'you take me for a bloody fool?'

Major Trelawney pulled down the steps and Father stared down at the astonished crowd. Holding his cane high in the air, his furious face somehow assumed a smile. 'Hear me. Listen. If you'll just be quiet...' he shouted, raising his voice above the rumble of loathing. 'I know you've your grievances. I know those tenements have long been unsafe and you deserve better but if you just listen to what I'm saying.' The crowd grew quieter, their faces full of mistrust.

Father raised his voice. 'I've already instigated plans for new houses to be built. On my desk are instructions for ten cottages – the *first* ten I

229

should say ... because I've plans to build more.' He nodded, smiling back at the shocked silence. 'And I've *other* plans, drawn up and ready to proceed for an alms-house for ten worthy citizens of this town.' Again he nodded his head, staring down at the wide eyes looking up in stunned disbelief. 'Six men and four women shall enjoy comfort in their old age. I have the plans drawn up and the building work will commence within the week.'

People at the back began pressing forward, desperate to hear what he was saying. Men at the front turned to tell those who had not heard. A cheer rose, followed by another. Soon a great roar swept round us, hands waving in the air. Charity flushed with pleasure. 'Oh, Father, that's wonderful. Nobody knows how much you really care.'

Bile turned my stomach. That was how he worked, using people to further his own gains; buying some, discrediting others. He was waving his cane in the air. 'Two families per cottage – there'll be plenty of space. And there'll be *more* cottages once they're finished. Give your names to my steward. He'll see you get the roof over your head that you deserve.'

Father was doubling his generosity so the word would spread. Major Trelawney was certainly thrilled. He stood watching the crowd, his hand on his sword, his face relaxing in a warm smile. He, too, had been fooled and I looked away, trying to hide my fury. Across the street, a man was standing on the step of a shop, slightly raised above the crowd. Framed by the doorway, he was staring at me, his eyes willing me to see him. A thrill of pleasure rushed through my body, my heart at once beginning to race.

His hair was loose, untidy, his chin unshaven. Rough stubble darkened his face. His clothes were dowdy, the cloth poor quality, his boots muddy and unpolished – a working man, indistinguishable from the men around him, except for his eyes. They were watchful, gazing at me with such intent.

I could hardly breathe. It was all I could do to stop myself smiling. I glanced back but he was gone, swallowed by the crowd around him. Why be dressed like that? Father held up his cane, trying to quieten the cheering crowd. 'Two barrels of ale at The Anchor,' he shouted, 'to help ease the pain. Tell the landlord to charge it to my account.' There was suddenly no doubting his popularity, the cheers were deafening, men pushing past us to claim the first jug. Father's smile faded. 'Major Trelawney, a word.'

He slumped angrily back into the carriage, scowling through the window. Major Trelawney climbed the steps, bowing to each of us in turn. 'I'm afraid the road ahead's blocked, Sir Charles. There's timber and rubble as high as any man – no cart can cross it, let alone a coach. I've my men working hard on it, but it's going to take a while. I've been waiting for your coach – I believe we've been invited to the same tea party.' He smiled at our expressions of delight, beaming with pleasure as Charity replied.

'How lovely you're coming. We've missed you up at the Hall.'

Father looked far from pleased. 'How the deuce

are we expected to get to the quay? We'll have to turn back and abandon the whole bloody idea.'

'Not at all, Sir Charles, we just need the help of six strong men. Instead of a sedan chair, you shall be taken by human chair. It's perfectly proper for the ladies – come down and I'll show you.' Major Trelawney climbed stiffly down the steps, calling men over to the now-deserted space around the carriage. Charity looked alarmed but my heart was leaping. Major Trelawney was beckoning Arnaud forward with five other men. 'There's nothing to it – it's a lift we use a lot when carrying the injured. Each man grasps his own wrist and a wrist of the other man. Like this. Here – a perfect square seat. All you have to do is sit back and put your hand on each shoulder.'

Father watched two men lift Major Trelawney in the air, vigorously shaking his head. To my mind it looked perfectly sturdy. 'Why ever not?' I snapped. 'Charity's engagement could be at risk and we can't miss this tea party or Mother will be furious.'

He glared at me but heaved himself down the steps, pointing to the smartest of the six men. 'You and you,' he shouted. As they linked hands, he lowered himself onto their hands. They held his weight, staggering forward, the pile of rubble looming in front of them. If they dropped him, they would have to run for their lives.

The remaining four men watched in relief. I was trying not to smile, looking anywhere but at the man who set my stomach fluttering and my heart thumping. Arnaud had been waiting for this, watching Major Trelawney practise this manoeuvre before we arrived. Major Trelawney looked at the four remaining men and hesitated. He would make sure I was taken next and would follow behind with Charity. Arnaud stepped forward. 'You and you,' he said. 'Miss Cavendish, are you ready? Let me help you.'

I smiled, trying to hide my excitement. Was I ready to be carried in the arms of the man I loved? How ready could I be? The two men gripped wrists, kneeling on the ground beside me and I sat back on their clasped hands as they lifted me up, my feet swinging beneath me like a carefree child. Behind me I heard Charity gasp as she, too, was swept up in the air to be carried across the muddy cobbles and over the pile of rubble.

The ditch smelt appalling, everything black and rotten. The ground was slippery and strewn with obstacles. Impatient mules shook their halters, stamping their hooves as they waited for their carts to be filled. Major Trelawney's soldiers were giving orders, directing the men with clear commands. There was so much to move. Some had buckets, some had wheelbarrows: others used spades, scraping them across the cobbles to pick up the broken glass.

Arnaud cried out as if in pain. 'It's no use – put her down. On my count of three...' I felt myself lowered slowly to the ground and stood clutching my skirts, desperate not to let the mud ruin my hem. He stretched, rubbing his back. 'It's no good, my back won't take that.' The other man looked crestfallen, staring at the filth in growing panic.

'Perhaps we could ... what if we swapped hands...?'

'No,' replied Arnaud. 'There's only one way to carry a lady.' He smiled, swooping to pick me up, holding me high in his arms as he strode effortlessly toward the pile of rubble. I wanted to laugh, clutch him tightly. I wanted to brush my cheek against the roughness of his stubble, breathe in every bit of him. His face was inches from my own, his arms strong and secure. How I belonged in those arms. We reached the top and he almost ran down the other side. Ahead of us, the quay was dwarfed by the huge naval frigate lying alongside. I leant against the man I adored and whispered, 'I'm going to run away ... anytime soon ... wait for me.'

He said nothing, but his arms tightened round me. We had reached the quayside and too many people were watching. Behind us, Major Trelawney looked livid. Arnaud put me down, bowing respectfully. 'I'm glad to have been of service, my lady – anytime, anytime at all.'

'I'm so sorry, Miss Cavendish ... so ... very ... sorry.' Major Trelawney winced in pain and shifted his leg, watching Arnaud disappear into the crowd of onlookers. 'If I see that man again, he'll answer for that appalling liberty. I can only apologise, Miss Cavendish – that was never meant to happen.'

I smiled, trying to control my leaping heart. Any time, Arnaud had said, anytime. 'Please don't apologise, Major Trelawney. You must know how grateful we are. It was terrifying back there in the coach and if it hadn't been for you, who knows what would've happened.' He bowed and I smiled. Above us, Lieutenant Carew was watching anxiously from the deck. 'You're quite a romantic, aren't you, Major Trelawney? For all your military bearing, I believe you're quite determined to play Cupid.'

His face relaxed into a warm smile. 'We both know they'll be very happy together.'

He left me, turning to supervise Charity and Father, and I breathed in the smell of the sea, the drying seaweed, the stench of rotting fish nets. The huge ship loomed above me, the masts reaching high in the air, blocking the light. 'What's she like?' asked Charity, coming to my side.

'She's jet black with a yellow stripe the colour of golden sunshine. She's got three masts, a long bowsprit and an almost indecently decent figure-head!'

Charity smiled. 'Is Lieutenant Carew there?'

'He's lining up the sailors. It's quite a to-do and I don't suppose he's allowed to come rushing down to meet us. The sailors are standing along the decks and the officers are lining up by the gang plank. They all look so splendid.'

She flushed with excitement. 'Oh, Cici. I hope I don't trip.'

Chapter Twenty-eight

I followed behind Father, Captain Penrose introducing the long line of officers. 'Lieutenant Saunders ... Warrant Officer Moyle ... Master Warren...' They bowed in turn and I smiled with pleasure. They looked so smart in their blue coats and white breeches, their gold buttons gleaming, their sashes so white. They were strong and lithe with sun-burnt faces and an irrepressible energy, worlds apart from Father's huge belly and bandaged leg. Captain Penrose stopped. He seemed disappointed in Father's lack of response, turning to me instead. 'Altogether, two hundred of His Majesty's finest men, Miss Cavendish.'

'I can certainly believe that, Captain Penrose – the finest men on the finest ship. What is she?'

'She's a sixth-rate frigate – five hundred and ninety-nine tons. Three years commissioned and she's already proved her worth.'

'She's certainly very beautiful and we're honoured to be invited. I thought women were considered unlucky on a ship.'

Captain Penrose smiled. 'Not if they're as sure-footed as you, Miss Cavendish.' I smiled back. I liked him. Mother would say he had risen through the ranks but he had charm, intelligent eyes and the easy manners of a man who did not need to impress. He must have been early forties, about my height, broad shoulders, impeccable uniform, a stern face but capable of humour. Yes, I liked him. He turned to Father. 'Easy to manoeuvre, heads close to wind, she's everything you want.'

Father looked bored. 'How many guns? You know my brother, Admiral Sir George Cavendish? He could barely get his frigate into the harbour.'

A flicker of annoyance crossed Edward Penrose's face. 'Thirty-four guns and, yes, I've heard of Admiral George Cavendish.' He turned to Major Trelawney. 'Not seasick, I hope, Henry? I know you military men don't like ships.'

Major Trelawney looked over the side at the glistening mud. 'Alright, so far, Captain Penrose.'

The men were dismissed to return to their work. HMS *Circe* was clearly well cherished; I could smell paint, varnish, and soap on the brushes. Her decks were scrubbed, the brass fittings gleaming, the wood polished to a smooth shine. Everything was neatly stowed and lashed to the decks, the rows of coiled ropes hanging securely to the sides. Ropes crisscrossed and looped across the yard arms, stretching like a spider's web above us. Frederick Carew tucked Charity's arm through his. 'A hundred and twenty feet.'

'And her width?'

'Thirty-three – she's not big, but she's sturdy and very fast.' He spoke with the same pride as his captain. 'Come and feel the wheel.' He smiled, indicating I should join them and I followed them up the steps as eager as a child. Two wheels were joined together, about two feet apart, the circles of beautifully crafted spokes polished to a shine. Charity gripped the wheel on her side and I gripped mine. To sail such a ship, to hold her steady while the ocean lashed. I felt suddenly afraid.

'Do you have a ship's cat?'

Charity looked puzzled but Frederick Carew smiled. 'We most certainly do, Miss Cavendish – rather more than we should.' The others had reached the forward hatch. 'Time for tea,' Frederick whispered, his voice turning conspiratorial, 'I can't tell you the trouble Captain Penrose has gone to. He's borrowed a beautiful Worcester tea set. He'd have had me scurrying all round town but, fortunately, Major Trelawney knew exactly where to get one. They were at school together, you know – Truro grammar school.' He smiled, the intimacy of his tone making Charity smile back. 'Cornwall's a small place – everyone seems to know everyone.'

Mist blurred the horizon. Gulls were screaming, swooping round the boats entering the river mouth. A cormorant stood with its wings held wide to dry, watching me from the top of a wooden pole. The wind was from the south, smelling of seaweed churned by an angry sea. From my vantage point, I searched the ships. Barges lay blocking the creek and small fishing boats crammed the inner harbour. Boats were beached on the tiny stretch of sand, their owners mending nets, but the boat I was looking for was nowhere to be seen.

Lieutenant Carew led the way, walking carefully down the polished stairs, ducking under the hatchway. It was tall enough for us, but not tall enough for him to walk without bowing. At the entrance to the wardroom, he removed his hat. Father was sitting at the large table, Captain Penrose waiting to seat us. He came eagerly forward. 'Do, please, come in. A bachelor captain has very little experience in offering tea, but I believe we'll not disappoint. Had it been dinner, you'd have been pleasantly surprised but ... well... I've been reliably informed ladies like caraway cake and frangipanes.'

The wardroom was larger than I expected with

seven large windows across the stern and a further two at either end. The windows were composed of small leaden squares but even on such a dull day, the room seemed bright and airy. Beautifully upholstered benches were carved into the deck sides and a lantern swung from the deckhead. Two paintings of the ship in full sail hung against the wooden panels. A central table stood bolted to the deck, its polished surface gleaming almost as much as the silver tray which held the borrowed china. Another tray held glasses and a crystal decanter.

'That's far more to my taste,' said Father. 'I believe I'll dispense with the tea.'

Captain Penrose laughed, seating us appropriately. Despite their busy schedule, some of the officers were to join us. Lieutenant Saunders drew out my chair. 'That collapsed building's delayed the loading of the ship.' He seemed nervous, ill at ease. 'We're waiting for some provisions – cabbages, turnips, potatoes, crate of chickens, that sort of thing, but most of the salted stuff's stashed away and we're almost ready.'

The tea was poured, the delicate cups chinking against their saucers. Father swilled his brandy round his glass. 'Orders at last, Captain Penrose. That must please you.'

'It certainly does, Sir Charles. I need to get back in the thick of things before Lieutenant Carew makes a civilised man of me.' He smiled broadly. 'I believe Lord Falmouth only sent us here so I could be taught manners and Lieutenant Carew could pursue his social life! Am I right? One word in your godfather's ear and we're off drinking tea in Fosse!'

'Captain Penrose, I must defend myself – you know very well that's not why we're here!' A slight blush coloured Frederick's boyish cheeks.

'Yes, it is, but the pleasure's all mine.' Captain Penrose's smile showed respect, teasing, even affection for the aristocrat who had been foisted on him. 'Do you like sailing, Miss Cavendish?'

I put down my cup. 'I'm afraid not. The sea frightens me. I was terribly sick when we came from Portsmouth.' My mind was racing – Lord Falmouth's godson? I had seen the look on Father's face. He was staring at Frederick Carew, the man he assumed to be without patronage. Lord Falmouth's word was law, even I knew that.

'Have you seen much action, Captain Penrose?' Father said with more courtesy than before.

'In thirty years? I should say. I ran from school at fourteen, couldn't wait to feel the waves beneath me. My father was a packet captain but it was always the navy for me. I've protected British interests all over the world – the Falkland Islands, the Indes, Newfoundland, Mediterranean. I've protected the colonies, chased every French ship I could find. I've been everywhere, seen more battles than you young ladies have had cups of tea – Valcour Island, Saratoga, Lisbon.' He turned and smiled at me, swapping his teacup for a glass of brandy. 'I've amassed enough prize money to buy a pile of stones and a large estate and I've a sister lining up every suitable bride she can find.' He took a sip of brandy. 'Trouble is ... my legs turn to jelly every time I leave my ship – too much sea-water in my blood. I'm frightened of the bulls in my fields and petrified by the geese in the orchards. But they're nothing to the ladies in my sister's drawing-room! They're absolutely terrifying.'

'Oh dear, Captain Penrose,' I said laughing. 'That won't do.' Somehow, I believed him.

'Are you still under Admiral Howe's command?' Major Trelawney asked, also swapping his teacup for a glass of brandy.

'Yes. We return to Falmouth then, I presume, it'll be back to France. The Duc of Orleans has been guillotined and the siege of Dunkirk has failed. The last dispatch made grim reading – at least thirty-two siege guns seized at Hondschoote. There's been a shameful retreat and heavy losses.' He looked up, glancing across at Charity's quick intake of breath. 'I'm so sorry. I shouldn't speak like this in front of you ladies. Forgive me – you see I'm a hopeless case.'

Charity paled. 'No, Captain Penrose, we need to know. We like to be informed – it's not knowing that makes us so fearful. I know you mean to spare our feelings but being wrapped in cotton and kept in ignorance is a lot worse than knowing.' She smiled, shrugging her shoulders. 'And it's particularly frustrating for me as I can't read the newspapers. I have to rely on others to read them to me and if they only read me what they want me to hear, I'll never be properly informed. Will we win this war, Captain Penrose? Are the French royalists capable of taking back control of their country?'

Captain Penrose looked surprised. 'Not on their own. Our problem is that we've been given orders to fight alongside their ships under Royalist command but we'd fare far better fighting under British command alone – British ships with British sailors.'

Charity smiled. 'Because you hate everything to do with the French and don't believe they can be trusted?'

Captain Penrose laughed and leant forward. 'In a nutshell, yes – but putting aside my years of hatred, we know the Royalist ships *can't* be trusted. They're full of pressed recruits, all swearing allegiance to the Royalist cause but in the midst of battle...' He clicked his fingers. 'Suddenly they switch sides and show their true colours – all of them seething revolutionaries, ready to knife their officers in the back.'

'That's terrible! Enemy ships within your formation.'

'Exactly so. Too many ships have turned sides in the midst of battle. The officers we can trust because they're from landed families, but the crew?' He shook his head. 'They're pressed into service and there's no knowing their true leanings.'

Father nodded to Lieutenant Saunders to refill his glass. 'Shouldn't trust a single one of them – officers included.'

'Some more tea, Miss Charity?' Major Trelawney stood poised, ready to refill Charity's cup. Frederick held out his hand but did not take the saucer from her. Instead, he held her hand steadily in his own, supporting hers while the tea was poured. I saw her blush and I smiled at Major Trelawney who smiled back. My beautiful, timid sister was really quite remarkable. Intelligent and beautiful, she had all three men eating out of her hand.

Lieutenant Carew spoke. 'We believe our orders will return us to France. The French are equipping at L'Orient, Rochefort and Brest but we don't know whether all the ships are manned or if they're lying up as hulks. We need to know which ships are *actually* equipping.'

I put down my cup. 'Do they want us to think they've more ships than they really have?'

'Yes – the old ruse – the Greeks did it, so did the Romans and I suppose we'll do the same. Knowledge is power, Miss Cavendish.'

A pang of fear shot through me. It was dangerous too, absolutely petrifying.

Father drained his glass. 'So what are you doing in Fosse if Lord Falmouth didn't send you to take tea with my daughters?'

Captain Penrose hid his dislike of Father very effectively. 'Surveillance, Sir Charles. We've been keeping a close watch until the batteries are manned.'

'And are they now manned? That was quick – I thought you said they were in a terrible state, Major Trelawney?'

Major Trelawney frowned. 'They'll not be fully operational for at least two weeks, but we've managed as best we can. A watch is now in place.'

'For French ships? Do you really fear an invasion?' If Father did not exactly sneer, his dismissive tone was enough to make Major Trelawney's mouth tighten.

'From tomorrow, all ships will need to signal.'

'And has everyone been informed?'

'All naval ships and any vessels with legitimate business have been informed. The Revenue will intercede and chase any ships not displaying the correct naval signal.'

'That's a bit drastic, isn't it?' scoffed Father.

Major Trelawney glanced at Captain Penrose, their unspoken thought hanging in the air. 'I'd say not – far from it. Until the cannons are in place, the men have orders to fire a musket over any vessel not displaying the signal. Two unanswered musket shots will result in the fires being lit. The beacons are already in place. Those are Lord Falmouth's orders, not mine.'

'Good God, man,' Father's flushed face paled considerably. 'I thought you said you were just preparing. That sounds like you're expecting an invasion.'

'Not an invasion, Sir Charles,' replied Captain Penrose.

'What then?'

Captain Penrose was no longer smiling. His voice hardened. 'We have it on good authority that French spies are operating from Fosse. We're watching certain establishments and it's only a matter of time before we catch them.'

'Here in Fosse? Surely not?'

'Fosse, Polperro or Mevagissy. They're hiding in the coves and wooded creeks – using the mists and fog to smuggle their people in and out. They know the coast like the back of their hand and have somehow managed to slip through our blockades and avoid our nets.' He finished his brandy. 'So far, they've had the devil's own luck, but we'll get them. The Revenue's watching, we're watching and traps have been set. Major Trelawney's men are on twenty-four-hour watch along the coast and I've got men positioned all over the harbour. We'll catch them – anytime now, their luck'll run out.'

The frangipane cake turned to salt in my mouth. I thought I would be sick. 'What makes you think they're French spies?' I managed to ask.

'Not *think*, Miss Cavendish, *know*. They've been followed at a distance and were nearly caught but slipped away – by a breath. As I said, they've the devil's own luck. They operate out of an abbey in Brittany, Abbaye Beauport, to be exact. It's near Saint-Malo, but there's no knowing who are the spies and who the monks. They dress alike, all hooded and bearded, skulking around, pretending to tend their bees – but they're wasps, the lot of them.'

I gripped my hands under the table. Charity's voice sounded far away. 'These spies – are they sending information back to France or bringing it from France?'

'Both, Miss Charity – but what's most important is we believe they send information to the Irish. They want Britain to split their resources, fight on two sides. They intend to use the Irish's dislike of the English to land their troops in Ireland. The United Irishmen make powerful allies – they're sympathetic to the Catholic faith and hate the English.'

The room was too warm, the blood rushing from my head. I tried to keep my voice steady. 'Could they not just be rescuing émigrés? I believe people are still risking their lives to save others from the guillotine.' But even as I spoke, I

245

knew the answer – émigrés only had to register, spies must be bundled ashore before daybreak, rowed to secret coves where men with covered wagons waited to transport them to a safe-house. My chest was rising and falling, my head spinning. I would have to get out before I fainted.

'They *are* spies, Miss Cavendish,' someone was replying – Major Trelawney, I think. 'They're very clever. They use all sorts of ciphers – musical scores that can't be played – poetry that barely scans. They use invisible ink made from freshly squeezed lemons and dress just like you and me. They blend in with the crowds and seem to slip through walls, vanish into thin air. That's why they're so hard to catch, but we'll get them, I promise.'

His voice was fading one moment, getting louder the next. I heard him through a blur of dizziness. I had seen everything, everything – the spyholes at Madame Merrick's, him vanishing into thin air, his sudden change of clothes. I put my handkerchief to my face, wincing from pain.

'Miss Cavendish, you look unwell.'

'It's just rather hot ... and it's a ship. Ships always make me feel queasy.' I tried to laugh, to control the pain shooting through me. What a fool I was. What a brazen, stupid fool. He was using me for information. I wanted to put my hands over my face and howl. 'Perhaps, if you don't mind, I think I'll get some air.'

Father heaved himself upright. 'We must leave – we've delayed you long enough. You've a ship to get ready and you must be wishing us away.'

Captain Penrose helped Father to his cane. 'Not

at all. I've enjoyed your company, Sir Charles, and that of your daughters. Tell me, Miss Charity, do all women like to be informed? Is it just possible that someone in my sister's drawing-room could be as interested as you?'

Frederick Carew drew back her chair and she smiled at both in turn. 'Yes, Captain Penrose,' she replied. 'You must trust your sister to select someone who shares your interests. It may not be considered seemly for women to think too deeply but, believe me, we do.'

Major Trelawney took hold of my arm, guiding me up the stairs and through the hatch. Once on deck, I gulped the salt-laden air, fighting back my tears. Lieutenant Carew was talking to Charity, asking whether his mother might invite her to stay. I should have been graciously thanking my hosts. I hoped I was walking with the dignity I needed, holding my head high, looking back to smile my appreciation, but all I knew was that my heart was breaking, the pain so intense I wanted to scream.

'Well, that went well enough,' said Father, settling himself in the coach. Major Trelawney bowed and slammed the door. Around us, people were cheering. Enough rubble had been cleared away and we drew slowly across the crowded quayside, Charity waving from the window, smiling, knowing to give the people our attention. Word must have got round that Father was to build the cottages, but I could not face any more lies.

I closed my eyes, forcing down the pain. Nothing was as it seemed. Nothing would ever be the same again.

Chapter Twenty-nine

Pendenning Hall
Wednesday 20th November 1793,
12:00 p.m.

The park was bathed in watery sunshine, the tips of the trees red against the green of the pasture. Sunlight glinted on the lake. There were moorhens, mallards, even some visiting geese but I hardly saw them; my head throbbed through lack of sleep. The same thoughts kept spinning round my mind. If I told Major Trelawney my reputation would be ruined, if I did not, my silence would make me a traitor. I had saved the life of a French spy. I had aided and abetted. I knew everything about them – the boat they sailed, their signals, the coves they used. I knew their names, their faces. One word from me and their whole operation would be exposed.

Yet even through the stabs of treachery, my heart burnt with longing. What if I warned him? Gave him a chance to leave and never come back? A knife twisted inside me, ripping me open, the pain so severe I thought I would be sick. Why could I not hate him the way I should? Why was my mind so clear, but my heart so weak? I needed more time – that was all.

No, time would not heal. I loved Arnaud so completely. With him, I was the person I should have been, the person I wanted to be, without him, the future seemed desolate. Had he been using me? Telling me he loved me because I was useful to him? I closed my eyes, the knife ripping me apart. Cynical manipulation – was that what it was? Or had fate brought us together, Venus doing her worst?

He felt part of me. I thought like him, laughed like him, anticipated his actions. I understood how his mind worked. From the very start, I knew him to be watchful, those dark-lashed eyes so quick and observant. When he told me he had a secret my heart had jumped. I felt so alive, as if living and breathing for the very first time; the thrill of the unknown, the hint of danger, the anticipation of risk sending shivers down my spine. I wanted that. How I wanted that.

I could not hate him, I admired him too much. In France he would be held in great awe, a man risking so much for the country he adored. I forced back my tears. Traitor – me, not him. I was the traitor. It was not him I hated, but me. I would soon forget the clothes he wore, his elegance, his humour. The way he cooked. How he wore a large white apron to shield his clothes. I would forget the way he adored Perdue, how he smiled, how the sea's reflection would turn his eyes an intense blue. How the wind ruffled his hair. I would forget the way he gazed at me, how he held me, the taste of his lips. I would soon stem the rush of pleasure every time I thought of him.

I turned round, twisting in my satin shoes. This was the tenth time I had passed that statue. The sun was hot, the blue sky stretching endlessly above me with no sign of clouds. Through the open door I heard Charity singing. She sounded so happy, her voice winging its way from the house, like Hope escaping Pandora's jar.

I forced back my tears. He had not lied to me – I had known not to delve too deeply. The desperate need to hold each other – that was real. He had not forced himself on me – I had willingly accepted his advances, even sought them, drawn by those hooded, secretive eyes, the windows to his soul. I had loved what I saw. Loved his kisses, the way he held me.

I took a deep breath. Always reining in when I wanted to gallop. This was no different. I was born to restraint and constraint; a daughter's duty, family bonds clamping me as firmly as any shackle. If I was French I could adore him, being English I must hate him – the accident of birth, the intrusion of politics. That was all.

I had not thought to bring my parasol. The sun was burning my arms, my bonnet insufficient to shield my face. I needed to go inside, but I could not face the others. Mrs Jennings would see my tears and Charity would sense my unhappiness. I would seek solace in the library and search the books. Perhaps it was not the same abbey – there must be any number of abbeys along that coast. Yet even as I made my way across the terrace and looked through the library window, I knew I could not hide from the truth.

I stepped into the silent library. The footman did not see me enter but stood to attention on the other side of the door. I was quite alone, un-watched and free, for once, able to swirl round and touch my toes. I did neither, but removed my bonnet, shut the terrace door and went quickly to the shelves, knowing there was an atlas and several religious tomes, all of them in French. I was bound to find something about Abbaye Beaufort.

A few books looked promising and I flicked quickly through them, mostly putting them back, but reaching down for an atlas, I caught sight of a large brown leather book with faded-gold lettering – *Les Éléments de l'Histoire … Abbé de Vallemont*. It was well used and my heart began racing – it definitely looked hopeful. Balancing three more books in a pile, I topped them with the huge atlas and tucked them under my chin.

The large wing-neck chair could easily accommodate me with all my books, so I settled down, plumping up a cushion behind me. The clock in the large glass dome had just struck one and Charity would sing for another hour. Even Georgina would not pester me – she would still be upstairs, watching Mother dress. I opened the atlas, turning over the pages, searching southeast by south from Fosse. Exactly twelve hours there and twelve hours back.

'Leave us, damn you. Wait outside.' Father's stick banged the marble floor and I froze in fear. 'Shut the door.' I heard laboured breathing, a man blowing his nose. Every instinct told me to rise and make my presence known, but one glance at my books and I turned to stone. They might not stay long, a quick bark of instructions, then back to the hall. If I stayed completely still, I might not be seen. I thought I could risk it – the chair was wide enough to hide me and even

251

Georgina never saw me. 'Well, have you got them?'

'It's bad news, Sir Charles. The certificates are in Polcarrow's hands. He's got everythin'.' Philip Randall's high-pitched whisper carried across the room.

'He can't have.'

'He's been in Falmouth. The bastard tricked us – all that time pretendin' to be dying, he's been in Falmouth, searchin' for Robert. Alice Polcarrow told him everythin' – squealed like a bloody pig, handed him her brother straight on a plate.'

'Damn the bitch.' Father was pacing backwards and forwards, turning on his heels. My heart was thumping, the drumming in my ears making it hard to hear.

'Polcarrow took the bloody lot – the forged papers, everythin'. The constable was with him ... they had Robert cornered and secured before he could escape. Matthew Reith was there too – Robert stood no chance. He's back in Bodmin.'

'Christ. They'll use this against us – Polcarrow's got all the evidence he needs. He'll ruin me. Damn Roskelly.' They were speaking in low whispers, restraining themselves so the footman could not hear but Father's voice had been rising and he checked himself, walking to the cabinet to pour himself a large drink. I held my breath, watching his reflection in the window, his hands shaking as he poured the brandy. Wiping his handkerchief across his brow, he strode back, out of my line of vision and I breathed again, willing them to leave. Another drink, or a move towards the table, and they could see my reflection.

Philip Randall cleared his throat. 'May I suggest–'

'Dammit, man, I'm thinking.'

The room went silent; only the ticking of the clock and the pounding in my ears. I sat rigid, hardly daring to draw breath. If I had been alone, I would have put my head between my legs to stop the dizziness, but I was too scared even to swallow. Father returned to pour himself another drink and my heart froze. My bonnet was on the table by the window. Raising his glass, he downed the contents in one. 'I believe this might work in our favour – it may be just what we need.' He walked back across the room and out of vision. 'Why did Polcarrow pretend he was dying? That cock and bull story he concocted? He's duped everyone – even Sir Richard and that idiot, Trelawney. Why pretend to everyone he was dying?'

'I'm sorry – you've lost me, Sir Charles.'

'Because he has a fast cutter at his disposal and needed to get to France, that's why. Because the navy are searching for French spies and because he speaks fluent French and his wife's a revolutionary peasant, that's why.' He drew breath. 'James Polcarrow's been away for over ten years and during that time he served on a French ship.' His voice was getting louder, he was almost shouting. 'Everyone knows that – but what they don't know is that James Polcarrow's a French spy. We've got all the evidence we need for his arrest.'

Philip Randall opened the door, no doubt to let the servants hear. His voice rose. 'Indeed, Sir Charles, James Polcarrow's a dangerous and vicious spy and must be stopped at all costs.'

'I've been trying to warn the town and now, finally, maybe the people of Fosse will listen to me. James Polcarrow's a traitor to his country. He runs a network of spies from his house. A tunnel links his study to the river – that's how he brings spies in and out of the town.' Father's voice was getting progressively louder, high-pitched and shrill. 'The captain of his cutter's also a French spy. They operate out of a bay near Saint-Malo, the north coast of France from an abbey called Abbaye Beaufort. The spies dress as monks and James Polcarrow acts as a channel of communication. He uses ciphers, invisible ink, secret codes – anything he can to betray his country. He ferries spies backwards and forwards to France and passes information to the Irish so they can aid the French with their invasion. He's a traitor to his country and must be stopped.'

'Will you have him arrested, Sir Charles?' The door closed again, their voices dropping to a whisper.

'No, people will think I've a vested interest. Send two anonymous expresses – one to Sir Richard Goldsworthy and one to Major Trelawney. He'll see to the arrests and Richard Goldsworthy to their conviction.'

'Has Sir Richard already left?'

'Yes. Send the express to the courts in Bodmin – the timing couldn't be better. Sir Richard's sitting in judgement. He's got another week of trials before the assizes and this is just what he needs. His other cases are sedition and riot but a high-profile case of treason will get his message across.

Two witnesses – that's all we need.'

'Sailors?'

'Two sailors to swear they've sailed with James Polcarrow and his wife across the channel to Abbaye Beaufort in Brittany. Get them to say they thought they were just picking up brandy, lace ... whatever. Tell them to swear they've brought people back to Fosse, dressed as monks. Got that? We'll go over the details later, but pay what you need. And get testimony from the doctor who tended the Polcarrows – he'll not lie on oath. It's our duty to keep our shores safe. James Polcarrow and his wife must hang for treason.'

There was a sudden silence and my hands began trembling against the map of France lying open on my lap. It was too quiet, as if they had both frozen like statues, Father's finger held against his lips, forbidding Philip Randall from speaking. 'See to it, Phillip.'

'I will, Sir Charles.' There was something feigned about their speech and I strained my ears, expecting to hear steps coming in my direction. I heard them move but it was towards the door and I held my breath, willing the door to open. Father's cane sliced the floor, his heavy footfall striding angrily away from me. The door opened and slammed and I felt the blood rush back to my heart. I knew I should grab my bonnet and run, but I could not move. Fear had turned me to stone.

That was how he worked – getting others to kill for him. So much better if the state hung Sir James for treason. All he needed were two witnesses and enough suspicion and another court case would be avoided, Father's name not even mentioned. I had to somehow warn Sir James. If Major Trelawney searched *L'Aigrette*, he would find all the evidence he needed.

A glimmer of light glinted across the white marble goddess – the briefest flash, vanishing almost as it appeared. I froze in terror. Something had caught the sun and reflected it back. A glass? A mirror? My heart seemed to stop. It could only be the reflection of a silver buckle. They had seen my bonnet and were still in the room.

Chapter Thirty

Father's stick tapped the floor. I lay with my forehead buried in the cushion, my arms lying limp across the books. I could feel their eyes boring into me, imagine Philip Randall's snake-eyes widening as he saw the books on my lap. I could smell the reek of tobacco, his stale sweat and foetid breath leaning over me. Until they woke me I must breathe slowly and deeply, hide the thumping of my heart.

I felt the atlas lift from my lap and jumped. 'Oh, Mr Randall, you frightened me.'

'So deeply asleep you didn't hear us?' Father sneered from the fireplace.

'I'm sorry.' I began gathering up my books, arranging them in a pile.

Phillip Randall grabbed the top one, turning the pages, his mouth tight with anger. 'Interested in abbeys are you, Miss Cavendish?' He looked at Father.

'Not interested, scared... I'm petrified – all this talk of the French invading our shores. We could be taken from our beds and murdered in our sleep, just like France. There are spies out there, helping the French invade. I haven't slept all night. I wish Captain Penrose could have stayed – I felt safe with him in the harbour.' Father's eyes were pin-prick cruel. Not just the greedy eyes I thought them, but cold and hard; the callous steel of a killer. 'I'm frightened. I don't like living so near the coast.'

'Then it's as well you're not going to live by the coast when you're married. Go back to the music room.'

'Yes, Father.' I started collecting up the books.

'Leave those. Just go.'

I reached for my bonnet, putting it slowly on my head as if I had all the time in the world. At the terrace door, I turned and smiled. 'I'm sorry, Father, Georgina tells me I shouldn't sit in that chair as I *always* fall asleep. I'm ... I'm sorry to be so afraid. I promise I won't scare the others with my fears.'

I walked slowly across the terrace. A buzzard was circling over the lake and I paused to watch, doing everything I would normally do. Any sign of hurry would be enough to alert them. I stood holding my bonnet, looking up at the huge bird, the sun making me squint. My mind was racing. I needed pen and paper. I had fifteen minutes before Charity finished her lesson and, any moment now, Georgina would leave Mother and come in search of me.

Not the music room. Not Mama's withdrawing-room. I walked quickly along the back corridor, mounting the stairs. On the first floor I began to hurry. I could not risk my own room so where could I go? I had to stop trembling and think. Mrs Jennings' room – no-one ever went there.

I rushed up the second set of steps, the third, hugging the wall, taking them two at a time. My shoes made no sound. I rarely ventured further than the nursery and never went to Mrs Jennings' room, but I knew she never locked it. No one was about and I ran along the nursery corridor, almost sliding on the polished wood floor. The nursery door was closed, as was Mrs McCreal's.

Mrs Jennings' room was at the end of the corridor and I caught my breath, glancing over my shoulder as I tried the latch. The room was almost bare – just an iron bed, a tiny wardrobe, a small desk and chair. The carpet on the floor was threadbare, the curtains dull and faded. Her room in Richmond was just as unadorned and I felt a surge of regret. She had no miniatures, no precious china, only the necessities – her brush and comb, and a glass decanter by the bed.

On the desk lay her writing equipment with musical scores, piled high on either side. I grabbed a sheet of paper, holding it flat, dipping the pen into the inkstand. My fingers were trembling, the ink in danger of smudging.

Sir James, you are in grave danger. You are to be arrested as a French spy. Lady Polcarrow will also be arrested. L'Aigrette *will be seized and you will be tried for treason.*

Without signing my name I folded it over, creasing it flat and addressed it to Lady Polcarrow. My hands were shaking so much I had difficulty scraping the flint across the tinder box. On the third stroke the flame caught and I lit the candle stub. The wax dripped onto the paper and I waited just long enough so my thumb would not scald. Straightening the paper, I replaced the quill exactly as I found it. Nothing looked different. The chair was back, the ink stand at the same slight angle. Only the faint smell of the candle, but that was already fading.

Hiding the note down my bodice, I kept close to the wall again, spiralling down the huge staircase, stopping only to walk slowly across the hall. The footman stood to attention, by his side a silver salver. Today's post was piled high, ready to be sent, and I stared at the pile of letters, my panic rising. How stupid even to contemplate putting my letter with the others. I turned slowly round, trying to think.

I would never find the maid, but the coachman? He seemed attentive in a way that was not familiar; there was kindness in his eyes almost as if he understood my clipped wings and gilded cage. He had already taken one parcel for me, so would not think it strange if I asked another favour. I crossed the hall, retracing my steps, knowing Mother would be watching from her window.

The courtyard was full of activity. A man wearing a leather apron stood shouting orders. There were oxen yoked to carts, mules laden with baskets. Men were unloading logs, rolling barrels, carrying sacks of vegetables to the kitchen. The sun was shining onto the cobbles, turning the stones a golden yellow. Two men were drawing water from the pump, two maids watching them through the grilles of the laundry. The coachhouse doors were shut and my panic rose. I looked round and smiled with relief. The coachman was walking towards me, removing his cap.

'I'm sorry, I don't know your name,' I said as he bowed.

'Walter Trellisk, m'lady.'

I stalled, still wondering if I could trust him. 'I see the swallows have gone.'

'Well gone – autumn's nearly over, though ye wouldn't know in this heat.'

'Cornwall's quite extraordinary, we don't have such changeable weather in Richmond – not that you notice, anyway.' He must have known I was not there to exchange polite conversation about the weather. He was wearing his leather apron and holding an oiled cloth. He must have been busy but he stood patiently squinting into the sun. 'I've a letter I'd like you to take to Lady Polcarrow. She's recovering from her illness and I want to send her my well-wishes, but...' I paused, trying not to sound too desperate. '...I'm in a difficult position because my father's no friend of the Polcarrows and I don't want to incur his displeasure.'

He looked up with the same pride of service I had seen in his face before. 'Would be a pleasure, m'lady. I understand what ye're sayin' and ye can be sure yer Father'll not know.' I smiled and would have reached for the letter, but he quickly shook his head. 'Ye're being watched, Miss Cavendish, so I'll shake me head, like this, as if yer askin' if there be meres for ridin'. When ye leave the courtyard, look for a drain pipe with a copper cover an' leave yer letter under there. I'll deliver it as soon as can be.' He bowed politely and I turned away.

Mother was watching the front, Phillip Randall the back. My prison doors were firmly closing. I had done everything in my power to warn James Polcarrow but was it enough? I walked slowly back to the house, fighting my tears. I was not a fool; I knew exactly what I had done. By warning one, another might go free.

I was not a traitor to my country but neither was I a traitor to my heart.

Charity wrapped her shawl around her. The window was open, the sound of owls hooting across the night's sky. Below us the park lay bathed in silver light, the folly eerie and ghostly in the moonlight. It seemed so peaceful.

'It's so still. Is the moon full?' she asked.

'So full you can see its face – it's almost as light as day. There are deer by the obelisk and rabbits darting everywhere. If we wait, the badgers may appear.'

'Will they be in Falmouth? Or do you think they've set sail for France?'

'It would be a beautiful night to sail.'

'You like him, don't you, Cici? We're doing the right thing, aren't we?'

I reached for her hand. 'I like him very much ... and I like the sound of his family. We're *definitely* doing the right thing.'

'But what if his family don't accept me? What if they realise my blindness is worse than they thought and forbid him ever to see me again?'

I hugged her to me. 'Frederick Carew's far too well connected to need money or patronage. He's one of the lucky few who can marry for love.'

'His mother probably only sent him out of politeness. She probably doesn't want anything to do with us. Not really.'

'Itty, it's so unfair. I wish you could see how his eyes soften when he looks at you. He can barely tear them away. Just for one amazing moment I wish you could see him.'

She squeezed my hand. 'I don't need to.'

She sat bathed by the light of the moon, her heart winging over the water, following the wake of an armed naval frigate. My heart lay shattered and broken, too heavy to skim the waves behind a small unarmed cutter. Two boats slicing through the sea, foam breaking over their bows, their sails arching gracefully against the moonlit sky: two men, intent on serving their country, each keeping his course, one man gripping a huge polished wheel, the other with his hand resting lightly on the tiller. The same moon would be shining down on them, the same wind blowing the lapels on their jackets, ruffling their hair.

It was too painful to contemplate.

Chapter Thirty-one

Pendenning Hall
Thursday 21st November 1793, 12:00 p.m.

We had been summoned to meet in the hall. We were to wear our bonnets and bring our parasols. We definitely needed gloves.

'What's this all about, Mrs Jennings?' asked Charity.

'Sir Charles thinks Lady April should be seen distributing alms. He believes it will enhance your family's reputation as caring for the sick and destitute.' She looked as shocked as I felt.

'But Mama never gives alms, and it's only twelve o'clock – she doesn't get dressed for another two hours. I can't believe she's agreed to it.'

Mrs Jennings seemed more flustered than usual. 'Yes ... well ... there's always a first time.' She straightened Charity's bonnet and touched her cheek. 'Don't breathe deeply ... and if you're near anyone who coughs, hold your herbs to your nose ... and don't enter any of the cottages. Try and distribute the loaves from the coach and don't touch any one. There's fever out there and heaven knows what else beside.'

'Who's going?'

'I'm not sure. Ah, there you are, Georgina, you do look lovely. Wrap that cloak around you ... it may be sunny but don't be fooled; it's nearly the end of November.' She was fussing like a mother hen. Outside, the coach had drawn up, the footmen loading two large baskets of loaves onto the back rails. Two other footmen stood holding smaller baskets of freshly baked bread and it was obvious the cooks had been up all night. 'Have you got your vinaigrettes, girls? Here comes Lady April.'

Mother swept down the stairs in her green and red travelling gown, her tall hat and a large veil covering most of her face. Saffron lay in one arm, a velvet muff hanging from the other. She stood scowling on the doorstep, incandescent with rage. I raised my eyebrows at Mrs Jennings and took Charity's arm, pulling her back as Georgina barged in front.

Mother stood at the carriage steps, angrily beckoning Mrs Jennings. She handed her Saffron. 'Keep her warm. I'll not take her anywhere near such filth. Sir Charles may not care one jot for the health of his wife and family, but I'll not put my dog in danger.'

Mrs Jennings smiled. 'Am I to stay behind, Lady April?'

'No, you're to go,' shouted a voice from behind. Mr Randall was standing at the door, feet apart, hands resting on his hips. A look of thunder darkened his face and I knew something was wrong – he sounded too authoritative, too sure of himself.

Mother bristled, delighted to vent her fury. 'It is not up to you, Mr Randall, who goes and who stays. Mrs Jennings will remain and take care of my dog.'

'It's not up to me – I'm just the messenger, but

264

Sir Charles believes Mrs Jennings should hand out the bread on your behalf and there's only room for four of you with all those baskets.'

Sudden dread filled my stomach and I tried to quell my fear. Walter Trellisk was staring straight ahead and something in the set of his shoulders increased my uneasiness. 'Georgina should stay behind,' I said, stepping in front of her. 'She's too young to be exposed to fever.' I began mounting the carriage but she pulled me back, pinching me painfully below my elbow.

'No, Mama promised me, didn't you, Mama? You said I could come. It's not fair, Celia always gets to go everywhere and do everything. She's so selfish – she never lets me have any fun.' She pulled me back, pinching me harder, almost ripping my shawl.

'For goodness sake,' snapped Mother, her face rigid with fury. 'Get in the coach, Georgina. Mrs Jennings, hand the dog to Celia and get in. I don't care if you don't have your cloak. Charity, stop looking like you're going to cry. Let's get this farce over and done with.'

I stood holding the whimpering dog, watching Georgina smoothing her skirts next to Mother. The baskets of bread were handed through the door, the steps pulled quickly up, and I stood watching the coach recede down the drive. Anxiety filled me. Father knew Georgina always got her way.

I put Saffron's soft little legs firmly on the gravel. She seemed bemused, looking up at me through her large, brown eyes. 'Walk!' I snapped, pushing her forward. She looked petrified, staring back at me, completely at a loss. 'Go sniff the fountain, chase those sparrows.' I began walking across the drive in the hope she might follow. There was something lying by the fountain – a small soft mound and I stifled my scream, beginning to run. She hurried behind me, her mouth open, intent on reaching it first. 'No, leave it!' I shouted.

Tears blurred my eyes. My beautiful ring-neck dove lay limp and lifeless, her eyes fixed and dull. I stared in horror at her blood-soaked feathers. They knew. Dear God, they knew. Footsteps crunched behind me. Philip Randall grabbed Saffron by the scruff of her neck, her body dangling in the air. She looked terrified. 'Sir Charles wants to see you.'

I laid the dove gently on the rim of the fountain, this symbol of constancy and peace. Her mate would be watching from the ledge above, no doubt already pining. Philip Randall's snake eyes were full of venom. I had always hated him, but now I was petrified of him. I walked towards the house, my legs turning to jelly. The dove's neck had fallen to one side, just like poor poisoned Hercules, lying in Alice Polcarrow's arms. My letter could not have reached Sir James. Neither Sir James nor...

We entered the hall and Philip Randall threw Saffron to the floor, staring in disgust, as she looked up and whimpered. 'In the study,' he said, pointing for me to go first. Walter Trellisk must have been caught when he tried to retrieve the note. Father had plenty of time to order the baking of the bread and set his plans in motion.

He wanted me alone in the house, no-one else there. I heard the door slam, the lock turn.

Father stood by his desk, his eyes blazing. I had expected fury, purple rage, but this silence seemed worse – like Mother's icy-calm. Philip Randall stood behind me, unquestionably my gaoler. He was too close, too sure of himself. I could smell his foul sweat, his acrid breath. Father had my note in his hand and was holding it in front of him. 'So you were asleep, were you? Heard nothing? Scared of the spies? Well, I've news for you, my dear. Walter Trellisk does not work for you – he works for me.'

The room began spinning, the blood rushing from my head. Father saw my fear and smiled. Behind me, Phillip Randall laughed. 'Made you feel you could trust him, did he? Gave you the look of one you could turn to?' I felt dizzy, breathless. I needed air. I had been so stupid, so utterly foolish. Walter Trellisk had seemed so genuine, as if he really cared, but I had walked straight into Father's trap.

Father reread the note, scowling with distaste. 'Who'd believe I'd a daughter who thinks nothing of alerting a known French spy? Is he your lover? The one you spend your nights with in the cottage?' He was icy-calm, but his eyes were blazing. Pin-points and cruel. I forced back my tears, staring at the twitch in the corner of his mouth – it was unstoppable, like his power.

'How dare you suggest such a thing!' My heart was pounding. Lies – that was how he worked, silencing people through lies and innuendo.

'Or perhaps he was just one of many? We know

you sneak out at night to your whores' den beneath the eaves,' Philip Randall's breath was hot
against my neck.

I swung round. 'How dare you!'

His eyes hardened. 'You're a traitor, Miss
Cavendish – a traitor and a liar. You tried to warn
a French spy so it's right to assume you must be
one of them.' He grabbed my arm, jerking me
towards him.

'Let me go!' He loosened his grip and I pulled
away. 'What you accuse me of is outrageous. How
dare you talk to me of whores' dens!' I was angry
now, every bit as angry as Father. A red mist filled
my head, a seething wave of anger sweeping
through me. I could feel my cheeks burning, my
eyes watering. But I needed to stay calm, think my
way through this. The last thing I needed was to
screech like an alley cat. I turned back to Father,
calming my voice. 'I've been so foolish, so very,
very foolish. I only wrote to Sir James because I
know he's innocent. That night I went missing, I
saw Viscount Vallenforth beat a young boy nearly
to death and I was scared...' Father was staring at
me, his face full of hatred. '...I thought he'd do the
same to me... I wasn't thinking, I just panicked
and ran. I took the path through the wood... I was
frightened... I thought only to take refuge with the
Polcarrows and beg you to release me from my
engagement–'

'You thought to take refuge with the *Polcarrows?*' Father snorted in contempt.

'At the time I thought I could never marry
Viscount Vallenforth ... but I was wrong – I can
see that now. I thought only to stay at Polcarrow

'... but Sir James and Lady Polcarrow were leaving – some other business called them to Falmouth so I *begged* them to take me with them.'

A flicker crossed his face. 'What business?' His eyes were steel – the eyes of a man who recognised fear.

'They didn't say and I didn't ask. I've no idea why they went.' I looked down, unable to keep his gaze. It was a mistake. I should have stayed looking at him. He knew I was lying. He was playing me, cat and mouse.

'And James Polcarrow agreed, of course.'

'No, he was very angry and refused, but I managed to persuade Lady Polcarrow. She lent me a cloak and smuggled me aboard. I was completely hidden ... no-one saw me and no-one could identify me – I promise you.'

Father's face turned so puce I thought he might choke. 'You expect me to believe you sailed to Falmouth?'

'It's the truth, Father. I'm ashamed I even thought to do such an outrageous thing ... but I was scared. I thought Viscount Vallenforth would whip me the way he did that boy. I was running in fear ... thinking only of the whip.'

'You expect us to believe that?' Philip Randall took hold of my arm again.

'I'm not talking to you. I'm talking to my father,' I shouted, angrily twisting my arm free. There was hatred in his eyes, no, not hatred, lust. He was enjoying watching me plead. I turned away, feeling totally repulsed. 'I knew Arbella was in Falmouth–'

'You knew what?' Father's fury erupted, his

bulbous nose flaring like an angry bull, his skin purple, blotched with pockmarks. He rushed towards me, his hand in the air, and I flinched, waiting for him to strike.

'Don't hit me, please, I'm telling you the truth. Please, please, listen ... let me explain. I'm not proud of what I did ... but I'm telling you the truth because you need to understand why I wrote that note.' He lowered his hand but stayed uncomfortably close. I could smell the lavender oil in his wig, tobacco on his breath. 'In Falmouth, I thought I found Arbella. It was the right place and I found people with the right name—'

'You knew where they were? This is outrageous – completely outrageous.' Beads of sweat glistened on his forehead.

'I know how terrible it sounds ... believe me, I know.' I fell to my knees, tears running down my cheeks. 'Please don't tell Mama ... please keep this our secret. I've learnt my lesson.' I knew to beg for my life – make him believe I knew nothing about the poisoning. He was going to silence me – dear God, he would silence me, just like the others. I gripped my hands together. '...Sir James was determined I stay with his friends but I told him I'd found Arbella and sent him away.'

'You expect me to believe this...?'

'It's the truth ... the absolute truth... Arbella wasn't there and I was frightened. I was alone in Falmouth ... I had no money, no friends... I had to get home so I rushed back to Sir James' ship and demanded the captain bring me straight back.' I caught my breath, looking up at Father. 'The rest you know...'

'The rest?'

'How I was locked in the cottage and had to wait until morning.' Tears filled my eyes, blurring my vision. 'I only wrote to Sir James because he'd shown me such consideration.'

Father stared down at me. 'You stupid idiot. James Polcarrow's a known French spy. He's fooled you, just as he's fooled everyone.'

'No, that's not true – he went to Falmouth, not France. The captain left him behind when he brought me back.' Tears were streaming down my cheeks. This was no pretence, I was pleading, really pleading. I reached forward like the supplicant I was, my palms sinking into the soft pile of the carpet. I could smell vinegar seeping through his bandage and held my breath. I was petrified, utterly petrified. There was no knowing what he would do.

He stepped away but I stayed on my knees, my head bowed. This changed everything. I would have to leave tonight, take my jewels, anything I could sell. This time I would be prepared. I would use the servants' stairs, take the tradesmen's road and make my way to Bodmin. I would walk all the way, if need be. I would find Matthew Reith and offer myself as a witness for James Polcarrow. I would tell him everything. 'Father, please, please, don't tell Mama. If Viscount Vallenforth finds out, I'll be ruined.'

'Get up,' replied Father. He was back at his desk, straightening his chair, picking up his quill, dipping it in the ink. 'James Polcarrow's a spy and you tried to warn him – that makes you culpable and it's my duty to have you watched.

Mr Randall, take my daughter to her room. Lock the door and bring me back the key.'

'Father, please... I'm so sorry – I should never have written that letter. I was so sure...'

'Not another word. Get out.' He began writing, his pen scratching across the paper. I felt my arm grabbed from behind, Philip Randall's bony fingers gripping me too harshly, lifting me to my feet with unnecessary force. He was pushing me to the door, his fingers sinking into my arm and I winced with pain but would not plead – that would give him too much satisfaction. He pressed harder, edging me quickly through the door, thrusting me in front of him as we left the study.

Half pushing, half pulling, he forced me across the hall, almost dragging me up the stairs. There was no-one there, no-one to see me, not even Georgina – Father had seen to that. Outside my room two men stood to attention and I stopped at the sight of them, pulling back against Phillip Randall's fierce grip. 'Are they to be my gaolers?'

'Get in,' he said, pushing me roughly through the door. The door locked behind me and I leant against it, my heart hammering, my breath coming so fast I could hardly breathe. I pulled up my sleeve and stared at the large red mark already forming.

I looked up. Something was different. A strong smell of camphor filled the room. A bag lay on the floor next to the chaise longue and I could hear rustling in the washroom. The door opened and a woman stood glaring at me – a thin woman with pinched cheeks and a drawn, grey face.

'Good afternoon,' she said, her thin lips barely moving. 'I'm Mrs Roach. Mrs Augustine Roach. I'm your new companion.'

Chapter Thirty-two

There was something familiar about her sinewy frame, the gleeful cruelty in her eyes. Deep lines radiated from her mouth, puckering in disapproval. I sensed the thrill of her power, her delight I had been brought so low. Her mousey-brown hair, tied tightly beneath her cotton mob cap, was streaked with grey, her dress dull worsted wool, as worn by most of the townswomen. 'My gaoler, you mean,' I said, brushing past her, trying the door to Charity's room. 'Am I to stay locked in for ever?'

She stood behind me, watching my efforts. 'That's not the best of starts, Miss Cavendish. If we're to pass the time together, you'd do better keepin' a civil tongue in your head. D'you think my brother hasn't ordered that door locked?'

Her brother, of course, who else would Phillip Randall choose? Fear twisted my stomach, filling me with dread. I let my cloak fall from my shoulders – she would have to pick it up – and crossed to the mirror, removing my diamond hat pin, throwing my bonnet to the chair, dropping my gloves to the carpet. Outside, the park looked deserted, no groundsmen, no gardeners, just the soft sun lighting the grass, the blue lake reflecting the azure sky. To be confined on such a day.

One glance at my writing table and my fury rose. 'Where are my pens and paper?'

She sniffed, glaring at my discarded clothes. 'There's to be no writin' notes. D'you think my brother didn't think of that?'

'Where's my sketch pad and chalks?'

'Put away.'

'And has your brother removed my embroidery in case I stab you with my needle?'

'You've yer book to read.'

Panic rose inside me. I had no way to signal, no way to write. Surely they could not keep me long like this – surely Charity would try the door and hear me. I would shout to her, tell her to get Mother to intervene. I took my cashmere shawl and wrapped it round my shoulders, sitting bolt upright by the window, desperate for the coach to return. From my window, I could see only a small section of the drive sweeping across the park and knew I would have to watch carefully for their return.

Augustine Roach stepped over my cloak and reached for a large tapestry bag, pulling out threads and bobbins. Sitting herself on a hard, upright chair by the door, she began making lace, her fingers flying over the cushion she placed on her lap. I stared at the open page of my book, not reading a word, my gloves still lying on the floor. Her fingers flew. Horrible bony fingers darting across her lap, like a witch conjuring a spell.

The clock chimed three. Three hours! I must have missed their return. My heart jolted in sudden realization – visiting the cottages would have involved going through the south gate. They would have returned by way of the stables. I had been such a fool, staring at the small length of drive for nearly three hours. In the distance a cart caught my attention and I looked again. It was a shabby donkey-cart, driven by the hunched figure of an old man. Jolting uncomfortably inside the cart was a lady wrapped in a black shawl and black bonnet, by her side a small portmanteau.

I stood up, pressing against the window. They were a long way away but I knew the bonnet would be trimmed with purple ribbon, the bag crammed full of closely written music. She was such a familiar figure, I recognised her at once, but in a donkey-cart? 'What's happened?' I shouted. 'What's Father done to Mrs Jennings?'

The witch fingers flew. She did not even look up. 'Your father's done nothin' – it's what she's done you should be askin'. Two days past, a large sum of money went missin' from Sir Charles' desk. My brother's been lookin' for the thief and this mornin' he found the money alongside several bits of silver – under the mattress in Mrs Jennin's' room. Thieves are hung, I believe, Miss Cavendish.'

'What?' I had to sit down, press my fingers against my forehead.

'She'll deny it, of course – throw herself at Sir Charles' feet. I can just see her, can't you? All her righteous, ladylike manners, that uppity, better-than-the-rest-of-us, snooty composure vanishin' as she begged for her life. Beggin' my brother on those precious knees of hers. She should've been less the lady and a bit more the maid.'

'She *is* a lady. And she's innocent.' I had to stop

myself from rushing over and hitting this foul-mouthed women with her vile talk and evil heart. Never before had I felt capable of violence, but as I watched the creases tighten round those puckered lips, the fingers jab at the bobbins, I felt capable of anything. 'Mother will believe her,' I said. But would she? The only thing that could save Mrs Jennings was Mother's fear of scandal. Even Father would not risk such public exposure, not with the legal case he was facing. I tried to breathe, think rationally. 'She was in a donkey cart. She's been dismissed, not arrested.'

'My brother'll give her a chance – considerin' the unlocked door, but she's out, you can be sure of that. Mrs Precious is now playin' a very different tune.'

'You seem to know a lot about it, considering you've been cooped up with me in this room.'

'I know all me brother's business. We're very close, you know. Since my poor husband died, he's been very good to me.'

I stared at the empty drive, the dust long settled. *Offer your services to Mrs Pengelly,* I willed, shutting my eyes. The clock chimed four, disturbing my thoughts. 'Am I to starve today?'

'The cook'll bring you broth at five. Your father's given your message to Lady April that you're not to be disturbed as your headache's taken away your appetite and you've no want of dinner.' They had thought of everything. This was no angry 'sending to my room' like a child, this had been carefully planned. Even if Charity came to my room, she would not see the gaolers for what they were. She would see only a blur of uniform, the familiar sight of footmen waiting to convey my messages, jump to my command.

The relentless threading continued; the lace now the size of a collar. My mind was clearing. I would need my hatpin to release the latch of the servants' door. I knew where to place it and exactly how to open it. It would be tonight, when Augustine Roach was asleep. I glanced at my desk – the silver inkpot was still there, so too the silver candle-holder by my bed. There was the filigree-silver glass stand, my silver-handled comb. She might wake if I searched for my jewellery, so I would take only the diamond earrings I was wearing and my silver compass, hidden under my pillow. My heart lurched in pain. I would sell it.

Outside my door I heard footsteps and the gentle knock I had been waiting for. I leapt from my chair, pushing past Mrs Roach but she was too quick for me. I tripped and fell over her out-stretched foot, tumbling headlong to the floor, my wrists taking the full force of my fall. Immediately she leapt on me, pinning me down by the weight of her body, her knees digging painfully into my back. She was every bit as strong as her brother, pulling my shawl tightly over my mouth, crushing my lips against my teeth, gagging me so I could hardly breathe.

I gasped for breath but the more I struggled, the tighter she wrenched my gag, her wrists pulling the shawl into a knot. I tried rolling sideways but she pulled my head backwards, stretching my neck so I thought it would snap.

'Sleepin' peacefully, m'lady, and asks not to be disturbed. I'll send word the moment she wakes.'

277

The respectful voice of the footman, Charity would know no difference. Augustine Roach was pulling my hair from its roots. I was choking, desperate to breathe. Charity must have gone. I could do nothing but stop struggling and lie limp.

'That was very foolish,' she hissed in my ear as she released the shawl. I gasped for breath, lying at her feet watching as she smoothed her skirts. 'My brother'll have to know 'bout this. Your tantrums aren't makin' this easy for me – I've an elixir to use, so bear that in mind, *Miss* Cavendish.'

I threw myself onto my bed. The maid would hand the footman my tray and the footman would bring it in. No chance at all to alert Charity. I would have to break my solemn promise and leave without saying goodbye. Worse still, I would have to abandon Charity to a house with no Mrs Jennings. I could hardly bear it. 'Use what you like,' I said, dissolving into the tears I had been struggling so long to hold back.

'I need the privy,' I said, pushing aside my evening tray. I had not touched the lukewarm broth.

Mrs Roach sniffed. 'It's where it's always been,' she replied, shrugging her shoulders. I reached for my comb, looking back at my pale reflection. My eyes looked haunted, fearful; no sign of defiance, no trace of the carefree girl who loved to gallop. I had picked my cloak off the floor and hung it on the back of the washroom door, slipping my hatpin up my sleeve as I tidied away my bonnet. Down my bodice lay my compass and the silver-filigree glass holder. I would slip the comb up my sleeve and take the silver candlestick into the washroom. 'Have you ordered hot water, or am I to wash in cold water from the jug?'

'No hot water. You've requested none because you want to sleep.'

'You will, at least, help me into my nightdress?'

She looked up. In the candlelight her cheeks looked hollow. 'Do it yourself. You just have to undo the ribbons ... sometimes they're buttons, sometimes clasps. Everyone else – and just about every man – knows how to undo stays, so it's time you learnt.' Years of anger and bitterness were etched across her face, each line vindictive, each crease clamping in the venom, the satisfaction of seeing others suffer.

I glared at her, but my heart raced. The comb was cold against my skin. The silver candlestick steady in my hand. The only problem I faced was my lack of outdoor shoes, other than that, I was ready. I picked up my nightgown. 'There may be ties round my back I can't reach – and without your help it'll take me forever. I'll call you if I need you.'

'Take as long as you like,' she said, smiling through the darkness.

I shut the door behind me. The key had been removed so I had no way of locking it. I grabbed my cloak, throwing it over my shoulders. There was enough light from the single candle to light the room. I would leave it burning, showing under the door to make her believe I was still undressing. I had been rehearsing the way in my mind, remembering it clearly – the third door after the second bend. Then two bends. I would trail my fingers along the wall – three doors, two bends, two flights of steps, then along the tiled corridor leading to the ironing room, the laundry and out to the stable yard.

I took my hatpin and knelt by the hidden door. There was hardly any light, the door impossible to see. I ran my fingers over the embossed paper, feeling for the outline. I felt the tiny gap and followed it up to the top, pushing the hatpin against the latch. The hatpin jolted in my fingers and I pulled it out, frantically pushing it back into the tiny gap, sliding it upwards with greater pressure. The same solid resistance, the same lack of movement. I began to panic, digging my fingernails into the thick wallpaper, clawing at the locked catch.

Behind me, the washroom door flung open. Augustine Roach was laughing, throwing back her head, the candlelight showing the crooked teeth crowding her mouth. 'D'you think I didn't know?' her eyes filled with tears. 'Lockin' that door was the first thing my brother did! I've been watchin' you collect your silver, believin' you're so clever. D'you really think my brother didn't think of that?'

Chapter Thirty-three

She stood in the doorway watching my courage turn to fear. Tears of anger filled my eyes – fury, frustration, but mostly panic. I pushed past her, undoing my curtain ties, pulling them round the bed and threw myself on the eiderdown, staring up at the heavy brocade, for once grateful that the dusty curtains would give me privacy. In the morning I would insist on seeing Mother. I would scream from the window, break the glass if necessary.

I began to feel calmer. She had taken me by surprise, that was all, tripping me up and suffocating me with the shawl. I was a match for her. I was strong enough. I just needed the advantage. The curtain ropes would do very well. I would tie her up and gag her, just like she had done to me. Tomorrow would be different.

I could hear her moving about, her candle lighting up various parts of the room – my wardrobe, my desk, my dressing table. I could hear her pulling open drawers, shuffling through their contents and I leant slowly forward, peering through a small gap in the curtains. She was going through my jewellery, placing most of it in a small bag. I watched her lift my pearls to her neck, holding them against her grey dress, the pearls shimmering in the candlelight. Her face hardened, her mouth tightened. There was greed in the eyes that looked back from the mirror. Thrusting them into the bag, she reached for my cashmere stole and threw it round her shoulders. She settled back on the chaise longue, her hideous shoes dirtying the satin cover.

My mind was now clear. I would take advantage of her while she slept. I would wait until I heard the sounds of heavy breathing. She had not drawn the curtains and long shafts of moonlight filled the room. It was stuffy behind the curtains, hot and uncomfortable. I lay in my gown, the silk crushed and ruined. The clock chimed eleven. I loved that clock, the delicate deep blue enamel with its intricate workings. It was French, signed, *Orange a Versailles.* I watched it for hours – the wheel clicking, the delicate pendulum suspended on silk. It had ticked away days that should have been lived and nights spent lying awake, dreaming of Arnaud. I wiped away my tears. Practicality, not sentimentality, was what was needed.

I sat suddenly upright and strained my ears, my stomach tightening. Someone had opened the washroom door and footsteps were crossing the room. I pulled back the curtains. A man stood by the bed, reaching forward, forcing a rag over my mouth, pushing me back against the bedclothes. The rag was tight against my face, caustic, sharp, burning my nose, catching my throat, making my eyes water. I began writhing under the force, pulling away from the hand pressing so firmly against me, but I could feel my senses swimming, spiralling away from me.

I was spinning, the bedposts whirling round me. I could hear distorted voices. 'Take this rope – bind her feet while I gag her. Get her out those clothes and into these.' The voices were coming and going. I was being pushed, pulled, twisted from side to side, the sharp, pungent smell burning my nostrils. 'Get those buttons done and tie her hands.'

'You're right – she knew 'bout the door.'

'She knows too much. Bitch has been spyin' on us.'

'I've got her jewellery.'

'Good. Ah, you're wakin'. I'm afraid there'll be no more sleep for you, tonight.' He began pulling me across the eiderdown, lifting me on his shoulder, thrusting me onto the chair by my desk. The room was spinning, the gag suffocating me. My hands were tied in front of me, my legs bound beneath my dress. 'What we need is a farewell note – you're elopin', my dear, runnin' away with one of your lovers you've been entertainin' in your whores' den.' Philip Randall smiled at his sister and even through my blurred senses I saw the satisfaction in her returned smile. 'You're goin' to write exactly what I say.'

She slid a piece of paper on the desk in front of me and forced a pen into my bound hand. I shook my head, sending the pen flying across the floor. Philip Randall forced my hands back onto the desk, holding me tightly round the waist, his chin pressing against my neck. I could feel his stubble scratch my skin, his nose rubbing against my jaw, his foul breath loathsome against my skin. 'Take the pen and write,' he said as his sister forced the pen back between my fingers.

I shook my head again, but Augustine Roach was ready, her bony fingers clamping over mine, her sharp nails digging into mine with enough force to draw blood. I was wrong. I was no match for her hatred. Suddenly I froze. Philip Randall had reached into his jacket and was holding a knife against my cheek. His grip tightened round my waist, his chin pressed harder against my face. 'You're wasting time – write. Don't think I won't slice this pretty cheek of yours. I would – easy. Just one slice and you'll be left with a hideous scar.'

My hands were shaking. He would do it, I knew he would. I grabbed the pen, holding it awkwardly in my bound hands. I could hardly write the words he hissed in my ear.

Dear Mama, I leave because I cannot live without the man I love. I know the disgrace I am inflicting on our family but I fear I must put my own happiness first. Your daughter, Celia.

It was my writing, my pen, my paper. There was nothing to show it had been written under duress. I felt myself jerked backwards, the rag once more forced against my nose but, this time, I was ready and held my breath. Even so, the acrid fumes were so pungent, so powerful, I felt my mind begin to swirl. If I struggled, they would keep the rag pressed across my face, if I shut my eyes and appeared senseless, they would think me harmless. I let myself go limp and my head loll to one side. I needed to breathe but, somehow, I held back, counting slowly, willing myself not to inhale. The rag was removed. 'She's out.'

I kept my eyes shut. I could feel a rough cloak wrapped around me, Phillip Randall dragging me towards the washroom. At the servants' door, he stopped to squeeze through the entrance before, once again, pulling me roughly behind him. Through barely open lids, I saw Augustine Roach following us, a candle in one hand, the tapestry bag containing her lace in the other. Father had thought of everything. The footmen would be replaced and Mother would never know anyone had been here.

Two bends, two flights of steps. No sign of any maids. It must be nearly half past one and the household would be sleeping. I saw the piles of laundry waiting to be delivered, the trolleys set for the morning. Philip Randall was cursing, dragging me behind him, his hands hooked under my shoulders, uncomfortably close to my breast. My stomach was turning with loathing. His hands began reaching beneath the rough cloak, fumbling with the ribbon on my stays. Vile, vile man. He did not believe I was asleep. He must think me awake.

Augustine Roach coughed, seemingly to bring him to his senses. He slowly withdrew his hands, hauling me over his shoulder, twisting down the two flights of narrow stairs, walking quickly along the corridor, my head and arms banging limply against his shoulders. I felt sick with disgust – sick and petrified, knowing my only chance was to stay awake. I could smell the lye, the scrubbed tables. I could feel him bend down, swerving to avoid the sheets hanging from the wires above.

He stopped by the door and I glimpsed my surroundings. Augustine Roach quietly shut the door behind us, checking to see if anyone was in the courtyard. Logs lay stacked in the woodshed; barrels piled high against the wall. She nodded and Philip Randall followed her into the shadows. Moonlight bathed the cobbles, lighting the water pump, the rows of buckets waiting in line but they kept to the shadows, skirting the buildings, out of sight of prying eyes.

We passed the stables, the coach-house, creeping silently under the arch to the tradesmen's drive. He shifted my position, my head jolting against his back, his hands now gripping my thighs beneath my dress. Foul, disgusting man. The rope binding my hands was too tight, the gag digging painfully into my mouth. I had to breathe through my nose, fighting the panic welling up inside me. Behind us, the house lay silent and undisturbed.

'The coach's behind those bushes. Walter's got the wheels muffled. Everythin's ready and I'll explain as we go. I'm comin' as far as the toll-gate. My horse's tethered to the coach – your bags are on the back.'

'And provisions?'

'You're well provided for – you won't need to stop. Just the change of horses but Walter'll see to that. You've done well, Augustine.'

'The payment's reward enough – it's you who's done well.'

'I made the bastard double it. Here's the coach. Walter, open the door.'

'It's open, sir – here, let me help. We'd best get goin', the horses are edgy – an owl disturbed them.' Another pair of hands grabbed me under the arms, Phillip Randall clutched my ankles.

'Get goin', I'll pull up the steps – use the verge, then cut behind the cottages. Once we're on the road, give them everythin'. It's a bright night – the road is clearly visible.'

'Perfect for a journey, sir.' I was half flung, half pushed into the carriage, left lying slumped on the filthy floor. 'Augustine, allow me to help you.'

The door slammed and I felt myself pulled onto the seat and propped roughly against the side. Old leather. Dusty curtains. No springs. My mind was racing. Philip Randall was going to leave us at the toll-gate. I would be alone with Augustine Roach. In her bag were scissors. I would use them to cut through my bindings. The carriage lurched forward, the wheels muffled by strong leather. As I thought, no suspension, the carriage rocking at the slightest dip, jolting us from side to side. Augustine Roach sat opposite me, Philip Randall by her side. Next to me was a small leather case – brass clasps, no initials.

'We won't use the lantern – I don't want us seen and there's enough light from the moon.' Philip Randall reached over, taking the bag onto his lap. 'It's very straightforward,' he said, undoing the clasp. 'The letters are in order. This one's for Dr Joseph Cox – owner of Fishponds. It's the letter of introduction so make sure you give it only to him. You're a long standin' friend of the family – you've been her confidante since early childhood and you're heartbroken it's come to this. Her name's Eleanor Morpass, wife of a strugglin' clergyman. She's become totally unmanageable, rantin' and ravin', insisting she's someone else.'

Chapter Thirty-four

Friday 22nd November 1793, 2:00 a.m.

I wanted to scream. I needed to fight my panic, stop the urge to struggle free. The coach was racing, hurtling along the drive. Even if I did manage to prise open the door, I would not be able to run. I would injure myself for nothing.

'These letters are from the physicians who've been attendin' her. This one's from Dr Hunter – he's an eminent doctor, registered with the Royal College of Physicians. And this letter's from Dr Bentley, a country doctor practicin' outside Taunton. Both tell of Mrs Morpass' developin' madness...'

'She's from Taunton?'

'Her husband's a curate on the Somerset levels. He's been told by the parish that her behaviour can no longer be tolerated. She's developed carnal cravin's ... she removes her clothes ... dances naked in the moonlight.' I could hear the lust in Philip Randall's voice. 'She frightens the servants, makes advances on the men. They're petrified of her rantin' ... and she scares the villagers. She denies her name, her marriage. She denies everythin' – says it's a conspiracy to silence her. The woman's quite mad.'

'You wrote the letters?'

'No, Sir Charles did. He knows Dr Hunter well. He's on the Commission for Visitin' Madhouses. It's worked before – no-one studies the signatures.' I could not breathe. Dear God, Father had done this before. Mrs White. Mrs Pelligrew. One had *gone mad with grief*, the other *rehoused at his own expense*. I had to stay calm. At the toll-gate I would leap from the carriage, if only I could open the door.

Philip Randall reached towards me, his hands diving beneath my skirt. As if checking my bindings, he began stroking my calf, reaching upwards to caress my knee. I lay limp before him, stifling my loathing. I was denying him the pleasure of watching my terror, but my panic was rising. My compass was in my garter, inches from his hand. If he found it, read those words and saw the engraving, he would guess. I felt sick with fear.

Slowly he withdrew his hand, reaching instead to his jacket pocket. 'Put this in your bag. She's out, but when she wakes use five or six drops – that should be enough.' Mrs Roach took the vial and he reached into the bag again, this time bringing out a pistol. 'Remember how to use this?'

'Of course.'

'Cock it at the first sign of danger. There may be highwaymen – she may get lively. Threaten her with the gun when you use the drops. Keep her asleep – if she soils herself, so much the better.'

Mrs Roach took the pistol, placing it carefully by her side. 'Where's the money?'

'Here.' He lifted out a package. 'Don't sell the jewellery 'til you get to Ireland. It's less likely to be traced.'

'We'll leave for Ireland the next day. Will you visit us, Brother?' She held out her bony fingers, taking the package firmly in her hands, stuffing it in the tapestry bag, along with the glass vial.

'In a year or two. You don't have to leave, Augustine. You know that.'

'Stay 'til you find a wife and be treated like a servant – by a woman who'd hate me? I'll not do that. Walter Trellisk has a way with horses and I feel sure he'll make his name. My payment's good but together our money'll count for more. There's money to be made in Ireland – he'll get the best stock, breed the finest horses.' She sniffed, her mouth clamping tight, her nose puckering into its accustomed distaste. 'I've no great likin' for him but he suits my needs. He'll breed horses an' make money – I'll have a house and servants.'

'He's been faithful, I can say that for him. He's honest and he'll do well. One day I'll buy a horse from him – I'll get Charles Cavendish and the whole bloody lot of them buyin' horses from him.' He was gathering up the letters, putting them in order, replacing them in the case. He slammed it shut. 'What was that?' The carriage swerved quickly to one side, then the other, sending me flying from my seat. I stifled my scream, lying limp on the floor. The carriage stopped and Philip Randall pulled down the window. 'What the hell happened?'

'I'm sorry, sir – wild boars ... runnin' straight for us. Are you alright?'

'No harm done. Where are we?'

'Edge of the moor, near the toll-gate. We'll see it over the next rise. I'm sorry 'bout the boars. They came straight at me.'

'Perhaps I'll leave you here. Pull over, Walter, strip the wheels.'

I lay hunched on the floor, my head inches from the heavy shoes of the woman who was trading my freedom for hers. The carriage jolted and came to a standstill. Philip Randall opened the door and climbed down the steps. The air smelt of moorland, of wild thyme and heather. It was so bright, almost as light as day. Reaching forward, he put his hands under my armpits, pulling me roughly to the seat again. I let my head loll back, my arms go limp. Through my lashes, I saw him do up his jacket and stare across the moor. He would be gone soon but, already, Augustine Roach had her hand on the pistol. She would use it. That woman was capable of anything.

Philip Randall walked to the rear of the carriage, untying his horse. 'You've got the list of inns for the change of horses?'

'Yes, sir – in the name of Warburton. We'll not be traced. I'll tell them at the toll we're headin' for Exeter.'

'It's a clear night, you'll make good progress. If you rest, make sure it's under cover of woodland. Keep the curtains drawn and don't let anyone see inside. Your payment's in the bag. The draft's dated a week from now – that gives us time to hear back from the doctor. Sir Charles must know she's arrived. After that, the money's yours. Use it well.'

'I will, sir. Opportunities like this don't come often.' His voice was hard, worlds apart from the gentle voice that had coaxed me to trust him.

'And be good to my sister. Treat her well.'

'I will, sir. I'll make a rich woman of her.'

'I believe you will.' Grabbing the reins in one hand, Phillip Randall placed his foot in the stirrup, swinging his leg quickly over the saddle. 'Get to Bristol as soon as you can.' He turned his horse, urging him on.

'I will, sir,' Walter Trellisk called after him. He climbed the steps, his face full of concern. 'Are ye alright, my dear? That jolt did yer no harm, I hope?'

'Not at all – you're kind to fret but I can take a few jolts.' Her voice was soft, cajoling.

'One day we'll have a fine carriage,' he replied, drawing the curtains and plunging us into darkness. He coughed slightly. 'D'you need to stop at all?'

'No, not yet.' I heard a rattle and my heart froze. 'Just get her chained.' A heavy object landed on my lap and I opened my eyes, staring in horror. Through the darkness, I caught the gleam of cruelty in Augustine Roach's eyes. 'See, she's awake. She may've fooled my brother, but she can't fool me. Chain her, Walter.'

Walter Trellisk pushed me roughly to one side, securing the chain round my ankles. It was cold and heavy, digging painfully into the skin above my shoes. But that was clearly not enough. Like a silver snake, he wound the chain round the metal beneath the seat, pulling it tight, bringing it back to my wrists, clamping two fetters firmly behind my bindings. He turned the key. I could smell oil on his belt – saddle oil.

I had smelt that oil before. It was the same oil permeating the wood in the servants' corridor. Not tobacco. It had been his belt pressing against the panels, his eyes peering through the holes to Father's study – Phillip Randall's spy, watching, listening, reporting back, waiting for his loyalty to be rewarded. I felt sickened, furious I had missed something so obvious. If I had recognised the oil, I would never have trusted him.

'She's goin' nowhere,' he said, looking at Augustine Roach with dog-like devotion.

I, too, was staring at her smile of satisfaction, the terrible gleam in her eyes. I looked away, unable to stop the tears rolling down my cheeks. Walter

Trellisk reached up to the luggage rack, took down a basket and started rummaging through its contents. He smiled shyly, proudly holding out a muslin bag tied with green ribbon. 'Most of the food's from the servants' pantry but I got these 'specially for you.'

'What are they?'

'Marrons glacés – they were made for Lady Cavendish but ye deserve them.' He undid the ribbon. 'They've got ginger and brandy in them.' They took one each, smiling in delight as they licked the loose sugar off their fingers. 'I'm goin' to look after ye, I promise. From now on, Augustine, ye'll only have the best.'

Augustine Roach smiled. She was almost purring. 'Get along with you, Walter Trellisk. Walk, don't run. I'm sure that's how you train your horses.'

He smiled back, drooling under her sugary sweetness. 'Ye could sit with me if ye like – after the toll-gate. We could watch the moon – catch the sunrise.'

She giggled sweetly. 'Perhaps I will, Walter Trellisk. Perhaps I will. Now get along with you.'

The door slammed shut and the coach started forward, Augustine Roach immediately reaching back into the bag of marrons glacés. Stuffing two in her mouth, she laughed her cruel laugh. 'I'm sorry you can't join me,' she mumbled, 'they're very good.' She crammed two more into her already full mouth. 'And it's too bad you're hungry, Mrs Morpass – but it's how the poor feel, most of the time.'

I turned away. The coach was gathering speed,

hurtling us down the hill. We must be over the crest and nearing the toll-gate. Reaching into her bag, she pulled out the glass vial, holding it in one hand as she grabbed the pistol in the other. 'One sound, Mrs Morpass, and I'll use these drops.' She straightened the curtain, leaving no gaps. Another two marrons glacés were stuffed into her mouth. 'No sound – not even the slightest movement.' I slumped back on the bench and shut my eyes. 'And my scissors can't cut chain,' she added.

Chapter Thirty-five

The carriage slowed and stopped. The pistol was pointed at my chest, the top of the glass vial on the bench beside me. She was standing above me, hesitating, poised to drop the contents of the vial on my gag. Outside, a door slammed, a man coughed. Footsteps were approaching.

'Been any robberies?' shouted down Walter Trellisk.

'None reported – a week since at Launceston but none tonight.' More coughing, followed by a loud spit. 'It's too bright – they'll not risk being seen. The weather's with ye...' Another cough. ''Tis a good night to travel. Where're ye headin'?'

'Plymouth. We've a mother to unite with her son.'

The voice grew muffled, the sound of blowing into a handkerchief. 'Two coaches have just passed for Bodmin and Falmouth but ye're the only one headin' east. Goin' to Torpoint?'

'Aye, with luck, we'll cross in the mornin'.'

'Does your lady need our rest room?' I could hear the clinking of coins.

'No – thank you. She's impatient to see her son.'

'Then I'd best not keep ye – safe journey.'

The coach lurched forward and with it all hope of escape. I felt petrified, knowing my chance had passed. I could do nothing but sit and stare at the vial, willing Augustine Roach not to tip it onto my gag. She seemed to be swaying, uncertain what to do, not knowing whether to stand or sit. She fell back against the seat, reaching out for the empty bag, turning it upside down in the hope of one last marron glacé. She began giggling, her eyes quite glazed. 'All gorn, nun leffed.' Her words were slurred, her laugh filling the carriage. 'Norra shingle one leffed.' The carriage was throwing her from side to side. She looked bemused, surprised, her eyes trying to focus on me. 'Gorr any moor? Jush one?'

My heart leapt, the marrons glacés – ginger and brandy. I had laughed like that, slurred my words. I had seen green eyes in the darkness. I remember the mixture burning my throat; the feeling of floating, the weightlessness. She was yawning, her foul crooked teeth opening like a crocodile. Her eyes were closing, her jaw dropping. She would be asleep soon. Already her jowls were slackening, her mouth gaping. I had been right to trust Walter Trellisk. Arnaud Lefèvre was one step ahead.

The road must have been good as the horses

were racing but I could endure anything, everything – the tight gag, the chains, the terrible suspension. Every bump, every jolt, was bringing me closer to the man I loved. Augustine Roach was now fast asleep, her snores loud and steady. The vial had fallen by her side, the contents spilling on the bench. The pistol lay abandoned beside her. I could reach neither but lay trussed and cramped, my heart singing.

Our pace slowed, the carriage coming to a silent stop. The door flung open and Arnaud Lefèvre stepped into the carriage, his eyes piercing mine through the darkness. He was dressed all in black, his hair tied neatly behind his neck. 'Are you alright, Cécile? Not hurt at all?' He was staring at me, his eyes searching mine, his fingers untying the gag clamping my mouth. Throwing it to the floor, he traced my lips with his fingers. 'Are you hurt?' he asked again.

'Just very thirsty.' My lips did hurt, my mouth felt bruised, my tongue swollen and sore, but somehow it did not matter. Seeing him re-kindled every flame in my body. He was cutting through my bindings, his knife flashing in the moonlight. Behind him, Walter Trellisk handed him the key.

'I'm so sorry you had to go through that, Miss Cavendish. Are you hurt?'

'No, I'm fine. I never guessed. You had me completely fooled.'

Arnaud turned the key and started uncoiling the chain. 'I hoped you might wonder about the marrons glacés but we'd no way of telling you. Everything happened so fast.' He threw the chain to the floor and held both my hands. Putting them

296

to his lips, he kissed them softly. His eyes were angry. 'Your father's an evil man – they all are.' He turned round. Augustine Roach was hunched against the side of the carriage, her mouth wide open.

'What will you do with her? Leave her here?' I asked, taking my hands away.

Stubble covered his chin. His shirt was freshly laundered, but his clothes were dusty, his black jacket and breeches merging into the night. His eyes hardened. 'Walter's being paid good money to deliver Mrs Morpass to the doctor. If she's not delivered, your father will come looking for you. He needs to know you're safely out of the way.'

'You mean take her in my place?' I must have sounded incredulous. Part of me was horrified, most of me thrilled.

'Of course – her brother's not expecting her back. She can scream all she likes that she's not Mrs Morpass. It's all in the letters and no-one will take the blind bit of notice. Let her suffer what she was prepared to inflict on you – for a while, at least.' He handed me a flagon of beer and I drank it eagerly, wiping my mouth with my hand. My wrists were sore, red marks left from my bindings.

'Chain her, just like she chained me,' I said, reaching for her tapestry bag. 'She stole my jewels.' I rummaged through the bag, my fingers touching the pouch of money. 'And I'll take Father's money, too. How much did Father pay?'

'Thirty guineas and fifty for Walter ... plus the horses. That's a considerable sum – your father clearly wants you out of the way.'

My hands were shaking. 'Blood money – thirty pieces of silver, how apt.' I reached forward, carefully picking up the pistol. It was the second time I had held a gun. 'How long will she sleep?'

Arnaud looked at the empty marrons glacés bag. 'Twelve hours, maybe more.'

I rubbed the marks on my wrists, looking at the scratches where her nails had dug into my hand. 'Do exactly what she did to me,' I said, watching him weave the chain round her feet. He secured it to the seat and clamped the fetters shut. I had no idea I could feel so angry.

Arnaud handed Walter the key. 'Can Walter have the pistol, Cécile, or do you think you might need it?' There was regret in his voice, a hint of resignation.

I handed over the pistol. 'Thank you, Walter. I owe you so much and I'll always be grateful. Promise me you'll stay safe – don't let Father find you.' I stood back, watching him mount the carriage. In a moment, my dream would come true. I would be alone on the moor with the man I loved. I wrapped my cloak around me, watching the carriage make its way down the moonlit road. I had dreamt of this. I had imagined everything; the moon, the smell of the heather. Arnaud stood beside me, his arm sliding round my shoulder. 'Where were they taking me?'

Moonlight bathed the two of us. 'Maddison's Madhouse – Fishponds,' he said softly. 'It's on the outskirts of Bristol.'

'How long will it take them?'

'Two days, maybe three – it's well over a hundred miles. Walter's been instructed to hire guards and a new driver at each inn. He's to change names every time and they won't stop until they get there.' I shivered. I hated Father. I loathed Philip Randall. I would never, ever let them near me again. Arnaud seemed to read my thoughts. 'Matthew Reith's got the reputation of being one of the best barristers in London. He knows his job. Don't for one minute doubt he'll let your father or Phillip Randall get away with their crimes.' His arm tightened round my shoulder. 'You're free, dearest Cécile. Free from the lot of them.'

The moor was so vast, so silent; just silver grass-land stretching for miles and miles. Deer stood grazing by a shimmering lake, in the distance huge boulders reached black against the pale night sky. The cool air smelt fresh, the scent of herbs mixing with the damp earth. I felt strangely light-headed, almost intoxicated, breathing in the heady mix of danger and relief. 'It's so beautiful,' I said, gazing round me.

'See the ring round the moon?' he whispered, 'It's going to get colder.' He bent down, swinging his bag over his shoulder. 'There are two horses in that copse over there. Where are we going, Cécile – *L'Aigrette* or Bodmin?'

I wanted to cry. How could he ask that? His hand slipped slowly into mine, pulling me gently behind him as we crossed the rough grass. They had changed my shoes and clothes. I wore stout leather, a foul woollen dress. My shawl was black and coarse – similar to the one I had worn before. I held his hand, following behind those broad shoulders, those arms that belonged around me. I loved him so much it hurt, hated him in equal measure, the pain of longing so severe I thought I would cry.

Two horses were tied to a tree – a chestnut mare and a grey gelding. As we approached they shook their heads, whinnying their pleasure at our arrival. It was dark beneath the trees. Shafts of moonlight filtered through the branches, landing like stars on the ground beneath us. It was like my dreams – two horses and vast open space, the freedom of being with the man I loved. My emptiness felt almost overwhelming.

'Bodmin's ten miles west from here,' he said, tightening the stirrups. 'James Polcarrow was arrested moments after I received Walter's warning. Rose as well. They're in Bodmin gaol and Matthew Reith's preparing their defence.' He put his arms round me, pulling me to him and I leant against his jacket, unable to stop myself. 'He's taken rooms at the London Inn – that's your starting point.' His lips brushed my hair, his chest rising and falling beneath my outstretched palms. 'No-one will recognise you if you keep your hood up.'

'Does Matthew Reith know you've singled him out to be my champion?'

I knew he was smiling, 'Not exactly,' he whispered.

The night was so bright, the horses impatient to be off. I had not ridden for what seemed an age. 'Let's gallop,' I whispered back.

His lips brushed my forehead. 'From now on, my dearest Cécile, you can gallop all you like.'

Chapter Thirty-six

The stones in the road glinted in the moonlight. We slowed our pace, walking side by side as if we had done it all our lives. My mare was strong, sure-footed, easy to handle, the two hired horses content in the knowledge they were returning home. Arnaud could ride – no doubt about it. He looked as comfortable in the saddle as he did on the foaming deck, his hands holding the reins so lightly, his back held straight. I could not speak, but breathed in every moment, wanting the night to go on for ever. This was how it was meant to be, the moon witnessing our stolen kisses, the heather a soft bed beneath us.

The road cut down to a vale, leaving the wild heathland with its barren rocks and boggy swamps. Windswept bushes gave way to straighter trees, rough moorland changing to farmed pasture. Hedges began to line our path, fences to keep the sheep from straying. There were no houses, just a vast patchwork of silver fields with moonlit ditches and owls hooting from the distant trees. We crossed a hump-backed bridge, winding along a brook thick with bulrushes. Somehow I managed to keep my tears from falling.

To our right, a ruined shepherd's hut stood bathed in light, the tumbledown stones sufficient to act as a seat. Arnaud pulled on his reins. 'Shall we stop?' he asked. 'I've some food and a bottle of wine.'

I nodded, turning my mare towards the stones, slipping from the saddle to hitch the reins to a nearby tree. Fine dew covered the grass, long threads of silver cobwebs carpeting the ground around us. The moon had lost none of its brilliance but the new day was already breaking. I could not look up. I did not want to see Venus gloating or the pink streaks of dawn stretching across the night sky.

Arnaud took off his jacket and spread it across the stones, his white shirt gleaming in the moonlight. He put his hand on my arm. 'Look, there ... in the grass. A female snipe. Can you see her long beak?' I could see nothing at first, only shadows but, suddenly, a large bird darted out. 'I'm surprised she's down here and not up in the boggy marshland. They nest on the ground and feed up on the moor. It's much safer up there ... fewer foxes. They're very shy birds, oh, she's gone.' He smiled and the pain inside me became almost unbearable.

'What have you brought?' I manage to ask.

'A rather nice cheese, some newly baked oat cakes and some chicken roasted with rosemary ... and a few unadulterated marrons glacés. Best of all, I've a very fine Chateau Margaux '88 – I hope it's not too shaken up. I've tried to keep it steady.' He opened his leather bag and brought out a brown paper parcel, spreading the contents on the stones between us. 'I've brought a knife and two glasses and I haven't forgotten napkins, though I was in rather a hurry.' He pulled the cork.

I wanted to scream with the pain. Someone was

302

tearing out my heart, ripping it from my chest. 'Was it Abbey Beauport you took me to, Arnaud?'

He paused, the beautiful fine stem glinting in his hand, 'How do you know that?'

'They're on to you – Captain Penrose, Admiral Howe, the whole British navy. They know all about you. Why did you swim ashore? Did you suspect a trap?'

He filled the glasses, handing me mine and leant slowly back, swilling his glass. His black eyes were watching me, guarded, like the first time we met. 'It was the old signal – we'd changed it. And it was the wrong place – too far north.' He put his glass to his lips, sipping slowly. 'It wasn't meant to be like that, Cécile. Normally they just row out to the boat with the documents hidden inside a brandy barrel.'

'Like the one we took ashore?' He nodded. 'Well, you've got careless – they're on to you and a good job, too. And I'm not Cécile, I'm Celia. And you'd no right taking me to so much danger and no right making advances to me.' I bit into a piece of chicken. It tasted of the moors, of wild herbs. I thought of Perdue and how much she would love it.

'I didn't make advances. Believe me, Cécile, I wanted to, but how could I?' His voice was hardly above a whisper. 'I loved you long before we met. For so long, I could do nothing but watch you, drawn by the way your eyes kept searching. You looked so restless and I felt such sadness. It was as if your spirit was bursting to break free and I wanted to help you.' He reached for my hands, pressing them to his lips. 'There's nothing contrived about falling in love, it just happens – the overwhelming desire to be with someone, to hold them.'

'That's enough. No more talk of love.'

'I have to. I must speak. I love you, Celia. I adore you. I love every inch of your beautiful body, every thought in your extraordinary brain. I adored you from afar but when we met ... when you flashed your haughty eyes at me across the deck, my adoration turned to the deepest love. And when I held you in my arms, when I kissed you, I knew that love would last for ever.' He drew my hands to his lips, kissing each in turn.

I wanted to cry. It was too painful to hear the words I'd longed to hear. My heart was breaking. It was not meant to be like this. Never like this.

'We're one, Cécile, you know we are – our thoughts, our interests, everything. We talk without speaking, we watch, we remember every detail ... we see what other people never see. Venus knew exactly what she was doing when she sent that arrow.' His voice was hoarse, almost pleading. 'I may be taking you to Bodmin but I'm coming back. Never, ever doubt I'm coming back.'

His eyes burnt with the intensity of his passion and I stared back into those yearning eyes, all hope of future happiness draining from me. An empty void filled the space where my heart had once been. 'Don't ever come back,' I said, pulling my hands sharply away. 'You've broken my heart – and I'll never forgive you ... you should never have encouraged me.' I fought back the tears blurring my eyes. In Pendenning I had hardened my heart; he was my enemy and I would never see him again. I could be angry, believe he had used me for his own ends, but staring back into those black eyes, I saw real pain. 'Arnaud, don't think ... for one moment ... that rescuing me from my father is enough to make me love you. I'll always be grateful, always, but I can never love you. Not now, not ever. Not even when this war's over.'

'You can love me–'

'No. Never!' His insistence triggered my anger. 'I can never love you – not now I know who you are. I've money and I've somewhere safe to go but if you follow me, I'll have you arrested.' My voice was steady, almost calm, certainly coming from every sense of duty, but also coming from my heart. I thought of Captain Penrose, Frederick Carew, the kind and dependable Major Trelawney – everyone put in jeopardy by this man's actions. 'How *can* you say we're one? You put my country in peril ... our brave soldiers... our wonderful navy, everything I hold dear. You put them all in peril.' I looked away, hiding my tears.

'I love you all the more for that,' he whispered.

'No, Arnaud ... stop! Stop talking about love. You're my enemy, fighting a violent cause in a disgusting and barbaric manner.' I pulled my cloak around me, shivering more from horror than cold. We were poles apart – not wrong time, wrong place, but wrong politics; a gulf so wide it was almost laughable. 'Find a woman who wants to see the heads of the aristocracy roll. Find someone who likes slaughter, someone who wants to support your blood-steeped tyranny. I hate your cause and don't ever, ever doubt I'll have you arrested.'

'I've never lied to you, Cécile.'

Never lied but never told the truth. 'Everything about you is a lie.' My voice was clipped with anger. 'The glasses, the fine wine – most likely plundered from some great house. Leave me, Arnaud, and never come back. Take your web of spies out of our country and never come back. I mean what I say – if I see any of you, I'll have you arrested.

He emptied the dregs of his glass to the ground. 'They're long gone.' He folded the brown paper into a parcel, bundling the remains of the meal into his bag. Only the wine remained – red wine, the colour of blood, of revolution, of young men dying for the sake of their country. Dawn was already breaking, *red sky in the morning, a sailor's warning.* I remembered my uncle's other favourite saying, *between the devil and the deep blue sea.* Why had I not heeded the warning?

He strapped up his bag. The leather was sturdy, indented holes spiralling in three lines around the base, the buckle tarnished. 'There's less than half a mile to go and it's too light to risk being seen together. I'll follow at a distance,' he said softly. 'At the fork in the road, leave your mare tethered to the post. Just outside the town there's a well with trees nearby. Hide in the trees until you see the Fosse coach – it's due at The White Hart at seven – then go to the London Inn and ask for Matthew Reith. Tell him you came by coach. It leaves from the Ferry Inn.' He slung his bag over his shoulder and walked quickly to the horses, cupping his hands for me to mount.

I slid easily into the saddle and took the reins,

the lump in my throat almost choking me. 'Good-bye, Arnaud,' I managed to say. 'Don't think I'm not grateful. Without you, I might have spent my whole life in Maddison's Madhouse.'

He looked up and I caught my breath. His eyes held such anguish, so full of love it wrenched my heart. 'There's no without you, Cécile,' he said. 'Adieu, my dearest love, we only part to meet again.'

I turned the mare, kicking her with more force than necessary. Tears blurred my eyes. Damn Arnaud Lefèvre. Damn him, damn him. I knew those words by heart.

Change as ye list, ye winds; my heart shall be
The faithful compass that still points to thee.

Adieu, not goodbye. I would never, ever be free of him, always looking over my shoulder, searching the crowds, every day petrified I would see him again. Every night, wishing I had.

Chapter Thirty-seven

Bodmin
Friday 22 November 1793, 7:15 a.m.

The coach came thundering past. The driver's capes were flapping, the horses foaming at the mouth. Dust and chickens went flying. It was packed, people crammed against each other, more passengers clinging to the back; the whole thing in danger of toppling over. A group of people gathered by the well and a queue had formed to draw water. It seemed so early yet already the street was busy. A long town, I could see that – one long, continuous street with lanes leading down on either side.

I wrapped my cloak around me, joining the steady stream of carts and wagons pressing together down the narrow road. A huge church stood on my right, no spire, slates missing and a tall chimney towered above me. I could smell fresh malt, wood smoke, the dung from the stables behind the brewery. The town was in a vale, a hill on both sides, a stream running in a ditch beside the road. Some of the houses looked newly built, some in desperate need of repair. It seemed so strange walking by myself, no-one looking at me and thinking it was odd.

The road narrowed, the houses pressing together and blocking out the light. The coach was making its way slowly in front of me, the coach driver waving his arms at the people in his way. Shops were already open, barrows being unloaded and stalls erected on the street. Every other building seemed to be an inn or guesthouse with signs hanging from the doors – *room available, no vacancies.* Even the coffee houses were opening. The window in the bakery was full of bread and boys were running down the street, carrying baskets on their heads.

There were no pavements, the street was in a terrible mess. Cobbles were missing, slabs broken, great potholes filled with mud and I was grateful for my ugly shoes – you would need stout leather to walk this street. Planks and poles were everywhere, huge piles of bricks, ropes, buckets and ladders waiting to trip the unwary. I made my way down the street, the sound of hammering echoing behind me.

The street widened with broad grass verges stretching in front of the houses. Tethered goats stood bleating, chickens pecked the dirt. The houses started to look smarter, new iron railings keeping everyone at bay. I walked past the brightly painted doors with their gleaming brass plaques – physician, attorney, printer and bookbinder. I read each in turn. This is what you did when you were free – you walked, you breathed, you joined the throng. How very different it could have been. I would never, ever take my freedom lightly.

The coach stopped outside a large inn. I could see the sign, the White Hart, hanging from the wall. The passengers began dismounting, spilling out, some being greeted, others marching quickly down the road. I stopped a woman with a small child. 'Where's the London Inn?' I asked. She nodded her head back the way I had come and I turned to retrace my steps.

To my right was a huge guildhall, further uphill I saw the law court. Men in wigs were already rushing along the street, clerks running after them carrying books and papers. I would need a new name, but not Miss Smith. I looked up. The London Inn crowded above me, the name of the proprietor proudly displayed, George Wells. That would do. It was an old building and had obviously seen better days.

'There's no work,' shouted a man in a large apron, his hands full of pewter tankards.

'I'm not after work, I'm after Mr Reith.' I stopped. His eyes had narrowed, sharpening considerably at the sound of my voice. 'I needs must speak with him,' I added.

'What's yer name?'

'What's it to you?' I hoped I sounded like the maids in Pendenning though I was not so convinced I did. He looked too interested and I sniffed, wiping my hand across my face. 'Can't wait all day – what's his room?'

'He don't like callers. I needs yer name, else I can't tell him ye're here.'

'Tell him Miss Wells wants him.' His eyes were too bright, too calculating. It was as if he was rubbing his hands with expectation, but he only nodded, beckoning me to follow him up the dark steps winding upwards from the heavily beamed hall. The place stank of pig fat, stale tobacco; the wood was black, the plaster in the walls crumbling in places. On the first floor he stopped outside a large door, two smaller doors on either side. He knocked loudly.

'Who is it?' called a voice.

'A woman wants yer – Miss Wells. Shall I tell 'er to come back?'

The door opened. 'Miss Wells?' Matthew Reith was fully dressed in a smart black jacket and breeches and a simple white cravat. His brown hair was greying at the temples, his eyes piercingly intelligent. He was tall, rather too thin, with a slight stoop to his shoulders and no laughter lines.

He stood staring at me, at once curious. 'Miss Wells? You've two minutes to state your business. Thank you, Jonah.' He opened the door, shutting it quickly behind me.

In front of me stood a desk piled high with papers and books. More books lay on the floor, periodicals stacked against a chair. In the grate a fire burnt, on the desk the last inch of a candle. He had been working – probably since the early hours. I walked straight to the desk and picked up his quill, writing quickly on a discarded piece of paper. He followed closely behind me, clearly surprised by the liberty I was taking.

I am Miss Celia Cavendish and your walls have ears. He read the note over my shoulder, obviously taken aback. I added *linen cupboards both sides* and turned and smiled. 'I'm from St Kew,' I said. 'You know, along the River Amble to the Camel Estuary? Major Trelawney's talked of your goodness, sir, and I'm hopin' you'll find me somewhere to stay.'

'Why are you here?' He was looking over my shoulder, suddenly conscious of the holes in the beams, the cracks in the wall.

'I'm a seamstress – lookin' for work, like everyone else. I can pay, mind. I've enough to last a week. I've run away and no-one knows I'm here.' I put the paper to the candle, watching the flame take hold, throwing it quickly into the fire.

'You have references – an employer's letter?'

'No, sir, only my word.'

'Then you stand no chance of getting a job.' He reached for more paper. 'The place is crawling with people seeking work. I don't know who

311

Major Trelawney is, but you can try Mrs Pomeroy round Back Street – tell her I sent you. But I think you've been very foolish – you'll get no position without a reference.' He began writing on the paper:

25 Bore Street. Don't use the front door. Tell Mrs Hambley I sent you. Alice Polcarrow is there – under the name of Mrs Thomas.

He put the paper to the candle, his eyes meeting mine. I could see I had shaken him, but the one thing I had learnt was that walls had ears. He walked me to the door. 'That's all the time I can spare. Good day, Miss Wells.'

I ran quickly down the stairs. Just as I thought – no sign of the man he called Jonah. At the door, a woman was sweeping the floor. 'Where's Back Street?' I asked.

She stared at me in disbelief. 'Round the back.'

I would have to hurry if I was not to be followed. Slipping into the street I dodged a cart and joined my step with a group of people making their way towards the coffee shop. Everywhere was busy, the noise of the building work almost deafening. I glanced round, relieved to see no sign of Jonah. 'Where's Bore Street?' I asked a young boy. He pointed towards the White Hart and, once again, I began to retrace my steps, searching everywhere for the numbers of the houses.

Number twenty-five was an old stone house with a slate roof. The house was set back from the road with shrubs down each side and an iron gate leading up to the painted front door. Another gate led down a small passage at the side. Three large windows looked out from the first floor, two from the ground floor. It looked clean and tidy, certainly well cared for and my relief was heartfelt. I nearly walked up the path but stopped in time.

A little further down the street a small lane ran to the right and I walked quickly along it, following the muddy path back to the garden gate. It seemed more of a farm than a garden. There were pigs in a sty, geese in a pen and rows and rows of neatly tended vegetables. It looked so welcoming. There were still apples on the trees, chickens scratching in the dirt by the water butt.

Sounds drifted through the open kitchen window, pans were clattering, a girl laughing. The door burst open and a young maid seemed to tumble out, a wooden bucket clutched in each hand. 'Can I help ye?' she said, straightening her back, wiping her hands on her apron.

'Mr Reith sent me. He says you've a spare room. I'm a friend of Mrs Thomas.'

Another woman put her head round the door. She was smiling, tying her white mob cap over her unruly curls. She must have been about my age, her smile as sensual as a temptress, her blonde hair refusing to be tamed. 'Ye'd best come in then,' she said. 'Mary, take towels to the top room. I'll get the water on.' Her eyes were an azure blue, her nose freckled by the sun, her mischief at once apparent. 'Ye're very welcome, miss,' she said, holding out her hand, indicating I was to go through before her.

'Miss Wells,' I replied.

She smiled. 'That'll do, at least 'tis not Miss

Smith. I'm Hannah and me mam's Sarah Hambley. She's at chapel so ye've come just the right time. No bag, Miss Wells?'

'My bag was stolen from the coach... I've come from St Ives – I'm a seamstress.'

Her smile broadened, her eyes danced, no young man would be safe from her. Even I was falling for her charms. 'No ye ain't, Miss Wells, ye're a fine-born lady and ye've run from home. Not that it matters – ye're safe here, that's what counts. Ye needs tell us nothing. Mrs Thomas isn't up yet – she keeps later hours so ye can bathe and rest first.'

I followed her into the warm kitchen and climbed the stairs behind her, the smell of baking filled the house. 'There's no need for water, Hannah – I think I'll just sleep.'

She opened the door of a large bedroom, crossing it quickly to close the pine shutters. 'I'll bring ye a nightdress,' she said. 'I'll not be long.'

A beautiful patchwork quilt covered the bed; the mattress was soft and inviting. I laid my head on the pillow. 'Thank you. It's just that I'm rather–'

Chapter Thirty-eight

'I'm sorry if I wake ye, but Mr Reith's sent notice he's to come at four.' Hannah unfolded the shutters, letting the last of the sun filter through the windows. 'I've a tray with tea and hot buttered scones and Mamm's making a lardy cake – 'tis

Mr Reith's favourite, what with him being so skinny and that she thinks he needs fattening.'

I stretched out. She had taken off my shoes and covered me with a blanket. 'What time is it?' I asked.

'Just gone two. I've hot water ready and I've found ye a brush and comb. There's a towel in the wash room – we've a wash room, ye know. Mamm's very particular about who she takes in. We've a bath, an' all.'

'That sounds perfectly marvellous, thank you, Hannah.'

She smiled. 'Mr Reith's Mamm's favourite. She offers him the rooms first. We used to have guests for the choosing but since the races stopped, 'tis only the fayres and assizes – and the hangings, of course. I'll get the water now and show ye what's where.' I returned her smile, sitting up to balance the tray on my lap. At the door she turned. 'Mamm's going to love ye.'

'Why's that?' I asked.

'Because ye're just the sort of guest she loves. She'll be hoping some of yer elegance and bearing will rub off on me.' She paused, her eyes laughing, her mischievous smile lighting the room. '*Well, if everything is perfectly marvellous, Miss Wells,*' she said, sounding just like Mother, '*I will leave you to enjoy your tea, but, please, do call me if there's anything you require.*'

I could hardly bear to put that hateful dress back on. Hannah helped fasten the bodice, her head shaking. 'Honest to God, 'tis a terrible dress. Ye really don't want to be seen, do ye? And do ye really want to wear yer hair plain like that? Honest, it's that awful.'

'It's perfect,' I said, looking back at my reflection. A hideous grey dress, a black shawl and my hair pinned severely down each side of my head. Only my eyes looked like me, the rest could be anyone in the street. Perfect. There was a knock on the door.

'That'll be Mrs Thomas – she said she'd give us half an hour.'

'Come in,' I said, rising from the stool.

Alice Polcarrow was a renowned beauty – how else had she captured Sir Francis Polcarrow? But as she peered tentatively round the door, she seemed fragile and timid. Her auburn hair was still so vibrant, but she looked tired, her thin hands clasped nervously in front of her. She walked slowly towards me, looking intently to see if she recognised me. 'I'm Mrs Thomas,' she said. 'Do I know you?'

We both glanced at Hannah. 'I'll leave ye now,' she said. 'I'll let ye know when Mr Reith arrives.'

I took a deep breath. 'You don't know me, I'm Celia Cavendish,' I whispered. She gasped, the colour draining from her already pale cheeks. 'I tried to warn Sir James – I sent him a note.'

'You sent a note? Forgive me if I appear shocked, but why? We believe your father's behind this, yet you sent a note?' Her voice was firmer than I imagined. There was bitterness in her tone, anger, resentment. She may look like a timid mouse, but her appearance hid her strength.

'It was intercepted ... it never got to you. Father is behind Sir James' arrest. I know that because I heard him tell Phillip Randall he must find two witnesses to swear, on oath, that Sir James Polcarrow was a French spy. I can't bear that my father seeks to falsely accuse a man and I'm prepared to stand up in court to tell the judge the truth.'

She looked shocked, reaching forward for a chair, indicating for me to join her at the small table. She was so much younger than I thought, not yet mid-thirties – hardly older than her stepson. Her manner was gentle, sad, her general air of vulnerability adding greatly to her beauty. 'Forgive me, but how do you know they'll be lying?'

I took a deep breath. My hatred for Father had not clouded all sense. Charity was not yet married and my younger sisters and brother still depended on him. I would tell them only what was necessary, the rest I would keep to myself. Certainly nothing about Father's involvement in the poisoning; I owed that to my siblings. Nothing about Arnaud Lefèvre, either, I would give him time to leave. I could not live another day if I was responsible for his death.

'This isn't the first time I've run away,' I said, choosing my words carefully. 'The first time, I went to Falmouth with your stepson and Rose. I was in the stable when your dog was poisoned and I overheard everything. I'm afraid I gave Sir James little choice though he was very reluctant to take me. That's how I know they went to Falmouth, not France, and that's why I'm here – to vouch that James Polcarrow is not a spy.'

She looked shocked, her beautiful hazel eyes wide with amazement. 'Does Matthew know?'

'Not yet – not unless Sir James has told him.'

'He hasn't been allowed to visit James. Honestly, Miss...'

'Wells...' I replied, looking back at the door.

'They're treating them as if they were guilty.' Her eyes filled with tears. Close up, she looked so drawn, dark circles shadowing her eyes. 'They're not together. They've been separated so they can't confer. It's really quite terrible, an appalling injustice.' She rose from her seat, going slowly to the window, looking out as tentatively as she had entered the room. At once she drew back. 'Oh no.'

I rose to join her looking down to the street. It was an excellent view, to the left the centre of town, to the right the distant crossroads and the countryside beyond. 'What is it?' I asked.

'You see that man, the one with the green jacket leaning against the horse trough? He's Marcus Babbinger.' I must have looked blank as the name meant nothing to me. She looked surprised. 'Haven't you seen the articles he writes in the *Gazette?*'

I shook my head. 'I hardly get to read anything, especially local papers. Mother considers them too provincial and never allows them anywhere near us.'

'He writes for the *Truro Gazette* but he also sends articles to London, to *The Times*. His articles are scurrilous ... he doesn't name people but he leaves everyone in no doubt who he means. He's here to dig up scandal about James. He hates James – he's tried to get him shamed before. He's a horrible man. It doesn't matter who you are because anyone's fair game – he pays people to spy for him.'

'Like Jonah at the London Inn,' I said, watching him from behind the shutter. 'Does he know you're here? Can we trust Hannah and her mother?'

'Yes, absolutely. Matthew got her son acquitted. He was up for theft and would've hung. We're safe here, trust me. I think only chance brings Marcus Babbinger to our door. He's here to watch the stagecoaches – they drop off at the White Hart. If someone rouses his interest, he'll follow them.' She stopped at the knock on the door.

'Mr Reith's just arrived. Ye best be quick as he's eating all the cake.'

Matthew Reith had found Jonah listening in the linen cupboard. Whether that gave me credibility or not, I could not tell. Perhaps he was like this with all his clients – he was certainly giving me a rough time and even going over everything without changing my story seemed to make no difference to his frown. 'How did you get here, once again, Miss Wells?'

'No wonder you've such a reputation, Mr Reith,' I said, trying to sound unconcerned. 'Out through the servants' quarters, round the back of the shrubbery, past the folly, through the wood to Polcarrow, across the ford, coach from the Ferry Inn, arrive at The White Hart.' *Please God let the tides tally.*

'Are you really prepared to put yourself on that witness stand? To swear the sailors did not take Sir James to France, but took him instead to Falmouth? Forgive me, Miss Wells, but I cannot make sense of your reasoning. You really felt the need to leave your father's home to stand witness against him? You've no faith that I could, *perhaps*, win this case for Sir James or that your reputation will be ruined?'

'Perhaps I was a bit hasty.' I was beginning not to like this man. Strange, I thought I would admire him, but there was something very disdainful in the way he looked at me.

'You run away often, do you, Miss Wells? Are you so bored at Pendenning that you need to seek adventure?'

'Matthew, must you be so strict? I think Miss Cavendish deserves better? I think you're being very hard on her – she's not on the witness stand.' Alice Polcarrow turned to me with a smile. 'He has the reputation of making even hardened thief-takers quiver.'

'I may sound fierce, Alice, but it's only so Miss Cavendish knows what to expect. *When* they let me see Sir James I'll ask him whether he thinks Miss Cavendish will further his cause or hinder it – but to my mind, Miss Cavendish, your presence is unnecessary. Your parents will be searching for you and with men like Marcus Babbinger about, it can only be a matter of days before your reputation's ruined for good. I take it you've money for your coach back? How much was your fare?'

His eyes were cold. It must have been high tide and I had absolutely no idea how much the coach fare was. 'Alright, Mr Reith,' I said, sighing, 'if it's the truth you want, then, no, I didn't get the coach. Father wanted me silenced... I was indecently assaulted by his steward, Phillip Randall, abducted by his sister – a woman called Augustine Roach – held bound and gagged in a carriage and should still be racing across the country to Maddison's Madhouse where letters from two doctors would incarcerate me under the name of Mrs Morpass but ... *fortunately* for me, a French spy drugged her, using marrons glacés, and rescued me just in time. We rode across Bodmin Moor in the moonlight ... and I waited for the coach so you would think I'd used it. My father believes I'm nicely out of the way and won't be searching for me ... and my mother thinks I've eloped and will be petrified of the scandal and desperate for my sister to marry Frederick Carew *before* Viscount Vallenforth hears of the scandal and cancels our engagement. I shall never marry him. He's a vicious brute who, by the way, takes great pleasure in beating children – I'm sorry, I left that bit out.'

Matthew Reith sucked in his already gaunt cheeks. 'You can stay here until I have discussed the matter with Sir James. And if you promise that Alice will stay safe with you here, and *not* be taken prisoner by pirates, transported halfway across the globe to be sold as a slave in some foreign land, then I will leave you two together. I'm more grateful than cross for you wasting my time. I've moved rooms and Jonah now works for me.' He cast a glimmer of a smile towards Alice Polcarrow but I saw his eyes soften.

A chink in his armour. I stood up, pursing my lips. 'I'll leave you two together – you must be wishing me away. No, don't get up. I've a letter to write – my governess has been dismissed. Money was planted in her room and she was falsely accused of stealing it. She's quite alone now, with no protection.' I left them staring after me but my priority was Charity – dearest Charity. She would be so worried. In the drawer upstairs pen and paper lay ready and a letter was already forming in my mind.

I just hoped it would arrive in time.

Chapter Thirty-nine

I dipped the pen in the ink. Despite Matthew Reith's reluctance, I would stay until James Polcarrow was acquitted. No-one knew what Father was capable of, but where could I go then? Certainly not to Madame Merrick's! I took a deep breath. I would think about that later. I had my jewels, I had father's blood money and, after all, I could always set up as a piano teacher or governess. I stared at the blank sheet of paper. Did Mrs Jennings go straight to Mrs Pengelly? She must have. She had no money and nobody else to turn to.

22nd November

My dear Mrs Jennings,

Please God you are still in Fosse. I am well and I am among friends. I have everything I need and am not in any danger but I am no longer at Pendenning and my only concern is that Charity is without either of us. As yet, I cannot tell you where I am, but I promise to write again when my circumstances are settled. Neither fear for me, nor scold me, but you must do exactly what I tell you. I have no time for niceties – I must simply give you instructions. Believe me, I know how this will shock you, but I believe it is the only way to ensure Charity marries Frederick Carew.

Today is Friday. With any luck you will receive this letter by Saturday. Once you have read it, go straight to Pendenning and insist on seeing Mother. Make enquiries first so that you know Father is not at home, or wait for him to be otherwise engaged. Tell Mother that you have written two letters, both of them addressed and left with people in Fosse. One letter is to Viscount Vallenforth, the other to Mr Marcus Babbinger, chief society reporter for both the Cornish Gazette *and* The Times *in London.*

Tell Mother that unless you are reinstated as governess and are seen with her in church on Sunday, the people holding your letters will have every reason to believe your reinstatement has failed or you are being wrongfully detained. Either way, they have instructions to send the letters, immediately.

Mother fears scandal more than any peasant uprising or invasion from France. Tell her you have detailed everything – the way I used the cottage to meet my lovers; how I remained for thirty-six hours in the arms of the coachman, finally eloping with him when I was confined to my room. It is as far from the truth as you can imagine, but tell her you know of my elopement letter, how I used the servants' corridors like my Cousin Arbella, and how we made a habit of slipping out of the house to meet our lovers.

Believe me, you must fear for your safety. Go everywhere with Charity. Insist that Mother allows you to accompany her to Lady Carew at Trenwyn House. Tell her, in no uncertain terms, that if this does not happen, those letters will be sent. Remember to add that Mr Marcus Babbinger pays well and you are confident in your reward from him but, should you disappear, and never be seen again, then the added scandal of how you were wrongfully dismissed and forced into a madhouse would be investigated by him. Either way, the scandal would ruin any chances of a good marriage for my sisters and would end Father's hope for a peerage.

My dear Mrs Jennings, I ask you to do this, not for me, but for Charity. Both your happiness and safety depends on this.

Your dearest friend,
CC

I read the letter – it was not perfect, but it would have to do. The room was already darkening, the sun no longer glinting on the window but dipping quickly behind the hill. They would have short days in this vale, not the long shadows stretching across the lawns in Pendenning. Would Mother tell Charity I had eloped? My stomach tightened. I could just see Father leaning against the mantelpiece, telling Mother he was scouring the countryside, following every lead, doing everything in his power to find me. I could hear his well-practised lies, his smooth tongue assuring her everything was being conducted with the utmost discretion and no hint of scandal could possibly arise.

I sealed the letter using the seal on the desk, but smudging it with my finger to prevent it being recognised. I wrote *Mrs Jennings, care of Mrs Pengelly, Combe House, Fosse* clearly across it and reached for my cloak, pulling the bell-cord as I blew the ink dry. My purse was still safely down my bodice.

'Ye want something, Miss Wells?'

'Ah, Hannah, yes, two things – no, three. First, do you have a large bonnet I can borrow until I get my own?'

'Ye're welcome to the one I wear to chapel – it's that ugly no-one will look at yer.' She seemed to fill the room with her energy, her smile immediately conspiratorial.

'Does it have a veil?'

'I can add some grey lace to cover yer face completely – wouldn't be the first time I was asked to do that!'

'Perfect. And is the post office still open?'

'Stays open till ten.'

'Could you take me there?'

'Do ye have money for stamps? Only Mr Reith left ye this.' She handed me a purse. 'He says ye're as like to have no money.'

'I do have money but only a five-pound note. I suppose that would draw too much attention?'

She threw her head back and laughed. 'Lord love ye, Miss Wells, stay close to me and don't let no-one have sight nor sound of yer five-pound note.' She seemed genuinely amused, taking hold of my arm, ushering me down the stairs and into the kitchen. 'Here's Miss Wells, Mamm,' she said, pushing me proudly forward. 'Miss Wells needs the post office so I said I'd take her.'

Mrs Hambley curtseyed deeply, wiping her hands on her apron, her eyes showing the respect her daughter obviously found unnecessary. She was a short woman, almost as broad as she was

325

tall, her pink cheeks aglow with health. 'Miss Wells, ye're very welcome. I hope yer room's to yer liking. I'm making rabbit pie and I've a lovely apple tart for yer supper.' The kitchen table groaned with produce. Flour dusted a large board, a rolling pin lay abandoned next to a pile of uncooked pastry. It seemed so strange, as if I was seeing everything through new eyes.

'My room's lovely, thank you. I suppose I need to ask the tariff?'

'No tariff, Miss Wells,' replied Mrs Hambley, smiling broadly. 'Mr Reith took all the rooms – paid for the lot, so Mrs Thomas don't get disturbed.' She lowered her voice, whispering proudly, 'Mr Reith knows we say nothing. Honest, Miss Wells, we're that happy to have ye.' She picked up her rolling pin, slamming it into the pile of pastry. 'Don't ye go taking Miss Wells all over the place, Hannah. Mind ye take her just to the post office an' back.'

There was nothing in Hannah's smile to indicate anything of the sort. She delved into a basket and drew out some lace, pinning it in place on her Sunday bonnet. She handed it to me and winked. 'Straight to the post office an' back.'

We passed through the garden, the hens gathering by the entrance of their henhouse. Hannah linked her arm through mine and we walked briefly down the muddy back path, cutting up through a lane to the main street. 'Mr Reith can do no wrong in our eyes. Our Ben was guilty – he'd done it alright, but Mr Reith got him off. They couldn't prove it was him so the jurymen gave him not guilty,' she said, smiling. 'He's going to break our hearts, the lousy toad.'

'Your brother or Mr Reith?'

'Me brother, of course,' she replied, laughing. 'Mamm thinks he's working down Falmouth Docks – unloading cargo. He's unloading cargo, right enough, but not at the docks!'

'You mean he's…?'

'The money he sends can't be lawfully earned. Not that much. Ye see, we've all got secrets. We never look and we never see. We certainly never tell. Could be us one day – ye get my meaning?'

The street was even busier than before, huge crowds standing round a lit fire, the smell of roasting meat wafting across the air. Musicians were playing by the roadside, a huge bare-chested man with a leopard skin round his shoulders juggling with lit torches. Flames were flying high in the air above him. 'Don't know why the circus players are here – it's market day tomorrow but it's not usually this busy. Here, don't let's be parted,' she said, grabbing my arm. 'Stick close and mind that purse I gave ye. There's thieves and pocket-pinchers everywhere.'

We pushed our way through the groups of men spilling from the taverns. Children played catch, women gossiped in huddles, nudging each other, throwing back their heads in sudden laughter. The steady stream of carts had lessened and only a few smart carriages were making their way slowly down the road. I turned round, looking quickly at a passing man. It was the briefest of glimpses but he looked familiar. It was Jacques, I was sure of it. I held Hannah back, searching the crowd, but he had rushed past so quickly and was out of sight. I was probably mistaken, the gathering dusk making it hard to see clearly.

My heart was still racing from the sight of him, a prick of fear running down my spine. It would always be like this – if not Jacques, Arnaud. If not Father, Phillip Randall. My freedom was illusionary. I would always be looking over my shoulder, watching my step. My joy turned to anxiety. Walk with your head bowed. No straight back or haughty expression. I had so much to learn.

At the door to the post office I pulled Hannah back. Marcus Babbinger was leaning against the counter, talking to a man emptying the post bag. Smoke from his pipe coiled around him and he looked in no hurry to go. 'Is there ... is there any one you'd trust with your life?' I whispered.

She nodded, understanding me at once, pulling me quickly back into the street and guiding me down a lane lined with blacksmiths. At the dip in the road we jumped the rivulet and started walking up a slight incline. The path widened to grass, the smell of dung strong and powerful. It was darker now, the light fading fast, only a few lanterns lighting the main street behind us. 'Ye can trust Adam Tremayne.'

'Is he your beau?'

She threw her head back and laughed. *Do beaux come covered in pig-shit, Miss Wells?* she answered in her cut-glass accent. *I rather think not...!* Don't ye tell him, mind – it's what's under the pig-shit what matters.' We crossed a yard and she pushed open a stable door. A young man was shovelling muck, piling it high on a barrow, the muscles on his naked chest clearly visible through the dying light. 'See what I mean?' she whispered. 'I've watched him at the pump, too.'

A man with a shovel, a man diving for lobsters, we both had our secret dreams. He saw us and stopped, grabbing his shirt before coming towards us. He was tall, muscular with thick brown hair and gentle eyes. Yes, I could trust him.

'Hannah! What a pleasure,' he said, smiling from ear to ear, not even a glance in my direction. 'This is a lovely surprise.'

'No surprise,' she replied coyly, 'I've come on purpose. Miss Wells needs a letter delivering. Will ye do it?'

'Of course,' his voice was strong, seemingly educated. He looked intelligent, even dignified, standing there with muck streaking across his forehead, his boots ankle-deep in filth. 'Miss Wells,' he said, bowing in my direction.

He had manners, too, and a nice smile. His eyes were honest, his attention immediately caught but without the slightest hint of self-interest or greed. Yes, I could trust him. 'My letter's to go to Mrs Jennings in Fosse. She must be handed it personally – don't leave it with anyone else. You understand?'

He nodded, his face serious. 'I understand.'

'No-one else must read it. If she's not there, could you find where she is and find her? I've good money – very good money. I can pay you well for your service.'

He smiled. 'If you're a friend of Hannah, then all the money I need is for the horse and something to eat. I can leave when I'm done – I've no more than an hour left to work.'

Hannah smiled, taking some money out of the purse I held open for her. It was as if she had guessed I would not know how much a horse would cost to hire, or a pie and ale. She took hardly anything, two crowns, maybe three. 'Adam Tremayne, ye're as daft as ye're sweet,' she said, placing the coins in his filthy hand. 'What's to be done with ye? All heart and no sense – and don't go getting pig-shit on that letter.' She turned to leave, smiling back at him. 'Ye're a good man, though, and I'm that grateful.'

A lost man, that was for certain. We walked back towards the main street. 'That's the debtor's gaol,' she said, pointing to the tall walls beside us. 'Adam's old man's in there. He went bankrupt a year back. It wasn't his fault – it was the greed of other people, but that's all it takes. One lying toad and everything's gone. Adam can't get work now – not proper work. He stays for his mamm, but they'll not give him work. The family's ruined.'

'That's terrible. I like him, Hannah.'

'So do I,' she said, smiling that rogue smile. 'Poor Mamm, it's going to break her heart when I marry him an' not the ones she's got lined up fer me!' She laughed, linking her arm once more through mine. 'And that's *after* I tell her I'm goin' to be an actress! Come, let's see what that crowd's all about. Something's going on – the town's too busy for just market day.'

We pushed our way through the revellers, walking slowly back to the house. A loud bell jangled behind us and a man's voice rose above the din. 'Hear ye, hear ye, hear ye ... tomorrow morning at the eighth hour of the twenty-third day of the eleventh month in the year of our Lord seventeen hundred and ninety three, Robert Roskelly will be taken from Bodmin Gaol and transported through the streets to Five Ways Gibbet where he will be hung from the neck until he dies...'

The crowd roared their approval, the band breaking into a lively jig. As people joined hands, ready to dance, Hannah drew me closer. 'We'd best get home – it gets too rowdy when there's a hanging.' She kept my arm firmly through hers, almost dragging me through the jostling crowd.

At the back door she paused. 'Poor Mrs Thomas ... I feel that sorry for her.' She seemed shocked by my look of surprise. 'Robert Roskelly's Alice Polcarrow's brother. I thought ye'd know that.'

Her beautiful frown cleared. 'Oh, I see – ye didn't think we know who Mrs Thomas is.'

Chapter Forty

Bodmin
Saturday 23rd November 1793, 7:15 a.m.

If Alice Polcarrow had slept at all, it would be a miracle. I had spent the night disturbed by revellers, the early hours woken by the crowd gathering outside my window. Already people were lining the street, two or three deep, each wrapped in a heavy cloak. With baskets of food at their feet, they were all there to watch the hanging and I shivered at the thought. Poor Alice.

A slight knock. 'Do I wake ye, Miss Wells? Oh, I see ye're up already.'

'Has everyone come to watch? It's so gruesome.'

''Tis good for business, the town makes money – the toll gates, the shopkeepers – everyone. Like I told ye, there's not a room to be had for love nor money. Traders do better at a hanging than they do all month and farmers love a hanging – hogs get roasted, pies get eaten, beer gets drunk. Honest, it's that busy for the town. If ye weren't here, we'd have filled yer room double.'

'It's horrible – it's just as bad as watching the guillotine. Is Mrs Thomas awake?'

'She is, poor lady. I've taken her some tea – here, drink yers. I shouldn't wonder if ye didn't sleep at all last night.'

'Is Mrs Thomas watching?'

Hannah nodded. 'She's the shutter back, just like ye have. She's watching all right.'

I tied the borrowed dressing gown round me, taking my tea with me as I slipped across the hall. Knocking on Alice's door, I pushed it gently open. 'Would you like company?' I asked softly.

She was standing by the window, wrapped in a blue silk housecoat, her thick hair falling round her shoulders. She had a brush in one hand, a miniature of a young boy in the other. She turned at my entrance and smiled. 'I don't suppose you slept either,' she said.

'No, and it's not even my brother they're hanging. I can't imagine how you must feel. Can I be of any comfort to you?'

She continued brushing her hair, the early sunlight catching the copper streaks, making them glow. 'Not really, but you can keep me company if you like – I'm always glad of company ... but as to comfort...' She turned round, staring down the street at the sound of cheering. 'There can be no comfort until he's dead.' Her words sliced through the air like ice. 'For my sake and the sake of my son, hanging's too good for him – I hope he suffers. Are you shocked?'

I stood beside her, putting my hand on hers, lifting the miniature portrait to the light. 'Your son's a lovely boy. I saw him that night in the stable. No, I'm not shocked. Was your brother cruel to you?'

She nodded, her lips pursed. 'I hope you never know such cruelty, Miss Cavendish, though I rather suspect you might. Have you run from Viscount Vallenforth? If that's the case, then you have my full support. Run for your life, escape cruelty by every means. Once they have you, they feed on your fear, delighting in every fresh quiver, every jump, every false hope they raise.' Her voice was hard, cold, her words ringing more true than she could possibly imagine.

'My brother was a cruel and ambitious man – he still is. I was seventeen when he thrust me like a tasty morsel on a plate in front of Sir Francis Polcarrow. Francis was thirty years my senior, a man of influence and power – a man who'd never remarried, despite every attempt from the high and lowly. But somehow I caught his eye.' She stopped, her face softening to a radiant smile, 'Me, simple Alice Roskelly, daughter of a penniless squire, too full of drink to see to his estates ...

kind, gentle Alice Roskelly, too naive and trusting to imagine her brother's cruelty.'

Her words puzzled me. 'Didn't you like Sir Francis?'

'Like him? I adored him. My only wish was to please him. I loved everything about him – his manner to me, his sense of justice, his compassion for those with nothing. He had suffered so long from his wife's death and I was his new solace. We loved each other ... so deeply. People thought me too young but our age meant nothing. My son was born only ten months later.' Her eyes narrowed, her mouth clamping hard with hatred.

'I'm sorry ... it must have been so awful for you–'

'My brother murdered him, Celia, in cold blood. He made it out to be a riding accident – claimed Francis had misjudged a low branch when he galloped under it and I never, ever guessed. Francis was a powerful rider but I just accepted the evidence – believed what he said. In truth, it was my brother who swung the log that killed him.' Her voice hardened. 'After he murdered Francis he set up another deception. He lured James down an alley and had him attacked. Again he got away with twisting the truth, he said James had attacked *him* and laid charges of grievous bodily harm and attempted murder against him. Again his deception worked and James was transported but thankfully not hung. Robert took over the estate and I had absolutely no idea of his evil. But now ... now his crime's come to light and he's going to hang for it.'

A chill passed over me. Father and Robert Roskelly were good company for each other. Alice Polcarrow stared at the miniature in her hands.

'I had just over a year with my dearest Francis, then twelve long years living under the constant threat of cruelty. Robert took everything from me – everything. If I complained, he would threaten to hurt my son, or, worse still, would threaten to have him taken from me. I lived in fear ... slept in fear, keeping my son in my room for as long as I could. I jumped at my own shadow, every day watching my brother grow in influence.' She held the miniature to the light, her son's eyes gazing back at her. 'But until my son came of age, he was his guardian – just one word about not being a fit mother and who knows where I'd be.'

She would be in Maddison's Madhouse – that was where she would be. Along with every other woman who tried to cross the path of a greedy, ambitious man. 'He'll be gone soon,' I whispered. 'Not long now and you'll be free of him.'

Her laugh was brittle. 'Last night I didn't sleep because I was scared he would escape again. Can you imagine that? Only when I hear the crowd roar will I be free from him, no longer living under his constant shadow. My dreams are full of terrible dread – dread that he'll escape and come back for me. He thinks he owns me. He killed my dog and threatened my child and truly believed I would poison James – that's how certain he is of his power over me.'

'*Was* certain but not any more,' I replied firmly. 'He's no hold over you now.' The crowd stirred, straining their necks, looking expectantly along the street. From our window we could see the distant crossroads and a ladder placed against the gallows. Three men were climbing slowly up it, edging their way across the triangular frame, tying a large rope round one of the beams. I looked away, the sound of a slow drum suddenly making my heart thump. 'What's that?' I asked.

'He's on the wagon,' she said slowly. 'Matthew explained it all to me yesterday. They'll take him from the gaol, down round the church, then through the town for everyone to get their full. He'll be handed drinks but mainly he'll be pelted with rotten fruit. The drummer walks by the side of the cart. He'll drum the whole way – it means they've started.'

'It's a horrible sound.'

'I've waited long enough to hear it. You don't like Matthew very much, do you?'

'I don't know him. My first impression is that he's very severe, but that's not a bad thing. I think I was a bit rude to him and I must apologise because he left me money for my letter. I've written to Mother telling her I'm safe and well and coming home soon. She'll be furious but I've done it before, several times – that's why they need to marry me off. Before anyone hears of my little adventures.'

Alice smiled. 'Matthew may think you're empty-headed and bored, but I'm not so convinced. You've shrewd eyes, Celia. There's nothing empty-headed about you at all.'

'Thank you,' I said, smiling back. 'And if we're talking shrewd eyes, then yes, I do see a lot of things. You know Matthew Reith's in love with you, don't you?'

A blush spread across her cheeks. 'Celia, really. He's just a good friend ... there's nothing between us. He's still grieving for his wife.'

'When did she die?'

'Two years ago. She died of fever – he has two young daughters.' Her hands were trembling.

'And he's left London to start again in Cornwall?' I said softly. 'He may still be grieving but his daughters need a mother and your son needs a father – and he admires you, anyone can see that.'

'Do you think so?'

I put my hand on hers. She felt cold, fragile, her courage hiding her desperate need. 'Yes I do,' I whispered.

The drumming grew louder, the jeers beginning to turn frantic. From our vantage point we could see the cart move slowly up the street. Men in black sashes walked in front, gesturing to the crowd to keep back. To no avail, it seemed. The crowd kept pressing forward, elbowing each other to get a better view. Pie-sellers stopped selling, turning to watch, and pedlars put down their wares, resting their arms on their barrows. Even the children stopped running and stood shaking their fists at the approaching cart.

Alice Polcarrow's eyes hardened. Robert Roskelly sat hunched on one side, his handcuffed hands desperately fending off the torrent of rotten fruit landing on his blue jacket. The once-immaculate lace at his neck, the frills at his wrists stained purple-red. People had come for miles to make sport of a hanging. He may be loathsome but the brutality of the crowd left me reeling and

I shivered in horror.

The cart stopped outside the White Hart and a jug of ale was handed to him through the rails. As Robert Roskelly gulped it down, Alice drew me quietly away. 'I've seen enough,' she said, taking hold of my arm and leading me back to her table and chairs. She sat down, all colour drained from her face.

Never had time stood so still, every minute lasting an eternity, every drum beat making my heart thump. The cart passed more slowly than ever, the crowd surging behind it, working their way slowly to the field where the five roads crossed. The old gibbet, Hannah had called it, positioned high on the hill with a good view of the gaol on one side, the town on the other. It could be seen from miles and miles, the men left hanging in irons, pecked by birds long after their lingering death. But Robert Roskelly was lucky. Times had moved on – he had the gallows and a cart. The horse would be whipped and the cart would jerk quickly away.

An uncanny silence fell and Alice Polcarrow reached for my hand. It felt almost unreal, an eerie quiet after all the shouting. Robert Roskelly would be standing under the gallows, his wig thrown to the crowd. The noose would be round his neck, the last prayer being slowly recited. Alice's grip was like iron, her eyes tightly shut. A pulse throbbed at her neck, a fast pulse that matched my own. Then we heard it – the sudden cheer, the thunderous roar echoing from the crossroads and across the town.

'It's done,' she said, letting go of my hand.

Chapter Forty-one

Bodmin
Saturday 23rd November 1793, 4:00 p.m.

The parlour downstairs was rather cosy. I had never sat in a parlour before but I liked the simplicity of the open fire. One wall was kept as stone, the others painted with limewash. The assorted colours in the rug seemed cheerful and inviting and the chairs were comfortable, the cushions plumped up every time we left them. A shaft of sunlight filtered through the window.

'It's easier to come from the top – if you pull your thread upward, you can't loop the bottom stich so easily. Here, let me show you again – you've nearly got it.' Hannah watched carefully, taking hold of her embroidery again. 'Yes, just like that. Now, thread it round the needle and pull it back ... but make sure you pick up that bottom stitch. There, perfect.'

She smiled. 'I said Mamm would love ye – she loves anyone teaching me to be genteel. *Ye needs learn from them,* she says. Poor Mamm wants me to be a lady. Oh bollocks – I've got blood all over it.'

The door opened. 'Ah, Hannah, yer stitchin's coming on lovely.'

'She has real talent, Mrs Hambley, very dainty and lady-like.'

Mrs Hambley beamed with pleasure. 'Ye really think so, Miss Wells? Well I'll be blest. Did ye hear that, Hannah? Ye get as dainty an' lady-like as ye can get. I'll take that tray, shall I? Mr Reith said four o'clock an' he's never late. That'll be him now – clear yer stitching, Hannah.'

Hannah winked as she rose. Alice was blushing. Had she really no idea of Matthew Reith's feelings?

'Go on through, Mr Reith, the ladies are waitin'. Ye knows yer way.'

He had obviously been rushing, his face was flushed, a sense of urgency ruffling his usual composure. He bowed to us in turn, but his eyes rested on Alice. 'I'm sorry I wasn't here. I'd have liked, so much, to be with you. Are you alright?'

She smiled sweetly, her hair catching the light, her green silk gown shimmering round her. 'I'm very alright, thank you, Matthew.' Her voice seemed more timid than before, as if she was shy of him for the first time. 'I feel nothing but relief and I wasn't alone, Celia was with me – we've become very well acquainted.'

'Good, I'm glad,' he said, turning much sterner eyes on me. 'I think I owe you an apology, Miss Cavendish. I checked the tides and you were right and I've been talking with Sir James.'

'That's wonderful – how is he?' cried Alice.

'As well as can be expected, he's in a private cell which's something, at least.'

'And Rose?'

'She's very angry, but as well as can be expected.'

'I'm sorry ... I interrupted you ... please go on.'

He turned back to me. 'It's apparent you *do* have a habit of doing this sort of thing. Sir James is very grateful for your concern – he told me of your ridiculous flight to Falmouth, but I take it you saw the error of your ways?'

'I came straight back. The journey home was uneventful.'

'No Spanish galleon full of gold coins? No damsels needing rescuing from pirates?' There was not even a flicker of amusement in those grey eyes. It was a shame, he had a pleasant face but his scowl was his most noticeable feature. He turned to Alice. 'It's good news – we've won the right for a trial by jury.'

'I thought you said Sir Richard would never give way?'

'He nearly didn't. He claims his powers are absolute and, legally, that's true. He does have the right to apprehend and imprison anyone without further trial but they've made a grave error. The indictment accuses the Polcarrows of *corresponding with the enemy* – not just sedition and spying. It's in the wording and as clear as anything.'

'But why can that be good?'

'That charge – since May this year – instantly invokes the charge of high treason. I showed them the act itself. Sir Richard's furious, but there's nothing he can do.'

'But high treason's terrible.'

'It sounds terrible, Alice, but, actually, it isn't.' His voice softened. 'It sounds like the worst possible outcome but it's better for us. Anyone accused of high treason is entitled to a full trial with a defence council and a jury of twelve men ... and

341

what's also good is that our witnesses will be under oath. That's not usually the case and it's vital.'

'Have they agreed?'

Matthew opened his bag, rummaging through the many papers. 'Sir Richard's livid but he knows I'm right and he can't contest it. If he refuses, he knows I'll call for Habeas Corpus. Parliament hasn't suspended Habeas Corpus yet – though I suspect it's on the cards. Either way, they have to allow for a trial.'

'But treason, Matthew?' She put her handkerchief to her eyes. 'They'll hang if they're found guilty. How could anyone charge James with treason?'

Matthew Reith's eyes cut mine. 'It's a case of Crown versus Polcarrow, but we all know who's behind it.' I felt hot, the terrible reality making my stomach churn. I had to look away, unable to bear those piercing eyes. It was as if he knew how father worked, how the crown prosecuted and disposed of his victims. His voice turned hard. 'Every witness I call will be sworn under oath. Are you prepared to stand witness, Miss Cavendish? To have every newspaper salivate over the scandal? You'll be ruined. A daughter giving evidence against her father – it's unheard of.'

My mouth felt dry, my heart thumping painfully. It would ruin my family – my sisters and brother thrown like lambs to the wolves; one injustice bringing on another, my family tumbling around me like a pack of cards. No wonder people kept silent. No wonder eyes were closed, ears were shut. 'Of course I don't want that,' I said. 'Do you think me so stupid? But Sir James was good to me and Lady Polcarrow is my friend. If that's what it takes to stop my father hanging innocent people, then I've no choice but to stand in the witness box.'

Alice reached over and took my hand. Matthew Reith sniffed, clearly taken aback. 'Well I doubt it'll come to that. I won't call you, Miss Cavendish, unless I absolutely have to. I've better witnesses and I think, in all honesty, you'd be laughed out of the dock. No-one will believe you.' He took out a sheaf of papers. 'Here's our copy of the indictment. I've gone over it, again and again, and can't find anything I can legally challenge. We've five days from yesterday to prepare our defence – any time after that and we could be called to court. They've the right to withhold the names of their witnesses but we know from Miss Cavendish, *if we didn't already know,* they'll be false witnesses and paid for their trouble. We'll get the names of the jury at least two days before the trial so we can see if they've been especially chosen. It'll be just a matter of proving the witnesses are lying – they'll slip up, they always do.'

Alice smiled shyly at me, as if in apology. 'Have they heard of your reputation, Matthew?'

'I hope so.'

'James has so little trust in the judicial system. There's so much corruption out there.'

'Corruption and ignorance – both about the presumption of innocence and the need to prove a case beyond all reasonable doubt.' He paused. 'Are you still determined to take the stand, Alice?'

'I'm prepared to tell them everything – about the poison, why James had to pretend to be ill. I'll tell them everything, whatever it takes.'

'I hope it doesn't come to it, but I must prepare you if it does...' Again, more rummaging through the leather bag. 'These are the questions I'd ask you. Read them carefully and think through your answers.' He handed her a closely written page. 'Oh, and before I forget, this's for you, too ... it's a letter from Francis. Mother's written as well. The children are very settled and Francis has taken to fishing.' He smiled and my heart melted. Yes, he was just what Alice needed.

Hannah knocked on the door, popping her head round before we answered. 'Can ye stay for supper, Mr Reith? Ye better say ye can as Mamm's gone to so much trouble. Suet dumplings with apple an' custard an' raisin crusted scones. There's chicken pie, too, but she knows ye likes yer puddings and says ye need feeding up. Ye must stay.' She smiled angelically, leaving before he could answer.

I was clearly not the only one with my thoughts.

Chapter Forty-two

Bodmin
Sunday 24th November 1793, 10:30 a.m.

Hannah burst through the door, grabbing her embroidery, throwing herself on the chair. 'Tell her ye want me to stay,' she whispered. 'I can't be doing with chapel this morning.'

344

'Ah, Hannah, there ye are. Not ready? We'll be late ... where's yer bonnet, love?'

'Is that the time already?' she sighed. 'How time flies when ye're having so much fun. I can hardly bear to put this embroidery down an' Miss Wells, promising to teach me how to be lady-like – ye know, offering me deportment lessons an' all.'

'*Deportment lessons?*'

'Ye know, walking round with a book on me head, riding crops under me arms. How to get in an' out of a chair – stuff like that. So I catch the eye of a rich man an' marry well!'

Mrs Hambley was clearly torn. 'But, what about chapel, Hannah love?'

'Would it be very terrible if she stayed, Mrs Hambley? We do so enjoy Hannah's company. We were thinking of practising her curtseys, but if you can't spare her...'

Mrs Hambley's frown faded. 'No, Miss Wells ... ye just go on as ye are. Learn her what ye can.'

The door closed and Alice looked up from her sewing. 'I'm not sure which of you is worst and on Sunday as well! I thought girls loved going to church to get a glimpse of their young men.'

'Ye don't get to glimpse anyone at chapel. If ye did, ye'd be scolded and taken home and beaten – not by Mamm, she couldn't scold no-one, but Mrs Best would do it. Besides, we need to visit the well.'

Hannah rolled away her embroidery and began searching the sewing box, drawing out a jar of pins. 'We needs wish – all of us – but don't tell Mamm. She's not one for the well.' She held up the jar, shaking it firmly. 'Take a pin, that's it, anyone what catches yer eye.' She offered us the jar in turn. 'Now, bend it slowly and when ye bend it, make a wish. Any wish. Just make sure ye're wishing as ye bend it. Like this.' She closed her eyes, her lovely face turning serious. 'There ... now ye do it.'

'Hannah, really, it's almost pagan.'

''Tis no more than betting on two horses – me dad always did that and he always won! No-one's watching ... give it yer all, wish and bend ye pin.'

I held the pin between my fingers. I had only one wish. So, too, must Alice. We both closed our eyes, bending the pins. 'This is nonsense, Hannah.'

'No it ain't,' she said. 'Ye'll see – it'll come true. Now, who's coming to the well?'

We let Hannah go by herself but she took our pins and assured us they would work just as well. Alice went to her room to write a letter and without Hannah's chatter I felt strangely lonely, immediately regretting I had not gone with her. I felt restless, the beautiful sunshine drawing me to the garden. It was unseasonably warm for so late in November and I stood under an apple tree, the foreboding presence of the gaol adding to my unease.

The kitchen door opened and Mary came shuffling out, two baskets of produce grasped in each hand. The baskets were fully laden and obviously very heavy. 'Here, let me help,' I said, rushing to her side. 'They're very full.'

'The last of the potatoes – that's for the prison ... an' that's for the alms-house.' She smiled shyly and began staggering down the path.

'Let me help. We can go together.'

'That's kind of ye,' she said, putting them down. 'The alms-house is just down the road.'

The back lane was drier than before; the mud was caked, cracking down the centre. Behind the prison the hill rose gently. Sheep were grazing the higher moorland, gleaners picking over the newly cut corn. Young boys were chasing away the crows. A small stream followed the contours of the vale, a slight breeze blowing from the west. Church bells were ringing. We reached a wicket gate. The alms-house looked neglected; slates were missing, the windows cracked. 'I won't be a moment. Best ye wait here.'

She opened the gate and walked up the path, knocking loudly on the arched door. The garden looked tended but picked of all fruit, the once-neat rows of vegetables churned and yellowing. A single pig rooted through the mud. Mary gave the basket to a white-haired man and ran quickly back, chased by the pig. 'He nearly got me last time,' she said, her toothy grin making her look so much younger.

It seemed so strange. I had always wanted to be free, walk the streets, carry baskets and laugh about the simplest of things but as Mary took my baskets and smiled her goodbye, I felt strangely empty. I needed Hannah's laughter to keep me buoyant; left to myself my sorrow felt almost overwhelming. It was as if I was only just coming to terms with Father's cruelty. I missed Charity and Mrs Jennings so much. I was missing my life before any of this happened.

I pulled my cloak round me and took a deep breath. No. I did not miss being traded like chattel, Mother's constant control, her vicious tongue, her resentment of our youth. I did not miss Father's vulgarity, his boorish manners or his cruelty. I must not despair; Charity would marry Frederick and I could live with them.

The bells were still ringing, the street quiet. A woman was sweeping the steps of the bakery. Empty buckets hung on their ropes, and a huge pile of bricks lay guarded by a growling dog. I passed the White Hart and stopped for a cart, glancing back at the inn. I glanced again, but my eyes had not deceived me. Jacques was sitting by the window, his fingers drumming the table as if he was waiting for someone.

What was Jacques doing so far from the sea? Was he here to watch me? Who was he waiting for? Excitement made my heart race. It was always the same – the terrible need to fulfil my curiosity. Lowering my head, I entered the door of the inn and pushed through the crowd.

He was dressed for town; fawn jacket, tricorn hat, his hair tied neatly behind his neck. One hand was holding his tankard, the other resting on the table. He reached inside his coat and drew out a watch, frowning as he put it back. Taking one last gulp, he rose and gathered up his bag, reaching quickly for his coat. He wiped the froth from his mouth and I stood quickly back, hiding behind the wooden partition as he passed. I watched him mount the steps to the rooms above.

It had been so fleeting, one moment later and I would have missed him. I glanced at the clock, a half past twelve. My heart was racing. How long would somebody wait?

Hannah gathered up the tea tray. 'Yes, definitely. Put it straight into her hand.'

'Did she ask any questions?'

'No, just took it and thanked him. Offered him some food but he thought it best not to stay.'

'Will you thank him again? I can't tell you how grateful I am. Are you sure it was Mrs Jennings who took the letter?'

'Honest, I promise. Adam always tells the truth. He said he handed it straight to Mrs Jennings, so ye can be sure she got it.' She smiled and turned.

'Hannah, before you go. What coaches come here on Sunday? Around twelve o'clock?'

She looked surprised. 'No stagecoaches, but private ones come all the time. The stagecoach comes Monday, Wednesday and Friday – that's Falmouth to Exeter. Takes two days ... they dine going Exeter-way and sleep going Falmouth-way.'

'So only private coaches come here on Sunday?'

'If there's trade, or someone's willing to pay, they come any time ... the Truro coach comes 'bout that time ... and Yoxall's wagon from Padstow arrives 'bout twelve, The wagons come and go all hours, but no stagecoach.' She balanced the tray on her knee and opened the door. 'Cotton wharf's wagon comes about two and there's one what leaves for Launceston about then. The Fosse coach leaves at four.' Her smile had faded. 'Ye're not thinking of leaving us, are ye?'

'No, not at all.'

She smiled again, 'Good, because Mrs Thomas likes having ye here. And if ye're not giving evidence, shall I get us a place to watch the trial?'

'Thank you, Hannah, I'd like that.' My mind was racing. Truro or Padstow?'

Chapter Forty-three

Bodmin
Monday 25th November 1793, 11:00 a.m.

'You're very restless this morning, Celia, walking about and staring out of the window. Come and sit down, you're making me dizzy.'

'There's so much to watch. That inn's so busy – night and day. I wish I had a map. You don't suppose they've a map, do you?'

Alice put down her sewing. 'Why do you need a map?'

'I'd just like to know where we are, that's all ... and where Padstow and St Ives are ... and where Truro is. I don't know anything about Cornwall – just where Fosse is. I can't believe I didn't study the maps when I had the time.'

She smiled. 'I've stared at a print of Cornwall for so long, I have it by memory – here, let me draw it for you.' She crossed the room, sitting elegantly at her writing desk, dipping her pen into the ink. 'It's long and pointed, a bit like this. It starts with Launceston about here and Plymouth's almost directly below. Here's Fosse, down here ... it's more like this really, and Bodmin's here – almost in the middle.'

'And Truro ... and Padstow?'

'Truro's further down ... at the top of this river which goes to Falmouth,' she smiled. 'You know Falmouth, I believe, but Padstow's up here...'

I looked at her map. 'So Bodmin's exactly midway between Fosse and Padstow?'

'It's right between everywhere – you can see why all the turnpikes lead through it.'

I stared at her map. Not Truro. Jacques would have sailed to Falmouth and gone upriver. 'What's Padstow like?' I asked.

'I don't know. This is my first time even in Bodmin – Robert never allowed me to go anywhere...' Her voice hardened. 'Not to a single ball, a single concert. But I believe Padstow's a fishing town – it has a harbour. Why don't you ask Hannah?'

I stared at the map again. Padstow was on the north coast, the nearest port to Ireland. I glanced at the clock – a quarter past eleven. 'Do you feel like coming to buy a bonnet?' I said as lightly as I could. 'It's just that I can't borrow Hannah's all the time.'

'No, my dear, take Hannah with you. I'm quite content with my sewing.'

I shut the door and raced across the landing, picking up my cloak and borrowed hat. It was already half past eleven and the wagon could come at any moment. Two empty baskets lay on the dresser so I grabbed the nearest, walking quickly into the garden and down the path.

The street was full of packhorses laden with corn and furze. Carriages and several smart curricles rushed past at great speed, but none of them stopped at the White Hart. Travellers were waiting outside and men with carts stood, beer in hand, flirting with the wenches from the inn. It was so much colder than yesterday, the sky laden with ominous black clouds. I wrapped my cloak around me and pushed through the door.

The tobacco smoke was thick and choking. The fires had been lit and people stood warming their hands, calling for ale. My eyes were immediately drawn to a group of women surrounded by bags and baskets and I decided to join them. I sat facing the window. From there I had a good view of the street and a perfect view of Jacques.

He was sitting in exactly the same place, wearing the same clothes, carrying the same bag. The Truro coach had just arrived and he looked up, his ale poised in the air. He pulled out his watch and checked the time. He was trying to act normally – just the occasional look over his shoulder – but his eyes were watchful and I could tell he was nervous. The passengers dismounted and the driver whipped the reins, directing the horses through the arch. Once again the street was clear.

At once Jacques stiffened. A huge wagon with Yoxall painted down the side was lumbering down the street. It was heavily laden, the four horses straining to take its weight. Three men sat next to the driver, another four passengers sitting facing the rear – a woman with a child, an old man and a huge man with dark features and curly black hair.

Jacques stood up, staring through the window, as the passengers alighted. The dark, curly-haired man had a bag in one hand, his coat over his other arm. He walked, not towards the door, but towards the window where he stood deliberating whether to come in or not. I watched them both carefully. They showed no sign of recognition; no nod, no smile, just blank faces looking past each other as if the other was not there. Suddenly Jacques turned for his coat and came brushing past me in his hurry to leave. As he flew past, I saw the button was missing from his top lapel.

My heart jumped. The same button had been missing on his jacket on the boat. It was too much of a coincidence. It must be their sign, their way of recognising each other. Jacques was halfway across the crowded inn and already disappearing through the door to the stables. The man from the wagon was at the front door, waiting his turn to enter. They were deliberately missing each other – one in, one out, no chance to be seen together, no way to be linked.

My mind was racing. It seemed so strange. Why wait all this time then leave so abruptly? I looked back at the bench. Jacques' bag was still underneath the seat. I could see the strap poking out from the dark recess beneath the window. I felt suddenly breathless. This was not a meeting but an exchange and that bag contained information the Irish must never get.

I looked quickly round. Jacques was nowhere to be seen and I saw my chance. I hardly thought what I was doing My heart was racing. Walking straight to the bench, I reached down, lifting the

bag quickly onto my lap, hiding it under my
cloak. Tightening my cloak, I walked slowly back
to the women's bench and picked up my basket.
The women were chatting, thrusting a baby in
my direction and I smiled at the baby, nodding at
the mother.

The traveller went straight to the seat, settling
himself down, holding up his hand to call for
some beer. He was a big man, late thirties, with
black curly hair. He had blue eyes and a larger
than average nose. He leant back, taking in the
room, his jovial smile not reaching his eyes. My
eyes were drawn straight to his missing button. I
was right.

His foot was trying to locate the bag. I saw a
sudden look of concern cloud his face and from
under the rim of my bonnet I watched his
concern turn to panic. He started looking round,
staring intently at everyone, judging the best time
to search under the bench. I sat smiling at the
baby, tickling his tummy, his delighted gurgles
making everyone laugh. Across the room the man
visibly paled, his eyes darting from person to
person. The baby gurgled and squealed, bringing
more laughter.

Another coach pulled up outside, the grooms
rushing from the stables to change the horses. As
the travellers dismounted, the women around me
began gathering up their belongings and I stood
holding the baby while everything was collected.
The mother had a bag and another child so I
nodded, indicating I would hold the baby a little
longer. I knew not to look his way. From the
corner of my eye, I saw his frantic searching, his

head bobbing up and down as he looked under the seats.

I handed the woman her baby and waved her goodbye. The coach was crowded, a mountain of bags and baskets piling ever higher, acting as the perfect screen. I crossed behind it, walking slowly past the house and round the back path. No-one followed me. As I walked up the path it started to rain.

'Just in time – that's quite a downpour. Did, ye find a bonnet, Miss Wells?' Mrs Hambley asked as she closed the door.

'No, I got a bit lost. Perhaps Hannah can join me next time.'

'Don't you go lettin' Hannah nowhere near that shop,' she laughed, 'or ye'll come back with all sorts of feathers and frills. Here, let me take yer cloak, and would ye like something to drink?'

'No thank you,' I said smiling. 'And my cloak's not wet at all.'

I walked quickly upstairs, shutting my door, going straight to the window to peer down. The coach had gone, the crowd dispersed, the street now empty. My whole body was tingling. I felt flushed with excitement, the danger more thrilling than I could ever imagine. My hands were shaking, my heart pounding but I had done it. I threw off my cloak and stared at the bag – at the indented holes spiralling in three lines round the base. If it was not exactly identical to Arnaud's, it was from the same workshop.

I tipped the contents onto my bed. There was a quill, an ink pot, a small leather notebook. I grabbed the notebook and flicked through its pages, once, twice, my desperation rising. The pages were empty, completely unused. There was no writing at all – *just 4:15 return coach* written on the first page. I laid it carefully on the bed and picked up the ink pot, opening it carefully so not to spill it. It matched the writing and the tip of the quill. A rush of disappointment flooded through me. This was not correspondence at all – just the time of his return coach.

But they were clever, I knew that. I looked again, remembering the talk of secret codes, musical scores, invisible ink. Rushing to the window, I held up the pages, desperate to see a message written in lemon juice. There was nothing. I would try candlelight. Fumbling for the tinder box, I struck the flint, holding the candle as close to the pages as possible. I stared at the pages, holding them against the candle but still nothing. The pages were blank. Nor was there a secret compartment in the bag; a false bottom or a lining that could be torn from the side.

I put the contents carefully back in the bag and hung it behind my dressing gown. Footsteps sounded on the stairs. 'Is that you, Hannah?'

'It is,' she replied, panting heavily.

'Do any coaches leave at four-fifteen?'

'Lord love ye, Miss Wells. Ye *do* want to leave. Just tell me where ye want to go and I'll tell ye what coach to get.'

'I'm not going anywhere, I promise. I'm interested, that's all.'

She looked as if she had heard it all before. 'There's nothing from the White Hart – not then. The Falmouth stagecoach leaves at two and the coach to Fosse is four. The wagons go back tomorrow an' the Truro coach is six.' She drew more breath, her hands on her hips. 'There's more from the Blue Hart but not around four. Launceston's eight in the morning and three in the afternoon. Where d'you want to go? Honest, ye secret's safe.'

I smiled, trying to hide my disappointment. 'I'm not going anywhere.'

'Good, 'cos I came to tell ye I can get us in to the courts – it's going to cost us and we've got to be quick. Honest to God, the bugger's making a fortune. I usually get in for free but everyone's clamourin' at his door and he's asking a shilling each. Can ye spare that?'

I rushed to the table and grabbed my purse. 'You know I can. Pay whatever it takes. A shilling, whatever – we have to get in.'

Chapter Forty-four

Bodmin
Tuesday 26th November 1793, 9:00 a.m.

My nightmare was so vivid. We had been running, Charity laughing behind me. It was mischievous, happy laughter, me holding Charity by the hand, both of us running down the corridor, hiding from Georgina. Then it had gone dark. We were in a wood, a forest, the gnarled tree trunks twisting in front of me. I was still running but Charity's

357

hand was slipping from mine and I could not hold her. She was slipping further and further away. My feet were sinking and I could do nothing but watch her disappear from view.

'Would ye like some more tea? Ye haven't drunk the last lot.'

I was calling her name. Then I saw Father. He was standing by the gallows, laughing, holding his hands on his belly. Someone was to be hung. I was screaming but no sound came. I was trying to run but my legs would not move.

'There now, drink this ... are ye alright, Miss Wells?'

'What time is it?'

'Just gone nine and ye're not alright. Ever since ye've got here ye've had sad eyes.'

Sad eyes, broken heart. My future was turned on its head. I thought always to protect Charity, keep her safe. As a child I promised never to leave her, yet, not once, but twice, I had left with no word. I tried to calm my terrible fear. Charity had Mrs Jennings and Frederick; they would never let Mother make her marry Viscount Vallenforth. But what if Mrs Jennings had been unsuccessful? What if I had not done enough to secure Charity's happiness?

'This is lovely...' I said, sipping my tea. I began to think rationally. Charity was strong and resilient; my timid little sister was no longer a child. She had stood up to Mother with the courage of a lion. She was intelligent and beautiful and would be loved wherever she went. The familiar pain shot through me – it was I who had no-one.

'When I'm an actress and needs be sad, I'll

think on ye. I'll act all brave and happy, but me eyes will look sad.' She smiled. 'Mamm tells me ye're after a new bonnet – well, I know just the place. Ye'll want feathers an' frills an' why not a robin like the one ye keep watching?'

'You can't put a robin on a bonnet!'

'Yes ye can. Ye can do anything ye want. Ye can put a whole nest on if ye like.'

'I'm not in the mood for shopping.' I was thinking of another actress, every bit as convincing as Hannah would be. One that could curtsey with the grace of a duchess, incline her long neck at just the right angle. Madame Merrick had learnt her trade well, so too, had Arnaud. Both of them fooling me so entirely; they must have watched the émigrés, copying them exactly. 'Why don't I keep your hideous bonnet and you buy yourself a new one? I can give you my money ... put anything you like on it ... apples, pears, I know you like fruit.'

No, I couldn't ... wouldn't be right, me having all the fun an' ye so sad.'

'No, honestly, I'd rather wear your bonnet to court – it'll keep me well hidden.'

She nodded, her eyes full of compassion. 'Ye really don't want to be seen, do ye? Well, ye can have me old bonnet with pleasure but ... if ye'll not come shoppin' then, at least, let me sort yer hair.'

I joined Alice in the parlour, my freshly washed hair catching me off guard. Hannah had cut and dressed it in a new style and I kept glancing at my reflection. Curls framed my face, bobbing around me, anything but curtailed. It made me feel lighter, brighter. Alice had immediately liked it and so did I.

'And Hannah's going to buy me a new dress. There's a shop selling handed-down dresses – like the ones we give away. I thought maids kept them to wear for best but they don't, they sell them and keep the money.'

'Of course they do, my dear. The money's far more important to them. Come, read this to me, the print's too small and I've left my magnifier upstairs.'

I spread the newspaper flat on the table. It was another stormy day, the sky still ominously black. Hardly any light was coming through the window and I needed the candle. I caught a headline on the first page. 'Did you read this? The French *Law of Suspects?* Any known or suspected enemy of the Revolution will be arrested.'

'How dreadful! Matthew says the Revolution's just a transfer of power into the hands of the greedy. The peasants thought they'd have a better life but they're worse off. He says the slaughter will go on.'

'*All avowed enemies, or likely enemies.*' I read the paragraphs that followed. 'It seems everyone must fear for their lives.'

'It's quite unimaginable. I fear for the young Dauphin – it must be petrifying. But, tell me ... are the court cases listed?

'Bodmin Courts, Wednesday 27th November ... *non-repair of highways ... misdemeanour ... non-repair of highways ... misdemeanour ... stealing goods...* There's nothing about Sir James.'

'Then it won't be tomorrow. Is there anything under the social pages?'

I stopped. The page opposite contained the social calendar for Truro and my eyes were drawn to the first entry. *It is with regret that owing to the sudden illness of Miss Celia Cavendish, Lady April Cavendish announces the postponement of her daughter's wedding to Viscount Vallenforth.* I stared at those three lines without a quiver of remorse. Mother would be in such turmoil and I felt not the slightest sympathy. There was another entry, further down the page. *Lady Carew is to host another splendid concert in aid of the new hospital. As patroness to the Hospital Charity Commission, this will be her third concert and, if the last two are anything to go by, expectations are high. Tickets are all sold.*

'Does it mention James at all?'

I looked back at the Bodmin page. 'Nothing about Sir James ... it's mainly about the ball tonight at Priory House. There's a long list of people expected to attend... *Sir William Molesworth ... Lord Camelford ... Colonel William Morshead...* Oh, look! *Sir Richard Goldsworthy's to be the guest of honour.*'

Alice jumped to her feet. 'They're closing ranks round Sir Richard – not one of them's sympathetic to James.'

I nodded but my hands were shaking. Father's name was next on the list. He was in Bodmin.

Alice turned sharply, looking out of the window. 'Wasn't that Matthew? He said he wouldn't come today.' Our eyes caught.

'He must have news.'

Chapter Forty-five

Matthew Reith looked tired, even gaunter, his hair slightly dishevelled. There was mud on his shoes and dust on his travelling coat. He held out his hands to Alice, taking hers gently in his as he led her back to the chair. 'It's tomorrow. I've just got back from Falmouth and found a note on my desk.'

'Tomorrow...? It isn't listed.'

'No ... they think to catch me off guard, but, legally, it's within the time frame. I've been given the list of jurymen and will go over their names very carefully. If I can't prove any patronage, I'll have to approve them.' He sounded as tense as he looked. 'Ah, thank you, Hannah,' he said, handing her his coat.

'There's whortleberry cake comin' . Ye're needs must eat, Mr Reith. Ye look that tired and ye need yer strength.'

He smiled back at her, 'I won't say no, Hannah.'

Alice had paled. 'Falmouth?'

'I went last night. I had to. What a journey! The roads are in a terrible state but we're back, thank God, and I've brought the witnesses.'

'Have you got everyone you need? Are you ... are you ... *hopeful?*' She reached for her handkerchief, her beautiful eyes filled with tears.

Anxiety flashed across his face. 'Yes, and so

must you be. I'll just keep going until I prove their witnesses are false. I'm known as The Terrier – I'll keep snapping at their heels until they trip! And they will trip, Alice, I promise you.' His love for his friend was driving him, but it was obvious his admiration for Alice was the spur.

'And I am to stand?' Alice said, looking into his eyes.

'If you feel you can.'

'I can, Matthew. Don't think, for one minute, I'm not prepared to tell the world about my brother's ill-doings. And Jenna, will she stand?'

He nodded. 'There'll be two cases. My intention is to get James cleared so Lady Polcarrow's case will be a swift, almost cursory affair – if one's not guilty, then neither's the other.' He smiled and reached for her hand. 'The prosecuting counsel's John Wallis. I've come across him before and I must warn you, he can be very rude. Remember, don't take it personally. Rise above his taunts and answer everything in a level-headed, quiet and dignified manner.'

Alice nodded. 'Will I go first?'

'No, I'll call you *only* if I have to. I don't know who the prosecution are bringing as witnesses but I know they're calling Dr Trefusis.'

'Oh, Matthew, I'm so scared.'

He took her hand back in his. 'The trial's scheduled for two o'clock. I want you to get to the courts for half past one. Go to the ante-chamber, round the back, and my clerk will see you settled. You'll sit at the front with the other witnesses.'

'And Celia?'

He looked at me, the softness draining from his

eyes. 'Miss Cavendish can sit where she likes. I'm not calling you, Miss Cavendish. Your father's to sit on the prosecution bench.'

True North

Chapter Forty-six

Bodmin court
Wednesday 27th November 1793,
12:30 p.m.

I could hardly breathe. We had no space, every-one pushing and elbowing each other. Without Hannah I would have been squashed, even trampled underfoot, but she knew exactly where she was going and how we would get there. 'Quick ... push past him... I'm sorry, sir, but if ye'd give me some room...' She flashed her smile and we squeezed past. Only the front seats would do. We were right at the top of the hall, looking down with an almost perfect view.

'That was terrible ... honestly, what a free-for-all.'

'We're here now and don't ye go anywhere. Just stand ye ground.' She smiled, lifting her basket onto her lap. 'We've whortleberry cake if we're hungry and I've cider ... and two apples.'

'And the cherries on your bonnet! You'd better be careful – they're so realistic, someone may eat them!'

'Can't thank ye enough for my bonnet. Ye like it, don't ye?' She shook her head, the cherries and ribbons fluttering freely. 'I'm that glad it stayed on. That was a terrible crush.'

I had never been so crammed in before,

crushed against greasy jackets smelling of offal and pig fat; the reek of tobacco, the stink of sweat; a great seething mass of unwashed bodies pressing together. Everyone was eating, drinking and shouting. The noise was deafening, the heat almost too much to bear. The clock on the wall showed one o'clock. Another whole hour before it started.

'I knew 'twas best to get here early. Are ye alright?' She lifted the lace just high enough to see my eyes. 'Ye don't look very well.' She reached into her bag. 'I don't suppose ye've ever been in a crowd like this before. Here, smell this lavender, I've brought two bunches ... an' they'll be lighting the herbs soon.' She held the small posy to my nose and I breathed in its welcome fragrance.

The ceiling stretched above us, vaulted with dark beams, a huge arched window to the east. It was the medieval friary church, now a vast hall with platforms and benches crammed against the sides. We had climbed wooden steps to reach our vantage point and large gaps yawned between the planks of the floor. The rail looked makeshift, anything but safe. Hannah seemed quite at home, waving across the sea of faces at people she recognised. Already she had the cake unwrapped. 'Like some?' she said, taking a large bite. 'They've squeezed in a deal more seats but I like it best here – ye get a better view. That's where the judge sits and that's the prosecution ... and that's the witness stand.'

'You seem to know an awful lot – do you often come to watch?'

'As often as we can – Adam an' I come together. He wants to be a doctor, not a lawyer but he likes to know what's going on. I watch the gentry.' She pointed to the front benches and I got a sudden glimpse of Mrs Pengelly. Poor lady, she looked so frightened.

A large gong sounded. Ten minutes to two. The front seats were already taken, only the jurymen's benches and the seats for the prosecution remained empty. Hannah squeezed my hand. 'Don't mind me, I know ye're one of them … look, they're coming – that's the jurymen … 'tis about to start.'

The crowd hushed and I watched the jurymen shuffle along the bench, settling down with an air of importance. One or two glanced up at the staring onlookers, most looked across at the empty dock, each one of them serious and unsmiling. A couple looked decidedly prosperous, a few with an air of authority. They were soberly dressed and I looked at Hannah. She was frowning. 'They look like they've judged him already,' she whispered.

The clerk banged his staff. 'Silence in the court. All rise for His Honour, Justice Sir Richard Goldsworthy. The court will now stand in silence.'

Four men entered the court – Sir Richard Goldsworthy, in a long red robe and large white wig, another man in judicial robes and one wearing the black robes of a barrister. The fourth man was Father. I tried to rise, but my legs felt weak and I gripped the handrail in front of me. He was searching the crowd for a face. Phillip Randall was in the front row. Their eyes met and through my lace I saw the look that passed between them.

I caught my breath in sudden realization. Father feared Philip Randall. He needed him, but he did not trust him. I had less time than I thought. Father was too astute to leave himself open to blackmail. If he had not already done so, he would soon make arrangements to have me moved to another madhouse. He would have me moved, again and again, each time, using different people, each time, with a new name.

Sir Richard took his seat, spreading out his vermilion cloak in expectant silence.

Chapter Forty-seven

'Bring in the prisoner,' shouted the clerk. There was jeering as everyone leant forward to watch James Polcarrow make his way across the court to the dock. He stood tall, erect, his clothes immaculate, but his face was drawn, his scowl deepening as he glared at Father. Sir Richard barely looked up, a mere cursory glance as he shuffled papers on the desk in front of him.

The clerk unrolled his scroll:

James Polcarrow ... you are indicted on the charge of High Treason. On the seventh day of November in the year of our Lord, seventeen hundred and ninety three, you did wilfully, grievously, and with malice aforethought, prejudice the safety of the State by passing on, and receiving, information calculated to be injurious to your King and Country ... and you did, wilfully, grievously and with malice aforethought, correspond with the enemy by receiving French spies onto your ship, with the express intent to bring them to the shores of your country and thus, you did, knowingly, and maliciously, endanger the life of the king. How do you plead?'

My stomach was in knots. Sir James looked furious. He could barely bring himself to answer. 'Not guilty.'

'Honest, poor man looks that shaken. Are ye alright? Only ye look so pale.'

I nodded. 'It's just the heat.' But it was the sight of Father still making me so unwell. I gripped the rail as Sir Richard's voice rose above the murmurs.

'The prosecution will now begin. Mr Wallis, proceed, if you please.'

Mr Wallis nodded. He was middle-aged, bespectacled, dressed in black, with barrister's wig and crisply starched white bands at his neck. 'Your Honour...'

Matthew Reith's voice soared across the courtroom. 'If I may interject, Your Honour...' Sir Richard looked up, raising his eyebrows in surprise. 'My lord, we are not in the Dark Ages and I believe the justice in this court equal to, if not superior to any other court in the country. As such, I presumes all prisoners are considered innocent until they are proved guilty. I ask, therefore, that Sir James' handcuffs be removed in accordance to the dignity we must afford an innocent man.'

Stunned silence greeted his request, everyone staring at Sir Richard, who stared at Matthew through half-closed eyes. 'Remove the prisoner's handcuffs,' he replied, nodding to the clerk. Matthew returned to his seat as Mr Wallis rose again from his.

'Your Honour, members of the jury, this is no ordinary assize court. We're not here to judge a man for theft, misdemeanour or even murder. We're here to judge this man for the most heinous crime of all ... treason. I will prove to you how this man, James Polcarrow, thinks nothing of endangering the life of his king and country. How he has maliciously, and knowingly, put each and every one of you, in the most gravest of danger. He is a traitor to his country...'

'Objection, Your Honour.' Matthew Reith rose to his feet.

'Objection granted...'

'I will prove to you that this man is a spy... A dangerous French spy who ferries other spies backwards and forwards to our Cornish shore, not twenty miles from this very building – not twenty miles from your wives and children.' He held up both hands, quietening the sudden surge of outrage; men were hurling insults, waving their fists. James Polcarrow shook his head in silent disbelief.

An innocent man, only there because of Father.

'That poor man, it's wicked what people shout ... but Mr Reith'll clear him – he'll find a way. Honest, ye should hear him, he's that good.'

'I call for Dr Obie.' The name echoed down the

corridor and a florid man came forward, dressed in sober clothes, black jacket, black breeches and a simple white cravat. 'Take the stand, if you please, Dr Obie.'

Dr Obie's voice was loud, authoritative, swearing the oath with no prompting. He had clearly done this before. He looked confidently round the court, up to our gallery, his manner leaving no-one in any doubt he was trustworthy. 'Dr Obie,' began Mr Wallis, 'you're an eminent doctor, a member of the Royal Society of Physicians, no less?'

'I am, sir.'

'You live and work in Fosse where you have a large practice and you're known for your excellent cures ... as well as your tinctures and your well-known tonic for dropsy. You are a man of honour, I believe?'

'I am, sir.'

'And you had not quarrelled or "fallen foul" of the accused or any other people living in Polcarrow – and by that I mean his wife or Lady Polcarrow, his stepmother? I believe you brought her child into the world. Am I right?'

'I did, sir. And there was no quarrel. I would have dropped everything *had* I been summoned.'

'But you were *not* summoned, were you, Dr Opie? On the night of Thursday seventh November you were, what, ten minutes, fifteen minutes from the house and yet you were not called to help a man and his wife who suspected they were dying of mushroom poisoning?'

'I was not, sir.'

A gasp filled the room. Mr Wallis turned to-

373

wards the crowd, lifting both eyebrows to encourage their incredulity. 'Thank you, doctor. No more questions.' He looked at Matthew who shook his head. 'And no questions from the defence, it seems. Your testimony is greatly appreciated. You may go now.' He flexed his hands in front of him and nodded to the clerk. 'I call on Dr Trefusis.'

Dr Trefusis was young, slim, tall and anxious, obviously unused to giving evidence. He kept his eyes on the floor, never once looking at Sir James. His voice was educated, firm, but clearly nervous. 'Dr Trefusis, you are a young man. Forgive me if I suggest you are just starting your career and yet to make your name.'

Dr Trefusis coughed. 'Yes, sir, that is true, though I've extensive experience and I'm appointed physician to the new hospital. Age should not always be held against the young when starting a career.'

'And you live and work in Truro?'

'I do, sir.'

'Yet on the day we speak of ... the seventh of November you were in Fosse?'

Dr Trefusis' voice faltered. 'No, sir. I was in Truro. I was woken in the middle of the night and made as much haste as I could. I reached Polcarrow the next day.'

Mr Wallis scratched his forehead, his eyebrows drawn tight with puzzlement. He put his hand up to quieten the whistles. 'Dr Opie might have attended them within fifteen minutes and yet you arrived the next day? How do you account for that, Dr Trefusis?' He looked to the jury. 'I'll tell

374

you why. You were summoned because it was an elaborate hoax. You're personally acquainted with Sir James and a friend of Mr Reith.' His voice grew louder. 'You were summoned because there were no patients to attend, were there? Empty beds ... no one there. You were summoned because a man starting his career does what he's told. Am I right?'

'No, sir ... I mean, yes, sir.'

'It was a hoax,' Mr Wallis shouted, the jeering so loud he could hardly be heard. 'A hoax, because Sir James Polcarrow and his wife had *other* business to attend ... other business that involved sneaking out of their house through the smugglers' tunnel we all know exists, in order to board their ship to go to France – *to pick up French spies.* Tell me, yes or no, were Sir James and Lady Polcarrow ill from poisoning?'

'No, sir.'

'Yet you told everyone they were?'

'Yes, sir.'

'Were they even there? Did you see them at all?'

'No, sir. They were not there.'

'Thank you, no more questions.' Mr Wallis sat down, flicking his coat-tails behind him. The jurymen were shaking their heads. If they looked grim before, they now looked thunderous.

Matthew Reith rose to his feet. 'Tell me, Dr Trefusis. Were you told, right from the start, that Sir James and Lady Polcarrow would not be there?'

'I was, sir. I was asked to pretend they were dying...'

There was complete silence, no-one moved. 'And why was that?'

'Sir James Polcarrow needed to get to Falmouth. He had heard Robert Roskelly had newly escaped from Bodmin and he believed him to be in Falmouth. He needed to find him.'

'And you were prepared to go along with their plan?'

Dr Trefusis looked straight at Sir James. 'I was. I consider it my honour to serve Sir James. His generosity to our new hospital is unmatched by any other benefactor.'

'Thank you, no further questions. You may step down.'

Mr Wallis rose, his frown deepening. 'Gentlemen, a good cover is needed for a good lie. If you're going on a clandestine journey, is it not expedient to tell everyone you're going to Falmouth? We're dealing with a man of intelligence, not a common man – a man who knows how to cover his tracks, keep the law off his trail.'

'I don't like him one bit,' whispered Hannah. 'But why lie like that? Sir James should've just gone to Falmouth and no-one would be the wiser.' She nodded at the jurymen. 'They don't like it, neither – not one bit.'

'I call on Mr Josiah Troon,' shouted the clerk.

Josiah Troon entered. So this was the sort of man Father bought. He was definitely a sailor, dark, black hair, weather-beaten face. His wrists were tattooed, his shoulders hunched. I could barely look at him. Lying, lying toad. He had not even opened his mouth but already I felt my fury mounting. He could not read so repeated the oath after the clerk. Not a Fosse accent, sounded more like Falmouth.

Mr Wallis smiled encouragingly. 'You are Josiah Troon, hired seaman on the cutter *L'Aigrette?*'

'I am, sir,' Josiah Troon replied, wringing his hat in his hands.

'And how long have you been in service on this vessel?'

'No more than two weeks. I was dismissed ... that is ... they said they didn't need me no more.' He stared at his boots.

'Tell me, again, Mr Troon. On the evening of the seventh of November, Sir James Polcarrow and his wife came aboard their ship and you sailed from Fosse, on, as yet, an undisclosed heading.'

''Tis the truth, sir.'

'Tell me, why was it an undisclosed heading?'

'Sir James took the tiller and we'd no notion where we was headin'. He didn't tell us but we thought 'twould be Jersey ... because 'twas Jersey the last time.'

'But it wasn't Jersey, was it, Mr Troon? When did you realise you were heading to France?'

'We didn't, not rightly. Not even after Sir James gave over the tiller ... but we'd a notion somethin' was wrong. T'was a rough sea, the waves strong – and ye can't always be sure where ye're headin'. Ye have to account for the tide.' He glanced up, quickly looking down again.

'I understand your nervousness, Mr Troon. You'd no notion *where* you were going, you'd *not been told* ... but as king's evidence you may fear no repercussions. The court is not judging you. It recoils with the same horror even hearing what you were *made* to do. You're a sailor and proud of your country?'

He was a big man, thick-set, bulky frame, yet there were tears in his eyes. He put his hand across his heart. 'I love me country, sir. I'd defend it with me life... I never knew ... honest to God... I never ... never ... knew what he was plannin' or I'd not have gone.'

'Of course you wouldn't, Mr Troon, nor would anyone else in this room. Nor anyone else in the country ... because we do not spy for the French...' He waited for the whistles of support to die down. It was theatre, sheer theatre – Sir Richard's red gown, the elaborate wigs, the gesturing to the crowd. He was playing the audience.

'And what happened on that journey?' He continued when enough time had elapsed. 'Tell the court when and where you stopped.'

'We stopped in a cove, alongside an abbey. By then, we knew 'twas France. Sir James told us we was to take on a few barrels – we was made to believe 'twas brandy we was goin' for–'

'But it wasn't brandy, was it, Mr Troon? Who boarded the boat and where did they come from?'

'Monks, sir, three of them. All clothed in brown with hoods. Ye couldn't see their faces, but we heard them right enough, an' they weren't speakin' the king's English.'

'Where was this?'

'I don't rightly know, sir. I had no sight of the charts. I just do the sailin' not the navigatin' but I know 'twas France.'

'It must have been a terrible ordeal for you, Mr Troon. The court's very grateful you put your country before your own safety and came forward with this testimony. Without you, James Polcarrow ... an *accused* spy would still be betraying his country.' Another roar of approval; a deafening, foot-stamping, thunderous bellow ripping through the hall. People were whistling, clapping their hands. Mr Troon smiled shyly, keeping his head down. I could imagine his brief. *Act humble ... be scared ... make the crowd grateful you've come forward.*

Matthew Reith jumped to his feet, no trace of a frown. He was smiling, rubbing his hands, holding up his open palms to quieten the crowd. 'Mr Troon ... forgive me, but you said Sir James was at the *tiller?*' He emphasised the last word, looking round the court, smiling like a fox. 'Perhaps you'd like to repeat that a little bit louder. Could you turn to the jury ... and remember, Mr Troon, you are under oath ... could you turn to the jury and say, very loudly ... that Sir James was on the *tiller* and that you also took turns to hold the *tiller.*' He smiled at Sir James, as if in triumph.

'I don't rightly understand ye...' Gone was his look of sheepish nervousness, in its place a look of sheer panic.

'You did sail the boat, didn't you? It's a long way to France and back. Sir James couldn't have sailed the whole way ... you said yourself he gave over the *tiller.*'

I held my breath. Everyone was holding their breath, everyone realising he was on to something. The colour drained from Josiah Troon's face, James Polcarrow looked down at his hands. So, too did Mrs Pengelly and Alice Polcarrow. My heart was racing. We were all thinking the same ...

say it … say it. I felt sick with nerves. I could feel the smooth wood in my hands, the boat obeying my slightest command.

'Mr Troon,' continued Matthew with a smile, his head high with confidence, 'I put it to you that you're a liar, a *paid* witness. You did not sail the boat that night nor have you *ever* sailed that boat. I put it to you that your evidence is fabricated because someone *in this very room* wants to discredit Sir James and see him falsely hung. I put it to you…'

'Objection, Your Honour. Supposition! There's absolutely no evidence for that.'

Sir Richard's eyes narrowed. He barely moved. 'Objection granted. Answer the question, Mr Troon. Did you, or did you not, sail the boat on the seventh of November?'

'I did, sir … I'm that put out bein' stood here. It's had me that confused … when I said the *tiller* … course I meant the wheel.'

Matthew Reith's face fell. His shoulders slumped, his voice at once disappointed. 'Are you sure about that? I thought you said there was a tiller.'

Josiah Troon's voice grew stronger, soaring out across the court. 'There was no tiller, just the wheel. I know there was a wheel – I remember holding it steady in the waves.'

Matthew fumbled for his handkerchief, wiping the sweat from his brow. 'I've no more questions,' he said as if defeated. It was so thrilling, so clever, such a simple, simple trip. I had to suppress my smile, try to look concerned.

'He's usually better than this,' whispered Han-

380

nah. 'It's as if he's given up without even trying. He's not himself...'

I felt like hugging her. Matthew Reith made it look so easy. He would win, I knew he would. James Polcarrow would go free and Father would be taken to court. I felt the knot leave my stomach. 'He'll have a plan, Hannah. You said yourself he was the best.'

John Wallis shrugged his shoulders, playing the crowd by encouraging their shouts. Sir James hardly moved, standing bolt upright, chin held high, his eyes fixed firmly on Mrs Pengelly. Neither gave any sign of emotion. Mr Wallis reached for a glass of water and shouted, 'I call upon Mr Samuel Spiller.'

Sir Richard Goldsworthy looked up, his piercing grey eyes sweeping over the crowd and up to the gallery. I looked away, desperate he should not catch my eye. There was power in those eyes. Power and cruelty. Fear shivered down my spine. My confidence was misplaced.

'Do you swear by almighty God to speak the truth, the whole truth, and nothing but the truth ... so help you God?'

'I do, sir.'

'Then please take the stand.'

Samuel Spiller was taller, thinner, with a shock of black hair. The sleeves of his borrowed jacket were too short, his cravat obviously choking him. He kept fiddling with it, trying to loosen it; his actions were jerky and uncomfortable, the oath he had just sworn clearly undoing his careful preparation. He glanced up at the jurymen and paled.

Mr Wallis stepped to his aid. 'Mr Spiller, I believe that, like Mr Troon, you are anxious about giving evidence. You fear you'll be judged alongside Sir James Polcarrow and you'll be thought a spy. Am I right?' He crossed his arms in front of his chest, one hand tapping his upper arm. It was a strange gesture. I only noticed it because he had done it twice before.

'Yes, sir,' replied Samuel Spiller.

'The court's not judging you – indeed it commends you on your bravery. We have no place in our society for traitors to our king and country.' He turned to the jury. 'And the court is grateful for that courage. Are you ready to proceed?'

Samuel Spiller nodded. 'I am, sir.'

'How long have you been a sailor on *L'Aigrette?*'

'A month.'

'Only a month?'

'They only hire ye for a short time. They pay ye good money fer yer silence, then ye're gone.'

'The court has been told what happened on the night in question, but could you tell us in your own words what happened? How did Sir James and Lady Polcarrow reach their boat?'

'A tunnel, sir – a secret tunnel runnin' from their house to the caves. Then they rowed out to us.'

'And was the captain on the boat?'

'He was, sir.'

'And what nationality was the captain?'

'He was French, sir...' This was too much for the crowd. Loud shouts drowned his next words. It was as if they had been holding back, rotten fruit now raining down on Sir James. He did not flinch but stood glowering at the witness, his mouth clamping tight with anger as an egg landed on his jacket.

Hannah looked horrified. 'Oh, poor Sir James ... but French – ye'd have thought he'd more sense than that. Poor Mrs Thomas...'

'Captain Lefèvre and Sir James Polcarrow knew *exactly* where they were going?'

'No doubt about it.'

'As if they had done it many times before?'

'No doubt about it. Many times. I thought we was after brandy, but it was monks we took aboard. We sailed them to Fosse but let 'em off before the excise men could get to them. I swear to God, I never knew they was French spies.'

'Of course you didn't. The court knows that. Where did they take them?'

'Just west of Polperro, sir.'

'Thank you, Mr Spiller, no more questions.'

Mr Wallis sat down as Matthew walked slowly across to the witness stand. 'Describe the captain if you would, Mr Spiller.'

'The captain?'

'Yes, Captain Lefèvre, this French captain you were quite happy to sail with. *L'Aigrette* is a very fine cutter, a good master, was he? You were able to understand him?'

'He was ... just like the rest. I understood him very well. His English was very good. He said he was from Jersey an' I've sailed with a lot of men from Jersey. He was no different. 'Twas only afterwards we realised he was French.'

'After Mr Wallis told you to say he was French?'

'Objection...! Your Honour ... I must protest. The defence has nothing to go on. His sole defence is to defame my witnesses.'

Sir Richard nodded. 'Continue, Mr Reith. I do not believe in wasting the court's time.'

'Tell me, if you'd be so kind, exactly what this French captain looked like.' He turned to the jurymen. 'I've several witnesses who know the captain well, and I intend to call on them directly. People like the harbour master of Fosse, the chief excise officer, the victuallers who regularly provision the boat...'

Samuel Spiller paled. 'He was ... like the rest of us ... like us all ... we're all sailors ... we all look alike.'

Matthew rubbed his finger across his chin. 'Try to remember *if* you can. Or at least, try and remember what you've been told to say. Was he old, was he young? Did he have grey hair ... black hair ... did he have whiskers ... a beard? And there's no point looking at Mr Wallis. He's no signal for you to answer this.'

'Objection, my lord ... this is outrageous. I demand Mr Reith withdraw that at once.'

'Objection agreed. Strike that from the records. Mr Reith, a warning.'

Matthew smiled at Samuel Spiller. 'I'm sorry but it's a very simple question and I'm surprised you've been so badly briefed. Captain Lefèvre is in his late sixties and is in very good shape for a man of his age ... he has grey hair and whiskers ... and yet you could not remember that?' His voice rose, his finger jabbing the air. 'I put it to you, Mr Spiller, that you're *not* telling the truth. I put it to you that, like the last witness, you've been paid money to spread vicious lies against my client.' He turned to the jurymen. 'Lies that, *if believed*, would hang an innocent man. I put it to the court that someone has wasted his money because he's too stupid or too ignorant to think I would not ask this man to describe the identity of the captain.'

Samuel Spiller glared at Matthew. 'The captain was grey-haired and whiskered. Ye didn't let me answer.'

'And does the boat have a *tiller* or a *wheel?*'

'No, sir ... not a tiller ... that ye can be sure of that ... 'twas definitely a wheel.'

'You heard the last witness?'

'No, sir ... we're not to confer. I heard nothing. No-one told me to say that.'

Matthew turned to Sir Richard. 'My lord justice, does the prosecution mean to waste the court's time much longer?' He shook his head, turning to the jury. 'Believe me, gentlemen, I've no wish to waste your time or insult your intelligence. Waiting outside are two, no, three witnesses. In fact, I have *any number* of witnesses to swear the boat has a tiller and Captain Lefèvre is an unusually young man.' His voice was steady, authoritative, his finger pointing at Samuel Spiller. 'This man, just like the last witness, was told there would be no trial. Neither of them expected to be questioned under oath, by a defence counsel.' He scowled at Samuel Spiller. 'What were you told? Just a brief testimony in front of a stipendiary magistrate? No court. No jury – just two witnesses and enough suspicion?'

'My lord, this is outrageous – sheer supposition. There's no proof.'

Sir Richard's eyes were almost closed. 'Your point, Mr Reith?'

'My point is that this man, just like the last witness, has never been near that ship. He has never met Captain Lefèvre ... I put it to him that he is a liar and a perjurer, lying under oath, and that in itself has serious consequences.' Samuel Spiller wiped the sweat from his brow. He looked petrified. Matthew Reith walked over to him, looking him straight in the eye. 'If you have the courage to admit to perjury, the court will act more leniently towards you...' He looked round. A commotion was disturbing the silence, everyone's eyes drawn to the justices' bench.

A man was standing at the other side of the court room, a letter, slowly making its way from hand to hand. It reached Mr Wallis and he slipped his finger under the seal. No-one was moving, everyone craning their neck to get a better view. Mr Wallis smiled, passing the letter quickly along the bench to Sir Richard. He, too, read the letter and smiled. I recognised the glint of anticipation and my fear returned.

'Something's wrong,' whispered Hannah. 'Mr Reith needs the verdict. He's got the jury for the taking...'

Sir Richard Goldsworthy waved his hand for silence. 'Mr Reith, one moment ... if you please.' He bent over the bench to talk to Mr Wallis, both nodding vigorously, their wigs bobbing up and down. In agreement, Sir Richard handed the letter straight to Sir William Molesworth. He, too, read it and nodded.

Matthew looked increasingly worried, casting

an anxious glance at Alice. She looked scared, her face pale beneath her feathered hat. 'I would like to call my next witness,' he said.

Sir Richard ignored Matthew and spoke to the jurymen. 'The case against Sir James Polcarrow is withdrawn—'

'Withdrawn!' Matthew looked furious. 'My lord, I must insist. This is a court of law and my client has been accused of treason. My client does not want the case withdrawn. Sir James is an innocent man and, therefore, I must *insist* his name be fully cleared. The case against him is false. The two witnesses against him are paid liars and Sir James deserves the unanimous agreement of not guilty.' Sir Richard did not even look up. He was gathering together the papers on the desk in front of him. Matthew's voice rose. He was clearly furious. 'This court has been witness to Mr Wallis' attempt to defame Sir James and I demand the trial continue until the jury reach their verdict and justice is served.' He stood glowering at Sir Richard.

A voice bellowed from the back of the court. 'Justice for Sir James.' Another voice repeated the cry, another and another. Immediately everyone around us started standing up, the whole room taking up the same chant: 'Justice for Sir James, justice ... justice...' The man next to me rose quickly, his heavy boots narrowly missing my shoe. His elbows dug into my shoulders as he waved his fist. It was so cramped, all of us crammed together with almost no air. The heat was terrible, the building cogged with smoke.

James Polcarrow stood rigid in his stand, his

hands clenched by his side. As he looked across the court I saw bewilderment in his eyes. Alice Polcarrow stared back, trying to smile. Sir Richard's normally grey face was flushed with anger. Holding up his hand, he sat waiting for silence. 'James Polcarrow *will* get justice,' he said coldly. 'Gentlemen of the jury, the crown dismisses the case against Sir James Polcarrow ... there will be no further prosecution. The case is dismissed.'

The noise was deafening, a loud whoop of delight filling the air. Sir James walked slowly down the steps, nodding to each of the jurymen, shaking Matthew Reith warmly by the hand. Only when he reached Alice Polcarrow did his frown give way to the briefest of smiles. But Matthew Reith was not smiling. I hardly knew the man, but his frown was deeper than I had ever seen.

'He's done it. I told ye he would – Sir James's free and I'm that glad...' Hannah began clapping her hands along with everyone else but I could not join her. *Dismissed, not innocent.* Something was wrong. A feeling of panic began to fill me. Father looked hot and flustered, waving a paper to cool his face. He was not scowling. He was smiling.

The clerk was trying his best to be heard above the crowd, his voice drowned to everyone but those nearest to him. Gradually his words filtered above the noise. 'Quiet please! The court will reconvene in fifteen minutes. Quiet! The court will break for fifteen minutes... After the break the court will hear the next case. Crown versus Lady Polcarrow...' The hush was instant. James Polcarrow looked as if he had been hit, staring straight at Matthew Reith.

'Your lordship...' Matthew Reith protested. 'I insist the case against Lady Polcarrow be dismissed as well. There can be no point in wasting the court's time.'

Sir Richard Goldsworthy looked up and smiled. 'The case against Lady Polcarrow will proceed.' He rose from his seat, straightening his robe as the court stood in stunned silence. It lasted only until the door shut behind him, then the hall erupted.

I was not the only one to recognise the cat and mouse smile playing on Father's lips.

Chapter Forty-eight

I sat back on the hard bench, holding Hannah's lavender against my veil. The herb burners had been re-lit but they made no difference. The air was almost too foul to breathe. 'Why'd he stop the trial? He can't do that ... can he? Ye alright, Miss Wells? Here, let me fan ye.'

'I don't think Mr Wallis had any idea those men were lying. Did you see his face? I think he honestly thought they were telling the truth.' I flapped my fan, trying to calm my anxiety. My nausea was not from the stench or crush but seeing the smile on Father's face.

'Something's wrong... I don't trust that judge. He looks like a ghoul. He could be dead for all we know – sitting there, not moving, his eyes all hooded an' that.'

'He's very much alive. He's like a reptile, waiting to flick out his forked tongue.'

Hannah passed me a jar of cider. 'Perhaps a drink may do ye good? We can't leave ... we'd never get back.' I took a sip. It was surprisingly thirst-quenching, not strong at all. 'Somethin's wrong,' she repeated, 'I don't like that judge.'

The jurymen had left the court, the judges' bench was empty and Matthew Reith had taken Sir James and his party out with him. No-one else had left; everyone remained shouting, eating or drinking. Bets were being honoured and money changing hands. New bets were being laid, everyone sensing the stakes had just been raised.

I flapped my fan and declined the last slice of cake. Hannah was talking to the woman next to her and I sat back, not looking down at the court, but sideways along the rows in the gallery. Suddenly my heart leapt. A man was standing at the end of the row, staring at me. Not any man, but Arnaud Lefèvre. My pulse started racing. He was staring straight at me, his gaze unwavering, no hint of a smile. He was dressed like every other man – brown jacket, cotton cravat, woollen waistcoat and working breeches; his hat was pulled low over his forehead, his beard quite grown. His eyes were boring into mine, intent on me seeing him. It was as if he had been willing me to look his way.

I stared back across the rows of people at those piercing eyes. He had recognised me. Even dressed as I was, he knew how to find me.

'More cider...? The woman next to me knows Mamm from chapel – I gave her the last of me apples, ye didn't want it, did ye? Oh dear God, ye're not alright, are ye?' She lifted up my lace. 'Ye look like ye've seen a ghost ... drink this ... 'tis far too hot in here.'

I drank the proffered cider, looking over the rim to where Arnaud had been standing. He was no longer there. Another man had taken his place, Arnaud nowhere to be seen. I wiped my mouth with my hand, searching the crowd but I knew it would be pointless. Arnaud had wanted me to see him, now he wanted to stay hidden. Just like the time in the square when he had stood on the step and stared at me. Why did he want me to know he was there? Why come to court when it was so dangerous?

I could not stop the excitement running through me; the sudden thrill, the rush of pleasure I felt at the sight of him. I had sworn to renounce this man yet the hidden danger made me feel so alive. Yet he had not smiled. His eyes held warning – as if he was trying to tell me something. I handed back the cider, searching the sea of faces. Suddenly I caught my breath. Of course! *Jacques' bag.* They wanted it back. He was warning me to give it back. Perhaps he thought I had it with me.

'They're coming back... Yes, here come the jurymen and Sir James. Ye alright? That's better – ye've a lot more colour to ye now.' I leant back against the wooden bench, watching the jurymen take their seats. Matthew Reith was escorting Sir James and Alice across the hall, Mrs Pengelly following closely behind. Father was making his way slowly along the bench.

The room was buzzing, all eyes expectant. 'I don't like this ... not one little bit...'

'Nor do I, Hannah.'

Chapter Forty-nine

The court settled quickly. There was silence even before Sir Richard waved his hand to proceed. The clerk stood up and nodded towards the door. 'Bring in the prisoner.'

James Polcarrow had his hands clasped in front of him, as if in prayer. The door opened and he stood up, gazing at his wife with such love and anguish. Rose Polcarrow looked pale, her thick chestnut ringlets cascading beneath her hat. She wore a green dress and soft cream leather gloves, her striking beauty causing an audible intake of breath. As she took the stand, her eyes were blazing.

Sir Richard waved his hands as if dismissing an irritating servant. 'Remove the cuffs...'

'She looks so beautiful but she's that angry...' whispered Hannah.

'Your name, please?'

'Rosehannon ... Polcarrow.'

'Rosehannon Polcarrow ... you are indicted with the charge of high treason. On the seventh day of November in the year of our Lord, seventeen hundred and

ninety-three, you did wilfully, grievously, and with malice aforethought, prejudice the safety of the state by passing on, and receiving, information calculated to be injurious to your king and country...'

'It's the same charge,' whispered Hannah. 'You'd think they'd learn.'

'...and thus you did, knowingly, and maliciously, endanger the life of the king. How do you plead?'

'Not guilty.' Her voice resonated across the court with unleashed fury.

Mr Wallis stood up, his stance confident and assured. As he walked across the court, there seemed a new arrogance in his gait. 'Gentlemen of the jury, you are familiar with the charge. I will prove to you that this woman, standing before you, a woman known for her radical views ... whose father is a known dissident in gaol *at this very minute* on the charge of sedition...'

'Objection ... Your Honour.' Matthew Reith looked furious.

Sir Richard waved his hand. 'Objection granted.'

Mr Wallis smiled. 'No matter, gentlemen of the jury, we've all the proof you need – you will decide for yourselves if this woman is guilty or not. I call on Mr Nathaniel Ellis.'

I felt suddenly winded. Nathaniel, the sailor I had threatened with a gun. I could hardly look as the door opened. It was definitely him, the same thick-set shoulders, the same bald head browned by the sun, but he was dressed differently; his clothes spotless, he was wearing the blue jacket and white trousers of a naval uniform. I had not seen this coming. Dear God, I had not seen this coming. Arnaud had been trying to warn me.

'Mr Ellis, you are a bosun in His Majesty's navy. Perhaps you could tell these gentlemen what you were doing and under whose orders.'

'Yes, sir. My orders came direct from Captain Penrose of His Majesty's frigate, HMS *Circe*. Three of us, sir, sent on special duties – to watch an' report back. We was to watch all the cutters, sniff round, keep our eyes open and our mouths shut. I saw the cutter *L'Aigrette* and I thought to watch her, but luck was with me...'

'In what way was luck with you?'

'Their man was down with the gripe an' couldn't sail. I was in the right place at the right time. I put meself forward for crew. I thought to search the boat, get an idea of the captain, but they took me straight to France...'

'Who took you to France? We need to know, exactly, who was on that ship the night of the seventh of November? Take your time, the jury need to know everything.'

'I thought we was goin' to Jersey. Least that was what the captain said.'

'Describe the captain ... if you please.'

'Young man – very young for a captain, but an excellent sailor. He knew his stuff and I couldn't better the way he sailed. Many wouldn't have put out on a night like that, but Captain Lefèvre crossed to France like it was child's play. He said he was from Jersey but he sounded French – spoke English just like you an' me, but sounded French.'

Mr Wallis nodded. 'And who else was on the ship?'

'Me, the captain and Jacques. We was about to pull the anchor when a boat comes alongside an' three people come aboard – two gentlemen an' a lady.'

Mr Wallis smiled. 'And who were they?'

'On my life, sir, I swear it was Sir James Polcarrow, Lady Polcarrow an' another man.'

'Indeed?' The jury looked shocked, shaking their heads, their mouths clamped in the severest disapproval. They raised their eyebrows, nodding to each other across the bench. James Polcarrow stared at Rose, watching the fury in her eyes turn to fear.

Mr Wallis held up his hand. 'And you immediately set sail?'

'We did, sir. We had wind an' tide so we made good progress. We were in Falmouth before the storm hit.' Nathaniel Ellis was standing tall, a perfect example of the best of our navy. His words were clear, his voice unfaltering. Everyone knew he was telling the truth.

'Falmouth?'

'Yes, sir. Once we anchored, Sir James rowed the others ashore.'

'How did you know it was Sir James?'

'I knew him, sir. He often walks among the people of the town. I knew him the moment I saw him, though he was dressed in common clothes – like a labourer.'

'And Lady Polcarrow?'

'She was there. She was wearing a heavy cloak and hidin' her face, but she was there.'

395

'But Falmouth isn't France, is it, Mr Ellis?'

'No, sir, the captain didn't want me to sail with them... The other sailor, Jacques, was one of them, French, like the captain. He rowed me to Falmouth, hoping to leave me there but the other man was no better and couldn't leave his bed ... so we came straight back to the ship.'

'Why did they risk taking you?'

'The storm, sir. They needed three to sail on a night like that.' Mr Wallis nodded and smiled. 'When we got back to the ship, I saw Sir James' rowing boat lying alongside. Straightaway Captain Lefèvre told us to stash it well down an' prepare to leave.'

'Yet the storm was coming?'

'I thought to question his command but Jacques was gettin' everythin' ready an' I had a feelin', deep inside, that somethin' wasn't right so I didn't question, I just prepared the sails.'

'And Sir James and Lady Polcarrow were on board?'

'I can't say that for certain, sir. I never saw Sir James again, but I saw Lady Polcarrow. I certainly saw her again.'

'No ... that's not true ... that's a lie...' shouted Rose, her eyes blazing.

James Polcarrow leapt to his feet. 'That's a dammed lie. She never went back ... she was with me all the time...' He was shaking with rage.

Matthew Reith reached for Sir James' arm, pulling him down. 'I'm sorry,' he said, trying to be heard above the sudden uproar. 'My clients will not interrupt again.' He shouted louder. 'They know to wait their turn ... please ... let the witness proceed.' I felt sick with fear. It was so hot, so cramped; I could not bend forward to stop the dizziness. If I had only confided in them, they would have been better prepared. I tried to breathe.

Mr Wallis nodded to a man standing by the door and he stepped forward, bearing a black cloak. 'Mr Ellis, have you ever seen this cloak before?' He nodded again and the man proceeded to carry it over to the witness stand, spreading the cloak out before reaching up with it.

'Yes, sir. That's the exact cloak Lady Polcarrow was wearin'.'

'Thank you. Can you show that exact same cloak to the members of the jury? They'll be interested to know that this cloak was found by Major Trelawney when he searched the home of Sir James and Lady Polcarrow.' He waited for the gasps to subside. 'And was Lady Polcarrow wearing this cloak when she pointed the gun at you? Perhaps you could tell the court what happened when you got to France.'

'Jacques told me it was Jersey, an' I pretended to believe him. I just kept me head down but I knew somethin' wasn't right. They were waitin' for someone. There was a flag wavin' at them from the beach but they weren't movin'. We were in a bay ... there was an abbey and a large wall – afterwards, I knew for certain it was Abbey Beauport but at the time I just kept me head down and got on with me jobs, as if I wasn't interested ... but I was watchin' them. They was actin' like they was only smugglin' but I knew somethin' was wrong. Not long afterwards, Captain Lefèvre

397

slipped from the stern an' swum ashore.'

'Captain Lefèvre *swam* ashore?'

'As God's my witness. I tried to see where he went but Jacques came lungin' at me. He had a knife an' I could tell he wanted me dead. I would've got the better of him but I never got the chance. Lady Polcarrow came up the steps with her pistol ready. She was pointin' it at me and swearin', saying she weren't afraid to use it. She meant it, too. She knew what she was doing alright.'

'You were in grave danger, Mr Ellis.'

'I was a dead man. If I didn't jump, they'd have shot me.' He waited for gasps of horror to quieten '...so I jumped ... but the good Lord was watching over me ... somehow I made it to the shore. I'm no swimmer but I made it, no thanks to Lady Polcarrow.' He glowered across the court at Rose.

'We're certainly very glad you did, Mr Ellis. Your king, your country ... indeed everyone in this hall is grateful you did. But what did you see then, Mr Ellis?'

'Men was runnin' along the beach and I feared for me life. I had to hide meself as best I could. When I thought it clear to look, I saw a boat alongside the ship. Captain Lefèvre was carryin' up an injured monk an' Lady Polcarrow was in the boat.'

'You saw Lady Polcarrow in the boat?'

'I did, sir. As God's my witness ... Lady Polcarrow rowed ashore to pick up the spy.'

Mr Wallis nodded at the jurymen. 'You say injured, Mr Ellis?'

'Yes, sir, I followed the blood. It led to a hidden

beach among the reeds, just in front of the abbey. They use the abbey as a hidin' place. It's a place no-one goes – the tide's too treacherous and there are rocks an' sandbanks everywhere. Most people leave it well alone.'

'And they sailed back without you? They left you in an enemy country in grave danger of your life?'

'They did, and I never thought to see England again. Lady Polcarrow cared nothin' about leavin' me there. I was in great peril and had to pretend I was dumb an' couldn't speak. I found a fishin' boat goin' to Jersey and I came straight back to tell Captain Penrose. Only the ship had sailed, so I got word to Major Trelawney. We searched the house, found the cloak an' he sent me straight here. I'm glad I've got here in time.'

'Thank you, Mr Ellis. The court commends your bravery. No more questions.' Mr Wallis smiled at the jury and walked back to his chair.

Chapter Fifty

Matthew Reith and James Polcarrow were deep in conversation, Matthew Reith nodding vigorously, firing questions; James Polcarrow was leaning forward, his hands clasped in front of him. Sir Richard looked up and scowled. 'Mr Reith ... is the court to wait much longer?'

Matthew Reith glanced up at the gallery, scanning the crowd and I knew he was searching for me. He owed me nothing. I was the daughter of the man who had falsely accused his friends. He recognised me at once, his glance cold, furious, leaving me in no doubt that by saving Rose he would implicate me – maybe not directly, maybe not by name, but by the trail I must have left behind. I could hardly hear Hannah for the shouting. 'She can't be guilty ... ye don't think she's done it, do ye? Only he wasn't lying, he was telling the truth...'

My mouth was almost too dry to speak. 'I'm sure she didn't do it ... it must have been someone else.'

She blew her nose. 'Ye think so? Mr Reith better get her off.'

'He will,' I said with absolute certainty. This changed everything, everything. My life was hanging in the balance and I could do nothing but watch it happen.

Matthew Reith stood up, suddenly smiling, giving every impression of enjoying himself. 'Mr Ellis, the court commends you and so do I ... and so, I'm sure, do the members of the jury. I have every respect for our brave navy and the work you do. Catching French spies is a difficult and dangerous task and everyone in this court is grateful there are men like you who put their lives in such danger. I do not doubt anything you have told the court. I believe you are telling the truth. I believe you are an honest, God-fearing man and would never perjure yourself. Indeed, I admire you.'

Nathaniel Ellis looked puzzled, glancing over to Mr Wallis. 'Thank you, sir.'

'Your brave actions have uncovered a network of spies – of that there's no doubt. The question we must ask, however, is ... who *exactly* are these spies? Who ... *beyond all reasonable doubt* are the men and women involved in such a heinous crime? Certainly, Captain Lefèvre ... certainly, the man, Jacques ... certainly, the woman in the black cloak, but who was she really, Mr Ellis? I put it to you that you are not lying but that you are mistaken in who you *thought* was Lady Polcarrow.'

Nathaniel Ellis shook his head. 'No, sir, I saw what I saw.'

'*You saw what you saw* but did you, Mr Ellis? I have three, no four, witnesses who are about to follow you to this very stand, who are also good, honest men and woman who, just like you, would never perjure themselves. Yet each and every one of them can swear, under oath, that on the night in question Lady Polcarrow *did* board *L'Aigrette* alongside her husband, but she was *dressed as a man.*'

The crowd drew breath, a collective gasp resounding across the hall. Matthew Reith waited, nodding his head. 'Two men and one lady did not board your ship, Mr Ellis, but one man and two ladies. Tell me, what is this Captain Lefèvre like? We know he's a young man ... would you say he's a healthy man ... and by that, I mean a man with healthy appetites? A man who might like a little bit of company on those long nights at sea?'

'He's a healthy man.'

'Would you say he's a ladies' man? Or rather, a man ladies might find irresistible? I believe all women love a sailor ... but a lusty, young captain?

Now, there's a thought. I often wish I'd chosen the sea instead of burying my head inside all those dusty law books...' He turned to the crowd, raising his eyebrows at their roar of laughter.

Nathaniel Ellis nodded. 'Perhaps, sir.'

'And how did our lusty captain greet the woman in the black cloak? Did he bow politely? Did he proffer due respect? After all, Sir James Polcarrow is his employer and the ship belongs to Lady Polcarrow ... how did he greet her, Mr Ellis?'

Nathaniel Ellis looked shaken. 'He helped her aboard...'

'How, exactly?' Matthew looked back at his audience, once again raising his eyebrows. 'Did he politely offer his hand or did he carry her up the ladder as if he could not wait to get her to his cabin?'

'He carried her up the ladder, sir. He could see she was in difficulty – the sea was rough, the boats were knocking together ... she was losing her grip and was in danger of slipping. He came down the ladder and helped her–'

'Helped her, or carried her?'

'Carried her, sir.'

'How, exactly?'

'Over his shoulder, sir.'

Matthew turned, once again, to his delighted audience, pursing his lips and rubbing his chin. 'Over his shoulder...' he repeated, with a knowing smile. 'Mr Ellis, I know Sir James very well. He has been married for only a few weeks. If his wife was dangling in danger over a heaving sea ... do you think he would allow another man the privilege of sweeping her into his arms ... let alone hoisting her over his shoulder like a willing wench?' He held out his hand to the roaring crowd, his finger pointing in the air. 'Especially, let me add, a lusty French captain known to be such a favourite with the ladies...'

Hannah was laughing like everyone else. The crowd was lapping it up like a cat with cream. They were whistling, stamping their feet. Even some of the jurymen could not hide their smiles. I tried to smile, to hide the fear ripping through me. Rose would be acquitted and that was all that mattered, but as soon as the verdict was passed they would start their search. They would ask everyone the identity of the woman – first Sir James and Rose, then Jenna, the man Joseph, the footman, the servants. Everyone would be asked. My heart jolted; Phillip Randall would use this as blackmail.

Matthew Reith was trying to be heard, his voice deadly serious. 'There's not a person in this hall who doubts your testimony, Mr Ellis ... I do not doubt your testimony but I ask you to consider, very carefully, whether you can, *beyond all reasonable doubt*, swear to the identity of the woman you are calling Lady Polcarrow. You must be sure of your facts because the life of an innocent woman lies in your hands.

'Think hard. This town is known for its woollen manufactory. There are trucking mills almost everywhere you look. And what do they make? Wool to be dyed and woven into cloaks – just like the one you have there ... and just like all the other ones that are here in this hall. I could ask every woman and every man present here, if they had seen this cloak ... and their answer would be yes ... because that cloak is like every other cloak worn in this town.' He turned to the jury. 'That black cloak is evidence that the woman wearing it did not want to be identified but Mr Ellis never saw the face of the woman hiding beneath it – the woman he *alleges* to be Lady Polcarrow. He never saw it, because she was not there.'

'Objection, My Lord. That cloak was found in Lady Polcarrow's room.' Mr Wallis was clearly flustered. He could see the jurymen shaking their heads.

'Objection dismissed. Get to the point, Mr Reith.'

'My point is that my next witnesses will prove that on that night Rose Polcarrow was dressed in men's clothes. Indeed, Captain Lefèvre must have recognised her at once because he had seen her dressed like that before. In Lady Polcarrow's defence, I shall call on Miss Marlow and other witnesses from Falmouth who *all* saw Lady Polcarrow *dressed as a man*. Their testimonies will stand any amount of questioning ... so my point is that you must think very carefully, Mr Ellis. Did you, or did you not, ever see the face of the woman in the cloak?'

'I did not, sir.'

'And when she was in the boat and you saw her from the shore. Did you see her clearly? Tell me, did she have chestnut-coloured hair?'

'It was some distance, sir. The sun was in my eyes ... I...' He looked at Mr Wallis. 'I cannot rightly say ... she was wearing a ruby-red dress. I

404

know she wore red ... but I can't swear as to the colour of her hair...'

I had to get out. I had very little time. I tried to remember what Hannah had told me. Four o'clock? That was it. I began gathering up my skirt, trying not to draw attention to my sudden movement. 'Hannah,' I whispered, 'it's too hot... I need the privy and some air. You stay and watch – I'm going to want to know every detail ... only I've got to go...'

I began edging along the row of people, all of them angry with me for blocking their view. The crowd was so dense, almost solid, reluctantly parting to let me through. At the bottom of the steps I used all my strength to squeeze towards the door, tumbling out of it with a gasp of relief. The meat market was in full swing, glazed pigs' eyes staring up at me from rows of severed heads. The smell was appalling and I raced to the gutter, retching behind the barrels spilling over with offal.

The clock in the market square chimed quarter past three.

Chapter Fifty-one

I ran past the friary gate-house, past the guildhall, jumping the potholes in the road. Carts were coming both ways, wagon of bricks blocking everyone. *Celia Cavendish you did wilfully, grievously and, with malice aforethought, prejudice the*

safety of the state by passing and receiving informa-
tion calculated to be injurious to your king and
country. The words were ringing in my head. I
stood no chance. Too many people knew it was
me. Too many people could swear to my identity.

I passed the Dog and could see the White Hart.
I was nearly there. I would have just enough time
to collect my things and buy my ticket ... *with*
malice aforethought you did correspond with the
enemy... No-one would believe me. If I was innocent, I would have come straight back and told
my parents. I stopped to catch my breath – they
would think my warning to Sir James was intended to warn my lover. *You will hang from the*
neck until you are dead.

I ran down the path to the front door. It was
shut. I knocked loudly, almost falling into the hall
as Mr Hambley opened the door. 'Ah, Miss Wells
... is it over...? No, don't tell me...' She put her
hands on her heart. 'Oh poor Mrs Thomas ...
poor Mr Reith. Both found guilty?'

'Oh, no ... wonderful news ... it's not over yet ...
but Sir James' case has been dismissed and Lady
Polcarrow will be acquitted... It's just I have to
catch the coach–'

'Ah, ye're not leavin' us, are you? Hannah will
be that sad... Can I help ye...?' she called after me
as I raced up the stairs.

I took off the hideous bonnet and opened the
drawer, reaching for my bag of jewels. Running
to the desk I grabbed a sheet of paper, dipping
the pen in the ink, my writing a terrible scrawl.
Dear Hannah, these are for you. Thank you for your
kindness. I slipped some earrings from the pouch

and left them with the bonnet. I had to hurry; I looked round the room a final time. On the wall there was an etching of a snipe; the timid bird that nested on higher ground. It had been there all the time yet I had been so blind. Already the coach was outside the inn, the horses waiting to be changed. I grabbed my money and Jacques' bag and tore down the stairs.

Mrs Hambley met me at the door. 'This is all I could gather in time, take it ... ye'll be hungry ... be safe, my love ... come back an' see us.' She thrust a package into my hand and I reached forward, kissing her cheek. She was a dear, sweet lady and I would never forget her.

Jacques' bag was hidden under my cloak, my hood drawn down to cover my face. A stable lad was leading round fresh horses, another swilling heavily caked mud off the coach's wheels. A small group of people gathered outside the door, portmanteaux and baskets ready to be loaded. I rushed past them, pushing my way to the huge oak bar. I had to find Arnaud.

'One ticket for the Fosse coach,' I shouted to the barman. It was ten to four.

'Return or single?' He was pouring a tankard of beer, watching the froth rise.

'Single.' *Come on, come on.* He seemed so slow. I handed him a guinea and scooped up the change, putting it in my purse without a second glance. Poor Matthew Reith, I still had no idea how much the coach cost. With the ticket firmly in my hand, I pushed past the crowded tables and out of the back door.

The courtyard was much bigger then I imagined; a forge was blazing, smoke and hammering filling the yard. Carriages were blocking the coach-house entrance, and vast stables stretched as far as the trees behind. Stable boys were running everywhere, tending horses, filling buckets from the pump. I looked quickly round. A line of packhorses were hitched together, huge barrels of manure strapped to either side. 'Which is the Fosse coach?' I called to a passing groom.

'Leaving just now ... if ye'd like to follow me... That's the coachman's whistle ... ye'd best be quick.'

From the corner of my eye I saw a familiar jacket and turned round. The man who had come to meet Jacques was standing by the door.

Chapter Fifty-two

Six of us crammed inside the coach; four men, two women crowding together on the hard benches. The men had fallen asleep, their heads nodding with the movement of the wheels, their chins wobbling from side to side.

The sky had darkened, dusk turning quickly to night. The lanterns were lit, glowing brightly on either side of the coach. I could see nothing through the window. The curtains were drawn, the journey seeming to take forever. I opened the cloth parcel and smiled. A chunk of bread, two slices of ham and a large slice of apple tart – just what I needed. I kept my cloak firmly round me, my hood covering my face. No-one must recognise me.

We bumped over yet another bad patch in the road, the horses still racing, the appalling suspension throwing us from side to side. I was trying to remember every detail of the trial, going over in my head what Nathaniel Ellis had said. He was definitely telling the truth, everyone could see that. That was what Arnaud was trying to warn me. He had come to tell me my life would be in danger the moment Nathaniel took the stand. He knew Nathaniel was going to be a witness and wanted me to be safe. He had come back for me, just like he said he would.

How long had we been going? We must be nearly there. The coach slowed, the wheels bumping over a cobbled road. The larger of my companions leant forward and pulled back the curtain. 'Not long now,' he said, straightening his hat and adjusting his cravat. I could smell the sea. We would soon be in Fosse.

I could imagine Mother sitting by the fire in her drawing-room, waiting expectantly for news of the trial. Charity would be with Mrs Jennings, Georgina allowed up for another hour. Little Sarah and Charles would be fast asleep in the nursery. Father would return either tonight or tomorrow. He would be furious, his plans in ruin.

Nathaniel had sworn on oath that Jacques had attacked him, yet Jacques claimed otherwise. The fight I witnessed was the clue to the whole thing. Jacques needed Nathaniel off the boat – he must have recognised him as a British sailor.

We began descending the hill, the coach

twisting round the bend, entering a narrow lane and I recognised the row of cottages I had seen before. The horses' hooves clattered noisily down the deserted street, a whistle pierced the air. Dogs began barking and we turned through an arch. 'Here we are … no harm done…' The lights in the courtyard made a welcome sight. Men came running over to hold the horses, one quickly opening the door, another pulling down the steps.

It must have been the landlord who rushed to greet us. A large man with a jovial face. 'Welcome, welcome everyone … you've made good time. Good journey, was it? Come in … come in. Here, miss, I've got yer. There's good ale to be had an' plenty of it. Ah, Mr Mitchell, welcome back, sir. How was Bodmin? Need a lift anywhere, miss?'

I shook my head. 'No, thank you.' My hood was pulled low over my face, my cloak wrapped tightly around me. No-one knew who I was and that was how it must stay. I ran across the courtyard and under the arch. The sea was beckoning, the salty air. It smelt so fresh and my heart began racing. I should be in time to return to my dressing room and prepare for supper. I should dress in my blue organza, sit stiffly with Mama, eat Madeira cake, play cards, drink sherry and plan my forthcoming wedding. Oh yes, I knew exactly what I *should* do.

I clutched my compass to my heart, excitement making my body tingle. I was smiling. Smiling and smiling, no longer reining in, but free to gallop. Philip Randall and Sir Richard Goldsworthy could search all they like. Celia Cavendish would just disappear. No more locked doors. No windows to stare through. No pleading, no running, no looking over my shoulder. No more pretending, no more heartache. Matthew Reith and the Polcarrows would be told I hurried onto the Fosse coach; Mother believed Father to be scouring the land and Father thought me safely in a madhouse. No-one would dare tell him otherwise. They would take his money and tell him what he wanted to hear.

For the first time in my life, I was free.

The river lay to my left. It was not yet high tide. A breeze blew against my cheek. I could smell seaweed, cockles, wood smoke. The night was pitch black, the air damp and full of mist. Clouds hung heavy in the sky. There was no moon to light my path, no stars, only the soft glow of the oil lamp and the light filtering through the windows of the inn. I could hardly breathe for excitement. The thrill of the unknown, the danger drawing me now like it had done all my life. I was born for this, born to breathe the air, live on my wits.

I raced along the road, hugging the river, the sound of waves lapping against the large wooden poles. Prosperous merchants' houses with newly painted railings lay to my right, lanterns burning either side of their large front doors. I pulled my hood lower, covering my face, hurrying past them as fast as I could. Arnaud said he would come back for me. He had been trying to tell me.

Cécile was the woman I wanted to be – brave, adventurous, able to do things for myself; waking to fresh coffee, breathing the salt-laden air. As

Cécile, I would feel the wind in my hair, the sun on my cheek. The road narrowed, turning away from the river, winding between two opposing taverns. Both were crowded and I held my breath, picking my skirts up to stride the foul black water spilling from the sewer. It would be so easy. Celia Cavendish would simply disappear.

I would haul up sails, navigate by the stars. I would swim in blue water and dive for lobsters. I would make bread from beer froth, cook fish on a bed of herbs. I would see birds I never thought to see. My smile broadened, my heart bursting. Every evening I would sit with the man I loved, watching the sun set over a red sea. Every night I would lie in his arms.

I passed the Ship Inn, walking quickly in front of it, taking the alley down to Madame Merrick's warehouse. I knew to approach it from the back – certainly not the front as Sir Richard's spies might still be watching. I would keep to the shadows, slip silently along the edge of the buildings. Arnaud would be there, I knew he would.

I made no noise, lifting my skirts, stepping over the piles of rubbish, edging my way carefully between the barrels. My eyes were accustomed to the dark, the end of the warehouse looming above me. I could see the chute, the huge pulley reaching out from the top. There must be a door. There must be. How else had Arnaud slipped so easily into Madame Merrick's store room? I would feel for it with my hands, find some sort of irregularity, a hollow sound, something obvious but completely unseen.

Chapter Fifty-three

I ran my hands over the wood. The other three sides of the warehouse were made of brick, but this end wall was constructed of wood panels, three foot square, each one surrounded by a thicker plank. No-one was there, the cobbles deserted, just the sound of voices drifting across from the distant inn. Two night-watchmen were sitting by a burning brazier on the boatyard slipway. They were talking and I was sure they could neither see nor hear me.

The panels were a perfect size for a door. I began tapping them quietly, working my way from side to side, knocking each in turn. On one side of the chute the wood sounded different, distinctly solid. On the other, definitely hollow. I stood back, knowing I was missing something. I had to think. Where would I hide a door? The chute was made of wooden planks, wide enough for the rolled sails to reach the ground from the third floor. The end of the chute was waist level, enabling the men to grasp the sails and load them onto a cart. It had to be there. My heart was racing. I would try that area again.

My fingers trembled as a vertical plank behind the chute wobbled in my hand. It was definitely loose and I slid it slowly upwards. It jammed in my hands and I tried easing it carefully, lifting it over the horizontal plank above. Suddenly, I could make sense of it; one move upwards then one move sideways – just like my secret Chinese box I had been given as a child. The plank slid smoothly upwards and I put my hand in the gap, carefully pushing the panel. It slid easily to one side and a pitch black hole opened before me. All I had to do was balance my foot on the ledge and I would be through the gap.

I stepped up, crowding into a space no bigger than a small cupboard. A set of narrow wooden steps hugged the side, going steeply up to the first floor and I turned round to slide the panel shut. It was completely dark, barely wide enough to climb the steps without snagging my cloak. My heart raced with excitement. At the top of the stairs a thin line of light showed beneath a closed door.

I crept silently up the stairs and opened the latch. It was a long, thin room, no more than six foot wide. Bookcases and cupboards lined the wall. There was small bed, a table with two chairs and a desk covered in papers. Two candles were burning in silver candlesticks. Arnaud was bending over a large basin of water, shaving soap on his face, a razor in his hand. He looked up and smiled, his wet hair falling forward, his chest stripped to the waist. 'You're early,' he said, wiping his face with a towel and grabbing his shirt.

'I couldn't wait a moment longer.' My heart was leaping, jumping, pounding in my chest. He was walking towards me, smiling, buttoning up his shirt.

'I was going to come and meet you. You've made good time. I thought I'd at least ten more minutes!' He held out his hands, our fingers touching, entwining. 'I'm only just ahead of you.' He clasped my hands quickly behind my back, drawing me against him, his lips poised against mine. 'Am I forgiven?' he whispered.

'I suppose you must be,' I whispered back. 'My reputation's in tatters, my countrymen want to hang me and I'm not going anywhere near Pendenning. You've rather left me with no choice.'

'Good,' he replied, his lips brushing mine. 'Never oppose the gods, everyone knows that.' His kisses travelled across my face, my eyelids, my ears, down my throat. I was smiling, laughing, reaching up with my own willing lips. This was my new home, these arms, this man. This was where I belonged. He let go of my hands, his arms closing round me, crushing me to him, kissing me hungrily and I let go all my upbringing; kissing him back, matching his passion, his unquenched desire. 'When did you know?' he whispered, kissing my ear.

My body burnt at his touch. 'Nathaniel's evidence...' I managed to whisper. 'Did you suspect him ... of being in the navy?'

'Not at first, but ... as we got going I spotted the way he did things...' He was kissing my throat, my neck. 'He obviously knew his stuff – did things just like a naval man. Jacques must have suspected him, too. I'm sorry, have I covered you with shaving soap?'

I reached forward, brushing the almond soap from his ear. 'I've got something you might want,' I said. 'I saw Jacques – he was in Bodmin.'

'You saw Jacques?' The smile fell from his lips.

He went rigid, his eyes at once wary. 'When was that?'

'Three days ago.' I slipped the cloak from my shoulders, pulling the leather bag quickly over my head. 'He left this under the bench in the window of the White Hart. A man off the Padstow wagon was meant to pick it up but I intercepted it. At the time it seemed the right thing to do ... but there's nothing in it. It's empty.' I held the bag for him to take.

He looked inside. 'It's not empty, Cécile ... the Irish need this very badly – it's the new code. With this the Irish will be able to read any letters or plans they intercept – without it, they won't be able to decipher the messages...' His voice hardened. 'Did you see who was meant to pick it up?'

'A big man, late thirties, black curly hair, blue eyes, larger than average nose.' I shut my eyes trying to remember every detail. 'He held his beer in his left hand and had the top button on his jacket missing ... but he's still in Bodmin. I saw him, just as the coach left. He was outside the inn.'

Arnaud smiled. 'So we might be in time to get it back to him.' He shook the contents of the bag onto the table and picked up the quill. 'The code's in here,' he said, 'hidden down the hollow.' He reached for a beautifully engraved box on the table and lifted out a pair of tweezers. Holding the quill to the candlelight, he carefully eased out a finely rolled piece of paper from inside the hollow.

'I never thought to look there,' I said, watching him unroll the slip of paper. 'I checked the pages for invisible ink but never thought anything would be in there.'

He held up the tiny roll of paper and reached for the notebook, opening it at the first page. 'These numbers ... here, these ones which look like a time – four-fifteen – that's where you start. I'll show you how it works.' He reached across for another pen, dipping it in the ink, copying the long line of letters in the same order. 'Twenty-six jumbled letters ... the four corresponds to the vowels, the fifteen to the consonants. Start with the vowels ... go along the line and take the fourth vowel. That becomes *A* so write that down and cross it out ... then count the next four, that becomes *E* ... always start where you've crossed off. Do you see?'

I nodded, leaning over his shoulder, watching him start on the fifteenth consonant. 'So that's *B*. It's very clever. Are the codes changed often?'

'Every six months. Or whenever they suspect the codes are broken.' A sudden bang, a loud crash and our eyes caught. Voices were coming from the other side of the wooden partition, heavy footsteps stamping across the adjoining floor. Arnaud leant quickly forward, scooping everything back into the bag. 'They're on to us,' he whispered, blowing out both candles.

He drew me closer, keeping hold of my hand, leading me across the pitch-black room without making a sound. He stopped and I sensed rather than saw him put his eye to the partition. 'They're searching the storeroom,' he whispered. 'Have a look – there's another peephole. Soldiers – a lot of them, fifteen, maybe more.'

I peered through the tiny hole. The room was

full of men in red coats, each holding up a lantern. The light shone on their grim faces, the muskets slung across their shoulders. One man looked particularly familiar. 'It's Major Trelawney,' I whispered.

'It was only a matter of time. He's been searching for me ever since Nathaniel returned. He's determined to find me. I never use the front entrance but he clearly has his suspicions.'

I kept my eye to the tiny hole. Major Trelawney was walking towards us, pointing straight at us. He must have been no more than a foot away, his voice as clear as if he was in the room. 'It's my guess this is *not* the end wall of the warehouse... I believe there's a hiding place behind here ... a hidden room where Madame Merrick can hide them. I believe she brings them food ... they probably brought the monk here.' He reached forward, knocking on the wood. 'They'll have a secret way in ... it's here, somewhere, but I'm dammed if I have the patience to find it. Joseph Tregony...?'

'Yes, sir.' A man stepped forward. A huge man, shoulders like an ox.

'Find an axe. Break into the smithy if you must, but bring me back anything we can use to break through this wood. There's a room behind here ... I can feel it.'

Arnaud squeezed my hand, bringing it to his lips. 'Are you sure you want this?' he whispered.

I felt fearless, the thrill of danger making me feel so alive. I was born for this; my prying eyes, my memory, my terrible desire to see what lay behind closed doors. I had dreamt of this, yearned for this. 'You know I do,' I whispered back.

'Then it's time we took *L'Aigrette* out of her hiding place – we need to leave Fosse and rather quickly. We need to regroup but, mostly, we need to get this code back to our waiting Irishman.'

Behind the partition Major Trelawney was shouting instructions. 'It'll be some sort of sliding panel. Try sliding the wood sideways ... or up and down.' He tapped the partition next to us. 'See what I mean? Sounds hollow ... there's a room behind here, I just know it. And that dammed Frenchman is hiding in it.'

'He's as clever as he is charming,' whispered Arnaud. 'We've no time at all.' He put his hand on my arm, ushering me towards the door, grabbing a bag that hung from a hook. Through the darkness came a splitting sound. 'Quick,' he said, 'they've got the axe.'

We rushed down the steep wooden steps, making no sound. Arnaud slid back the panel and peered into the darkness. There was no-one there, just the pitch-black alley, the cobbles and the night-watchmen sitting by their glowing embers. He reached for a large stone by my hand and threw it hard against a barrel. The stone struck with a thud, clattering down to the cobbles and, immediately, two soldiers ran towards it, blowing their whistles. Arnaud grabbed my hand and we ran into the darkness of the opposite direction.

We were heading down a narrow alley, the stones wet, slippery and covered in slime. Lobster pots were stacked high on both sides, mounds of fishing nets stinking of dead crabs. Ropes lay coiled like sleeping snakes. As we slowed to catch our breath, I recognised the quayside, the stone steps leading down to the river. By the dim light of the oil burner I saw the water lap silently against the second step. 'Not yet high tide,' he whispered.

'Where's *L'Aigrette?*' I whispered back.

He smiled, not his tender smile that came straight from his heart, but his mischievous smile that made my stomach flutter and my senses swirl. 'Right here – right under their noses,' he whispered, 'and we're in luck – the ferry's just leaving.'

Chapter Fifty-four

We squeezed together into the bow, looking down at the still black water. The lights of Porthruan shone ahead of us; Arnaud's arm was warm around my shoulders, only the faintest breeze blowing against our faces. It was cold and misty, the water so silent with barely a ripple. Above us a sliver of moon broke through the heavy black clouds and through the river mouth, the sea started to glisten. As the ferry pulled out, I leant against Arnaud, revelling in the smell of the sea, the salt, the sound of the oars.

We were halfway across. Porthruan Harbour looked crowded, a few ships busy with last-minute provisioning but most seemed ready to leave. Men were pacing the decks, watching the sea. Arnaud followed my gaze. 'They can't leave until the tide turns and, even then, there's not enough wind for them to put to sea. They've been waiting all day.'

'Jesus Christ!' muttered the ferryman. 'What's goin' on? Soldiers scurryin' everywhere.' He was facing Fosse and we all turned round, staring back at a line of red coats running along the quayside.

Some soldiers stood in a half circle, pointing at someone. They raised their muskets, their white sashes glowing in the moonlight. Major Trelawney walked stiffly towards them, the uncanny stillness causing his voice to echo across the river. 'Stay just where you are. Do not move. My soldiers are trained to shoot.'

A man in the boat whistled. 'They've got some poor bugger cornered – got their muskets right on him.'

'They're lookin' for smugglers,' said Arnaud, matching their accents exactly. 'The major's clampin' down, hard.'

He was met by cries of horror. 'Bloody hell!'... 'Better not be'... 'Shit.'

The ferryman heaved on the oars, doubling his pace. 'Not tonight. Ye hear? Not tonight – tell the others.'

We watched the man come slowly out from behind the barrels. Major Trelawney shook his head and the soldiers once again renewed their search. They split into groups, running everywhere, some jumping onto moored vessels, others looking behind the barrels. Major Trelawney remained standing on the edge of the quay, looking across the river. Boats were rowing upstream, some downstream, but we were the only boat crossing to Porthruan. He seemed to be staring straight at us. His hand stretched out, his finger pointed and a piercing sound filled the air.

Everyone must have heard it. The soldiers came running back, at least ten of them searching for rowing boats to follow us across. 'For chrissake, hurry–' A fellow passenger slipped quickly next to the ferryman and took an oar, heaving the boat through the water. The boat picked up speed and I caught the glint in Arnaud's eye.

We were alongside the inner harbour, tying up against the wall. The men leapt from the boat, running quickly up the steep lane and into the night. Arnaud helped me onto the quayside, keeping hold of my hand, leading me quickly to the shadows behind a row of cottages. The path narrowed to a mere track, clinging to the river's edge. A dense wood lay to our right, the track winding through the trees, staying close to the water. Arnaud held my hand tightly, pulling me after him and I ran like never before, racing behind, dodging the low branches, my hood slipping from my head, my hair falling round my shoulders.

A stone cottage came into view and we stopped. 'Are you alright? We're nearly there.' I nodded, catching my breath, and we turned to watch the soldiers getting into their requisitioned boats. The clouds had dispersed and it was suddenly so bright, the moon bathing the river in silver light. 'You see that breakers' yard?' I nodded. '*L'Aigrette*'s lying alongside the hulls of those old wrecks. They search every creek and every river but they never think of searching the wrecks.' He smiled and bent to kiss me, '...which is just as well...' His lips were warm and tender '...because it's very convenient.' Another kiss, longer this time and deeper, '...and it's one of my best hiding places...'

We drew apart and I followed him through the trees, shafts of moonlight lighting our way. The wood was dark, the track barely visible. Beside us the water lapped the lower branches of the trees. Dogs were barking in the distance, lights bobbing up and down on the anchored ships – just like the first time we set sail, yet how different it now felt.

We turned a bend and the breakers' yard lay at the entrance to a small wooded creek. It was untidy, cramped, huge piles of rusting shackles, chains and large anchors blocking our way. Planks of wood had been sorted into sizes, spurs and masts lying alongside the yard wall. There were large barrels of rope, coils of chains, two figure-heads leaning drunkenly against each other. A huge dog was chained to the entrance, his vicious barking at once turning to ecstatic pleasure. 'Quiet, Endymion, you'll alert the soldiers.'

'Endymion?' I laughed.

'He bays at the moon. I thought it apt. Come, round here … we'll go round the back.'

'It's alright, I'm here.' A man was walking towards us, hardly visible in the dark. A large man, broad shoulders, thick-set neck and white hair beneath his cap. I had already seen the wagon and recognised him at once. 'You've brought the Pendenning *maid,* I see.' His voice was gruff, his scowl more visible as he came nearer.

Arnaud drew me closer, his arm around my shoulders. 'It's alright ... she's one of us, now. We're gathering to regroup. Is Jacques on board?'

Jago shook his head. 'Left just after you did. Said he'd be back – I'm expecting him any day.'

'He'll not be back. We've got soldiers on our trail and it won't take them long to find us. You heard the dogs? They'll follow us straight here.'

'Regrouping, ye say?'

'We certainly are.'

Jago unchained the dog who bounded ahead, leading us round the front of the cottage and down some steps along a stone jetty. He was a huge dog, very nimble, constantly looking over his shoulder to see what kept us. The hulks lay crammed together in a jumbled mess – rotting planks, burnt timbers, masts at half tilt and spurs at all angles. The creek was wooded and dark, the stones wet. Jago stepped onto the blackened ribs of the nearest hull and held out his hand. 'Mind you don't slip, lass.'

We crossed the steeply angled deck of the next ship and stopped. *L'Aigrette* was tied alongside, her decks covered by rotting nets, her mast completely hidden by a criss-cross of broken yard-arms. Arnaud stood behind me, his arms encircling me. 'Here she is,' he whispered. 'Welcome home, dearest Cécile.'

I knew he would lift me up and carry me over the gunwale. Of course he would. Jago frowned and shook his head. Endymion barked, wagging his tail. He was a brute of a dog; shaggy coat, huge paws, teeth designed to bite. He ran straight along the deck, jumping onto the coach roof and leaping to the bow as if taking up his position of command.

Arnaud put me down. 'The tide's turned.' He was watching a log bob slowly towards the river mouth. 'We'll pole her out – Jago, pole from the bow. Cécile, take the helm, I'll tell you exactly where to point. I'll pole from the stern so I'll be right behind you. When we've cleared the hulks, set the sails to starboard – there's just the slightest southerly so we'll make the most of it.'

The two men began untying the ropes, hauling away the nets that covered her decks, hurling everything onto the adjacent wreck – crates and lobster pots, old planks left lying at odd angles. She had been well disguised and as the sacking was removed, she looked pristine again, her sleek black hull almost indistinguishable in the inky water. The only thing that remained covered was her name painted on the stern. Jago stood at the bow, a huge pole in his hand; Arnaud was on the stern, heaving his pole against the jetty behind us. 'We're off,' he said. 'Are you alright, Cécile?'

I nodded, holding the tiller firmly in both hands. Inch by inch, the boat edged slowly forward, slipping silently from her eerie graveyard. 'Just hold her steady ... once we've cleared these hulks we'll swing round.'

The mouth of the creek was barely wider than the boat. *L'Aigrette* lay straight across it, pushed sideways by the tide. Jago ran to starboard, jamming his pole against a disused jetty on the bank opposite. 'Now swing right round.' Arnaud was right behind me, '...keep pointing to the church.' He joined Jago on starboard, both heaving on their poles, stretching high in the air as they thrust them against the stones opposite.

The bow swung round to face the narrow gap that would take us out to open sea. To our right the lights of Fosse, to our left the harbour of Porthruan. We were at the widest part of the river, the tide with us. Arnaud stood with one leg on the deck, the other on the gunwale. His hair was ruffled, his eyes alight. 'There's hardly any wind – we'll need every breath. Hold her steady while we get the sails up.'

I nodded, keeping my course towards the narrow entrance. Jago and Arnaud hauled in unison, heaving up the sails and securing them in place. We were inching forward. The turn of the tide; no wind, no other boats, just *L'Aigrette* unfurling her sails, ready to slip out on a breath and the daring of her captain.

A light flashed. A blast of gunshot. Another red flash, another and another. 'Jesu ... what the hell...?' Jago crouched to the deck. 'Get down, both of you.'

The soldiers were running along the harbour wall. Another flash, another shot. Arnaud tied the last rope and leapt to my side. 'I thought we'd have more time.' He took the tiller, heading across the river, the smell of cordite drifting towards us. Men were shouting from the moored ships, dogs barking, Endymion standing on the deck, barking furiously back.

'Get down, dog!' yelled Jago. He grabbed the dog and crouched low at the bow. 'They're getting into boats. They're rowing over.' He looked up. 'Come on, girl ... fill your sails ... you know

426

you can.'

Major Trelawney stood on the harbour wall, pointing straight at us. A soldier ran to his side and saluted. He was holding a burning torch. Major Trelawney grabbed it and started waving it from side to side. Arnaud put his hand on my shoulder. 'What's he playing at?' The torch was raised for three counts ... down for two. Up for three ... down for two.

'He's signalling the forts – Jesu, he's got the guns working.' On either side of the narrow gap a light signalled back, first one side, then the other. Moonlight shone on the cliffs, lighting up the stone batteries, the crenulated walls. We could see soldiers running along the battlements, lamps swinging in their hands. 'They're loadin' up the cannon.'

The other soldiers were back in their boats, kneeling in the bows, their muskets pointing towards us. They were making headway, their oars splashing noisily towards us but the firing had stopped. 'They know we'll have to tack soon. We can't risk the cannons – we'll be a sitting duck.'

At once I remembered. 'We need Major Trelawney's code...' My mind was racing. What had he said? 'The naval code – that should clear us.'

Arnaud smiled. 'Three lights abreast each other, port and starboard,' he shouted. 'Hold this course, Cécile...'

I held the tiller with white knuckles. I felt a pull and looked up. *L'Aigrette's* sails had caught the slight breeze and were tilting to one side, leaning with the wind. Water rippled against the bow, a slight, but steady wake.

Arnaud lit the lanterns and began securing them to the gunwales. He was working fast, jumping onto the coach roof, running along the deck. 'If this doesn't work, we've got enough wind to gibe. We'll go up river and hide... Get ready, Cécile ... you'll have to swing her round ... but not now ... wait for my command.' He tied the last lantern and looked round. The soldiers were local men, born to row these waters. Their boats were racing behind us, their muskets pointing straight at us. More soldiers lined Porthruan Harbour.

Arnaud stood on the coach roof, leaning against the mast. 'We must hold our nerve. They're not firing because Major Trelawney expects us to surrender. He wants us alive.'

The way he smiled, the way he stood; I knew he had done this many times before. Not here, perhaps, but this was his life and this was to be my life; slipping from under gunfire, the smell of cordite. I relished the danger; I accepted the risks. My cheeks were flushed, the thrill of adventure coursing through my veins.

Sailors' shouts echoed across the water. Angry shouts, encouraging the soldiers to row faster. No other ships were leaving. Even if they could, Major Trelawney would have told them to wait. He had the river mouth covered, the moon in his favour. Silver light bathed the river, *L'Aigrette* an easy target. Arnaud's lanterns were in place, shining brightly. All we could do was hold our nerve and wait to see what Major Trelawney would do.

He raised his torch, up, down, up, down, three times. Behind us the sound of splashing stopped and the oarsmen leant forward to catch their breath. Jago left Endymion to stand sentry on the bow. Shaking his head vigorously, he joined us in the cockpit. Arnaud put his arms around me, holding me tightly. His hair was tousled, his eyes full of mischief.

'He's called off the batteries. Take her out, Cécile. Take her out right under their noses.' He smiled at Jago. 'Poor Major Trelawney, he doesn't deserve this – he's really rather a nice man.'

'Nice man be buggered,' grumbled Jago. 'And it's all coming back to me – why I stopped sailing with you, Captain Lefèvre.'

Arnaud's laughter drifted over the water. 'You love it, Jago ... and you miss it.'

The sails were filling, the ripples getting deeper. *L'Aigrette* was flying. The fastest cutter in the channel was taking her leave. I held the tiller, pointing her out to open sea. As we passed between the forts Arnaud raised his hand in salute to the soldiers looking down from the batteries. I returned his smile. Living not watching, doing not dreaming. I could feel the tide pulling us, the sudden swell of the waves as we reached open sea. The air smelt so fresh, so full of adventure. I was smiling. Smiling and smiling. No more stuffy rooms, no more embroidery. No more jumping to Mother's command. No more peering out of windows. No more yearning for the man I could never have.

'Where to?' growled Jago.

'Straight to Mylor,' replied Arnaud, squeezing my shoulder.

Jago looked up and, for the first time, I saw him smile. 'No wonder you're in such a hurry, lad,' he said, his eyes full of love. 'I take it we're going to Flushing first.'

'No, straight to Mylor.'

'Flushing it is, then,' replied Jago, walking back to the bow. 'Sailing with you is one thing. I can take any amount of gunfire and cannons but your mother's wrath? Never that!'

Chapter Fifty-five

The Channel
28th November 1793, 1:00 a.m.

I held the tiller. Moonlight shimmered over the sea, bathing us in silver light, catching the sails, turning them ghostly grey. I could see the dark outline of the coast, the curve of the land, the jagged rocks spilling down from the cliffs. Foam frothed across the deck, the movement gentle, mesmerizing, just the faintest splash of waves against the bow. The wind blew from the south, the sails arching to starboard. Arnaud sat down beside me, his arms folding around me. 'The stove's lit, the coffee's on but Perdue's still not speaking to me.'

We looked round. Perdue had followed Arnaud up the steps and was glowering at us from the hatchway. 'She looks very angry.'

'She's going to need a lot of fish with Endymion on board – she hates him!'

'I'm not surprised. He's so fearsome.' Endymion was sitting by the bowsprit, staring out to sea like a figurehead. Jago was beside him, smoking his pipe – two old friends sitting in companionable silence.

'She thought she'd seen him off. He's quite petrified of her and stays well away, but that's not enough – she wants him off her boat.' He smiled, drawing back a lock of hair blowing across my face, his voice turning suddenly serious. 'I couldn't tell you, Celia. You must know how much I wanted to but I'm bound by a strict code of conduct. We can't say anything, tell anyone – not even to the woman you adore.' He kissed my cheek, his eyes entreating, searching mine. 'I wanted you to know ... I've always wanted you to know.'

'You tried to tell me. Not directly, of course. You said I could love you ... you told me you were coming back and only a Cornishman would know snipes preferred to nest on the moor. There was an etching of a snipe in my room and yet I never thought ... not until the end.' My head was against his shoulder, his arm around me.

'When did you guess?'

'Nathaniel Ellis was no liar – everyone knew he was telling the truth. When he said Jacques attacked him, I couldn't understand it. Why lie about that and be so honest about everything else? Then everything became clear – it was Jacques who had lied. If you were to be caught, Jacques needed Nathaniel out of the way. We were sailing straight into Jacques' trap but you didn't know it. Even the signal was wrong.'

He nodded. 'Everything was wrong.'

'Nathanial's evidence made sense of it all – the way Jacques tried to take the pistol from me, the way he anchored to delay us. Did you suspect Jacques was working for the French?'

'Not when we set out, only when he anchored when he didn't need to ... and the fact he sent you ashore – he probably thought you couldn't row. Darling Cécile ... keeping silent has been the hardest thing I've had to do. I run a network ... a line of correspondence going straight to the very heart of Paris. Too many people rely on our silence – living in danger, risking everything to provide us with information.' He held my hand to his lips, his eyes no longer laughing, but alive with passion, devotion to his country. 'These people offer safe houses. They work as servants to spy for us, carry information back to us. Through them we know where the troops are massing, who commands what.'

'I understand ... honestly, I do. You were sworn to secrecy. You couldn't tell me and I'm proud you didn't.' My heart felt as if it would burst. 'I couldn't understand why you were in court – then I realised you were waiting to step forward if James Polcarrow was found guilty. You were there to save him.'

'Anyone wishing to break silence or leave the network has to get permission. I had to ride to London – I galloped there and back, desperate to be in time...' The mischief returned to his eyes. 'I didn't recognise you, at first. That was an awful bonnet.'

A rush of pleasure made my heart race. My face was burning, his touch making me tingle – the feel of his arms, the scent of almond soap. 'Who are you?' I whispered. 'I don't even know your name.'

'Arnaud's my middle name, used only by my family. To everyone else, I'm Lieutenant Edward Pendarvis.'

'That's a very fine name. I think I can get used to it.' The name sounded familiar.

'When the slaughter started, my mother's family were still in France. I brought most of them to Britain but a couple of my cousins remained behind. They wanted to help overthrow the tyranny. We set up a channel of communication, passing information directly to Mr Pitt. He called me to his office one day and told me I was to leave my ship and work directly for Mr Dundas, his War Secretary. Mr Pitt calls us his secret service – Mr Dundas' spies. Even the other cabinet members don't know about us. Are you warm enough?'

He leant over and reached for a cashmere blanket, wrapping it round my shoulders, tucking it down my back. The air was full of moisture, the wind picking up, blowing steadily from the south. 'I run an organisation known as the Channel Island Correspondence; any information we collect goes straight to the Foreign Office. I needed a fast cutter so I bid for *L'Aigrette*.'

'But Sir James wanted her for Rose.'

'The bidding was fierce but then I saw the beauty of it.' The lines around his eyes creased. 'In fact, the perfect cover.'

'Did the man we rescued survive?'

His lips lingered on my cheek. 'The man you helped save was William Wickham, Mr Dundas'

433

spy master. He's based in London, under the wing of the Alien Office but he'd been in Switzerland, setting up new channels. He had all the information with him – names, codes, addresses ... everything. It was all in that barrel we handed over the side.' I nodded. I had guessed as much. 'He was in grave danger and we were only just in time to get him to safety.'

There was no trace of his borrowed French accent, just a beautifully modulated voice with West Country vowels. Edward Pendarvis, brave, handsome, a Cornishman, full of honour and integrity, an officer in the Royal Navy, risking his life for his king and country. How I adored him. He frowned, his eyes dark in the moonlight. 'The only time I think Jacques could have seen the code was when I was showing you how to gut the fish. The tiller was tied down – he must have rushed down and copied it when our backs were turned.'

'I take it your plan is to replace it with a false code?'

He smiled. 'See how good you are? I knew you'd make the perfect spy. If your Irishman's still there, we'll leave him a false code, followed by false information.'

'My lodgings were just opposite ... I may be recognised.'

His eyes creased. 'You can wear Jacques' clothes.'

'Why didn't you have Jacques arrested?'

'Jacques wasn't my choice. I chose everyone else, but Jacques was foisted on me by Mr Dundas. His friend, the Comte de Trevaunes, swore to his loyalty and I had to tell Mr Pitt I suspected he was working for the French.' He paused, turning my chin slowly so he could reach my lips, 'and I had to tell Mr Pitt I was going to marry you.'

It was hard to keep my course – the touch of his lips, the taste of his kiss, his hand caressing my throat, twirling the silver compass in his fingers.

'I'm a man of honour and I must act to restore your reputation. How long was it? Thirty-six hours alone with a captain who could not wait to get you into his cabin? Matthew Reith had absolutely no idea how right he was. Dearest, bravest Cécile ... will you do me the very great honour of becoming my wife?'

'I would love to,' I whispered.

We watched the coastline, both of us smiling. The night was so clear, the silver light shimmering on the sea around us. Celia Pendarvis, Cécile Lefèvre, both sounded wonderful. I had so much to learn about this man I adored.

'Dodman on the starboard beam,' called Jago from the bow. 'Wind's picking up. Should be in Flushing in no time.'

Edward stood up. 'All sails out – let her run.' His movements were strong, decisive, just like the first time I watched him. It seemed a lifetime ago. He released the rope, one hand in front of the other, the wind filling the sail. *L'Aigrette* was flying.

'Just the wind we need,' he shouted. 'It's backing south-east – it'll blow us straight to Mylor.'

Chapter Fifty-six

Edward handed us a cup of steaming coffee. Jago took it with one hand, the other on the tiller. 'Ye can't do this – not to yer mother.'

A look of resignation crossed Edward's face. He raised his eyebrows and sighed. 'I'm an only child and sometimes, well ... sometimes ... Mother can be a little...' He left the words unsaid.

'Dear Madame Merrick. You can look just like her sometimes. You've got her long fingers and high cheekbones. And you've got the same eyes – watchful, secretive, never giving anything away. I'm very fond of your mother – we already get along very well.'

'Well, I know she adores you.' Edward was still frowning. 'But that's not our problem ... our problem is that Mother will insist on making your wedding dress and that'll take forever.' He put his hand through his hair. 'And I can just see the list they'll start to make. They'll want to invite all their friends – Lord Falmouth, my godfather, Lord Carew, my uncle, Lord Camelford ... not to mention all my English cousins. And Father will want to invite all his Admiralty friends. The list will go on and on and it'll take months to organise.' He shook his head. 'We can't wait that long, can we, Cécile?'

Admiralty friends. The excitement had clouded my mind. 'Admiral Sir Alexander Pendarvis, soon

436

to have a large house built in Fosse with plans for a row of cottages and an alms-house?' I asked.

Arnaud's eyebrow shot up, his smile lighting his face. 'You've met him, by the way – you gave him alms.'

'That beggar was your father?'

'He's been watching the shipyard, keeping a close eye on the Irish bookkeeper. He saw Jacques go there a couple of times. The bookkeeper must have been his contact and once he was arrested, Jacques had no choice but to take the code to Bodmin himself.'

Jago was still shaking his head. 'Yer Mother won't like it – not one bit.'

Arnaud frowned. 'But there's all her family, Jago – you know what they're like! All four brothers will have to travel from London and the Marquis de Barthélémy will *insist* on giving a ball in Celia's honour. He'll want me to go to his vineyards to collect the wine and that'll take for ever.' He looked up. A terrible howl was echoing along the decks and across the open sea. 'Oh no … there goes Endymion…'

Endymion sat in the bow, his neck outstretched. He looked so happy baying up to the moon with heartfelt love. Purdue's tail thumped and she sprang to her feet. 'Endymion used to sail with us until he learnt to bay – then he had to go. It's not very convenient, hiding up a creek when Endymion starts howling.' He drew me closer, holding me tightly. 'We're eloping, Jago. Celia's run away from home and doesn't want her family to know anything about me.' He leant closer. 'That's right, isn't it?'

I tried to smile. I was being silly, wanting too much.

His voice dropped to a whisper. 'You'd like Charity to be there, wouldn't you?'

I nodded, feeling suddenly sad. 'And Mrs Jennings ... but it's alright, I know it's impossible. Mrs Jennings knows your Mother as Madame Merrick and if you're to keep your cover, no-one must recognise you. She knows you, too, remember?' I put my cup down, feeling increasingly queasy. The waves were building, the boat rising and falling with greater force. My lips felt dry, my mouth full of salt. It had been a mistake to drink the coffee. I tried breathing deeply. 'How much longer?' I asked.

Edward smiled. 'Not long – perhaps two hours.'

'Two hours!' I could not believe I could feel so wretched. Not again. Please not again.

Edward leapt to his feet. 'I'll get some ginger ... and some peppermint tea. That helped last time, didn't it?'

Jago shook his head. 'It'll pass. Ye'll get yer sea legs soon enough.' My hand flew to my mouth. 'Quick, captain, bring a bucket,' he yelled.

If I stayed completely still, my sickness might be held at bay. I kept my eyes fixed firmly on the sea, watching the white crests. It was not even as if it was rough; the wind was perfect, the waves hardly moving. Edward handed me the exquisite china cup, the strong smell of mint filling the air. He wrapped the blanket round me and kissed my cheek. I tried to smile.

'This is what we're going to do,' he whispered. 'We'll drop Jago off in Falmouth and you and I will ride to Bodmin and leave the false code. Jago, tell Mother and Father to meet us in Mylor Creek at midnight on the third of December. If I'm right, and I have every reason to believe I am, Charity and Mrs Jennings are expected in Trenwyn House in three days' time and it's just across the river from Mylor.' He drew breath, but not for long. 'We'll get a note to them that Jago will be waiting for them on the river just before midnight on the third.'

'Mylor Creek? We're to be married on the boat?'

'No, in the church. Reverend Milles has a romantic disposition. My family have known him for years and he won't be hard to persuade. It'll be just the thing. At the door, Mrs Jennings will be blindfolded. She and Charity will be sworn to secrecy and Mother, I promise, will sound like any other Englishwoman. Charity won't recognise her as Madame Merrick and Mrs Jennings will see no-one through her blindfold. That way, they'll be there for you and can witness you becoming Mrs Edward Pendarvis – there, I think that covers everything.'

'Sounds as good a plan as any,' muttered Jago. 'So I'm to arrange it all, am I?' He smiled. 'Take the tiller – I'll quieten that dog.'

The baying stopped. I held the ginger jar in my hand. Of course it was Ming, what else would it be? Edward was holding me tightly but when he spoke it was as Arnaud Lefèvre. 'You'll love the River Fal, Cécile, and you'll love Mylor Creek. Kingfishers flash across the water and egrets swoop down from the trees. Herons stand like statues by the water's edge and seals swim round the boat. Sometimes I swim with them.' He kissed my hand, keeping it to his lips. 'When the tide's out, sandpipers scurry across the mud and god-wits dig for molluscs. It's so beautiful. And when night falls, we'll hear the curlews calling, the owls hooting.'

I took another piece of ginger.

'We'll be based in Jersey, but we'll come back to the creek and anchor below Trenwyn House. We can watch Lady Carew's concerts. You'll be able to see Charity whenever you want.' The wind was blowing his hair, ruffling his collar, his hand resting lightly on the tiller. 'There's so much to show you, I hardly know where to start.'

We looked up. Jago was leaning over the bow, holding the bowsprit. 'Dolphins,' he shouted, 'more than I can count.'

Tears stung my eyes. The sea was rippling, black shapes diving in the water around us. Dolphins, riding the bow waves, the man I loved, standing by my side.

Better than my dreams. Better than my wildest, wildest dreams.

Acknowledgements

I would like to extend another huge thank-you to my family and friends; to my agent Teresa Chris and my editor Sara O'Keeffe and her team at Atlantic books. Also to everyone in the Cornwall Record Office, Truro. Thank you, each and every one of you for your continuing enthusiasm and support.

The publishers hope that this book has given you enjoyable reading. Large Print Books are especially designed to be as easy to see and hold as possible. If you wish a complete list of our books please ask at your local library or write directly to:

Magna Large Print Books
Magna House, Long Preston,
Skipton, North Yorkshire.
BD23 4ND